AN IMPULSIVE KISS

Feiyan lowered her gaze to Dougal's mouth—his wry, exquisite, enticing mouth, where the traces of a smile lingered—and she couldn't resist.

She had split, bruised, smashed, and swollen men's lips. She'd never once kissed them. She'd never before had the desire. But now a kiss seemed the perfect celebration of their triumph.

On instinct, she snagged the front of his gambeson and pulled him toward her. Then she closed her eyes and pressed her lips to his.

Her breath quickened. Her flesh tingled. Her head vibrated.

And then he responded.

Glynnis Campbell – Publisher
P.O. Box 341144
Arleta, California 91331
Contact: glynnis@glynnis.net

Cover design by Richard Campbell
Formatting by Author E.M.S.

ISBN-13: 978-1-63480-121-8

Published in the United States of America

BRIDE OF MIST

The Warrior Daughters of Rivenloch, Book 3

DEDICATION

To my quarantine team...
my husband Rich, my mom, and my son Dylan...
for making lockdown bearable,
and to my dear readers
who had the patience to wait
until the world was no longer on fire
and I could find the courage and heart
to write for them.

OTHER BOOKS BY GLYNNIS CAMPBELL

THE WARRIOR MAIDS OF RIVENLOCH
The Shipwreck (novella)
A Yuletide Kiss (short story)
Lady Danger
Captive Heart
Knight's Prize

THE WARRIOR DAUGHTER OF RIVENLOCH
The Storming (novella)
A Rivenloch Christmas (short story)
Bride of Fire
Bride of Ice
Bride of Mist

THE KNIGHTS OF DE WARE
The Handfasting (novella)
My Champion
My Warrior
My Hero

MEDIEVAL OUTLAWS
The Reiver (novella)
Danger's Kiss
Passion's Exile
Desire's Ransom

THE SCOTTISH LASSES
The Outcast (novella)
MacFarland's Lass
MacAdam's Lass
MacKenzie's Lass

THE CALIFORNIA LEGENDS
Native Gold
Native Wolf
Native Hawk

ACKNOWLEDGMENTS

Special thanks to

Rachael Gavan from Wilderness Scotland for the route,

Emilia Clarke and Richard Armitage for their inspiration,

Amy and Kirby for taking me the last mile,

and my daughter Brynna
for making the journey a pleasure

PROLOGUE

Castle Giric, Scotland
1146

Banished...

The harsh curse cut through the crisp air like winter's icy breath.

To Fergus and Morris mac Giric, not yet seventeen years old, abandoned to the rugged shores and wild woods of western Scotland, the punishment may as well be execution.

Discarded by their laird in dishonor, they were exiled forever, never to return.

Forgotten by the clan.

Damned.

Left to rot.

And they didn't deserve it.

They weren't the villains. It was Colban, that high-and-mighty foundling runt, who should have been cast out. Not Fergus and Morris. For shite's sake, they were blood kin to the laird himself.

But cunning Colban had found an ally in the laird's young son. Morgan mac Giric had welcomed the filthy bastard into the clan as if he were a long-lost brother.

The ten-year-old lads did everything together. Morgan trained with Colban. Rode with him. God's blood! Colban even supped at Morgan's right hand, the place that had once belonged to Fergus and Morris. Like a conniving cuckoo, Colban had usurped their nest. And he'd begun to believe he was as good as *they* were.

Young Morgan was too naive to see how the devious orphan had insinuated his way into the household. Too stupid to realize the kind of disgrace the whelp of a harlot would bring to the clan.

Fergus and Morris, older and wiser, had simply taken it upon themselves to compensate for Morgan's lack of good judgment.

They meant to show Colban his place. Teach him that the nameless son of a whore could not assume their rank in the proper order of things. That he would never be their equal. Prove to the bastard, once and for all, that blood was thicker than water. And leave him with scars that would remind him of that for the rest of his life.

But then Morgan had spoiled it all. He'd squealed to his father. Once he'd brought the laird their bloody whip and shown him the bastard lad's bloody back, there was to be no forgiveness.

They never imagined Laird Giric would react so harshly. After all, they'd only given the lofty Colban what they deemed a much-needed lesson.

Now they were banished for their pains. *Banished.*

The laird had treated a nameless cur that had shown up at his door with more respect than two youths born of his line. And now they were nothing. *Less* than nothing.

But if the incident had taught them one thing, it was that good fortune was seized, not won. If the son of a harlot could rise to greatness from nothing, so could they.

So, seething with hurt and anger, cursing the name of mac Giric, Fergus and Morris christened themselves anew—the Fortanach brothers. Against his skin, close to his heart, Fergus wore the mac Giric clan badge to serve as a cold reminder of unhealed wounds.

One day, they swore, no matter how long it took, they would seek retribution.

Find a way to ruin the clan that had ruined them.

Bury Morgan mac Giric.

And destroy the mac Giric legacy forever.

CHAPTER 1

Castle Darragh near Ayr, Scotland
Spring 1156, 10 years later

Dougal mac Darragh had heard the rumors.

There was a price on his head.

His brother had put it there.

For weeks now, Laird Gaufrid had offered a reward to any warrior in the clan who could bring Dougal down on the sparring field.

He was sure his brother didn't mean to have him killed. Gaufrid only meant to humiliate him. To punish Dougal for his *own* lack of self-worth.

But the warrior facing Dougal now didn't know that. He circled Dougal with murder and desperation in his eyes.

Dougal couldn't blame him. The man needed that reward money. Maybe for his family. For his bairns. For food.

The trouble had started two years ago, when Dougal and Gaufrid's father had died unexpectedly. By tradition, the clan had chosen the oldest son as the new laird.

But Gaufrid knew nothing of leadership. He was no more qualified to be a leader of men than a harlot was to be a nun. He couldn't read. He couldn't do sums. Too

10

frequently, he found solace at the bottom of a bottle. And he was a poor judge of character, a fact made clear by the company he kept.

Gaufrid's closest companions were the Fortanach brothers, a pair of miserable vagabonds who'd ingratiated themselves to him shortly after the laird's death.

Dougal didn't trust them from the beginning. Fergus and Morris Fortanach claimed no home. No history. No background. And they reeked of vice, intrigue, and mischief.

But Gaufrid had been grieving for their father. Dougal didn't have the heart to tear away his brother's newfound friends in his time of need.

Perhaps if he hadn't had his hands full, holding the clan together under his brother's neglect, Dougal might have intervened sooner. But by the time he grew aware of the changes in Gaufrid, it was too late.

The Fortanachs had already sunk their claws deep into Gaufrid's malleable mind. Toying with his affections. Drinking with him. Whoring with him. Poisoning his soul. Using gushing flattery, free-flowing ale, and carefully chosen whispers, they bent Gaufrid to their will.

Under their influence, Gaufrid gradually replaced his father's once loyal soldiers with brutes and mercenaries gleaned by the Fortanach brothers from God knew where.

Dougal devoted himself to protecting those harmed by his brother's excesses and cruelty. The villagers. The servants. The crofters. But since Gaufrid was laird, Dougal had only limited power.

When the Fortanachs' exorbitant tastes quickly drained the Darragh coffers, Gaufrid—eager to fulfill their demands and prove his own merit and power—filled them again by raising taxes on the surrounding villages.

Gaufrid's efforts were misguided, of course. Taxing the villagers didn't buy their respect. It made them hate him more.

What it did buy, however, was an army of bloodthirsty warriors willing to fight for the laird—to the death, if necessary—if it meant their survival.

Which was why, when the warrior's sword swept with killing force toward Dougal's ribs, he responded in equal measure. He thrust up his targe with enough power to both knock away the blade and send the man stumbling backward into the dust.

No sooner had one foe fallen than another came to take his place.

And another.

And another.

Dougal defeated them all.

But he felt no thrill of glory as he watched them depart from the field one by one, hanging their heads in disappointment.

He felt grateful that he'd live to fight another day for what was left of his father's noble legacy.

He also felt the need to get away from the castle for a while. Leave the stench of hate and hopelessness behind. Fill his lungs with fresh sea breeze.

"Campbell," he called out to the stable lad. "Saddle Urramach, will ye? I'll stretch his legs today."

He'd ride out from the sea cliff to the countryside. Check on the crofters. There had been a christening at Kirkoswald this morn. He'd make an appearance on behalf of the laird. Give the new parents a wee gift of coin. Look after the villagers in whom his brother took no interest.

"Congratulations, brother!"

There was Gaufrid now. Drunk again. Already, and not yet noon. He leaned against the gate of the wattle fence that bordered the field, beaming, as if pleased by Dougal's victory.

Dougal knew better.

Gaufrid's smile might be indulgent. But his eyes simmered with long-burning, deep-seated, rumor-nourished resentment.

His brother wanted nothing more than to see Dougal soundly defeated. Only when Dougal was felled in shame would Gaufrid finally feel like he'd triumphed. Like he'd earned the lairdship. Like he deserved it.

But they both knew Gaufrid wasn't fit to be laird. Nor would he ever be.

The brothers might be similar in appearance. Both had their mother's coal black hair and their father's keen blue eyes. They were striking enough to turn the lasses' heads. They were tall and powerful in stature, with wide shoulders and commanding voices that demanded attention and deference.

But in character, Dougal was nothing like his brother. Gaufrid was petty, greedy, foolish, insecure, and utterly lacking in empathy. A weak and wheedling bully.

Nonetheless, he was the chosen head of the clan. He deserved Dougal's deference, if not his respect.

Dougal acknowledged him with a nod. "M'laird."

The new maidservant, a timid, young red-haired lass, came up beside Gaufrid, bearing a cup on a tray. When she hesitated, Gaufrid seized her roughly by the arm, shoving her through the gate. "Well, go on. Can't ye see our champion needs refreshment?"

The lass blushed and stumbled toward Dougal. She slowed as she approached, eyeing his claymore with trepidation.

She needn't have worried. Dougal was nothing like his brother. He didn't assuage his own inadequacies by browbeating others. And he would never raise his blade— or his hand—to a lass.

To put her at ease, he laid down his sword and hauled off his helm. Scraping the damp locks of his hair back from his sweaty brow, he managed a disarming smile. "Merraid, isn't it?"

She smiled in pleased surprise. "Aye."

There was an awkward moment of distraction as she stared up at him in wonder, almost as if she'd forgotten what she was doing.

"Hand me the cup, lass," he softly warned, "lest ye want to suffer the laird's disapproval."

She blinked. "Och. Aye."

He downed the ale all at once. It soothed his dusty throat. But it couldn't wash the bitter taste of injustice from his mouth.

It was a travesty that maidservants like Merraid should have to cringe from the laird who was supposed to protect them.

It was outrageous that warriors like those he'd just defeated were driven to murder to keep from starving.

"Go on now," he urged the lass. She was looking up at him with the sort of lovesick gaze that would only get her into trouble.

As she scurried off, Campbell brought Urramach, saddled and ready, to the field. The destrier had shied at his last battle and was worthless in tournament. But Dougal didn't have the heart to get rid of him. Besides, the beast loved to run. Dougal took the reins, giving the horse a pat on the neck, and then narrowed his gaze at his brother.

Ordinarily, the daily trouncing that Dougal gave the laird's warriors tested Gaufrid's temper. His eyes would glitter with rage. His teeth would grind with frustration. He'd try to wound Dougal with his sharp tongue.

Today he didn't seem as out of sorts as usual. Instead, he gave Dougal a simpering smirk, looking curiously pleased with himself, as if Dougal had *not* just defeated his entire army of warriors.

Before Dougal could wonder what his brother's good mood meant, he heard desperate bellows from the courtyard.

"Help!"

"Come quick!"

He acted at once, snatching up his claymore and tugging Urramach toward the cries.

Gaufrid was still sputtering in confusion when Dougal raced past him to see what was going on.

The two Fortanach brothers stood in the courtyard, bent over and heaving. Sweaty, breathless, and exhausted, they looked as if they'd been chased by a devil. Their faces were smudged with char. Their hair was coated in ash. They reeked of smoke. Their garments were torn and bloody where cloth and skin had been scraped.

"What's happened?" Dougal demanded, wondering what foul mischief the troublesome brothers had gotten into now.

"Fire," Fergus wheezed.

"An attack," Morris rasped out.

Dougal's heart raced. This was more than mere mischief. "Where?"

"In Kirk—" Morris's words ended in a series of racking coughs.

By now, others had gathered. Murmurs of "fire" circled the courtyard like an ominous wind.

"Kirkoswald?" Dougal asked, his heart in his throat.

Fergus nodded.

Bloody hell. That was where the christening was to be. East of Castle Darragh. Roughly three miles away.

"Fetch buckets!" Dougal called out to the bystanders. "We'll need all the able-bodied folk we can muster to put out the fire." He turned back to the Fortanachs. "How bad is it?"

"They burned the whole village," Morris muttered.

Dougal fist tightened in Urramach's bridle. "Who?"

Fergus shook his head. "We didn't see them." Then he held out a tarnished medallion. "But they dropped this."

Gaufrid had finally arrived. "Let me see that."

Dougal had to go to Kirkoswald. There was no time to waste. He hauled himself into the saddle and shoved the helm down over his head.

"Men, saddle up and follow me as soon as ye can!" he commanded the warriors.

"Wait!" Gaufrid countermanded him. "I know this badge. 'Tis the mac Giric's."

Beneath him, Urramach danced impatiently, eager to run. "And?"

Gaufrid frowned. "The mac Giric stronghold is three days' ride from here, at...at..." He glanced up at Morris.

"Creagor," Morris said.

Gaufrid nodded. "Creagor, aye, that's it. The mac Girics at Creagor."

Dougal didn't see how that mattered. "Whoever attacked Kirkoswald, I'll chase them to the ends o' the earth."

"Nay!" Gaufrid suddenly seized Urramach's bridle. "Not with my men!"

Dougal's brows slammed together. "What?"

"He's right," Fergus interjected. "What if the marauders return?"

Morris said, "Ye can't leave the clan defenseless."

"Besides, brother," Gaufrid sneered, "ye do not command my warriors."

"Kirkoswald is on fire," Dougal bit out. "Every moment we delay..." He didn't want to think about it. "Let go."

Dougal knew he'd suffer later for defying his brother. Defying and humiliating him in front of the clan. But he'd gladly pay the price to save the village. "Let. Go."

Gaufrid's eyes squinched with fury as his knuckles tightened on the bridle.

This was no time for sibling rivalry. Time was slipping away. Dougal had to save Kirkoswald. Even if he had to do it himself.

Out of patience, he gave Urramach a quick jab with his heels, and the steed bolted. If his brother hadn't released his grip at the last instant, he might have lost a finger.

But Dougal never looked back. He rode like the wind toward Kirkoswald.

Once again, it was up to Dougal to do what his brother could not. Pick up the reins when Gaufrid dropped them. Pay heed to the matters the laird neglected. Heal the wounds he inflicted. Hold the clan together.

He never resented what he was required to do on his brother's behalf. It only troubled him when Gaufrid tried to get in his way.

Even at Urramach's thundering pace, it took a long and anxious quarter of an hour to reach the village.

Nothing could have prepared him for the devastation.

He was too late. The fire was already out. Not because it had been extinguished. But because there was nothing left to burn.

The flames had fed on everything in the village. Every thatched roof. Every wattle fence. Every wooden post. Nothing remained but flattened and charred shadows of what had been.

Wisps of white smoke coiled from the smoldering black bones of the cottages, like final gasps of the fire that had greedily consumed the flesh of Kirkoswald.

As he removed his helm and rode gingerly through the village, Dougal noticed something else.

Silence.

Where were the fiends who had wrought such destruction?

And where were the villagers?

There should be lasses wailing over their lost homes. Men calling out orders for buckets of water. Children bawling in fright.

Where was everyone?

Only one structure remained standing. The church.

Its roof was gone. Black beams protruded upward from the scorched and crumbling stone walls, like fingers reaching for heaven. The high and slim stained glass windows had cracked from the heat. Through the fissures leaked threads of smoke. The thick oak double doors were still intact.

He dismounted and slowly climbed the stone steps.

What he saw made his blood run cold. Wedged through the twin handles of the doors, locking them together, was a pair of heavy blacksmith tongs.

Later he would learn he'd burned his fingers as he wrested the tongs from the door. But in the moment, he was numb.

When he tried to push the doors inward, he was met with resistance. And then the odor hit him. A sweet, sulfur, acrid smell.

Unmistakable.

Unforgettable.

The horrible stench of burnt flesh.

Dread gripped his throat like a vise. It took all of his strength to shove the doors inward just a few inches. And then he saw why.

Bodies were piled up against the doors.

Bodies with charred skulls and twisted limbs.

Their clothing had melded with their flesh.

Nothing but black holes gaped where their eyes had been.

Their bony fingers grasped and clawed at an unseen enemy.

Their teeth opened wide in silent screams.

The church had been set on fire. And the only exit had been blocked.

They'd been burned alive. Intentionally.

Men. Women. Children. The entire village.

Stunned sick and weakened by horror, Dougal sank to his knees. His grief was too deep for words or tears.

He'd known these people. He'd brought them food when they were hungry. Helped them bring new livestock into the world. Celebrated their weddings with them. Only two days ago, he'd sent the castle midwife to assist the birthing mother here. They'd been christening the bairn in the church when the attackers came.

Dougal's heart sank as he realized that somewhere among the bodies was a wee lass only two days old.

Suddenly he couldn't breathe. His chest ached, as if a mill stone pressed upon his ribs. As if they would crack under the unbearable weight of tragedy.

When at last he was able to draw in a ragged gasp, it came with the sudden, searing pain of guilt.

This was his fault.

He was supposed to protect the villagers. They depended on him to keep them safe. His brother couldn't do it. So it was up to Dougal alone. He was supposed to look after them.

But he hadn't. He'd failed them.

He'd allowed vandals to destroy their village. To murder them all.

They were dead because of him.

Behind him, Urramach neighed and stamped at the ground, anxious to be away from this noxious place of death.

For a long while, Dougal couldn't move. He was frozen by grief. Burdened by remorse. Dead inside.

But deep within the smoldering ruins of his heart began to burn a hot ember of rage. Rage for the ones who had done this. For their wanton slaughter and savage cruelty. The mindless, senseless violence perpetrated against innocent victims.

The ember slowly bloomed to life. Burning higher and hotter. Purifying his guilt with fiery intention. Coalescing into a single white-hot flame of vengeance.

He steeled his jaw. Narrowed his eyes. Clenched his fists. And rose like a phoenix from the ashes of annihilation.

"Mac Giric," he hissed between his teeth like a bitter vow. That was the badge the Fortanachs had found. That was the clan that must pay.

Dougal the noble warrior was no more. The man who rode east like a demon possessed was a new champion.

Forged in the fires of retribution, he was ruthless.

Unforgiving.

Deadly.

CHAPTER 2

Creagor, The Borders

Feiyan la Nuit couldn't breathe.

In the blink of an eye, the unimaginable had happened. The friendly tournament melee had been transformed into a bloody battleground.

The first tournament at Creagor, celebrating the recent union between her Rivenloch cousin Jenefer and Morgan Mor mac Giric, was supposed to finish with a lighthearted free-for-all with blunted blades.

At least that was how it started.

The clang of metal weapons and the playful taunting of jovial opponents filled the balmy spring air. More than a hundred competitors had come from faraway lands to test their mettle against the infamous Rivenloch warriors. They now joined in the mock battle, young and old alike. Even Feiyan's nephews were allowed to take part, since the worst they would likely suffer were a few scrapes and bruises.

Feiyan grinned as she sparred with a large mac Giric knight, confounding him as she pitted her pair of blunt, forked *sais* from the East against his dulled longsword.

Then, out of nowhere, a sharp claymore intruded upon their sport.

Whistling through the air, it landed with killing force.

Breaking swords.

Breaking bones.

Hacking through chain mail and gambeson.

Savagely wounding and slashing everything in its path.

Shrieks of disbelief and screams of pain suddenly rent the air. But they didn't stop the one wielding the blade. They only fueled his fury.

The brutal knight behind the cruel attack was large, dark, aggressive, and merciless. He swung his great blade in wide swaths, like a ruthless reaper harvesting souls. And though Feiyan couldn't discern his face in the shadows of his black helm, she could feel the pure rage and beastly violence emanating from his armor.

It was his final blow, striking her cousin Hallie's head—a blow that knocked off Hallie's helm and sent her to the ground with a horrible, deadly thud—that stopped Feiyan's breath.

In one fateful instant, fierce and vital Hallie was rendered still. Silent.

For Feiyan, time slowed to a crawl.

Her eyes widened while her brain tried to deny what she saw. Weighed down in the moment, she couldn't drag her gaze away from the dreadful sight.

Outside sounds grew muffled, until all she could hear was the sluggish pounding of her own heart, like dull blows beating the drum of her soul.

It wasn't possible.

Hallie couldn't be dead.

The three Rivenloch cousins—Hallie, Feiyan, and Jenefer—were as close as sisters. From the time they were small, they'd done everything together.

Made mischief.

Battled foes.

Grown to womanhood.

The three of them were an unstoppable force.

That Hallie could be gone forever—and so suddenly—was unimaginable.

Yet there she lay, motionless on the ground.

Even the monster responsible for her defeat seemed stricken by what he'd done. Jarred from his furious onslaught, he dropped his claymore with a ragged gasp. Staggered back. And fled.

Some of her clan bolted after him in pursuit, shaking their useless, dulled weapons. But before anyone could reach him, the man swung up onto an enormous black charger and dug his heels into the horse's flanks. Man and beast thundered across the sod, disappearing out the palisade gates of Creagor.

Meanwhile, a knight sank to his knees beside Hallie. Morgan Mor mac Giric's right hand man, Colban an Curaidh. Colban the Champion. The Highlander Hallie had once captured. The man Hallie's matchmaking sister had called The One.

He wouldn't accept that Hallie was dead. Whether by a miracle born of desperation, the man's stubbornness, or the sheer strength of his love, Colban somehow managed to breathe life back into the woman without whom he couldn't live.

At Hallie's first gasp of precious breath, Feiyan's heart swelled with gratitude.

Her chest ached.

Her eyes filled with tears.

But while everyone else crowded around, exclaiming in awe and relief—murmuring over Hallie, sighing over Colban and the power of love—Feiyan backed away, trembling.

Not with fear now. But with rage.

An intruder had burst into her world.

Threatened the ones she loved.

Rained destruction and mayhem down on her clan.

Nearly stolen her cousin from her.

He must pay.

She would make him pay.

As she retreated, separating herself from the crowd, her gaze alit on a great sword abandoned on the field, sharp and bloody and damning. His claymore.

The fiend had left it behind.

Feiyan tucked her *sais* away and quietly picked up the strange blade. She studied the hilt. The crossbar was carved with an insignia. A great oak tree with a single word below it. She traced a finger over the letters. Mac DARRAGH.

She had the savage's name.

With that, she could hunt him down.

Urramach chewed up the muddy road at neck-breaking speed. Branches whipped at the horse's sides. Trees passed in a blur. Every impact of hoof on sod sent a shudder through Dougal's chain mail. And a shiver through his soul.

The wind rushed by his ears, whispering the harsh accusation.

Murderer.

No matter how fast he rode, Dougal couldn't outrun the truth that pursued him. He couldn't escape what he'd just done.

Never had he imagined the moment of sweet reckoning would turn so bitter.

Never had he imagined, when he finally reached the mac Giric's stronghold, three days of pent-up hunger for vengeance would erupt in violence so overwhelming, it would render him blind. With his head swimming in a blood-red miasma of rage, he'd surged forward into the heart of danger like a wild animal. Slashing with his sword again and again. Hacking, breaking, destroying everything in his path.

For one glorious instant on the field of battle, holding his blade aloft, he'd felt like an avenging angel. Felt his ache for justice rewarded. Felt the weight of all the souls he'd lost at Kirkoswald lifted from his shoulders. Doing God's work, he'd sliced through the ranks of the mac Giric devils. Punishing them with an eye for an eye.

He meant to continue until he cut down every last one of them or died in the attempt. At least then he'd know he'd done everything he could to make things right.

Then he struck the woman.

The pale beauty of her face and the golden spill of her hair as she fell to the ground reminded him of the ones he'd left behind. The fallen lasses. The silenced children. The ones he'd been too late to save.

And when the woman's innocent lips exhaled their last breath, the red haze had suddenly lifted from his eyes.

Bloody hell. What was he doing?

A shuddering had begun deep inside him then.

Not fear.

Not revulsion.

But pure horror.

For the first time in three days, he saw clearly. What he saw was that he'd become the monster he despised.

His chest sank. The claymore dropped from his nerveless fingers. He staggered under the crushing weight of the atrocity he'd committed.

But ultimately, his instinct for survival took over.

Now, riding for his life through the darkening wood, he realized how rash and reckless he'd been in coming here. His judgment had been clouded by anguish. His thirst for revenge had been fed by grief and guilt.

Nothing had come of it but tragedy. More death. More suffering.

Despite tearing up the ground to flee Creagor, he knew that no amount of distance he put between himself and his sin would diminish the truth.

Dougal was no better than the savages he'd set out to punish.

Feiyan had to act now.

The monster had to be stopped.

And time was of the essence.

It didn't matter that Hallie had survived. The brute with the claymore had intended to kill her. He'd intended to kill everyone on the field.

Under different circumstances, Feiyan would have rounded up Hallie and Jenefer for the journey. The three cousins did almost everything together, working hand-in-hand to mete out justice and protect the clan.

But for the first time in her life, she realized that where she was going, her cousins couldn't follow. This particular kind of revenge required stealth, speed, shrewdness, and nerves of steel. A cold heart and a steady hand. Qualities only Feiyan possessed.

Hallie was cool, measured, and thoughtful. She would likely try to reason with the villain, hoping to make him see the error of his ways, and get herself killed for her efforts.

Jenefer was brash and hotheaded. She would strike first, ask questions later, and end up with her head in a noose.

Besides, her cousins' lives had changed. They were married now. They had husbands, leadership, new responsibilities. Now that the immediate threat was gone, they wouldn't want to tag along on Feiyan's mission of vengeance.

It was time for her to prove herself. To prove to her

illustrious cousins and to the clan that Feiyan la Nuit was worthy to be a warrior daughter of Rivenloch.

All her life, she'd been considered the *wee* lass of the three. Small and dark-haired, she'd always stood in the shadow of her towering, golden cousins. When she *was* noticed, she was seen as young, quiet, harmless. Sometimes she wasn't seen at all.

No one remembered that it was Feiyan last year who had escaped Creagor on her own, stealing past the guard, when the three cousins were taken hostage. That she'd been the one to warn Rivenloch of the English attack.

But it was that same invisibility that would serve her well now.

Besides, she knew something about herself that not even her cousins suspected.

Of the three of them, Feiyan was the most ruthless.

The most cunning.

The most deadly.

The same demure manner that allowed Feiyan to disappear in the wake of her magnificent cousins also enabled her to steal up on her enemy, to do what needed to be done, quietly and efficiently.

It was up to her—and her alone—to take on the unsavory task of assassination. She was the only one with the will and the nerve to do it. And the safety of the clan depended upon it.

She studied the claymore once more before dropping it back on the sod. Then she slipped through the crowd toward the pavilion where her weapons were stored.

She armed herself for battle, hiding her exotic blades in the secret folds and pockets of her dark green gambeson. As she tucked away her *yan zi fei dao*, her swallow tail darts, she furrowed her brows.

Mac Darragh. That name belonged to a clan in the west of Scotland, by the sea near Ayr, more than a hundred miles away. What quarrel could a Westlander possibly have with the border clan at Creagor?

It didn't matter. He'd tried to slaughter her clansmen and her cousin. He deserved to die.

She donned her leaf-colored mask and coif and pulled the dark green hood over her head, leaving only her eyes visible. Then she shouldered her pack of belongings, and disappeared into the shadows of the wood.

There was only one westward road wide enough to accommodate a fugitive on horseback. Situated several miles north of Creagor, the main thoroughfare roughly followed the river.

By the time she reached the road hours later, the sun was already setting. On foot, she was clearly no match for a rider.

But she had several advantages.

She was patient. Persistent. Tireless. Motivated. Unafraid of the dark. And she knew several detours through the forest that would shave hours off her journey.

She was also blessed by a nearly full moon, which would guide her when night fell. She didn't intend to sleep until justice was served. Until the monster's cold blood dripped down her hot blade of revenge.

As she'd expected, the ground was gouged and scarred by the charger's heavy hooves. The man had made no effort to disguise his passage, riding at a reckless speed to elude pursuit.

Also as expected, he was headed west, probably fleeing toward Ayr.

Fortunately, Feiyan knew a shorter path through the wood.

It would still be a long while before she'd catch up to a man on horseback. Maybe a day. Maybe two. But she *would* catch up to him.

She'd be damned if she'd let the Westland devil run loose through her Scotland.

Dougal couldn't keep up this manic pace forever. He'd already run Urramach half to death to get to Creagor in three days. The return trip to the coast would surely finish the animal.

Still, there was no time to waste. The bright moon was not his friend tonight. Sooner or later, the mac Giric men would catch up with him. He'd killed one of their womenfolk. And he'd left behind the claymore that had done the deed. A blade that damned all of Darragh.

His foes' eyes would be full of bloodlust. Their hearts full of vengeance. From what he'd experienced against their blunted blades, Dougal doubted he'd last long against their sharpened swords. He might be a feared fighter in his own clan. But he was no match for a company of seasoned border warriors.

He had to reach Ayr before they did. Warn his clan before the enemy descended upon them, bringing a deadly tempest of revenge.

He'd been a fool to come so unprepared. He'd assumed the bloodthirsty mac Girics were nothing but a cowering band of outlaws. He'd never imagined they would turn out to be an organized army.

An hour later, he had no choice but to rein back the wheezing charger, slowing him to a walk.

The steed's sides were heaving. His flanks glistened with sweat. Flecks of foam blew out with every breath. Without rest and water, the horse would die.

The road generally followed the river. A gap between the trees led downhill, toward the distant hiss of rushing current. Dougal dismounted and led Urramach through the brush, using his dagger to clear the way.

A few hundred yards brought them to the river's edge. Dougal fell to his knees in the silt, scooping his hand into the shallows and slurping up the cool water.

But the charger only stood and stared at the river. The proverb about leading a horse to water echoed in Dougal's head. Surely Urramach was thirsty. But the stubborn beast took no interest in the water, jerking back when Dougal lifted a palm full of it to the horse's lips.

He muttered a curse. This was not going to work. If Urramach didn't drink, he would exhaust himself and collapse on the trail. And Dougal had no time to wait for him to work up a good thirst.

After several fruitless attempts at coaxing him to drink, Dougal made up his mind. As much as it pained him, for his beloved destrier had served him well, and traveling on foot would slow Dougal's progress, the only answer was to abandon the beast.

The mac Girics would be searching for a man on horseback, after all. Without the horse, Dougal could slip in and out of the forest, concealing the signs of his passage, throwing his pursuers off his trail.

He pitched his helm, shield, chausses, and hauberk into the bushes. Chain mail might protect him in battle, but it would burden him now. Besides, he could hardly bear to look at his armor, stained red with innocent blood.

Taking only what provisions he could carry, he led Urramach back to the road. There he continued at an amble for a mile or so until he found a suitable place to leave the beast. With a heavy sigh and a bitter heart, he tied his faithful destrier to a tree. Then he shouldered his belongings and ducked into the woods, following a narrow deer trail that branched off the road.

The trail eventually opened onto a small moonlit glen. On the far side of the meadow was a wider footpath that continued in a westerly direction through the trees.

With each mile, the pines grew thicker and more menacing, until they blocked out the moonlight, and he could no longer see the trail.

Surely he was out of danger now. Far from the main road. Far from his horse. Deep in the wood.

He needed to sleep for a few hours. If sleep was possible.

After that, he'd have to eat. If he could. He'd gone days without a decent meal.

Using cracked branches and twisted rushes, he assembled a primitive snare. Perhaps while he slept, some small, hapless night creature would volunteer to be his breakfast.

Then, bundling up in his plaid, he burrowed under a bed of pine needles beside the trail.

Exhaustion made him fall asleep in moments. He was immediately drawn into a world of harrowing nightmares.

Kirkoswald was engulfed in fire. Smoke boiled out of every thatched roof, coiling like dragon's breath into the sky. Men and women, lads and lasses—trapped in the hellish inferno inside the church—scrabbled and pounded in panic at the doors, shrieking in agony and screaming his name.

And the blonde warrior angel he'd struck down at Creagor stood in the flames of the burning church rooftop to brandish an accusing finger at him.

CHAPTER 3

Feiyan traveled all night before the detour brought her back to the main road. The moon sank into the west. The stars winked out. The sky faded like a bruise, from deep indigo to soft purple. In another hour, the sun would rise.

When she emerged from the wood, she was disappointed to find the road unmarked. There was no sign a rider had passed this way.

Had he taken a different road? Had he stopped somewhere for the night? Or, she wondered with a leaden heart, had he managed to elude her? Was he even now perpetrating violence on more unsuspecting victims?

Her jaw tightened with worry as she cast a reluctant gaze back down the road. She'd have to backtrack. Find the place where he'd changed direction.

After half an hour, in the pale lavender light just before dawn, she spotted the dark silhouette of his destrier beside the road. Even a hundred yards away, the beast was unmistakable.

Enormous. Black. Magnificent.

It was tethered to a tree at the edge of a croft.

Feiyan curled her fingers around the leather grip of her *shoudao*, the deadly single-edged sword from the Orient she wore on her hip. She had to proceed with caution.

The man may have left the horse as bait. He could very well be hiding in the woods nearby with a bow and arrows.

Or he could have availed himself of the crofter's cottage, killing the occupants and lodging there for the night.

She slipped her blade silently out of its sheath and approached the horse with caution.

When she was a dozen yards away, she heard the creak of the cottage door. She ducked quickly behind a pine and watched as a woman with a basket emerged from the cottage.

The woman suddenly stopped in her tracks, taken aback by the sight of the strange horse at the edge of her property.

"Robert!" she called out. "Come quick!"

A tall, gangly man hobbled out the door. "What the devil?"

Feiyan froze as the couple came near for a closer look.

The villain must not be in their cottage. Maybe he'd spent the night in one of their sheds. Maybe he was lurking inside, planning to waylay them when they came to investigate. Maybe he meant to slay them in cold blood.

She waited with bated breath as the woman cooed over the beautiful beast. The man took the horse's bridle, calming the animal with soothing speech.

The woman nodded toward the horse's head. "What's that?"

The man pulled out a sooty rag tucked into the bridle. "A missive?"

"Are those letters?"

"Aye. Fetch Gille Christ."

The woman hurried off toward the stable.

Feiyan bit her lip. What if the monster was hiding inside?

She was about to shout a warning when the woman yelled out, "Gille Christ!"

A moment later, a scrawny, redheaded young lad in monk's robes stumbled sleepily out the stable door. "Aye?"

The lad didn't seem to be in any immediate danger. No villain held a knife to his throat.

The crofter called out, "See if you can make out these letters, son."

The lad rubbed his tonsured head, glared suspiciously at the big black horse, and then studied the scrap of cloth.

"D.O.N.U.M. E.S.T." He frowned. "'Tis Latin."

"What's it say?" the woman asked.

"Donum est," he told her. "Gift. 'Tis a gift for ye."

The crofter stepped beyond the horse to look down the road both ways. "A gift? From whom?"

The woman seized the horse's bridle. Already her eyes were lighting up with gratitude. Or greed. Feiyan wasn't sure which. Certainly such a horse was not suited to pulling a crofter's cart. But it would bring a handsome price at market.

Still, what did it mean?

Surely a brute capable of cutting down warriors in cold blood would never make a gift of his valuable destrier to a pair of poor crofters and a novice monk.

He must have sacrificed the horse to throw his pursuers off his scent. Which meant he'd proceeded on foot.

Fortunately, he'd taken as little care to disguise his own tracks as he had with the horse's. Beside the road, leading away from the charger, were fresh depressions in the mud. Made by large boots, one with a distinct crack in the heel, they led down a deer trail into the forest.

Feiyan's lip curled up in a calculating smile.

He'd assumed he'd be harder to track in the wilds of the woods. What he didn't know was Feiyan was now in her element, as comfortable in the forest as a fish in water.

Still, a curious thought pestered her as she traveled silently through the wood.

How did mac Darragh—a Highlander of mindless savagery and beast-like rage—know how to read and write?

Dougal woke to the sound of frantic thrashing in the snare he'd set.

Exhaustion sat like an anvil on his chest. Still he struggled up onto his elbows. Sunlight was already filtering through the boughs of the pines. He hadn't meant to sleep so late. But he felt as if he'd gotten no rest at all.

Again and again in his dreams, like some infernal punishment, he'd been forced to deliver the fatal blow to the blonde woman. Blindly shoving his elbow out. Driving the pommel of his claymore into her steel helm with enough force to knock it off. And then watching the spill of golden tresses as his victim—a beautiful lass—dropped to the ground.

He hadn't intended to do it.

He wasn't a killer of women.

He'd only meant to slaughter those who deserved death—the demons of mac Giric.

How could he have known there was a lass on the field?

Bloody hell. What kind of a clan let its lasses fight in a melee?

He snorted back his remorse, casting it off like a broken targe. It was too late for regrets. What was done was done. He'd have to suffer with the nightmares. After all, he deserved them.

But while he was awake, guilt would only burden him and slow his progress. He had to cast it off as he had his armor.

He scrubbed at his raw eyes and ruffled the dead leaves from his hair. Then he squinted into the underbrush, where a small coney was struggling in the trap.

How long had it been since he'd eaten? He couldn't remember. He hadn't felt like eating in days. He didn't feel like eating now.

It was just as well. The moment he unsheathed his dagger, the lucky coney nibbled through the noose of rushes around its leg and raced away. With a curse of disgust, Dougal hurled the dagger at the creature. Missing it by a yard.

He grimaced and kicked at the leaves, wishing for the hundredth time that he'd stayed in Ayr. He should never have set foot on this hostile soil. This wild part of Scotland, where coneys were as wily as foxes and lasses wielded weapons of war.

Feiyan was so weary from traveling all night and day, she could hardly place one foot in front of the other. Her eyes were gritty and sore. Her eyelids were heavy. Her bones ached. Her mind kept wandering. As she trudged along, the combination of soothing birdsong and afternoon sunlight on her face began to beckon her to sleep.

Then she stumbled across the remains of an animal snare. She grew alert at once. The villain must have left it behind.

The snare was a simple device. A pliable branch with a noose made of rushes that had been triggered by a notched twig.

He'd caught something. But there was no ash to indicate a fire.

She grimaced. Whatever he'd snared, he must have eaten raw.

But what else would she expect from a barbarian?

She'd wisely packed a bit of sustenance from the pavilion. She had little appetite, but she needed to keep up her strength. She dug in her pack and pulled out a linen-wrapped hunk of hard cheese and an oatcake.

Though she'd sworn she wouldn't rest until she'd punished the murderous mac Darragh, she knew she'd be useless without a break.

Hunting prey while the trail was warm was wise.

Exercising patience was wiser.

She would lull the man into believing he was safe. Catch him off his guard. Surprise him when he least expected it.

She bit into an oatcake and chewed thoughtfully.

She still wasn't sure what she'd do when she finally caught him.

Feiyan had always believed in mind over muscle. Relying on wit rather than power. Turning a foe's own strengths against him.

In a world conquered by might, a young lass like Feiyan was viewed as small, weak, vulnerable. Such misperceptions were useful. The principles of fighting her mother Miriel had taught her—agility, evasiveness, speed, flexibility— served her well.

As her mother's teacher Sung Li often claimed, the greatest weapon was the one no one knew you possessed.

There was no question in Feiyan's mind she possessed the skills to take the monster down. As long as she could practice patience.

What remained in question was whether she'd allow him the opportunity to defend himself.

In her mind, he deserved death without mercy.

Hardly tasting the rest of the meal, she finished it with a swig from her aleskin.

But a full belly made her even groggier.

Lying back on the bed of pine needles, she pulled her hood down over her eyes to block out the light. A short rest would do her good, refreshing her and giving her the strength to resume the hunt.

She wouldn't sleep long. Just a wee nap.

CHAPTER 4

Dougal had to eat. Soon. Even if he had no appetite. Hunger was making him delirious. He'd begun to wonder if it was possible to snatch a bird in mid-flight or scoop up a trout from the river with his bare hands. His famished body had almost convinced him to try the plump black berries of the poisonous nightshade growing along the path.

After the slaughter at Kirkoswald, he'd been too full of grief to think of food. In his haste to ride after the murderous mac Girics, he'd had only one thought on his mind. Driving the bloodthirsty clan out of Scotland.

And now, the fact that he had killed a woman left the bitter taste of sin on his tongue. A taste that no food or drink would ever wash from his mouth.

Still, time had dulled his grief and sharpened the hunger in his belly. If he had any hope of returning home, he needed to eat. He was past waiting for a coney to wander into a snare.

He'd brought no coin with him. But he could be resourceful.

Lightheaded, he made his way back to the main road. It was a risk. In broad daylight, he'd be much easier to spot. But perhaps, without his horse and armor, he'd be unrecognizable to the mac Girics tracking him.

Pulling his hood forward and staying in the shadows of the trees that arched over the road, he walked for nigh an hour, until he heard a cart approaching behind him.

The mac Giric knights wouldn't be traveling by cart. It was safe enough to step into the sunlight to give the driver a friendly wave.

A man and a lad, probably his son, were driving a cart loaded with peat.

For one ugly moment, Dougal consdered overpowering the pair, stealing the cart, and making his escape. No one knew him here. No one knew he was the brother of the mac Darragh laird. Here he was only a common outlaw. A woman-killer and a fugitive. What did one more crime matter?

As the cart neared, the man pulled back on the reins.

"Ho there, fine sir!" the driver called out with a tug at his hat, no doubt taking note of Dougal's well-made boots and gambeson, his fine woolen plaid, and the jeweled dagger tucked into his sheath.

"Good day," Dougal replied.

"May I ask where you're headed, sir?"

It was best not to be specific. "Just travelin' through."

"I see. Then you might be grateful for a word of warning."

"Aye? What's that?"

"This forest is thick with outlaws. A man of your... standing...could prove a temptation to their sort."

"Is that so?"

The young lad pointed at Dougal's dagger. "Someone might want to take that. Look at the jewels, Da."

"Aye," the man agreed. Suddenly his eyes gleamed with something more than admiration.

"This?" Dougal's voice was light, but he drew the blade, flipping it in his hand in an unspoken warning, just in case the driver had any unsavory motives. "Hmm. I suppose ye're right."

The man's eyes glittered with enterprise as he eyed the jewels. "For a shilling," he offered, thoughtfully stroking his chin, "I could take you to the next town."

"A shillin'," he pretended to muse.

It was an outrageous price, bordering on robbery. And it occurred to him again that he could probably take the cart by force. Abscond with the horse and peat and leave these two in the dust.

But the idea soured his stomach. Despite his recent failures, chivalry still burned inside his heart, preventing him from doing what was expedient. Forcing him to do what was right.

"I don't need a ride," he decided.

"Half a shilling," the man revised.

Even if he'd had the coin, Dougal would never give it to a man who would take such clear and callous advantage of a stranger.

He sauntered toward the horse and patted its cheek, casually looping his hand around the bridle so the horse couldn't bolt.

The guileless lad stood up and moved to the edge of the cart seat. "You could sit here, sir, between—"

The father, realizing he'd misjudged Dougal's intent, took his son's arm and pulled him back down onto the cart seat.

"You're a thief, aren't you?" the man grumbled. "Lucifer's luck. I should have known."

"Me?" Dougal scoffed. "Ye wanted a shillin' for a ride to town. Who's a thief?"

The man glared at him. "We've got nothing of value, only piles of peat."

The lad, trying to be helpful, offered, "We do have a wee bit of silver, Da, from the last village."

The man's mouth tensed as he eyed Dougal's dagger.

But Dougal replied, "I don't want your coin."

"You can't take my cart."

"I won't."

The man eased a protective arm around his son. "Then what do you want?"

Dougal nodded to the basket lodged between them. "Just a wee bit o' whate'er ye have in there."

"That's nothin' but our sup-" The man looked shocked for a moment. Then, making a hasty decision, he snatched up the basket and tossed it at Dougal's head.

The instant Dougal released the bridle, throwing up his arms to block the basket, the driver slapped the reins down. The horse shot off, and the cart careened down the road so fast that the lad nearly bounced off his seat.

As they bolted away, Dougal scowled and put away his dagger. There was no need for them to panic. He only wanted a bit of food.

He hunkered down to examine the damage.

Aside from a pair of cracked apple coffyns, bruised berries, and a small chunk of bacon that would require rinsing, everything seemed sufficiently edible to his watering mouth. There was a small round of ruayn cheese, a half dozen oatcakes, and even a skin of watered wine. Gathering everything back into the basket, he returned to his less-traveled path and sat down to feast.

A full belly revived him enough to proceed several miles more. But as the afternoon shadows lengthened and the woods grew dim, the cart driver's words returned to haunt him. Was the forest indeed "thick with outlaws"?

Though his purse was empty, Dougal mac Darragh was obviously a man of means. He had the body of a warrior and the bearing of a noble. Even the cart driver had seen that.

A thief might be tempted to pilfer Dougal's only weapon for its jewels.

Steal the valuable clothes off his back.

Take him captive with an eye toward ransom.

This time, before he made a mossy bed under a sprawling ash tree, Dougal took extra precautions. It was dangerous enough to be pursued by an angry clan. He wasn't about to be surprised by a band of outlaws.

Feiyan woke with a start.

"Oh, for shite's sake," she muttered.

Her wee nap had turned into an all-day drowse. The sun was long gone. The moon peered through the pines with its pale, round eye, and midnight mist clung to the forest floor.

How much distance had the villain gained while she slumbered on, blissfully unaware? Had he stuck to the path or turned off at some point? She'd wasted the daylight. By night and in the fog, he'd be doubly hard to track.

At least she was fully alert now. If need be, she could pursue him all night.

She hurried along the path. Perhaps she could catch the villain sleeping.

A few hours later, she spotted a scrap of beeswax-coated linen beside the trail, the kind of cloth one wrapped around cheese. Near it were crumbs of pastry. And next to that was a depression in the leafy bank, roughly the size of a knight's hindquarters.

He had eaten here. How long ago, she couldn't tell. But this time he'd apparently procured something more palatable than a raw rodent.

This close to the river, the mud was damp and yielding. She could easily discern the tracks of his crack-heeled boot. The food must have invigorated him, for his stride had lengthened. She had to take three steps for his two.

A few times she hesitated, startled by the scuffling of mice or the chirring of a nightjar. But the rising fog muffled her steps as she crept through the woods in the hours after midnight.

Indeed, she was so focused on stealth and speed, intent on closing the distance between her and her prey, when she finally spotted him, she almost sailed past.

Her heart leaped into her throat when she suddenly glimpsed a dark shape in the gray mist, several yards off the path, beneath an enormous tree. For an instant, she thought it was a wolf or a boar, and she clapped a hand to her *shoudao*.

Then she heard a loud, ragged snore, and she soundlessly drew her blade.

It was him. The monster. She had him now. He was utterly helpless.

As silent as a spider, she approached.

With her sharp blade of folded steel, she could slash his throat. Stab him through the heart. Chop off his head.

But as she came closer—five yards away, four, three—doubt began to filter through her thoughts.

What if this was the wrong man?

She'd never actually seen his face or even gotten a good look at his armor. This man didn't have a shield or a helm. All she recalled about the brute at Creagor was that he was large and dark and menacing.

What if she'd followed the wrong set of tracks into the wood?

What if the man she sought had abandoned his horse at the croft and then climbed onto the back of a hay cart and gone back the way he'd come?

What if he'd given away his crack-heeled boots, as he had his charger, as a "gift"?

She hesitated, gazing down at the slumbering bulk.

Once she saw his face, she'd know. She'd recognize the manic violence in his cold eyes. The dead and ruthless twist to his mouth. His empty, insatiable hunger. There was no hiding the disturbed countenance of a man capable of thoughtless savagery.

She'd wake him. Poke him with the slanted point of her sword, keeping it at the ready. If he lunged toward her, she'd stop him swiftly. Do what must be done.

She edged closer, wary of triggering any small animal snares he might have set in the night.

His snores were even now. Peaceful. Almost soothing. They didn't seem like the snores of a demon.

She halfway hoped she was wrong. That this wasn't the right man.

Hearing the soft sawing of his breath, she knew it would be no simple feat to extinguish it. Taking a life wasn't easy.

It wasn't that killing was physically difficult. Even at her young age, she'd been forced to take a handful of lives in wartime. With her skill and fine weaponry, all it required was will, good aim, and opportunity. In the heat of battle, killing was a necessary evil, a matter of slaying or being slain.

But the thought of ending the life of a defenseless man, a man who was the son of a mother, who might well be the sweetheart of a maid, the father of children...slaying someone outside the chaos of war... That was not so easy.

And no matter how much this devil deserved to be dispatched back to hell, Feiyan couldn't send him there without being absolutely certain he was the demon she believed him to be.

In her moment of hesitation, the man stirred and rolled from his side onto his back. She froze as his features were revealed in the milky blue moonlight.

And then her heart tripped.

He was more eye-catching than she'd expected. Surprisingly handsome. Curiously captivating. As magnificent, wild, and noble as his destrier.

Locks of black hair tumbled across his troubled brow.

His cheek was swarthy with several days' growth of beard. His face was lean and angular, with a straight, elegant nose. His mouth was soft with slumber.

And he was young. Much younger than she'd imagined. Probably not much older than her.

She gulped. Was she making a mistake? Surely this dark Adonis wasn't the savage who'd ravaged the knights at Creagor.

Flustered, she realized she had to extricate herself from this awkward situation until she was sure. She had no wish to explain to a handsome young nobleman innocently hunting in the forest why she was stalking him in the middle of the night.

Carefully sheathing her sword, she retreated, taking a step backwards.

All at once, she heard a snap, and something slithered around her ankle. Before she could draw in a gasp, she was yanked off her feet. The world abruptly flipped upside down. She found herself dangling by her ankle, swaying at the end of a rope.

In one painful instant of clarity, her heart leaped into her throat. She'd been trapped like a coney in a snare.

Whatever qualms she had about harming the sleeping stranger vanished into thin air. He was no guileless gentleman. She had indeed found the cunning devil of mac Darragh.

CHAPTER 5

Dougal was jerked out of a dead sleep. He instinctively clapped the ground beside him, where he usually kept his claymore. It wasn't there.

Memory flooded back as he blinked awake in the misty moonlight. He remembered now. He was in the woods. Fleeing Creagor. Pursued by mac Girics. And he'd left his claymore behind.

A dark shape suddenly swung through the shadows above him. He ducked, half expecting a giant owl had swooped at his head.

Then he remembered the snare.

Scrambling to his feet, he backed away from the swinging captive.

It appeared the cart driver was right. The woods *were* teeming with thieves. It was a good thing he'd set the trap.

"Who goes there?" he demanded.

There was no reply. The robber swung past a few more times, curling the fog in his wake, before Dougal reached out a hand to stop him.

The inverted thief's cloak fell over his face like great wings, making him look more like a bat than an owl. From what Dougal could see of the culprit, he was either a very large bird or a rather small human. But he had a very dangerous weapon. A sword was belted around his hips.

The thief was at a clear disadvantage, strung up and dangling by one leg. But his hands were free. If he drew his blade, he could do some damage.

Before that could happen, Dougal loosened the leather belt around the lad's hips.

"I'll take that," he said.

There was a furious, strangling sound from the thief as his suddenly liberated tabard fell even farther over his head, revealing a pair of dark-stockinged legs and pale linen braies. The robber jerked in frustration at the end of the rope.

Dougal unsheathed the sword. It was an unusual single-edged weapon with an angled point, a small oval guard, and an iron ring in place of a pommel. Why a common thief would have such a unique sword, he didn't know. He sliced once through the air, impressed by the way the light blade whistled as it passed.

"So are your minions close by?" Dougal asked. "Or are ye just robbin' folk on your own?"

There was no reply, but the thief went still, as if considering the best answer.

"Perhaps I'll leave ye strung up here as bait and catch the rest o' your band of outlaws."

The thief squirmed at that. Was he afraid that his fellows would be killed? Or that they'd leave him alone to die?

Dougal would do neither, of course. He knew about the desperation of poor folk and what drove a youth to a life of robbery. If no one came out of the trees in the next few moments, Dougal would give the lad a dire warning, box his ears, cut him down, and send him on his way.

That was his plan. Unfortunately, the thief had other ideas.

While Dougal swished the curious blade through the air once more, marveling at the way its sharp edge sliced through the fog, the lad took quick action.

Like a great spider reeling itself back up its silky web,

the thief seized the rope above his ankle and clambered up into the ash tree.

As Dougal watched with his jaw agape, the outlaw loosened the noose and slipped free. Then, issuing a hiss of frustration, the lad leaped off one branch and onto another. He disappeared into the misty forest, as silent as he'd arrived.

Dougal was mystified. What the hell had just happened?

He glanced again at the sword. He felt like he was in some fantastical tale where he'd thwarted a dark faerie, and this shining talisman was his reward.

Surely the thief wouldn't just let him keep the thing. It was far too valuable.

He'd probably left to fetch his fellows and return in full force to reclaim his weapon.

Whatever the outlaw and his cohorts intended, Dougal was wide awake now. He might as well travel onward. It made no difference whether the lad and his band of outlaws were following him. What was one more foe when he was being pursued by an entire army?

Feiyan was furious.

Mostly with herself.

Furious for being caught. For surrendering her sword. For not killing the lout as he lay sleeping. No matter how innocent he appeared.

At least she'd escaped. And she'd managed to hold on to the rest of her weapons, which were tightly secured in the folds of her gambeson. But now that the knave had her *shoudao*, she had all the more reason to stay on his trail.

The conniving villain would assume she was long gone. But she intended to stick close. Keep an eye on him. Watch for an opportunity to reclaim her blade. Reclaim it and *stab* him with it.

Next time, she wouldn't hesitate. Meanwhile, her blunder had cost her the element of surprise. Now that he was alerted to her presence, he would be more wary. And she would have to be more cautious.

Fortunately, she was bloody good at concealment. She would shadow him, steal silently through the trees until he grew careless.

Retrieving her sword might not be easy. She'd seen the way he handled the *shoudao*. Dangling from the rope, she'd caught a glimpse of him testing the blade. He was no inelegant mercenary. He had the bearing of a skilled warrior.

But she was no ordinary outlaw. And she wasn't about to let him get away with stealing her favorite weapon.

She tracked him for hours, avoiding detection by alternating her strategy. Sometimes she traveled through the underbrush, sometimes through the canopy. For a mile she would trail him at a distance, then surge ahead to lead the way. At some times she'd watch him through a dense thicket of trees. At others, she'd hide behind a boulder so close to the trail that she felt the breeze of his passing.

As for mac Darragh, he strode with confidence and purpose, not at all what she would have expected from a shiftless, mayhem-making vagabond. His forthright manner belied his capacity for irrational violence.

Of course, Feiyan knew better. She might have glimpsed the Westlander's handsome face. But she'd also seen his dark heart. And she let that memory inform her as she screwed up the courage to do what she knew must ultimately be done.

She saw no need to linger over the deed. She had no stomach for torture. Once she had her *shoudao* back in her possession, she'd commit his soul to the afterlife swiftly and surely, just as he'd felled Hallie with one blow.

Meanwhile, he continued on, ignorant of her dire

intentions. Indeed, he seemed completely oblivious to her presence, a fact reinforced when he stopped on the trail, unceremoniously loosened his trews, and relieved himself behind the very tree in which she was perched.

She averted her eyes—mostly.

Hitching up his trews, he continued on, but it was a long while before she worked up the nerve to follow.

Gradually the fog lifted. The sky, visible between the spires of pines, grew light. The stars slowly dissolved. Like a woad-dyed kirtle that softened with each washing, the heavens faded from indigo to azure to cerulean as the sun cast its light on the waking world.

Feiyan could no longer rely on the shadows and the mist for cover. She drew up the green hood to conceal her hair and masked the lower part of her face, leaving a slit for her eyes, rendering her imperceptible.

The day brought a new camouflage of sound. Larks and sparrows twittered madly for mates. Woodpeckers knocked at oak trees. Families of quail and scampering coneys skittered through the leaf-fall. Squirrels and crows scolded one another from the branches.

It was midday when the man turned from the path, taking a winding deer trail that led down to the river. Here the water rushed past at great speed, frothing over rocks and coiling into deep currents along the shore. As Feiyan took cover in the rushes, the whisper and roar thankfully disguised the rumbling in her belly.

In her haste to escape, she'd been forced to leave behind the last of her food. Now she was beginning to feel pangs of hunger.

He must have been hungry as well. Making his way along the edge of the riverbank, he located a large boulder where an eddy swirled above a dark and shady pool. It was a perfect spot for trout.

He broke a long, finger-thick branch from an alder and

used his dagger to strip off the twigs. Tying together several fibrous reeds, he made a fishing line. One end he tied to the pole. To the other, he attached a hook he carved out of wood. Then he dug in the mud until he found a lively earthworm to use for bait.

After that, he stood on the bank for a long while, dribbling his line into the water while Feiyan quietly climbed a nearby oak to observe.

From her perch on the oak limb, she could study every detail of his appearance, every nuance of his movement, every expression in his face. She hoped to work up a good loathing for the man so that killing him would be easy.

But as she watched him, it was difficult to imagine him as the demon who had charged through her clansmen. While he had the size and strength of the man who'd tried to single-handedly cut down an entire company of knights, his behavior as he fished was far different. Peaceful. Measured. Coaxing. Patient.

She studied his clothing. Somewhere along the way, he'd discarded his armor, his shield, and his helm. What remained was practical, but well-made, not at all the attire she'd expect of a feral madman.

His boots were of finely tooled black leather. His jeweled dagger was tucked into a sheath secured with a leather tie around his waist. His quilted black gambeson fit him closely, hugging his broad chest and clinging to his hips, split at the legs and extending just past his knees. Beneath his gambeson, the loose folds of a muted black-and-grey plaid hung nearly to the ground. And knotted around it all, to her exasperation, was her own sword belt and her precious *shoudao*.

His gaze was pensive as he stared into the water. Occasionally his brow would crease and his eyes would dim. Was he feeling the weight of guilt for what he'd done? Or only wishing something would nibble at his line?

She wished something would nibble at his line. She intended to let him land a nice, fat trout before she dispatched him and stole his supper.

A half hour later, he still hadn't caught anything and decided to change his strategy. He stepped onto the boulder to attack the pool from a different angle.

Feiyan settled back against the trunk of the oak. Now she had an even clearer view of him as he hunkered down atop the rock with the sun shining on his face.

She tried to force his countenance into that of a villain.

The locks slashing across his neck and falling in reckless tangles over his brow were as black as sin. His hollow cheeks and square chin were grave-grim. His nose was sharp, like a reaper's scythe. His brow was as dark as death. His eyes reminded her of a deep loch—bright and blue on the surface, with murky and menacing currents beneath. When he'd spoken before, his lips had twisted into a wry, wicked curve. And his voice with its slight Highland cadence had rolled out like thunder, low and threatening.

Yet no matter how she tried to mold mac Darragh's features into those of Lucifer himself, she couldn't deny the fact that if he was a devil, he was a handsome devil indeed.

"There ye are."

His sudden words nearly startled her out of the tree.

But he wasn't speaking to her. He was staring intently at the water. Something was tugging at his line. As it bent the branch of his fishing pole, he came to his feet. Feiyan held her breath, as eager as *he* was for a fish to take the bait.

It continued pulling on the line, and Feiyan could see by the bend in the rod it must be of a considerable size. She tightened her fists, as if she could will the man to set the hook quickly before his catch swam away.

Finally he did, giving his wrist a quick, firm jerk. Man

and fish grappled for a few moments. But when he tried to pull the trout from the water, it proved too heavy for the pole. The last foot of the branch snapped off.

While Feiyan watched in dismay, the line and the fish began to escape downstream.

"Och, nay, ye don't!" he shouted.

He was having none of that. He charged into the water—gambeson, boots, and all—and grabbed the broken branch with its line still attached before it could float away. Hand over hand, he hauled in his prize, battling the current, stumbling over the rocks of the riverbed, and drenching himself in the process.

But persistence won the day. He finally trapped the slippery, flopping fish against his gambeson, crowing in triumph. The trout, almost as long as his chest was wide, would make a decent meal.

She grinned in response.

But her smile faded fast when she remembered her purpose. This was the man she meant to kill. She shouldn't be smiling. Bloody hell. She shouldn't be feeling... anything...for him.

He lumbered forward through the current, hampered by his soaking gambeson. He knocked the trout against the boulder to kill it swiftly before tossing it onto the grassy bank. When he emerged dripping from the water, Feiyan's first thought was that he looked more like magnificent Neptune than wicked Lucifer.

That was before he removed her sword belt, tossing it onto the bank with as little care as he'd given the fish.

Damn the lout! That was a valuable sword. If he didn't dry off the steel blade and rub it with sheep fat, it would rust.

While she silently fumed over his callous mistreatment of her priceless weapon, he unknotted the ties of his gambeson and wrenched the sopping coat from his shoulders.

Her breath caught. The sheer, wet linen of his white leine left little to the imagination. His well-muscled chest looked as if it was carved of marble, smooth and perfect.

Draping his gambeson over a low-hanging alder limb, he grabbed the branch for balance and tugged off his boots.

When his hands fell to the leather belt holding up his drenched and dragging plaid, Feiyan squeezed her eyes shut.

She couldn't keep them closed for long. When she at last dared take a peek, his plaid was stretched out over a bush to dry, and he was strutting about in nothing but his soaking leine, which barely reached his knees.

Feiyan swallowed hard.

Not because she'd never glimpsed a half-naked man. On the contrary, she saw clansmen in various states of undress all the time in her parents' armory.

Not because mac Darragh was so well-formed. Any warrior who did a fair amount of drills developed muscles like his.

Not because her heart fluttered at the idea that she was wickedly spying on him without his knowledge. Feiyan la Nuit had a rich history of spying.

Nay, what stuck in her throat was the knowledge that she was supposed to slay him. She meant to steal back her sword and plunge it into that flawless body.

It was her duty. She knew that. For Rivenloch. For Scotland. For Hallie. She couldn't let a monster like him loose on any more unsuspecting victims.

Still, the idea left a nauseating taste in her mouth.

She swallowed it down. It didn't matter. Her feelings didn't matter. This was a task that had to be done without emotion. Without mercy.

And the sooner she got to it, the sooner she could go home.

Balance the accounts, as her mother said.

Put the unpleasantness behind her.

And earn the respect of the clan.

So she steeled her jaw against the amusing sight of him traipsing through the brush in his undergarments.

She fought the instinct to take pity on him as he battled to start a fire with his wet flint.

She stopped her ears against his voice as he coaxed the tiny flame to life, alternately cooing to it with the tenderness of a dove urging its fledglings to fly and cursing at its stubborn reluctance to take hold.

While he busied himself with the fire, she glanced at her sword, lying on the grass, mere inches from the trout. She bit her lip. Could she steal down from the tree and retrieve it while he was distracted by the blaze?

Just as she extended one leg to start her descent, he came abruptly to his feet.

She froze.

CHAPTER 6

ougal wasn't alone.

He couldn't explain how he knew.

But suddenly, the suspicion that had been troubling him all day—that someone was shadowing him—blossomed from a vague threat to an impending hazard.

Someone was very near. Watching. Waiting.

Maybe it was the mac Girics. Maybe it was the wee outlaw. Maybe it was a pack of hungry wolves.

Whatever the danger, it would do no good to make any sudden moves. Not until he knew more. Until he could locate what was sending a shiver of foreboding along his spine, it was best to act as if he didn't know it was there.

So he whistled with nonchalance as he retrieved the trout and his dagger, heading to the riverbank to gut the fish. All the while, he casually scanned the brush, the reeds, the trees.

It was only when he was skewering the cleaned fish on a makeshift spit that he caught something out of the corner of his eye. Something out of place. A branch that didn't look like a branch. A shadow that was more than a shadow.

In the tree behind his shoulder, a dark shape hugged the trunk.

It had to be the thief. Who else would travel through the branches of trees?

Dougal was impressed the outlaw had followed him so far. Perhaps the lad *was* a dark faerie, after all, come to reclaim his valuable talisman.

Had he brought his fellows with him? Or was he alone?

Dougal supposed he'd find out soon enough.

In the meantime, he'd keep the strange blade close. If the lad was determined enough to follow him so far, there was no telling what he'd do once he had the sword in his hands.

Leaving the fish over the fire to roast, he fetched the lad's weapon and removed it from its sheath. He pretended to examine the blade while keeping an eye on the dark shape in the tree.

The youth didn't move a muscle. Not when Dougal took a few practice swings with the sword. Not when he ventured close to collect more fallen tinder for the fire. Not when he turned the fish on the spit.

As the coals glowed, crisping the skin of the trout, Dougal began to feel sorry for the lad. Surely he was hungry. He was as thin as a post. That was likely why he was an outlaw.

The people of Kirkoswald had been in the same dire situation since Dougal's father had died, faced with stealing or starving.

Dougal had always done what he could to remedy their poverty.

A wave of pain washed over him as he realized he'd never be able to help them again. He'd failed them when they'd needed him most. He could no longer call himself a champion.

Still, his instincts wouldn't let him look the other way. Perhaps the people here had no champion at all. Perhaps they had no choice but to turn to thievery for survival.

Once the trout was done—nicely crisp on the outside,

tender and sweet on the inside—he lifted the skewer from the fire and settled onto a large, flat rock.

Without looking up, he called out, "Ye must be hungry, lad. Come on down, and I'll give ye a wee bite."

Feiyan blinked in alarm. How had he known she was there?

No one ever spotted Feiyan la Nuit. She could spy on lovers from the trees. Watch the servants without their knowing. Steal through the armory unseen.

In short, she'd always been able to hide in plain sight.

Observing mac Darragh, she'd taken special pains to be cautious. In the last half-hour, despite the aching in her muscles, she hadn't budged an inch.

She wished she could say the same for her thoughts. But they'd rattled about in her head like a frenzied hailstorm. Perhaps it was the clatter in her brain he'd detected.

But curse the Westlander! What should have been a simple task was turning into a major undertaking.

She'd figured when the time came to kill the man, she'd do it with the *shoudao*. After all, it was her most efficient, most deadly weapon. The last thing an assassin wanted to do was to leave a target wounded and not dead.

But once he'd doffed his gambeson, leaving himself vulnerable, she realized her other weapons would prove just as effective. She might not need to reclaim her *shoudao* to finish him.

First she considered attacking him with a pair of swiftly fired *yan zi fei dao,* aiming the darts at his vulnerable neck.

Then she decided to do it while he built the fire. Stab him between the ribs with her forked *sais* as he gathered kindling.

Then she meant to do it as he cleaned the trout by the

river. Sneak up behind him with her short but keen-bladed *duandao* and slash his throat.

Then she thought she'd do it when he busied himself with cooking. Push him onto the hot coals and thrust him through with her awl-like *bishou.*

Each time, the idea left a sick gnawing in her gut.

She blamed her nausea on hunger. Perhaps she had no stomach for killing because her stomach was empty.

She'd finally opted to wait until after he finished cooking the trout. That way, at least she'd get a good meal out of it. Maybe the prospect of food would settle her stomach and make what she'd come to do easier.

Now he was offering supper to her freely. That changed everything. It tied her stomach into even tighter knots.

How could she accept charity from a man she meant to kill?

The answer came to her in a flash.

She couldn't murder mac Darragh. Not in cold blood.

If they were to spar, however... Then she would have no qualms about killing him. She'd be giving him a fighting chance. Battling him face to face. She could kill him with a clear conscience.

Already her stomach eased.

She would challenge the Westlander to battle. Naturally she would win. Then, and only then—when he was laid out flat on his back, at her mercy—would she claim revenge for Rivenloch, for Hallie. Take up her sword and give him a swift and noble death.

A death that wouldn't trouble her conscience.

A death that would let her sleep at night.

"Come on. I'm not goin' to hurt ye," he said, coaxing her forward with a wave of his hand. "And I can't eat this enormous fish all by myself."

Feiyan smirked. Enormous? Now he was boasting. She pulled salmon twice that size out of Rivenloch all the time.

Still, her belly growled as she caught a whiff of the roasted trout. Surely there was no harm in supping first and fighting afterward.

Keeping her hood over her head, she crept down from the oak. She edged toward the fire and sat on a mossy stone.

He plucked an alder leaf to fashion a makeshift platter. Then he divided the trout, blowing on his fingers when he burned them, and placed half of his catch on the leaf for her.

She ate carefully, facing away from him to lower her mask and take a bite. Despite her hunger, she lingered over the supper. She hardly tasted the trout, knowing what was to come after she finished eating would be far less appetizing.

Finally she tossed the bones onto the fire and replaced her mask.

Long ago, she'd learned the wisdom of hiding her features. Not only did a mask conceal her identity and gender. In battle, it disguised the merest hint of hesitation and uncertainty. It ensured she wouldn't betray her next move by the clenching of her teeth or the sudden intake of breath.

She let him finish his supper. He might as well enjoy his last meal.

After he'd stripped the trout clean, while he was smacking his lips and licking his fingers, she stood up and braced herself for combat.

"Sit down," he said, arching a brow up at her. "I know ye want your weapon back. But that's not goin' to happen. I won't have ye slayin' me in the middle o' the night."

She didn't need her sword. Not yet. She was confident she could overpower him without it.

She gestured for him to get up. Then, angling her body to give him the smallest target, she flexed her knees, lifted her arms, and summoned him with a wave of her hand.

"Ye wish to grapple for it?" he guessed with a dubious smirk.

She was used to scorn. Men always judged her by her size and underestimated her skill.

She nodded.

He shook his head. "Ye're only a wee lad. Leave while ye can. Save yourself some breaks and bruises."

She raised her fists, insisting he accept her challenge.

"Look," he said. "Ye've taken my charity. Ye've had a nice meal. Go on now. Maybe without your nasty blade, ye'll find a way to make an honest livin'."

She narrowed her eyes. He imagined she was a common outlaw. He didn't realize she was an assassin. That miscalculation would cost him his life.

She lifted her chin and clenched her fists.

"Nay," he said, folding his arms over his chest. "I'm not goin' to fight ye."

This she hadn't foreseen. What villain would walk away from an easy conquest? She bit the inside of her cheek.

He added, "Run along home. I've got no quarrel with ye." He ignored her completely then, sniffing and staring into the flames.

No quarrel with her? This monster had brought destruction into her peaceful world. He'd ravaged her clan folk as if they were rats to be exterminated. And worst of all, he'd thrown down her cousin—fierce, strong, brave Hallie—and left her for dead.

The memory riled up something powerful inside her. The crouching beast within—the creature that had sat in the shadows for days now, waiting for the chance to take vengeance for the horror she'd witnessed—sprang to life.

With a growl deep in her throat, she flung herself forward at the brute that—worse than calling her his foe— dismissed her as if she were nothing.

It was rare that Dougal could be taken unawares. But the wee thief came at him before he could brace for the impact.

He'd assumed, once the lad had a full belly and was soothed of his anger, once he realized the disparity in their size, once he understood Dougal wasn't going to fight him, he might take a few harmless kicks at the dust in frustration and slink off into the woods.

The last thing Dougal expected was to be bowled off the rock.

The lad was a scrappy thing. That was certain. Legs and arms twined about Dougal's body like vines strangling a tree. Knees and elbows jabbed him with painful precision, bruising his flesh and nearly cracking his ribs. The lad scrabbled and scrambled at him with dogged persistence.

Indeed, so unaccustomed was Dougal to wrestling someone half his size, he almost couldn't work up a good defense.

Only when the lad's hand shot out toward the lethal blade lying on the grass beside him did Dougal suddenly spring to life.

With a roar of denial, he surged upward against the lighter weight of his wee attacker, forcing him out of reach of the weapon.

The lad would have dodged past him, but Dougal seized his arm.

Immediately, the lad's other fist shot forward, jabbing him in the throat.

Pain incapacitated Dougal. For a stunned instant, he couldn't breathe. Then he couldn't stop coughing.

But that wasn't the only trick the youth had in his arsenal. He stamped his boot down with great force on top of Dougal's bare foot.

While Dougal was gasping from the new agony coursing

through his bones, the lad plowed his knuckles with sudden force into the tender spot just below his ribs. A dull throbbing radiated out through his stomach, and Dougal wondered if he might lose his hard-won supper.

Somehow, through it all, he managed to hold fast to the outlaw.

Until the lad turned all at once in his grip, pushing forward instead of pulling away. With the sharp point of his elbow, he clipped the tip of Dougal's chin, dazing him and rocking his head back.

Dougal staggered backward, taking his attacker with him. He hadn't wanted to hurt the lad. But this wily thief could obviously take care of himself. So Dougal had to rely on his superior might.

He shook his head to clear the fog from his brain. Then, with a determined grunt, he picked the lad up bodily. Enclosing him in his steely arms, he crushed the youth against his chest until the lad could do nothing but squirm in frustration.

Still the outlaw managed to amaze him. This time the wicked lad jabbed a knee with breathtaking accuracy betwixt his legs.

Dougal moaned and crumpled in pain. Hobbled by aching agony, he was forced to drop the lad.

Once free, the lad swept Dougal's leg out from under him, toppling him onto his back on the forest floor.

But the careless youth made one mistake. He didn't count on Dougal's tenacity. Even as he was falling to the ground, Dougal seized the lad about the shoulders, and they dropped together.

Dougal's back bore the brunt of the fall. He winced as his shoulder blade struck the sharp edge of a rock, and it took a moment to get his breath back.

The outlaw was splayed atop him like a feather coverlet. Indeed, the lad wasn't much *heavier* than a feather coverlet. But this coverlet seemed as if it was filled, not with feathers, but with live birds.

The lad immediately attempted to wriggle out of his grasp. He wrested his shoulders loose and gave Dougal's stomach a hard shove with the heels of his hands.

Then he turned his head toward the sword. In another moment, he might have sprung to his feet and laid hands on the weapon.

But Dougal overpowered the youth, heaving him sideways, rolling him onto his back, and pinning him there with the weight of his body.

Still the lad wouldn't surrender. He flailed beneath Dougal until Dougal finally captured his wrists against the ground and rocked back to sit astride the wild lad's hips, rendering his legs useless.

As he caught his breath, the lad seared him with a smoldering gray glare. Dougal was sure that behind the mask, the youth was cursing him to hell. Every muscle of the lad's body was tense as he tried fruitlessly to twist free, and he looked as if he wished to commit murder.

Then Dougal noticed something disturbing in the outlaw's burning gaze.

Something curious about the startling pair of silvery eyes and the dark brows that lowered over them with hatred.

A delicate vulnerability that belied the lad's strength.

Dougal frowned. It couldn't be.

Risking the release of one of the lad's wrists, he reached up and snatched down the outlaw's mask.

CHAPTER 7

A scream of outrage gathered in Feiyan's throat.

The target wasn't supposed to *see* her.

Assassins were faceless.

Murder was cold and clean.

Without emotion. Without hesitation. Without mercy.

Now the villain had stripped away her emotional armor.

Now he could see, not only the glittering purpose in her gaze and the determination in her jaw that made her capable of killing him, but also the trembling in her lips, the flaring of her nostrils, and the blush of her cheek that indicated her reluctance to do it. Her distaste. Her regret.

She swallowed her scream.

As much as she hated this compromised situation, her objective hadn't changed. She still had to find a way to slay him. But now she was forced to resort to a less lethal weapon in her arsenal. A weapon she didn't like to use. But an effective one. One that worked on most men. One that had worked on him before, bringing his violent rampage at Creagor to a screeching halt.

Her femininity.

As he gaped at her, his eyes wide with shock, she fought the instinct to plow her fist into his ribs while his defenses were down. Instead of closing her eyes to angry slits, baring her teeth at him, and snarling, *get off me,* she softened her features, lowered her eyes, and bit her lip.

He inhaled in surprise.

When she lifted her gaze again, she'd extinguished the flame of fury.

As he looked into her guileless eyes, his face crumpled. His brow furrowed. His mouth turned down. His gaze dimmed. And his grip on her loosened.

With a sound that was half-sigh, half-sob, he released her. Then he fell away onto his haunches and hung his head.

For one uneasy instant, she hesitated. She hadn't expected her ploy to work so well. For the blink of an eye, she felt sorry for the man.

She'd glimpsed pain in his face. A sort of dispirited surrender. He clearly didn't wish to hurt a woman.

Yet he *had,* she reminded herself.

He'd nearly killed Hallie.

And for that, he must pay with his life.

No matter how ill-at-ease she felt, she had to act now, while he was vulnerable.

Rolling swiftly away, she reclaimed her *shoudao,* then sprang to her feet and unsheathed. With a single powerful sweep of the keen-edged blade, she could lop his head from his shoulders.

She gripped the sword in both hands, drew it back, and stepped forward for the killing blow. But as she swung the blade round, her courage faltered. She made the mistake of squeezing her eyes shut and aimed high.

Without the concealment of her mask, her intentions and her weakness were exposed. At the last instant, he dropped, and her sword whistled through empty air. The combination of her momentum and his sudden dive toward her shins knocked her off her feet.

She hit the ground hard this time. Hard enough to force

all the air from her chest. Hard enough to loosen her grip on the *shoudao,* which skipped out of her reach.

Suddenly she could rasp no air into her collapsed lungs. She opened her mouth, struggling to breathe, and failed. The edges of her vision began to darken. She clawed frantically at her throat.

The man snapped up her *shoudao* and scowled down at her. Then he grabbed her by the front of her gambeson and hauled her up to a sitting position.

For one terrible moment, she thought he meant to pay her back in kind, cleave her head from her shoulders. She fumbled at the front of her tabard, seeking her secondary weapons. Her *duandao* or her *yan zi fei dao.*

Mistaking her scrabbling for panic, he cast aside the *shoudao* and hunkered down beside her, "Slow. Breathe slow and deep. Ye've just had the wind knocked out o' ye."

Once she followed his advice, her muscles eased, her vision cleared, and she could breathe again. But why he should help her, she didn't know. She'd tried to kill him. He had every reason to let her suffocate.

"Better?"

She frowned, perplexed. Aye, she was better. But this wasn't how things were supposed to happen. Her target wasn't supposed to come to her rescue.

Mac Darragh had saved her life. Or at least he hadn't taken it. He'd had the opportunity to slay her, yet had not. He'd spared her. Which was *almost* like saving her.

And now he was gazing down at her with something resembling pity. Pity she neither needed nor deserved.

She'd meant to kill him. Indeed, she might still be able to reach inside her boot and slip out her *bishou.* Drive its point into his heart while he crouched before her.

But she couldn't bring herself to hurt him while he was looking at her like that. Not while his penetrating blue eyes seemed to stare into her naked soul.

Later, she promised herself. Another opportunity would arise, a more prodigious moment, one that would allow her to crow in triumph rather than wallow in guilt. She simply needed to feign defeat and wait till the time was right.

Dougal was sure it had been an accident. The lass couldn't mean to kill him.

She wasn't helpless, as she'd first pretended. But neither was she a murderer.

He'd met a dozen lasses in similar situations. Desperate. Starving. Unable to envision a life that didn't rely on stealing to survive.

This was the first lass he'd met, however, who had such skill with a blade.

He corrected himself. The second.

The first lass he'd left dead on the tournament field.

Indeed, it was that horrific memory that had struck him when he first slipped off the outlaw's mask. A memory that had distracted him and almost cost him his head.

He couldn't let it happen again. He had to keep that guilt buried deep. Locked away.

If he surrendered to it, if he dared to think too long on the truth—that his blindness, his recklessness, had led to the death of an innocent...that he'd menaced a melee field full of defenseless knights...that an entire village had been massacred on his watch...

Nay. Revisiting such thoughts would unman him.

He would lose his grip on what was right, what was fair, what was just.

He would lose his purpose for being.

He would lose the will to live.

And next time, he might well let the lass's stray blade do its work.

A woman's blood was on his hands. The blood of Kirkoswald stained his soul. Their deaths were on his conscience. It was too late to undo what he'd done. And useless to dwell on it.

So for now, he would survive. He would stuff down those self-destructive thoughts and survive. It was what he knew how to do.

The lass too was a survivor. A miserable waif reduced to a life of crime just to stay alive. A woman so full of fear and cynicism that she would kill rather than become a victim. She was a tragic reminder of what the cruel greed of people like his brother did to ordinary folk. Folk who deserved, not punishment, but mercy.

"What's your name, lass?"

He half expected her to spit in his face.

Instead, she was silent.

"Shall I call ye Outlaw then? Thief? Murderer?"

She met his challenge with the proud, bold truth. "Feiyan la Nuit."

"Feiyan," he repeated.

It was a curious name, but appropriate. The lass seemed almost fey. She was a bonnie wee thing, with chestnut hair and shimmering silver eyes. Her dark brows were expressive, her chin came to a charming point, and her lips looked soft and full.

Yet it was no wonder, before glimpsing the delicate beauty of her face, he'd believed she was a lad. She was small in stature, and her close-fitting dark garb disguised whatever curves might have revealed her gender.

Feiyan wasn't interested in his name, only his intentions. "What will you do with me?"

What indeed? If he let her go, he'd only give her a second chance to kill him. The wise thing was to keep her where he could see her.

Yet he couldn't take her with him. She'd only slow him

down. He didn't have the resources to look after her. Besides, he traveled best alone.

His only choice was to leave her behind, just as he had his destrier. Stash her somewhere she'd be safe. Protected. Cared for. A nunnery perhaps. Or a noble household.

"I'm goin' to help ye," he decided.

"I don't need your help," she murmured, raising her chin with pride.

He expected she'd say that. Even if it wasn't true.

Outcasts forced to live on their own grew fiercely independent. They relied on no one, trusted no one, living like orphaned hounds at the edge of starvation.

"Let's find ye a real bed, aye?"

Her eyes darted to him, clouding with suspicion. Their bright silver dimmed to a cynical gray. "Yours?"

He winced. She may have earned her way in the past by selling her favors. But she would do so no longer.

"Nay." He offered her a hand. "Come with me, Feiyan. I won't hurt ye."

She scrutinized his hand with mistrustful eyes.

"I promise," he said.

She scoffed at that.

Lasses like her doubted everyone. They had faith only in themselves.

He would prove himself to her. Convince her that he could be trusted. That he was a man of his word. That he wasn't a monster.

Maybe in convincing her, he could convince himself.

When Feiyan was a wee lass, she'd spied a heron in the marshes near her home. Fascinated by the beautiful bird, she kicked off her slippers and waded into the muck for a closer look. But each time she took a step forward, the bird edged a few inches farther away. By the time the heron tired of the game and flew off, Feiyan was up to her neck in the marsh, forced to cry for help as her feet stuck fast in the sticky, sucking mud.

That was how she felt now. Torn between curiosity, frustration, and the sinking feeling that she was being pulled under by shifting ground. Heading for perilous depths from which she might never emerge.

Yet, as always, she was unable to resist the allure of the unknown. She told herself she was no longer that wee lass. She was older and wiser. A woman grown. A deadly assassin. She could pull herself out of the mire if she started sinking too deep. What harm could there be in seeing where letting mac Darragh "help" her led?

She would never be in fear for her life, after all. Not really. She still had several weapons at her disposal.

Once she caught him off his guard, once she lulled him into complacency, she could easily subdue him.

Once he was subdued, she could easily finish him.

The earnestness in his eyes almost made her rue the wicked bent of her thoughts. On the other hand, she was certain he had some nefarious motive for offering her assistance.

He probably wished to torture her.

Or enslave her.

Or swive her to death.

"Where will you take me?" she asked.

"To the main road. By my reckonin', we're not far from Biggar. We'll find an inn there."

She lifted her brows. That was interesting. If he simply wanted to molest her, why would he take her to an inn? Cross an innkeeper's palms with enough silver, and she supposed he would turn a blind eye to a man's face and a deaf ear to a woman's cries. But it would be far easier to assault her in the middle of the forest, where the only witnesses would be the woodland creatures.

As he eased his garments over the injuries she'd inflicted, she noted with some satisfaction that he grimaced in pain. She might be small. But his bruises were proof that even a wee bit of force applied in a concentrated spot could do damage.

"Ye're a scrappy lass with your fists," he admitted, pulling on his trews.

She smirked. He had no idea just how lethal she could be.

"Have ye got any other skills?" he asked.

"Give me my blade," she dared him, "and I'll show you."

One corner of his lip curved up. "I think that would be unwise."

He was only half-dressed, still vulnerable. If she could coax him into a sword fight...

"Why?" she taunted. "Are you afraid?"

He slipped on his still-damp gambeson. "I'm afraid o' doin' ye harm."

She allowed herself a secret smile. The man's over-confidence would be his undoing.

He forced his feet into his wet, crack-heeled boots.

"Have ye e'er swept a chamber?" he asked. "Or served a meal?"

Her eyes smoldered. Her suspicions were correct. He meant to make her his slave. "Nay."

"Ne'er?"

"Never."

That was a lie. Since, as the oldest child, she spent most of her time in sparring and study, she had servants who cooked and cleaned for her. But as part of her training, Sung Li had insisted she learn humility by doing all the tasks required of her servants. Feiyan knew how to gather eggs, brew ale, milk cows, polish armor, herd sheep, launder linens, and even empty chamberpots.

That didn't mean she enjoyed it. Nor would she do any of those tasks for a man she meant to kill.

He snorted. "Ye seem bright enough. I'm sure ye can learn."

She seethed in silent aggravation. Damn the brute. She was a seasoned warrior. Not a serving lass.

When he fastened her sword belt around his hips *as if it belonged there,* she clenched her teeth together so tightly she thought they would crack. And when he slid her *shoudao* into its sheath with smug grace, it took all her willpower to resist throttling him with her bare hands.

CHAPTER 8

To Dougal, the inn at Biggar seemed as decent a place as any to deposit a wayward lass. The rushes on the floor were clean. A fire blazed on the hearth. A few lodgers guzzled ale and chatted at worn tables. A cauldron of pottage bubbled over the fire.

The gray-bearded innkeeper gave him a welcoming nod when Dougal closed the door behind him.

The lass immediately retreated to the farthest table from the entrance. Dougal kept an eye on her as he went to speak with the innkeeper.

"So just the one night for you and your...?" the man said, glancing at Feiyan, hooded, masked, and glowering from the shadowy corner.

Dougal frowned. Clearly he hadn't thought things through. "Sister."

The innkeeper raised a brow. "Your sister." He had probably heard such unlikely tales before.

Dougal held his jaw firm. It was a good enough lie. "Listen. I can't take her with me. Where I'm goin', 'tisn't safe. I promised our father I'd let no harm come to her. I'll pay ye handsomely to keep her here."

The man took another look at Feiyan. "For how long?"

Dougal bit the inside of his cheek. Outdistancing her

would take only a day. But he'd meant what he said. He intended to help her.

When he thought about the wayward waif, hope flickered at the edges of his shadowy, self-loathing soul.

True redemption for what he'd done was impossible, of course. He would be forever scarred by his actions. His was a debt of sin from which there was no absolution.

But if he could save one lost soul, keep one innocent from falling into darkness...

Perhaps he could save the life of one woman to help pay for the death of another. Perhaps he could begin to wash away the stain of dishonor. Make a sacrifice of the heart for a crumb of forgiveness. And quell the demons of self-hatred that haunted his dreams.

Surely it was worth the attempt. He had nothing to lose.

Running a pensive hand over his jaw, he considered the lass in the shadows. How long would it take before she abandoned her outlaw ways and became used to creature comforts? A month? Two?

"Can ye keep her till Michaelmas?" he asked.

"Michaelmas?" The innkeeper's eyes went wide. But they both knew he'd be foolish to turn down half a year's lodging for the right price.

"Maybe longer if ye can find some task to help her earn her keep."

The innkeeper scratched his cheek. "Can she cook? My wife could use a lass to make the morning frumenty."

"Aye. Sure." Dougal had no idea whether she could cook. It was hard to imagine her stirring a frumenty pot with her resplendent sword.

The innkeeper stroked his beard. "When you say handsomely..."

Dougal untied his sheathed dagger and placed it on the counter with a sigh. "I can give ye this."

The innkeeper emitted a breathy whistle when he saw the jeweled hilt. He'd likely never seen such wealth.

The dagger had belonged to Laird Darragh. It was all Dougal had left of his father, now that his brother had sold off everything else. It pained him to part with it. But he no longer felt worthy of the noble piece. Better it should be spent in gallant sacrifice.

The innkeeper drew the dagger and held it up to a candle, examining it to be sure the emeralds and rubies were real. Then he cast a glance at Feiyan, as if judging her worth as well.

"She's not another man's wife, is she?" he asked. "I don't want any trouble."

Dougal lowered his brows. That was something he hadn't considered. But he doubted the lass would be running loose in the wood, were she wed. If Dougal had such a lovely bride, he'd never let her out of his sight.

On the other hand, perhaps she'd grown tired of her husband and lopped off his head.

"She'll be no trouble," he promised.

He had no way of knowing that. In truth, she'd been nothing *but* trouble for him. But he suspected, after a night in a warm bed with a full belly and the prospect of a roof over her head from now on, she'd be grateful enough to be civil to her host.

They were served a hefty supper of lamb and leek pottage. Clapbread. Strong ale. And sweet custards made by the innkeeper's wife.

Aside from murmuring her thanks for the meal, Feiyan spoke not a word. Despite appearing half-starved, she dawdled at her supper, picking at her food, sipping at her ale. But that gave him time to think.

He meant to steal a few hours of sleep and leave before dawn. He'd let the innkeeper tell Feiyan about the arrangements in the morn. Let the lass know she had a room until Michaelmas.

With any luck, a night at the inn would throw the mac Girics off his scent. They were seeking a man alone, in armor, on a horse. They would pay no heed to a traveler on foot, lodging at an inn with his "sister."

She still hadn't finished eating. He got the impression the lass was trying to delay him. No doubt she'd drag her feet all the way up the stairs as well.

She needn't fret. He had no intention of hurting her. He'd give her no cause to defend herself. He meant to keep his word. He also meant to keep her sword.

"Are ye nearly finished?" he murmured, eager to retire.

Being seen with a female companion gave him good cover. But enemies could be anywhere. He dared not linger in the common room.

Feiyan had done all she could to delay the inevitable. She could guess what would happen next. Once mac Darragh dragged her up the stairs and secured the door, he'd throw her onto the bed, intending to have his way with her.

She'd naturally prevent him. There would be a struggle. And in the midst of it, she'd slip out her *bishou*—in defense of her virtue, she'd later explain to the innkeeper—and drive it into his evil heart.

It was a perfect plan.

It was the perfect time.

The other guests had left, and the innkeeper had started banking the fire.

She kept one hand on the hilt of her hidden *duandao* as she rose from the table and began to climb the steps. He followed close behind her.

At the stop of the stairs, he unlocked the first door off

the hallway and swung it open onto a chamber with a single bed.

The room was small, but decent and cozy. A modest fire already crackled on the hearth, warming the air.

The lecherous devil, wasting no time, immediately crossed to the bed and threw back the coverlet.

"The linens are clean," he announced.

He pressed down on the pallet. A pleasant mint fragrance issued forth. The dried herb must have been sprinkled into the straw-stuffed mattress, assuring no fleas infested the bed.

That was good, she supposed. After she...did what she'd come to do...she might wish to steal a few hours of sleep before returning to Rivenloch.

On the other hand, how easy would she find it to sleep, with the Westlander dead on the floor of the chamber?

Sauntering toward the window, she casually opened the shutters and eyed the drop to the ground, in the event she had to make a more clandestine escape.

"Don't even think of it," he warned, closing the chamber door.

She lifted back her hood, affecting her most guileless expression while mentally calculating the distance between them. "Think of what?"

"Runnin' away." He shook his head. "I'm no fool. I paid a hefty price for this chamber. I won't have it wasted."

Her eyes glittered. He might not be a fool. But he was still capable of being gulled. Every man was. She'd already gulled him into thinking she was helpless.

She catalogued each weapon on her person—*duandau, bishou, yan zi fei dao, sais*—preparing to engage him at the first sign of aggression.

He looked anything but aggressive. Still, when he came toward her to secure the shutters, she moved to the corner of the room.

"I told ye I don't mean to hurt ye," he said.

"Oh aye. You only mean to swive me."

"Swive ye?" he said with an irksome smirk. "I assure ye, 'tis the last thing on my mind. I'll bed down by the hearth. Ye can have the pallet."

She furrowed her brow. This wasn't how things were supposed to progress. He was supposed to corner her, tear off her clothing, and try to have his way with her.

Then she would snarl in fury, pull out whichever lethal weapon was nearest at hand, and finish him in a potent and justifiable rage.

"You don't mean to bed me?" she asked, just to be certain.

"Ye sound disappointed," he said, picking up the poker to jab at the coals.

Flummoxed, she couldn't even sputter out a reply.

"Look, ye're as bonnie as a blossom," he explained. "But when it comes to beddin' lasses, I prefer daisies to thistles."

"Thistles?" she said, bristling at the insult.

"I'd suggest ye get some rest," he said, sitting on a three-legged stool by the fire to take off his boots. "We don't want to miss breakfast."

His dismissal was infuriating.

Damn the knave! If he didn't at least *try* to molest her, he would ruin everything. Somehow she had to goad him into action.

If he wouldn't be provoked, perhaps he could be enticed. Her aunt Helena had taught all the cousins how to use feminine wiles to disarm men. It wasn't Feiyan's favorite defense. But she could make an attempt.

She removed her cloak and hung it on a peg. When she turned back, emulating her aunt, she made sure her surcoat had "slipped" off to one side.

When his gaze alit on her bare shoulder, the

Westlander's jaw slackened, and his hands froze on his boots.

She gave him her most wide-eyed and winsome gaze. "You'll need help with those."

Before he could close his mouth, she knelt strategically before him, giving him a clear view of her bosom as she took hold of his crack-heeled boot. Granted, her breasts weren't as ample as her aunt Helena's, but she could still use them to good effect.

His leather boot was still damp from the river, stuck tight. Still, she struggled at the task longer than necessary, letting him feast his eyes.

When the boot finally came off all at once, she would have tipped over backwards. But he caught her by the shoulder, preventing her from falling. She gasped. An inch more, and he would have felt the point of the *yan zi fei dao* hidden in her sleeve.

Smiling sweetly, she placed his boot beside the stool, then held her hands out for the second boot, inclining forward again in sultry invitation. She was playing a dangerous game. But she was at her best when facing peril.

His silence as she tugged at his boot was as taut as the boot itself, relieved only when she slid it from his foot.

"Thank ye," he choked out. He swiftly averted his eyes, but not before she glimpsed the naked longing in them.

This was working surprisingly well, considering she possessed fewer curves than her cousins and had little experience with such tactics. The sensation of empowerment and superiority was satisfying.

She rose then, retreating to the bed, where she perched on the pallet to take off her own boots. Slowly, languorously, she tugged at one of them, careful not to reveal the *bishou* tucked inside, while exposing a good bit of her leg.

Determined to draw him into an attack, she untied her

stocking and slid it off with forced leisure. As she bared her foot, she felt his gaze slip to her ankle for an instant before flitting away.

She crossed her leg to take off the second boot. But for this one, she feigned difficulty, scowling and straining at the thing.

By his disgruntled frown, he clearly wanted nothing to do with undressing her.

He just as clearly couldn't refuse to help her.

With a glower that made him look as if he'd been ordered to scrub a garderobe, he strode across the room.

"Here," he said, offering his hand.

She leaned back on her hands and placed her heel in his palm.

Intentionally flexing her ankle in resistance as he tugged on the boot, she kept him close, allowing him a good long look.

She smirked to herself. Her aunt Helena was right. Men were ridiculously easy to bait.

As he tried to gently remove the boot, his gaze predictably strayed elsewhere. Coursed up the length of her leg. Skimmed over her hips. Grazed her shoulders.

Eventually, she relinquished the boot with a seductive sigh of relief and a breathy "Thank you."

As he hunkered down to place her boot on the floor, she made a sensuous show of rolling off her stocking, slipping it down her thigh, inch by inch, before his eyes.

The sky blue of his gaze clouded over with the haze of desire. His jaw tensed. His brow furrowed. Then he gulped, as if his lust could be swallowed away and forgotten.

She dropped her stocking onto the floor. Dangling her bare feet over the edge of the pallet, she kicked playfully at the coverlet, melting him with a sultry smile.

But the smoke in his azure eyes as he looked up at her began to have a curious effect. Her smile faltered. Her breath grew shallow. Her cheeks grew hot. Wherever his gaze touched her, it felt like a burning brand searing his mark into her flesh.

The longer he stared, the more uneasy she became. What had started as heady triumph quickly splintered into dangerous uncertainty.

At this proximity, she could see the glaze of sweat on his brow. Inhale his spicy male scent. Hear the rasp of his breathing. Feel his breath on her knees.

Her eyelids grew heavy. Her ears hummed. The back of her neck tingled. Her skin grew warm. She felt simultaneously powerful and powerless.

The feeling was unbearable and wrong. It was utterly abhorrent to be attracted to a murderous Highland savage. So her mind told her.

Her body, however, wholeheartedly disagreed. It seemed perfectly content to fall under his seductive influence.

She had lured him into a loch of desire, deep and treacherous.

But the knave had dragged her in with him. And her only hope was that he'd succumb soon, before she did.

Once he began thrashing at her in a clumsy attempt at seduction, maybe then she could drown the brute once and for all.

Against his will, against his nature, against all that was right and chivalrous and honorable, Dougal felt himself bewitched by the beautiful lass.

It wasn't right. It was irresponsible. He was supposed to be rescuing her. Saving her from a life of scrounging and thievery and selling her favors.

To a lass like her, he supposed all men were alike. A man was either a mark or a client.

If Dougal succumbed to lust, he'd only prove her right. Besides, he'd done enough damage in the last week. He didn't deserve a woman's charms or affection.

So, fighting back the urge to take her up on her unspoken invitation, to enfold her in his arms, to taste her soft lips, caress her silken skin, and sink his aching dagger into her welcome sheath—to cast out the demons that made him feel inhuman—he lowered his gaze, came to his feet, and backed away.

"Go on now," he said hoarsely. "Get some rest."

But the lass wasn't finished attempting to seduce him. She was merciless. And as persistent as a wasp.

While he tried to busy himself—stirring the coals, taking off his gambeson, lining up his boots by the fire to dry—he couldn't help but steal peeks at the lovely maid.

Moving her hands to the back of her head, she released the ribbon securing her coiled braid. Then she fingered loose the tendrils of her hair until they fell over her shoulders like the wide, dark waves of the sea.

He felt her eyes on him as he brushed the dust from his gambeson and laid it across the stool.

From the corner of his eye, he saw her curl a lock of hair around her finger again and again while he unbelted his plaid and shook out the folds.

As he laid out his plaid to make a rough bed on the floor, she drew up her knees to watch him, tucking her legs under her surcoat and wrapping her arms about them. Her pale toes peeped out beneath the green hem, reminding him of the wee white shells he often found along the beach.

If he hadn't been determined to ignore her advances, he would have found her seductions irresistible.

Finally, as he folded his gambeson into a makeshift pillow, she let out a sigh.

"I suppose you'll be tying me up," she said.

"What? Nay." He scowled. Sweet Mary, what sort of

perversions was the lass accustomed to? "Why would I do that?"

She shrugged her bare shoulder. "So I won't escape."

"Ah." He resumed folding his gambeson. "Ye're not my prisoner."

"But you've forbidden me to run away."

"Aye, for your own safety."

"You're not holding me here?"

"Nay."

She cocked her head. "How do you know I won't rob you blind?"

He smirked. "I have naught left to take. I spent the last o' what I had on this chamber."

Taken aback by his confession, she suddenly released her knees, letting her legs drop over the edge of the bed. "You did?"

"Aye," he said. "So I'd prefer 'twasn't wasted."

"Why would you do that?" She sounded irked. "Why would you spend all you have on this?" She gestured to the chamber. "On me?"

He frowned. Perhaps she deserved an explanation. But he didn't feel like baring his soul to her. He didn't feel like telling her about his moral failings. He didn't want to speak of the tragedy at Kirkoswald. And she certainly wouldn't want to hear that he'd slain a woman.

So he simply shrugged. "Why not?"

She clearly wasn't satisfied with that answer. "What do you want from me?"

Absolution, he thought. *Forgiveness.* He punched his gambeson-pillow into a comfortable shape and replied instead, "Naught. I want naught. Just enjoy a good night's sleep."

"But..." She seemed exasperated. "But how do you know I won't take back my sword and...and slay you in the middle of the night?"

"Will ye?"

"Maybe."

"Well, then..." He nestled into his makeshift bed, wrapping the plaid over him, and tucked her sheathed blade against his chest, in his grip. "I'll just have to keep it in arm's reach."

CHAPTER 9

Feiyan bit back a curse, flouncing under the covers before he could see her frustration.

How had this happened?

Not only had mac Darragh completely defied all her expectations, but she'd blurted out her plans to him. And now he had her most lethal weapon in his grasp.

"Good night," he called out to her.

She gave him a vexed mumble in return.

She supposed it should come as no surprise that he meant to sleep with a sword in his hand. So did she, most of the time.

It wouldn't change her plans. She still meant to finish what she'd come to do. And she was fairly certain he couldn't unsheathe and slash at her before she could deliver a killing blow.

But once again she was faced with the unsavory prospect of slaying him in his sleep. Something that went against everything she'd ever been taught. An underhanded, unfair, unchivalrous idea that turned her stomach and filled her heart with dread.

She tried to distract herself from the macabre details, watching the shadows of flames flicker across the plaster ceiling. She focused her breath—inhaling slowly for strength, exhaling evenly for calm—the way her mother had taught her when preparing for combat.

If she could breathe out anxiety and breathe in composure, she could find the steady mind and hand required to take the necessary action.

Quickly.

Efficiently.

Without hesitation.

Without emotion.

Without regret.

Those were the soothing thoughts that eased her mind...settled her stomach...steadied her nerves. And, unfortunately, allowed her to drift off to sleep.

When she awoke, it was not in the dark quiet of midnight, where she could perform her unpleasant deed and slip away like mist.

Instead, she woke to the sound of the chamber door closing.

She sat upright. By the light seeping in through the shutters, it was nearly dawn.

She scanned the dim room.

Mac Darragh was gone.

He'd taken all his things.

His boots.

His pack.

Her sword.

"Shite."

He was fleeing.

Scrambling up from the bed, she stabbed her legs into her stockings, muttering to herself. "You think you're so clever, mac Darragh?" She wrenched on her boots. "Well, you won't escape me so easily." She swept her cloak off the peg and swirled it around her shoulders. "We have affairs to settle, you and I."

She whisked her hair back, braided it quickly, and wasted several moments searching for her coif before she finally found it tucked under the edge of the pallet.

"I swear, Westlander, before this day is done," she vowed, tying the coif under her chin with a decisive yank, "I *will* plunge my hot blade of justice into your cold black heart."

She clambered down the stairs and into the common room. The innkeeper was just stirring the fire to life.

"Where is he?" she demanded.

"Your brother?" he replied, startled. "I'm afraid he's gone."

"Gone where?"

"Well, now..." He regarded her with pity. "He asked me not to say."

She bit out a foul curse that made the innkeeper blink.

"He' only trying to keep you safe, lass."

"Ballocks!"

He flinched in surprise at her outburst and tried to placate her with an upraised palm. "Now I don't want any trouble. He's paid for your stay. And I told him you could even earn a coin or two helping my wife with the frumenty."

Stunned, for a moment she only simmered in silent rage. God's eyes! Help his wife with the frumenty? Feiyan was a warrior. Not a cook.

"Your wife is going to have to find someone else," she muttered. "I'm leaving."

"But lass, he's paid for your lodging through Michaelmas."

Her eyes went round. "Michaelmas?" The lout had planned to leave her here for half a year?

"Aye."

She spoke through clenched teeth. "Then I'll have his payment back, because I'm going now."

"Och, lass," he said, scratching his chin. "I don't know if I can give it back."

Before he could even blink, she'd drawn her *bishou* from her boot and leveled it at his throat. "I'm sure you can."

"Wait. I...I..." The innkeeper's throat bobbed and his eyes widened as he raised trembling hands in surrender. "I'll see what I can do."

She kept a threatening eye trained on him and her weapon at the ready as he rummaged behind the counter and pulled out the Westlander's jeweled dagger.

"Here," the innkeeper said. "He paid with this. Take it."

She confiscated the dagger and nodded to a basket of bannocks sitting on the counter. "I'll take three of those as well."

He slid the whole basket in front of her.

She picked out three wedges and stuffed them into her gambeson.

But though Feiyan was ruthless, she was also fair. Using the point of her *bishou,* she pried the tiniest gem out of the dagger's hilt and flipped it onto the counter. "There. For the meal and the night's lodging."

The innkeeper gulped.

Stuffing the *bishou* back into her boot and tying mac Darragh's dagger about her hips, she raised her mask, lowered her hood, and gave the innkeeper a curt nod of farewell.

Then she slipped out into the misty dawn.

Her step was silent.

Her eyes were sharp.

Her purpose was clear.

As he trudged through the fog-wet forest, Dougal couldn't stop thinking about the wee lass he'd left snoring at the inn. Never had a woman stirred him quite like she did.

He wanted to believe it was only agitation. His world was naturally rocked by having to tangle with an outlaw lass on top of all the other crises of the past few days. Surely the disruption would be fleeting.

But something else tugged at his spirit and teased at his heart. A nameless fascination that kept her image fixed in his mind's eye.

He was half-convinced she'd enchanted him. It was easy to imagine her as a child of the forest. An elfin princess. A fey creature who stole through the trees as silently as shadow and slipped through the branches on gossamer wings.

It wasn't only her physical features, which were unique, beautiful, and enticing. There was also something compelling about her quicksilver moods. Her unexpected strength. The lively intelligence in her eyes.

She was like no one he'd ever met before.

The white mist softening the distant black branches reminded him of the mutable shade of her smoky-gray-silver eyes. Eyes that sulked one moment and glittered the next, hardening like flint and then melting into liquid pools, changing form as readily as iron in a blacksmith's hands. Eyes that were shaded by lush and expressive brows that arched and lowered to reveal her every emotion.

Her supple mouth had been an almost irresistible invitation. It had been a long while since he'd stolen a kiss from a maid. But when her pouting lips blossomed into a coy smile, he'd been sorely tempted to taste the rosy petals.

The curve of her shoulder had beckoned to him as well, emerging from her surcoat like the pillow of a mushroom from the forest floor. Pale. Soft. Round. He'd longed to brush his lips against her tender flesh.

And when she'd leaned forward, affording him a view of the shallow slope of her breasts, his head had spun with desire, and his breath had been snatched away.

It was good that he'd left while he could, before she could awaken and work her charms on him. She might have convinced him to linger. To enjoy her company a while longer. To forget about the army bearing down upon him and his clan.

But had he done the right thing, leaving her at the inn?

Would she grow to appreciate the gift he'd given her? Would she be grateful for his rescue? Or would she think he'd imprisoned her like a caged bird, trapped her in a life not of her own making?

Perhaps in a few months when all this was over, if—God willing—he was no longer a wanted man and his clan was safe from retribution, he'd return to see how she was faring.

In the meantime, as he slogged through the wood, burdened by the dark memories of his failures—the souls he'd lost at Kirkoswald, the mac Girics he'd wounded, the woman he'd slain with his careless hand—he would hold Feiyan's image as a wee candle in the dark.

A candle that flickered with hope. Promise. And salvation.

Vengeance burned hot in Feiyan as she coursed down the main road, her cloak flapping about her like the wings of a great raven.

Now she had no qualms about killing the cursed Westlander. Not after he'd tried to indenture her to an innkeeper. And the fact he'd crept away before dawn, like a thief in the night...

The man was not only a knave. He was a coward.

She shuddered to think she'd actually felt pity for him.

She'd been fooled by his tragic blue eyes and his halfhearted smile. Moved to mercy by his melancholy.

Now she knew the truth. He'd never wanted to help her. He only wanted to be rid of her. He'd discarded her without a backward glance, just as he'd done his armor and his horse.

He'd said he was no fool. It seemed he was right. He'd sneaked away early, before anyone could witness his leaving.

But he hadn't counted on Feiyan's keen tracking abilities. Or her determination.

He'd probably return to the forest trail. It was the safest route for a fugitive. But it was also slow going. By taking the main road, Feiyan could surge ahead of him, cut back into the woods, and lie in wait.

There she would waylay the craven knave before he could even draw breath. Take vengeance for her clan. Seal the Westlander's fate. Reclaim her sword. And keep his jeweled dagger as payment for her trouble.

At a hectic pace fueled by fury, she stormed down the road. In the cold air of the morn, her hot breath chuffed out, curdling the fog in its wake.

Eventually the mist lifted, merging with heavy gray clouds that hung low in the sky.

A few carts passed by, laden with parcels and goods for market. A monk rode past on a donkey. A man herded a pair of oxen along the road.

But they paid her no mind. Feiyan was just another traveler, inconspicuous to most. Hours later, she was still silently cursing the Westland devil who had tricked her with his generous gestures.

Charmed her with his words of compassion.

Distracted her with his handsome face.

When she was sure she had outdistanced him, she left the main road and headed toward the water. The underbrush was thicker here, and the trees, fed by the deep river, grew to great height. The soft mud of the deer trail that followed the banks showed no sign of fresh footprints.

He hadn't yet passed this way.

But he could arrive at any time.

Choosing a stately elm near the path, she clambered up the trunk to perch in a fork that afforded her a good view for twenty yards in both directions. Then she waited.

Again and again, she planned her attack, with every variation possible. Leaping in front of him with her *duandao.* Waiting till he passed and surprising him from behind with the spike of her *bishou.* Firing her *yan zi fei dao* at him from the tree.

When she was satisfied she'd considered every possible outcome, she relaxed back against the trunk and pulled out a bannock. She'd have one of them now to break her fast and save the other two for journey home.

She had just finished eating and was brushing the crumbs from her gambeson when she heard a rustling.

She froze at the first flicker of leaves in the distance. By the measured, heavy footfalls, she knew it was a man.

A moment later, by his long stride, broad shoulders, and the *shindao* hung at his hips, she knew it was mac Darragh.

She pulled up her mask and braced herself, ready to act. She decided to use the *duandao,* since he was coming at great speed. Startling him would give him no time to draw his blade. And no time for her to falter.

She silently slipped the dagger from its sheath.

Then he stopped.

She held her breath. Had he heard her? Had he somehow sensed she was near?

He brushed off a mossy fallen log beside the path and took a seat. Then he dug in his pack, drew out a parcel, unwrapped it, and took a bite.

She frowned in disbelief. Was he actually stopping to eat? Right there? Not twenty yards from where she waited, ready to slay him?

She'd been so ready to act. Mentally prepared to finish him off in a swift, efficient manner. Without a second glance. Without hesitation.

Now she'd have to wait until he was finished eating.

Not only did it seem like a waste of perfectly good food—food that would do him no good where he was going—but it gave her time to reconsider what she was going to do.

Time to remember details about him. His char-black locks. His swarthy jaw. His soulful blue eyes.

Time to reflect on what it would be like to slay a defenseless man.

She tried to cast her gaze elsewhere. To ignore him. After all, she knew where he was going. She didn't need to keep an eye on him. When he was done, he'd pick up where he'd left off and continue along the path. When he was close enough, she would spring into action.

But even after he dusted the crumbs from his hands, instead of continuing down the path, he lingered where he was.

She clenched her teeth. What was he doing? Why was he stalling?

At last, he rose from the log, and she tightened her grip on the *duandao*. But when he hunkered down to scrape leaves together into a makeshift bed, she wanted to scream in frustration.

Was he actually going to take a nap? Now? While she was in striking distance, poised to kill him?

The man clearly had no instinct for survival.

Meanwhile, he was making things difficult for her. Unless she wanted to wait for him to snooze off his full belly, waken, and proceed down the path, she would have to come to him. And then, though it grated against her sense of honor and decency, she would indeed have to slay him in his sleep.

Perhaps it was best this way, after all. It would be much easier to slit his throat while he lay sleeping. He would die peacefully, not knowing who had ended his life. And she wouldn't have to stare into his riveting blue eyes to do it.

She didn't have to wait long. Soon his chest was rising and falling with the sawing sounds of slumber.

After several moments, when she was sure he was fast asleep, she sheathed her *duandao* and began making her way toward him. The dense trees formed a network of intersecting branches, so it was simple enough to climb from ash to elm to oak without ever touching the ground.

A thick sycamore limb crossed the path just beyond where he slept. From there she could drop down, as silent as a wildcat, steal up behind him, and slash his throat.

Crouching on the adjacent oak branch, she leaned out to make a leap for the sycamore. But at the last instant, something shifted, and she heard a crack.

The limb split under her feet, and she dropped to the forest floor, landing with a thud that jarred her bones.

Dislodged her mask.

Shook her nerves.

And roused her quarry.

CHAPTER 10

Well-trained for warfare, Dougal's body reacted to the crash before he knew what was happening. He was on his feet, sword in hand, before he could understand why what looked like a broken limb and a pile of clothing were plopped in the middle of the trail.

But he quickly recognized the fair face that peered up at him in pale shock.

"What the devil?" He lowered the sword. "How did *ye* get here?"

"Bloody shite," the lass breathed, wincing in pain. She struggled to stand, swatting her cloak out of the way.

"Are ye hurt?"

She spit leaves and dirt from her mouth. She was apparently more angered than injured.

"Ye fell out o' the tree," he realized.

She responded with a glare.

He had questions. "Did ye follow me all the way from the inn? Why? And how did ye get here so fast?" He gave her a quick perusal. "Are ye sure ye're not injured?"

"I'm fine," she bit out.

"What are ye doin' here? Why didn't ye stay where I left ye?"

She beat the dust from her cloak. "We have unfinished business."

He blinked in disbelief. "Och, for the love o'... Ye don't mean this, do ye?" He whipped her blade up smartly. "Does it mean so much to ye?" The lass seemed obsessed with reclaiming the thing. He shook his head, then ran his fingers back through his hair. "Don't ye understand, lass? I was tryin' to save ye from a life o' desperation. Takin' ye away from the outlaw life. Givin' ye somethin' productive to do besides robbin' strangers."

She stopped for a moment, studying him, as if she wondered whether to believe him.

Then her eyes went flat and gray. She flipped back the edge of her cloak to reveal another shining silver blade in her grip. It wasn't as long or impressive as the one he was holding. More like a large knife than a sword. But it was just as sharp.

"Where the hell did *that* come from?"

She didn't answer. Instead, she tossed her head and squared off against him, clearly spoiling for a fight.

"Ye don't want to do that," he warned.

"Aye, I do."

He steeled his jaw. He wasn't going to fight a lass. Not again.

"I don't want to hurt ye, lass."

But as he lowered his head to sheathe his sword, something flew past his ear like a swift silver bird. A thunk in the oak trunk behind him made him turn. A razor-sharp dart protruded from the rugged bark.

He reeled around to face her.

She was reaching inside her surcoat. "But *I* want to hurt *you*."

As she flung her arm forward, he dodged aside, drew steel, and knocked the second flying dart aside with a violent clang that sent it careening into the brush.

When he turned back, she was charging toward him with her large knife in one hand, a pointed dagger in the other, and murder in her eyes.

Marveling at her animosity—and her ability to conjure up weapons out of thin air—he faced the oncoming threat.

He didn't want to fight her.

But he wasn't willing to die.

He had the advantage of power and reach. Extending the blade, he kept her at a distance as she thrust and spun and slashed at him. If she had more of those lethal flying darts, she didn't use them.

A wily foe, she slipped under his guard. Fought with her feet. Moved about like an imp with its tail on fire.

A few times, he could have ended the skirmish with one powerful blow. But that was what had happened at the tournament. And he meant what he said. He didn't want to hurt her. He never wanted to hurt a woman again.

As long as he was cautious, he could wage a defensive battle until she tired herself out.

A few times, as he blocked one weapon, her other came round and did some damage. He earned two nicks on his arm and one on his chin from her short sword, and her pointed dagger jabbed through his gambeson once to pierce the skin of his chest.

But he was accustomed to minor injuries.

What he wasn't accustomed to was receiving them from women.

"What is it..." he wondered aloud through his teeth, "...about Border lasses..." He finally used his long sword to knock the shorter one out of her grip, sending it skittering down the trail. "...and blades?"

No sooner had she lost her sword than she retrieved another curious weapon from her gambeson. One with a head like a trident.

The next time he slid his sword forward to block her

dagger, she caught his blade between the forks of the strange weapon. The metals ground together, sparking as she diverted his sword. She probably could have snapped the steel between the tines. That was doubtless what the trident was made for. But that would have damaged her precious sword.

The longer she continued to spar with him, the more he realized that curing the lass of her wicked ways was a fruitless pursuit. She had a whole cache of weapons, and she obviously knew how to use them. Keeping one sword away from her wasn't going to change anything.

"Fine, lass," he said, withdrawing his weapon, stepping back, holding both arms up in peace. "Stop fightin', and I'll give ye back your blade."

She was still poised to attack. "Give it to me now."

"Put down your trident, *Neptune,* and I will."

But she wasn't about to surrender. She stabbed forward at him with the thing, and he narrowly missed having his lungs pierced. He threw up his arm at the last instant to deflect the blow.

"Lay down your weapons," he warned.

"I can't do that," she bit out, circling him with the trident in one hand and the pointed dagger in the other.

"Aye, ye can. Put them down on the ground. I'll lay your sword down next to them. We'll make peace and say farewell." He sighed in disappointment. "And ye can take your arsenal and go back to your life o' crime."

She shook her head. Her brows were lowered. Her mouth was grim. And the hostile storm brewing in her churning gray eyes told him the truth.

It wasn't about her sword.

It had never been about her sword.

There was a darker purpose behind her violence.

The wee outlaw was playing a deadly game.

Why he was the focus of her rage, he didn't know.

Maybe she'd been hurt by men before. Maybe she despised them all.

But by the quiet fury in her murderous glare, she meant to do him great harm. Perhaps even kill him.

He had to stop her before she did something she'd regret.

Something irreversible.

Something that would haunt her—as he was haunted—for the rest of her life.

Feiyan saw the change in his eyes. The sudden realization that this was no mere battle over property, but a fight to the death.

Now she would have to redouble her efforts. Relinquish any thoughts of a merciful slaying and kill him in any way possible.

With an assassin's cold focus, she circled him, watching for a wavering in his stare, a dip of his blade, anything that would reveal vulnerability in his defenses or an instant of weakness.

He showed none.

Anxious to be done, she made a jab for his heart with the *bishou.*

He turned sideways, pushing her arm aside with his left hand.

When she made an unexpected return slash, the finely honed point of the *bishou* grazed his neck.

He sucked a quick breath through his teeth as a thin red line bloomed across his flesh.

Her heart pounded. An inch deeper, and he might have been slain.

He lifted his fingers to his throat, then withdrew them, frowning when he saw blood.

He clenched his jaw. His eyes grew as dark and heavy

and threatening as a thundercloud. She would find no chink in his armor now.

But to her frustration, he still refused to attack.

Tension made her impatient. She tried to rattle him, clanging her forked *sais* against his blade.

But he shook off her advances like a duck shaking off rain.

Desperation made her careless. She made another impulsive stab forward with her *bishou.* If she could impale his heart, this standoff would come to a swift end.

But he anticipated the charge. While he diverted the *bishou* with his sword, his left hand snagged her wrist.

She gasped as he applied sudden, hard, painful pressure with his thumb, forcing her to drop the weapon.

She wrenched her empty hand out of his grip and took a backward step to regroup. Reaching inside her gambeson, she withdrew the second *sais* and then swept the pair down together in an X that whistled through the air with menace. They were defensive weapons with blunt prongs, but with enough force behind them, they could still kill.

He blew out a forceful breath. Pinned her with a glare of smoldering resolve. And transformed into the monster she'd seen at the tournament. Capable of violence and cruelty. Savage. Brutal. Unyielding.

In his gaze, for the first time, she saw the possibility of her own death.

Dread made her shaky. But she couldn't afford fear. Too many souls depended upon her. So with an aggressive cry, she lunged forward with both *sais.*

He knocked one of them aside with the flat of his sword and spun away, but not before she caught the end of his blade between the tines of the second.

Trying not to think about the damage to her precious *shoudao*—the weapon she'd proudly earned at the age of twelve—Feiyan used brute strength to hold the blade aloft and trapped. The weapons made an awful grating noise as she slid the *sais* halfway up the length of the sword.

She intended to snap the blade.

What she didn't foresee was that he would surrender it.

As he released the sword, her own strength worked against her. Momentum sent her staggering forward.

As she stumbled, he stepped in and wrenched the second *sais* from her grasp, flinging it aside.

When the handle of the entangled *duandao* abruptly struck the ground, angling the sharp tip toward her, she was still clinging to the first *sais*. And she was still falling.

For Dougal, there was no time for tact.

He instinctively tackled the lass, moving her out of the path of the sword's point.

They tumbled together in the dirt and leaves. The sword fell harmlessly onto the forest floor, its blade still caught up in the forks of the trident. She wound up in his arms, on top of him, stunned and breathless.

He expected she'd be grateful. Aye, he'd been rough with her. But he'd saved her life.

He never imagined she'd resume her attack.

But as soon as she blinked away her shock, her gaze hardened again. She shoved herself up from his chest. Wrapped her hands around his neck. And pressed her thumbs with killing force into his throat.

Gagging, he grabbed her wrists and quickly pried them apart, forcing her to collapse down on him again.

Her face was inches from his. Behind the mask, she spat at him in rage and frustration. But he was close enough to see the truth in her eyes. Mixed in with her bloodlust was very real fear.

Under any other circumstance, he would have released her. It was against his nature to frighten small creatures.

He was nothing like his brother, proud of the terror he inspired. He was nothing like the mac Giric clan, sowing horror against innocents. Nor was he anything like the monster he'd briefly become at Creagor, panicking crowds with his unleashed fury.

From his bruised throat, he grated out, "I'm not goin' to hurt ye, lass. I swear it."

She didn't look like she believed him.

"I've got the advantage now," he told her, wheezing. "I've disarmed ye. And I've got a good hold on your wrists. If I wished to do ye harm, I'd have done it by now." He stopped to cough. "But I don't. And I won't. God's hooks, I saved your—"

Without warning, she brought her thigh up hard against his groin.

Pain shot through his loins. To his credit, he didn't let go of her. But as a dull ache began to spread low in his belly, it took great fortitude not to push her as far away from him as possible, where she could do him no injury.

Instead, he rolled her onto her back and pinned her to the forest floor.

Her eyes shot silver sparks at him, and her mask fluttered with every angry breath.

She was like a wild kitten caught in the high branches of a tree. Stuck in a place she didn't want to be. Unaware of how she'd gotten there or how to get down.

Dougal could have helped her. He could have calmed her. Guided her back to reason. But like the cat, she was too stubborn or feral to realize that.

So she left him no choice but to physically restrain her until she stopped trying to kill him.

Her gaze steamed like a blacksmith's forge, and her mask began to suck in hard as she gasped. With Dougal crushing her ribs, he realized she might be having trouble breathing.

Since his arms were occupied, he resorted to lowering his head and using his teeth to tug down her obstructing mask.

If he'd lingered an instant longer, he was sure she would have bitten off his nose. She screamed in rage, thrashing beneath him, as if he'd just torn off every stitch of her clothing and meant to ruin her.

That was the last thing on his mind. In fact, if she weren't so desperately fighting against him, he'd laugh at such a suggestion.

Dougal was hardly a ravager of women. He was a champion. A protector. Kind. Gentle. Compassionate.

But of course, she wouldn't believe that. To her, he was the enemy.

Eager to be out of biting range, he sat back, anchoring her hips. There he felt the poke of something hard under his right thigh. Sweet Saints! Did she have yet another weapon?

"What's this?"

When she didn't answer, he forced her arms together above her head and held her wrists there with one hand. With the other, he rummaged under her cloak to see what she concealed.

"Get your hands off me!" she shrieked. "Stop! How dare you? Help! *Help!*"

Her loud screeches of outrage made him wish he'd stuffed her mask into her mouth. He hoped no one was near. To unknowing eyes, it would appear he was a ruffian accosting an innocent maid.

As soon as he laid hands on the grip of the weapon, he recognized his dagger.

"How did ye come by this?" he asked, drawing it from its sheath.

"Let me go, you son of a whore!" She squirmed in frustration.

"Did ye steal it from the innkeeper?"

"Get off of me!" She bucked up, trying to dislodge him. "Satan's spawn!"

He held the dagger up to give it a closer inspection. A jewel was missing. "And where's my damned emerald?"

"Unhand me, mac Darragh," she spat, "or I swear I'll..."

CHAPTER 11

Feiyan knew she'd made a grievous mistake the instant the words left her lips. Which was one instant *before* mac Darragh's eyes darkened, his brows lowered, and his lips pressed together into a grim line.

In the damning silence that followed, his deathly quiet whisper rang in her ears like the bells before an execution. "What did ye say?"

She bit her lip. It was too late to take back her words. Too late to pretend she didn't know exactly who he was.

"How do ye know my name?" he demanded.

"The...innkeeper," she improvised. "The innkeeper told me."

He shook his head. "'Tisn't the name I gave him."

She gulped. Of course it wasn't. And he didn't need a soothsayer to work out how she recognized him.

"Ye were there," he accused in a harsh whisper. "At Creagor. Ye were there. Ye're one o' them. Ye must have found my claymore. Ye've been trackin' me."

There was no point in denying the truth. He'd already figured out that she wanted to kill him. It didn't matter if he knew *why* she wanted to kill him.

But now she was helpless. And he was armed.

Her eyes flitted to the jeweled dagger. His knuckles had grown white on the handle. At her glance, he loosened his grip. But he didn't lower the dagger.

"Don't fret. I won't murder ye," he said through his teeth, reading her thoughts. "I've got a much better use for ye."

She swallowed the bitter tang of dread. What did that mean?

Mac Darragh might have feigned to care for her welfare when he assumed she was a hapless outlaw lass. But now he knew she was more than that. And Feiyan knew who he was. She'd seen him at Creagor. She knew the violence of which he was capable.

She'd lost the element of surprise.

She'd lost her disguise.

And she'd lost her weapons.

The only way she could survive now was by her wits.

She raised her chin with smug assurance, bluffing for all she was worth. "They know where you are."

"Who?"

"My clan."

"So ye're a scout?"

"That's right. I've been following you. And they've been following me." She beamed up at him. "In fact, they should be here any—"

She ended with a gasp as he swept the dagger down to her throat. She felt its steely tip against her throbbing pulse.

"On your belly," he commanded, lifting an inch off of her.

She hesitated for an instant. But she had little choice with his weapon at her throat. He might not *intend* to kill her. But she was damned sure, given the option of her sacrifice or his own survival, his dagger could make a swift decision for him.

"Slowly," he said, releasing her wrists.

She obeyed. But for one instant, she still thought she might be able to gather her limbs beneath her and leap away.

That instant was short-lived.

The moment she rolled over, he pressed his knee into the small of her back. She felt the point of his dagger at the nape of her neck.

A shudder of horror passed through her. Every assassin knew the fastest way to ensure death was a deep stab to the base of the skull. She dug her fingers into the soil, afraid to move, afraid to *not* move.

He didn't kill her. Instead, he cut through the ties of her mask and dragged it from around her neck. Seizing one wrist and then the other, he wound the cloth of the mask to bind her hands together behind her back.

Satisfied she was helpless, he quickly gathered up her weapons, all except the *yan zi fei dao*, which he left stuck in the tree. Then he sheathed her *duandao* and stuffed the rest into his pack.

She'd almost inched her knees forward enough to make a final spring for freedom when he thrust an arm under her belly, picked her up bodily, and set her on her feet.

"Let's go."

He grabbed her by the arm and propelled her forward. But the long-legged warrior walked at so brisk a pace, it was difficult for her to keep up.

"Where are we going?" she asked. She didn't expect an answer. He didn't give her one.

For nearly a mile, the only sounds were the leaf-scuffing passage of their boots, the flap of cloaks, and her labored breathing.

Finally he muttered, "How did ye track me?"

She lifted her chin with pride. "You have a crack in the heel of your boot." Then, just to twist the knife, she added, "A child could have tracked you."

"Maybe. But ye've had no contact with your clan," he reasoned. "So I'm guessin' they're still lookin' for a man on horseback."

She bit back a curse. He was right about that. No one would guess he'd abandon such a fine warhorse.

In truth, she wondered if her clan was in pursuit at all. Once they found his claymore, they would know who he was and where he was headed. They would see no need to rush when they could simply let him return home and march on his castle as an organized army.

Only Feiyan had recognized the need for expediency. A sheer madness in the Westlander's manner. An other-worldly rage that couldn't be reasoned with and had to be addressed without delay.

To her, mac Darragh was an arrow loosed in a wild wind. No one could predict where he would land. He might well return to finish what he'd started at Creagor. To triumph where he'd failed. And next time, he might send Hallie to her grave.

She couldn't let that happen. She couldn't wait for the Rivenloch army. Which was why she'd gone after him herself.

Now, however, she regretted leaving no crumb for her clan to follow.

If only she'd killed mac Darragh when she first had the chance. While he was sleeping helplessly under a tree...his face pale in the moonlight...his hair as dark as a raven's wing...his mouth curved up slightly in the sweet depths of slumber...

"How many are there?" he asked, startling her from her reverie. "How many o' your clansmen are in pursuit?"

She arched a defiant brow. "All of them."

He smirked. "How many mac Girics *are* there?"

She blinked. "Mac Girics?"

All at once, she realized that his hostility wasn't against Rivenloch at all. How could she have been so wrong? Mac Darragh had turned up at Creagor, not because it was the site of the Rivenloch tournament, but because it was a *mac Giric* holding.

That changed things.

"Aye," he said. "How many are there?"

"Thousands."

He scoffed at the obvious lie.

"They... We're scattered all o'er Scotland," she boasted. That was almost true. The main Giric stronghold was in the Highlands. Then she asked carefully, "What grudge do you have against...my clan?"

The sudden tightening of his jaw and the blaze that flared in his eyes made her regret her question. His stony cold silence for the next mile was the only answer he gave.

The sky reflected his mood. Dark and ominous clouds lowered like his brow, stormy and threatening. The quiet was not the quiet of calm, but of the uneasy stillness before a violent maelstrom. The sharp chill in the pregnant air was as unsettling as his frigid gaze.

Despite the cold, Feiyan's brow was dotted with sweat. Hot and breathless from his ground-swallowing pace, she tried to force him to a slower walk, dragging her feet.

"I'll carry ye if I have to," he warned.

Feiyan scowled. "Nay." She'd been slung over a warrior's shoulder once already this month, helping her cousin Jenefer win a castle. She had no desire to be packed around again like a sack of grain.

"Then keep up. We don't want to get caught in the storm."

A few heart-pounding miles later, she realized she had to slow him down. Once they reached his castle, once he realized his clan wasn't in danger, he'd have no reason not to get rid of her.

So she exaggerated her fatigue. When they reached a grassy glen in the wood, she yanked away from his grip and sank onto one of the bare boulders in the middle of the expansive meadow.

"I have to stop," she wheezed.

"Here?" He cast a nervous glance around the clearing. It was risky to be so exposed. The woods at the perimeter were deep and dark enough to harbor hungry wolves. But he was probably more worried about vengeful clansmen.

She said breathlessly, "You intend to use me...as a hostage...aye?"

Of *course* that was his intent. Otherwise, he would have abandoned her by the trailside and made better progress on his own.

"If it comes to that," he muttered.

"Well, if I take another step...I'll collapse...and I'm no use to you dead."

He seemed to hear the wisdom in her words. "Fine." He hunkered down beside her and uncorked his costrel of ale. "Only a few moments, though, aye?"

She nodded. She didn't want to be left behind either. She still had a mission to finish. If she let him go on without her, she'd lose his trail in the rain.

He offered her the first sips of ale, tipping her chin back with surprisingly gentle fingers. It tasted like ambrosia, wetting her dry throat. If her hands had been free, she might have snatched away the costrel and guzzled the entire contents in one thirst-quenching gulp.

"I don't *want* to harm ye," he murmured as she drank. "Ye know that, aye?"

She almost choked on the ale.

He said, "But I may have no choice."

Choice. Choice? His words made her blood simmer.

"No choice," she echoed bitterly. "Just like you had no choice, going after my kinsmen at Creagor?"

"Shite."

His lips compressed into a grim line. He popped the cork back into the costrel and drilled her with a dangerous gaze of warning.

But she was too stirred up to heed it. "You attacked men who were armed with blunted weapons," she snarled.

With a growl, he stormed to his feet and wrenched her up by her arm.

Uncowed, she spat, "Some of them were children."

His grip tightened.

"And you almost killed my cousin Hallie." Her voice broke.

"I never meant..." Then he stopped with a subtle intake of breath. His grip abruptly loosened. His eyes searched hers with a curious intensity. "What did ye say?"

As she opened her mouth to reply, the heavens opened, loosing their store of rain all at once in a pounding downpour that drowned out all other sound.

Pulling his hood over his head, he tugged her forward at a run. The rain fell with a roar, thrashing the grass and bouncing on the muddy trail. Fat drops pelted Feiyan, peppering her face, drenching her hair, soaking her woolen cloak.

He'd headed for the stand of pines a hundred yards ahead, where they could shelter beneath the thick-needled branches. But the meadow turned to marsh along the way, and by the time they reached safety, she was muddy up to the knees, wet to the bone, and shivering with cold.

Feiyan half-collapsed onto her hindquarters in a pile of pine needles as the storm bristled around them. She couldn't even summon the energy to resist when he sat down beside her, wrapping his cloak around both of them to keep them dry.

The storm continued. Rattling tree limbs. Spraying off rocks. Flattening the grass. Turning the trail to a pitted mire. Shrouding the glen with a watery veil of destruction.

As the maelstrom made the world a bleary mess, Feiyan thought about her *yan zi fei dao*—one stuck in the tree, one left in the bushes—getting drenched. They would be worthless now. The rain would turn them to rust.

Bitter discouragement filled her. How had things gone so wrong?

She'd been trained for just this kind of mission. To be quick and sly. To act on instinct, not emotion. To steal in, strike, and disappear.

She was Feiyan the invisible. Untraceable. Untrackable.

But this target knew her. To him, she had a face. She had a name. He knew she meant to kill him. He also knew she was hesitant to do so.

Worse, he was being kind to her. Even knowing her intentions, he'd rushed her to safety, enfolded her in his cloak. These weren't the actions of a merciless savage.

He sat close enough to her that she smelled the wet wool of his gambeson and felt the subtle warmth of his body. Lifting her eyes, she could see every detail of the man she was supposed to kill. A stray drop of rain trickling off of his wet hair and rolling down his temple. Each black bristle on his stubbled jaw. The red mark from the scrape of her *bishou* across his throat. The wisp of his warm breath on the cold air. The keen focus in his azure eyes as he watched the storm.

If this was the Devil, he'd taken on a pleasing form. And how she would ever work up enough cold courage to slay him now, she didn't know. She was having trouble even thinking straight.

"What ye said before the storm…" he murmured, staring out at the falling rain. "About your cousin."

"Hallie?" Her voice came out on a croak. God's eyes, what was wrong with her?

"Ye said I almost killed her?"

"Aye."

"Almost?" He waited with tense and bated breath, as if his fate depended on her answer.

She hesitated. Of course. He didn't know. He assumed

he *had* killed Hallie. He hadn't stayed around long enough to learn the truth.

Part of her wanted to be cruel. To punish him for his savagery by telling him Hallie had died from her injuries. After all, it was only by a miracle that she hadn't.

But something about the way he'd asked her—the vulnerability in his eyes, the tenuousness in his voice, and the memory of how he'd staggered away after the near fatal blow—made her feel sorry for him.

"Aye," she said.

"She's not dead?"

She sighed. "Nay."

Dougal couldn't speak. His throat was a knot of relief. Relief he dared not express for fear of dissolving into grateful tears. So he clenched his jaw to check his emotions and nodded.

It didn't exonerate him, of course. Far from it. He had stormed through the ranks of the mac Girics like a Viking berserker, heedless of whom he injured or killed. His reckless violence could not be absolved.

But now he could taste the sweet hope of redemption. A possibility for forgiveness.

He was not a monster.

He was not a savage.

He was not a killer of women.

His chest tightened as he stared at the unrelenting rain.

At least not yet.

He didn't want to think about the future.

Huddled beside the shivering lass—holding her in his protective embrace, feeling tendrils of her wet hair against his cheek, smelling the damp linen of her garments—it was easy to believe they were simply friends waiting out the storm.

Part of him wished it could be so. That he could sit here in this island of time with the fey lass, holding off what was to come.

But he knew the truth.

If and when the mac Girics found him, a valuable hostage might be the only way to protect his clan. And when that time came, he would have to find the strength to hold a dagger against the lovely lass's throat.

CHAPTER 12

The market at Melrose was loud and lively, despite the storm that had blown in from the west, frowning down from the clouds in dire threat, ready to loose a deluge at any moment. But even the pouring rain wouldn't keep the four Rivenloch lads from enjoying this rare taste of freedom.

They were on their own. Four dashing cousins, in the prime of life, eager for adventure. Even if that only meant browsing through the market a dozen or so miles from their home.

Gellir was in charge, of course—of the cousins and the coin. At sixteen, he was the oldest. He was the son of the laird, Deirdre of Rivenloch. And he was the most levelheaded. It was his task to make sure none of them wasted silver on a charlatan's goods, picked a quarrel with someone they couldn't trounce, or fell prey to the maids of questionable virtue who strolled the lanes.

His cousin Hew was only a few months younger, but he was cursed with the temper of his mother, hotheaded Helena. Hew was useful in a fight, not so handy for haggling over prices. The hardest thing to rein in, of course, would be Hew's raging lust. Lately, anything in a skirt might become the target of his affections. It was up to Gellir to keep him out of trouble.

Gellir's younger brother Brand, on the other hand, had nothing but disdain for lasses, whom he considered an inferior species. Brand's particular foible was an obsession with arms and armor. If Gellir didn't keep an eye on him, Brand could easily spend most of his coin in the first hour and have to beg for the funds for a cart to transport it all home.

Like Brand, Adam was fourteen years old, but the two cousins could not have been more different. Adam was deviously brilliant, as elusive as his mother Miriel. With his quiet charm and clever mind, he could convince a merchant to part with his goods at a loss, which was one reason Gellir had brought him along.

The other reason was to get Adam's mind off of his sister, Feiyan. She was missing, though no one had really noticed except Adam. He hadn't seen her since the fateful melee at Creagor, and he was worried about her, sure she'd gone after the perpetrator of the violence. The claymore left behind bore the name of clan mac Darragh, a stronghold more than thirty leagues away. Much could happen on the long journey, and Adam couldn't shake the feeling that Feiyan was in trouble.

Suddenly Hew waved two silk ribbons in Gellir's face—one blue, one red. "Which one do you think?"

Gellir smirked. "I think green is more your color."

Hew elbowed him. "Not for me, you dolt. For *her*." He nodded to a simpering lass at the next pavilion who was running a teasing finger along the neck of her surcoat.

Gellir clucked his tongue, then leaned close to whisper, "She'll have that ribbon tied round your ballocks—and your purse empty—faster than you can say 'kiss me.'"

Hew's face heated at once, making the ugly black eye he'd earned at the tournament stand out in harsh relief. "How dare you insult the woman I love!"

Gellir crossed his arms and nodded toward the lass,

who was now winking and waving at a pair of young nobles. "The woman you love seems to be...generous...with her affections."

Before Hew could retort, Brand came running up, poking Gellir in the arm repeatedly with his bandaged finger, another injury from the tournament. "Hey, brother, get me two shillings."

Gellir frowned. "What do you need two shillings for?"

"There's a wicked pair of Toledo steel daggers in Armorers Lane."

"Toledo steel? For two shillings?"

"I know! Amazing, aye?" Brand gushed. "Quick, before they're gone." He waggled his fingers out for coin.

Gellir rolled his eyes. "For that price, they're likely made of English lead."

Brand groaned in exasperation. "Will you at least come look?"

"Och, fine." He clapped Hew on the shoulder. "Come along, cousin. Maybe we can find you a dagger to thrust through your broken heart."

As the three strolled down the lane, Adam came striding briskly toward them. His expression was grim. His brow was furrowed. His face was pale.

"What is it?" Gellir asked.

"I think I found him," Adam replied. His hand went instinctively to the new bruise that colored his cheek, a souvenir given to him by the savage at the tournament.

"Found who?"

Hew stepped forward, guessing at once. "Mac Darragh?"

Adam nodded.

Hew had his blade halfway drawn when Gellir put out a restraining hand, murmuring, "You can't just murder the man in the broad light of day, Hew."

"Where is he?" Hew asked Adam.

Adam grimaced. "I didn't actually see him."

"What?" Hew barked.

Adam continued, "But I'm almost sure I found his horse."

"His horse?" Brand asked. "Then he must be here. Somewhere."

"That's just it," Adam said. "The horse is...for sale."

"For sale?" the three others echoed.

"Take us there," Gellir said.

They walked together through the market. With news that mac Darragh might be lurking nearby, Brand forgot about his Toledo daggers, and Hew forgot about his lady love. All eyes were alert for the demon knight in black armor.

When they reached the livestock pens, Gellir knew there was no mistake. The magnificent black horse belonged to the man who had savaged the melee at Creagor.

"Why would he sell his charger?" Brand wondered. "Doesn't he need it to get home?"

Hew nodded toward the man selling the beast. "Maybe he traded it in for a fresh mount."

Glum Adam had a different idea. "Maybe he's dead."

No one had to state the obvious—that Feiyan might have killed mac Darragh.

That idea sent a shiver through Gellir. Despite her small size, his cousin Feiyan wasn't as fragile or innocent as she seemed. But singlehanded assassination...

"Let's go find out," Gellir suggested, heading toward the merchant and his wife. Adopting an air of noble authority, he demanded, "Sir, how came you by this beast?"

When the man stuttered, the wife intervened. "I assure you, m'laird, we came by it honestly."

"Who sold it to you?"

"'Twas given to us," the man replied.

"As a gift," the woman added.

Gellir scowled and perused the sleek animal with its powerful musculature and shiny coat. No one in his right mind would give such an expensive gift to a stranger, unless he was in a hurry to disappear. On the other hand, this couple didn't look conniving enough to have stolen the horse. "A gift from whom? Is he still here at the market?"

"Och, no. 'Twas a few days past."

"What did he look like, this fellow who gave you the horse?"

"No way to tell, m'laird," the man replied. "He only left a note, saying 'twas a gift."

Hew asked, "But he took another horse in exchange, aye?"

They shook their heads.

"We've only got the one affer," the man said, "for ploughing the field."

By this time, the woman had slipped her fingers around the reins, holding them knotted in her fist, as if she feared the horse would be taken from her.

Gellir pulled open the pouch of coin and began digging in it. "How much do you want for him?"

The woman blinked. "You wish to buy him?"

"Aye!" Brand said under his breath with a grin of approval.

"If the price is fair," Gellir amended.

"Twenty shillings," the man said.

His wife gave him a chiding cuff. "*Thirty* shillings."

Gellir frowned. It was a lot of coin. Almost all he'd brought. But he couldn't help but believe fate had delivered the horse to him. He was sure the beast was a vital key to finding and punishing the culprit at Creagor—if Feiyan hadn't already finished him. Besides, the destrier was probably worth *fifty* shillings. And by his cousins' breathless silence, they knew that as well.

"Done," he said, counting out the coin. "And you'll

include the bridle?" They couldn't afford a saddle. But that was fine. For what Gellir intended, the saddle would only be a hindrance.

"Of course," the man gushed.

The woman too looked pleased. It was likely more money than they'd make in five years.

Gellir gave her the coin and led the horse out of the pen.

The cousins hadn't gone ten paces before the chattering began.

"What shall we call him?" Brand asked. "I like Goliath. Do you like Goliath?"

"Where will we keep him?" Hew asked.

"The laird's stables, of course," Brand said.

"There's more room at du Lac," Hew argued.

"Who's going to ride him home?" Brand wanted to know.

Hew answered, "We'll take turns."

Gellir stopped them with an upraised hand. "We're not going home. Not all of us anyway."

"What? Why?" Hew demanded.

"Adam's sister is still missing," he said. "And now that we have mac Darragh's horse..."

"Ah, I see," Hew realized. "If he's holding Feiyan, we can trade the destrier for her."

Brand scowled in disappointment. "We aren't going to trade him for a lass, are we? We just bought him."

Adam shoved Brand. "You lobcock! You're talking about my sister!" Then he shoved Hew. "And you! Feiyan's worth more than thirty shillings! Bloody arses!"

Gellir raise his hand again. "Cease!" After some residual jostling between the lads, he resumed. "Feiyan is still out there. 'Tis likely she's tracking mac Darragh." For Adam's benefit, he added, "But she can take care of herself."

He didn't say whether he thought she'd assassinated the man. He wasn't sure about that. Feiyan could be mysterious, unpredictable, and—he suspected—ruthless.

"Here's what we're going to do. Adam and I will look for his sister. We'll take the charger. The horse knows the way home. He'll take us straight to mac Darragh's keep."

"Wait." Hew was noticeably unhappy about being left out. "Why should the two of you get to ride to the rescue while—"

"I need you and Brand to make all haste to Rivenloch," Gellir said. "Tell the laird what has transpired here. Gather forces to go straightaway to the mac Darragh stronghold. We don't know what we're facing. 'Tis best to be prepared."

Brand's eyes glittered. "Come on, Hew! We've a war to wage."

Hew straightened, placated by the prospect of an important duty. He gave Gellir a grim nod. "Don't start the battle without us."

With somber salutes, they parted ways.

When they'd gone, Gellir turned to Adam. "We're a few days behind, but with the horse, we can travel twenty miles a day, make up for lost time."

Adam nodded, then cast a glance at the ominous sky. "And if the weather turns, we can find lodging at an inn."

Gellir grimaced. "I spent almost all our coin on the horse. We'll need what's left for food."

"We'll need no coin," Adam said. "Leave it to me."

They arrived at an inn by nightfall, just as a drenching storm was moving in from the west.

Adam proved true to his word. Whatever he said to the innkeeper, the man gave them a chamber, a hot supper, and hay for the horse at no charge. It was only when the man doffed his cap, made a quick bow, and bid Gellir "Good night, Majesty" that he realized Adam had somehow managed to pass Gellir off as Scotland's new young king.

As they climbed into bed, the storm was rattling the shutters.

Adam's brows lowered as he touched the bruise on his cheek. "I hope Feiyan's all right."

"Don't worry." Gellir punched the pillow and settled in for a good night's sleep. "Your sister is a survivor. If she's half as clever as you, she'll be fine."

CHAPTER 13

Feiyan shivered against the trunk of the damp oak as the wet ground seeped through her wool cloak.

Thankfully, mac Darragh had been able to find enough dry tinder to start a small blaze. But it would dwindle soon, now that he'd fallen asleep. The flames cast a golden glow on the Westlander's handsome face as he began to snore softly beside the evening fire.

He believed he was safe, sleeping with the *shoudao* within hand's reach.

He also believed his hostage was helpless, bound to the tree just a few yards away.

But he'd obviously never tied up a person before. When he'd secured the ropes around her, she'd simply arched away from the trunk, expanding her chest, puffing herself up to become much larger.

Now that he was deep in slumber, she sank back against the tree and let out all her air, loosening the ropes and squeezing out from under her bonds.

Whatever attack she planned, she would have to be quick about it. Gather her nerve and her weapon and do the deed swiftly before...

Graphic images of his murder—the blood, the struggle, the gurgling—flashed into her head like lightning, leaving a singed, metallic aftertaste in her mouth and making her feel sick. She paused to swallow it away.

She could do this. She must.

She closed her eyes and remembered her clan folk falling under his chopping claymore.

The helplessness of her young cousins as he slashed his way through their ranks.

The hollow ache in her heart when she thought Hallie was dead.

She closed her hands into determined fists. She never wanted to feel that again.

As silent as mist, she crept toward his satchel, where he'd stashed her *duandao*. The whisper of steel as she slipped the weapon out of its sheath made the only sound in the rain-sopped wood.

After that, three cautious steps brought her to his side.

She didn't want to look at him. Didn't want to see his handsome face. His chiseled jaw. His noble nose. His soft lips.

She focused on his throat, at the pulse that throbbed there. Her target.

Her hand tightened on the *duandao* as she counted the slow pulses. One. Two. Three. Four. Five.

Then they began to increase in speed. His throat bobbed. His face twitched. His eyes fluttered. His brow creased.

He must be dreaming.

She bit her lip, shifting her grip on the dagger. Should she wait until he stopped? Wasn't it bad luck to slay a person in the middle of a dream?

As the blade hovered inches from his throat, his mouth fell open, and he began to gasp. Shallow, uneven breaths of frantic fright.

She raised the dagger, torn between wanting to put a stop to the dreadful sounds and fearing she might be the stuff of his nightmares.

Grunts of alarm caught in his throat. All at once, his chest heaved upward as he struggled against the bonds of the dream.

Panicking, she slammed her left hand flat on his chest. Pressed him down. Braced herself to make the cut across his neck.

Then he uttered a sound in the empty quiet. A sound that racked his chest. A sound that shook her to her core. A single, anguished sob that came from the depths of his soul.

Her heart plummeted.

Pity weakened her will.

Her grip faltered on the dagger.

She couldn't do this. She couldn't kill him. Not now. Not while he suffered in the grips of whatever nightmarish beast had him in its clutches.

She began to wonder if she could kill him at all.

Silently cursing her inconvenient compassion and her disappointing lack of conviction, she jostled his chest, trying to wake him from his torment.

"Wake up," she whispered. "Wake up, damn you. 'Tis only a bad dream."

Trapped in his delusion, he writhed under her hand.

She raised her voice. "Come on, mac Darragh. Wake up."

Still he wrestled with invisible demons.

Finally she clapped at his cheek to rouse him. "Wake! Up!"

When his eyes blinked open, they were still glazed and unseeing, as if he languished in the land of dreams.

"You're fine. You're safe," she told him. "'Twas only a nightmare."

He turned his head then to look at her. The mist vanished from his eyes. But the horror lingered.

"Nay," he breathed. "'Twasn't. 'Twasn't a nightmare. 'Twas real." His brow crumpled in torment, and his voice was hoarse. "'Twas real."

Then he spied the dagger in her hand. "How did ye..." He didn't finish the question. He made no move to counter her or defend himself. He didn't raise the sword. He didn't throw her off his body. In fact, his chest caved beneath her hand in defeat.

Then he uttered one raw whisper that chilled her heart. "Do it."

She gulped.

"Go on," he insisted. "Do it." The agony in his voice sliced across her spirit like a knife.

She felt an appalling lump in her own throat. Damn it! What was happening?

Was he calling her bluff? Did he think she wouldn't go through with it? Was he testing her mettle?

She ground out a warning. "I mean to."

He closed his eyes. A stray tear leaked from the edge of his eye and trickled across his temple, disappearing into his hair.

"I *will* do it," she insisted. "I'll kill you."

When he opened his eyes, they were bleak and empty. "I'm already dead."

What did he mean? The dagger began to tremble in her hand. She was fast losing control of it.

Then he did something completely unexpected. He seized her wrist, steadying it, guiding the sharp edge of the blade to his throat. "Go on. Kill me."

Horrified, she tried to pull back. Assassinating him was one thing. But being forced to do so was unthinkable.

"Nay," she gasped.

"Do it. Ye said ye would. So do it."

"Nay!" She tried to wrench her wrist away, but he held it fast. "Let go," she bit out.

She lent both hands to the task, joining them on the hilt, using all her strength to pull the dagger away, afraid if she let up, the blade would recoil and plunge haphazardly into his neck.

"Cease!" she screamed. "I don't want to kill you."

The instant the words left her lips, she realized it was the truth. Dispatching him was her duty to the clan. But she didn't wish to do it.

"Why not?" he groaned bitterly. "Isn't that what ye do? Kill helpless victims?"

Her eyes widened in alarm. "What are you talking about?"

He shook his head.

The moment to assassinate him had come and gone. She wasn't going to kill him. Not now. Probably not ever.

Against all her warrior instincts, she loosened her hands around the hilt and let the *duandao* clatter uselessly onto the leaves.

He was still clinging to her wrist, but a curious disappointment tarnished his gaze.

A part of him had truly *wanted* her to kill him.

Why?

His bleary gaze drifted away again as he mindlessly stroked his thumb against the inside of her wrist—back and forth, back and forth.

"'Tis my fault," he murmured, so softly she almost didn't hear it.

Was he talking about Creagor? Did he finally understand the act of senseless violence he'd committed? Was it possible he regretted his actions?

"I should ne'er have left them so unprotected," he said, talking as if to himself. "I should have been there."

"Where?" she asked.

"I should have gone to the christenin'," he muttered.

"Christening? What christening?"

"I should have been at Kirkoswald."

"Kirkoswald?"

He turned fevered eyes on her in accusation. "And ye... ye were part of it. How could ye have..." His voice broke. "God's eyes! There were lasses inside the church. Children. A newborn."

"Bloody hell, what are you talking about?" she burst out in frustration. "You've only had a nightmare. I've never even heard of Kirkoswald."

For Dougal, threads of the nightmare clung like the sticky web of a spider. But he knew very well it was more than a dream. The images burned into his brain were all too real. The scorched clothing. Gaping mouths. Smoldering corpses. The stench of charred wood and melting flesh.

When he'd first wakened from the hellish landscape, his heart had sunk like a dead lead weight. It was all his fault, he realized. The tragedy at Kirkoswald had happened because of him. The villagers' deaths were on his head. And he would be haunted forever by their wronged spirits.

If only he hadn't lingered at the castle, compelled to spar with Gaufrid's knights...

If only he'd gone to the christening instead, like Gaufrid should have done...

If only he'd never promised the people of Kirkoswald his protection from the beginning...

The torment of his failure sat like a yoke upon his shoulders, a yoke from which he'd never be free.

For a few brief moments as the lass held a dagger to his throat, death had seemed like a welcome friend. An end to his suffering. Payment for his sins.

He might not deserve heaven. But he could fight his way through purgatory. Forfeiting his life as penance, he believed he might make peace with the victims he'd failed. Find redemption in the realm of the dead.

Now, however, the lass's lies were filling him with

affront and outrage, dragging him back to the land of the living.

How dared she deny the massacre and her clan's part in it?

How dared she refuse to acknowledge what he'd witnessed with his own eyes?

How dared she erase the fallen as if they'd never been?

That kind of denial went far beyond villainy. It was cruel. Inhuman. Infuriating.

His temper rose, and his blood began to boil.

His longing for death disappeared. He suddenly felt a fierce need, not to be punished for his sins, but to seek redemption for them. He had to stay alive, to protect the remaining villages from her bloodthirsty clan. To watch over Darragh's vassals.

Vassals his brother had abused and abandoned.

Vassals who looked to Dougal for protection, as a champion to keep them safe.

Vassals who could so easily fall prey to the torches of an enemy clan, like Feiyan's.

And now she had the gall to claim she'd never heard of Kirkoswald.

He shuddered with fury.

"Do not lie to me, wench," he bit out. "Your kin was there only days ago. Do not feign ignorance."

"I'm feigning noth-"

"Your clan badge was found there. One o' your marauders dropped it."

"That's impossible. The entire clan has been busy planning the tournament." She added pointedly. "The tournament you ruined."

"Is that so?" he challenged. "Not a single mac Giric rode to Kirkoswald to burn the village?"

"I told you, I don't know Kirkoswald. But nobody burned any village."

Her disavowal enraged him. And now he sought to punish her. Tightening his grip on her wrist, he chewed out the words with nasty malice.

"So your clan never boasted about their exploits?" he prodded. "About how they barricaded the bloody door and torched the church? For the love o' Mary! The poor souls trapped inside must have pounded at it until their bones cracked. Clawed at the wood until their fingernails bled. Screamed until the flames licked—"

"Stop it!" she cried, upset by his words. "I don't know about any of that."

"Maybe ye do. Maybe ye don't," he admitted. "But the fact remains 'twas your clan committed the atrocity, whether ye were with them or not."

"I don't believe you. The mac Girics are a noble clan. They would never burn a church."

"I saw it with my own eyes. The ashes. The corpses. I intend to make the mac Girics pay."

"Is that why you came to Creagor? To exact revenge for some imagined—"

"'Twas not imagined!" he roared. "And I mean to take vengeance, even if I have to use ye as leverage."

Unintimidated by his vehement threat, a threat that would make most men tremble, she looked him in the eye and said, "That would be a mistake."

"I doubt that."

"You can't use me for leverage."

"Watch me," he challenged.

"Nay. I mean you can't use me for leverage," she said, arching a fine dark brow, "because I'm not a mac Giric."

He blinked, startled. "What?"

"I'm not a mac Giric. And neither is the woman you almost killed."

Stunned speechless, he could only stare at her with his jaw slack.

"So you see?" she said. "Your berserker outburst at the tournament was wasted on the wrong clan."

Surely that was untrue. "Ye don't deny Creagor belongs to the mac Girics?"

"Partly," she admitted. "But Morgan Mor mac Giric was only awarded Creagor when he married into *my* clan."

"Your clan?"

She answered proudly. "Rivenloch."

Dougal's heart dropped into his stomach.

"Rivenloch?" His voice came out on a frayed thread.

Not the warrior clan of Rivenloch? The one that generations of kings had stationed at the border to keep out the English? *That* Rivenloch?

Those were the knights he'd mowed down at Creagor?

They were the men hunting him through the woods?

This was the army planning an assault on Castle Darragh?

He felt ill.

He'd heard the tales. Everyone had. But he'd always imagined the legends of the famed border clan of Rivenloch were highly exaggerated. He'd never actually believed that maids wore mail and fought in battle.

Now he realized the legends must be true. And to his chagrin and at his peril, he'd had the misfortune to capture one of the intrepid lasses.

"Shite."

CHAPTER 14

The blood drained from the Westlander's face. Feiyan lifted her chin with satisfaction. So he *had* heard of Rivenloch.

"You've poked the hornet's nest now," she told him. "There's nothing to do but wait for the swarm to arrive."

But he apparently didn't intend to sit idly by. With his free hand, he swept the *shoudao* from the ground.

"Wrong," he said. "I've still got a hostage." He leveled the angled tip at her throat. "Maybe ye should have killed me when ye had the chance."

She glanced at the sharp edge. She wasn't afraid. He wouldn't slit her throat. He didn't have the stomach for killing a woman. And the idea of him holding her hostage was laughable.

"You won't have a hostage for long if you don't learn to tie better knots."

He grimaced. He was clearly out of his element when it came to tying up captives. She wondered if he'd ever taken a prisoner before. Despite his sword at her throat, she could have easily escaped. A quick knock at the flat of the blade with her left hand, a quick twist to free her right hand, and she could have fled into the wood before he snapped his gaping jaw shut.

But now she didn't want to escape.

His story intrigued her. He seemed so convinced of what he'd witnessed, of the mac Girics' part in it.

She was just as certain there was no way the chivalrous mac Girics could have had anything to do with the cruelty he described.

But things were not always as they appeared. Villains sometimes came in the guise of heroes. Heroes sometimes resembled villains. Though she appeared to be a blood-thirsty assassin, Feiyan was a force for good. Perhaps it was the same for mac Darragh. Perhaps he wasn't the reckless monster he seemed.

She felt compelled to find the truth. To untangle the threads of what had really happened. And it would be much easier without a sword at her throat.

"What if we call a truce?" she suggested.

"I don't negotiate with murderers."

"Murderers? I'm not a—"

"Unless I'm mistaken, ye were goin' to kill me in my sleep."

She flushed and lowered her eyes. "I..." She couldn't finish the sentence.

"So ye'll understand if I'm a wee bit reluctant to trust ye."

He had a point. "Fair enough."

"First, ye should know I have no quarrel with *Rivenloch*," he told her.

Of *course* he would say that. A person would have to be mad to want Rivenloch as an enemy.

"You do now," she pointed out. "You cut down several of our knights, almost killed my cousin, and now you're holding me hostage."

"'Twas a mistake."

"Och aye, 'twas a mistake," she agreed, "because now the entire clan of Rivenloch is about to descend upon your castle."

That was unlikely. But it was a useful fabrication. No one wanted to face the formidable Rivenloch army. The lie might protect her from harm.

"Then we should leave at once," he decided.

She opened her mouth and closed it again. She hadn't anticipated that response, and it was the last thing she wanted. The sooner they arrived at Castle Darragh, the sooner he'd realize she was bluffing about Rivenloch.

"Wait," she said. She chewed on her bottom lip, wondering if she was about to do the wise thing or wading deeper into the muck. "Maybe I can intervene. Stop their advance."

He gave her a dubious glance. "How? In my experience, warrior clans slash first and ask questions later."

"If I knew the truth, if you can tell me exactly what happened..."

"What happened?" he scoffed. "Why don't ye ask the mac Girics?"

"I haven't got the mac Girics. I've only got you."

He lowered his brows. He compressed his lips. He ground his teeth. The attack was obviously something he didn't wish to relive.

"Bloody hell," he said at last on a vexed breath. "Fine. Ye want to know what happened? I'll tell ye what happened."

Apparently unsure whether to trust her, he continued to grasp her wrist, as if his human shackle could prevent her escape. He lowered the sword, however, and pushed himself up until he was sitting on his woolen plaid. Then he nodded to the cloth, indicating she could sit beside him.

As he began to speak through clenched teeth, he worked his thumb back and forth over his clasped fingertips in agitation. It couldn't be easy to recount a massacre.

"There was to be a christenin' at Kirkoswald," he said.

She lowered herself onto the plaid. "Where exactly is Kirkoswald?"

"A few miles from Castle Darragh."

"But that's four days' ride from Creagor."

"Three if ye've got a fast mount."

She frowned. That made no sense. "What dispute could the mac Girics have with villagers a hundred miles away?"

"How am I to know?"

She tapped thoughtfully at her lip. It was possible, though unlikely, that a few rogue mac Girics might have slipped away to perpetrate the violence.

"How many men attacked the village?" she asked.

"I don't know."

She blinked. "But you saw...mac Girics...setting fire to the church?"

He sighed. "Nay."

She was taken aback. "Nay?"

He stared morosely into the flames.

"Nay?" she repeated.

He cursed under his breath. Then he choked out, "I arrived too late."

"I see."

She nodded. So he'd only seen the aftermath. And he likely blamed himself for what had transpired. For not arriving earlier.

No wonder he had nightmares.

Despite wishing to kill him only moments ago, she felt sorry for the Westlander.

"The villagers," she continued gently, "they didn't say how many attackers there were?"

"The villagers?" His voice was bitter. "What villagers?" A muscle twitched along his clenched jaw. "There were none left. The mac Girics killed them all."

"What about the women? The children?"

"Everyone."

Feiyan felt all the air go out of her lungs.

He couldn't mean the whole village. Lads in their prime?

Lasses in the bloom of youth? Bairns in the cradle?

"Surely that's not poss—"

"Every. Last. One." His voice broke on the words.

A frisson of horror struck her heart.

No wonder he'd sought vengeance.

No wonder he'd ridden a hundred miles for retribution, slashing through the melee at Creagor like a man driven wild.

Outside the realm of a full-scale war between countries, at the direction of a cruel king, what kind of monsters would decimate an entire village?

Surely not the mac Girics.

This was an atrocity of the worst kind.

Unnecessary bloodshed and collateral casualties of war were abhorrent to Feiyan and her clan. Rivenloch's battles might be aggressive, but they were always carefully targeted. Rivenloch warriors were fierce, but merciful.

Whoever was responsible for this slaughter had abandoned all compassion. They deserved Rivenloch's wrath. It was just the sort of lawless villainy Rivenloch punished, the kind of battle the warrior clan was trained to wage.

And finding the culprit behind the bloodlust was just the sort of mystery Feiyan was born to unravel.

"I don't know who committed this massacre," she breathed. "But I tell you this, mac Darragh. I'll bloody well find out who did."

The border lass's fervent vow almost broke Dougal.

He clenched his jaw, fighting back emotion.

He'd wanted to put what had happened behind him. To bury it deep. To avenge their deaths and speak of it no more. He had no desire to relive the devastation, dwell on the details, give voice to the unspeakable horror.

Not to a stranger. Certainly not to a lass from the most powerful border clan in Scotland. A lass who might yet prove to have been an accessory to the massacre.

But now that he'd broken his silence, now that he was being heard, he felt as if the spirits of the people of Kirkoswald were lurking in the darkness around him. Waiting for the truth. Waiting to be freed.

Did she mean what she said? Would she help him seek the truth? Could he rely on her? Should he? And if he did, would he find closure? Justice? Redemption?

In the end, he had no choice. Her clan could decimate his in the blink of an eye. Lives were at stake. He had to trust her.

"Dougal," he said when he found his voice.

"What?"

"My name is Dougal." If the enemy of his enemy was to be his friend, he supposed she should know his name.

"Dougal," she repeated.

The word sounded curious, spoken with her Lowland lilt, and strangely beautiful on her lips. Under less dire circumstances, he could have listened to her murmur his name all day and never tire of hearing it.

"Then know this, Dougal mac Darragh." To his astonishment, she faced him squarely and clasped her left hand over his, at the place where he gripped her wrist. "We'll get to the crux of this, I swear."

He held his breath. Her wrist felt so fragile in his grip. He could break it like a branch. Yet the touch of her hand was powerful, capable, and curiously reassuring.

"Whoever is responsible for the slaughter of the villagers, whether 'tis a mac Giric or the Devil himself," she vowed, "I'll be the first to avenge their deaths. And I promise you, I'll have the force of Rivenloch behind me."

Her earnest eyes blazed into his with fierce silver fire. From the resolve in her words and the ferocity of her gaze,

Dougal came to one instant revelation. Everything he'd heard about the magnificent warrior maids of Rivenloch was true.

For the first time in days, he sensed that truth might prevail.

That justice was possible.

That he was no longer alone in this fight.

He sensed something else in her eyes. Something that went beyond the camaraderie of their newfound alliance. A soft spark that emanated from the smoldering depths of her gaze. Igniting his affections. Forging a connection. Warming his heart.

Before he could fully explore what he perceived there, she released his hand, blushing and lowering her eyes to her lap.

He immediately missed the warmth of her fingers and her gaze. Which was absurd. He barely knew the lass. How could he have tender thoughts toward a warrior maid who had just tried to murder him?

Yet there was no denying he felt...something...for the beautiful Rivenloch lass who had just vowed to brandish her avenging sword on his behalf. And it was more than mere gratitude.

He still held onto her wrist, ostensibly to keep her from fleeing. But now he fought the desire to bring her forearm to his lips, to press a kiss on the delicate inner flesh where her pulse raced with fervor.

Feiyan didn't know what was wrong with her.

Her heart was pounding against her ribs, and she couldn't draw in a decent breath.

For one mad moment, she thought the Westlander meant to kiss her.

Of course, that was ridiculous. She'd just tried to

assassinate him. And while he might feel grateful for her offer of aid, he still didn't trust her. He certainly couldn't feel affection for her.

Worse than imagining he wished to kiss her, however, was confessing that she might *want* him to. Which was even more ludicrous.

Only moments ago, she'd had her blade at his throat. If he hadn't been asleep and dreaming, she would have slain him. One small twist of fate, and she would be watching his blood spill all over the ground instead of averting her eyes from the heart-melting warmth of his gaze.

Where he held her wrist captive, her pulse throbbed under his fingers. Not with fear. But with a strange longing.

What had they been talking about? She couldn't remember.

As the silence dragged on between them, her nerves stretched tighter and tighter, like the string of a drawn bow.

What would have happened after that, she didn't know. In the next instant, the charged clouds burst forth in a heavy hail, taking her breath away as the forest suddenly clattered to life in the downpour.

Dougal immediately released her, and she exhaled a sigh of relief. But her wrist still tingled where his fingers had pressed into her flesh. And it would be a long while before her heart calmed.

Enfolding her in his cloak, he shielded her from the worst of the icy nuggets. They huddled with their heads together, watching the pellets fall through the firelight to bounce off the shivering branches and mossy rocks.

As if hurled by the warring Frost Giants of her Viking grandfather's stories, the shards of ice began to strike with angry force. Rattling the bones of the pines. Gouging the floor of the forest. Pummeling mac Darragh's woolen cloak. Spitting on the sizzling fire.

Eventually the hail won that battle, extinguishing the flames. They were left in the dark while the shattering destruction went on and on. Yet even in the blackest, bleakest moment, when the last spark died and the storm raged all around them, Feiyan found curious comfort in Dougal's arms.

As he clung to her, sharing his warmth, keeping her safe, she forgot about ever wanting to kill him. Forgot about the melee. And Hallie. And vengeance.

She forgot everything but the way she felt next to him right now, as chaos crashed down all around them. *That* she would remember forever. The damp, musky smell of his wool cloak. The soft caress of his wet hair as it brushed her cheek. The strength of his body as he tucked her against his chest. The moist heat of his breath across her face.

It was those sensations that calmed her thoughts, soothed her spirit, and gradually made her drift off to sleep, dreaming of staying forever in his arms.

CHAPTER 15

ougal was afraid to move. The lass seemed so comfortable, cradled in the crook of his shoulder.

She'd slept there all night. Amid the maelstrom of hail, in the relentless dark, whether from overwhelming fear or mere exhaustion, his wee captive had surrendered to sleep in his arms. Soon after, the hail had ceased, and he'd succumbed to slumber as well.

He smirked. If his captive was truly an assassin, she'd failed miserably at the task.

Now, however, he was the one held captive. Fearful of disturbing her peaceful slumber, he was compelled to stay immobile, despite the numbness in his arm.

In the gaps of the pines, the ground was patchy white with residual hail. But the first fingers of sunlight were already melting any lingering evidence of the storm. Where golden beams appeared through the branches, wisps of mist escaped the mulch of the forest floor and steamed off the black trunks of oak and ash to vanish into the air, like faeries of the night fleeing the sun.

He half expected his fey hostage to vanish as well. She was certainly as beautiful and enchanting as a creature of the faerie realm. As he gazed down at her sweet face, he found it difficult to imagine she'd come to kill him.

Dark tendrils of her hair curled across her pale cheek. Her delicate nostrils fluttered subtly as she breathed. Her lush brows arched over tender eyelids fringed by thick, long lashes. And her supple pink mouth, like a budding rose blossom, opened as if in invitation.

In another time and place, he might have stolen a kiss from such delicate lips. If she were a coy maiden like the servant Merraid, who flushed pink and giggled in his presence, he might have availed himself of her unspoken request.

But Feiyan was no blushing servant.

She was a warrior maid.

He gazed down again at her lovely face. To be honest, she looked nothing like any warrior maid he'd imagined. But he didn't dare underestimate her. She'd proved a formidable opponent before. If her impressive mastery of various weapons was any indication, she was a force to be reckoned with, despite her small size.

It was by sheer luck that she hadn't made good on her assassination attempts.

He doubted he would be so lucky when it came to her clan, which even now was bearing down on Darragh.

Whatever happened, he had to make sure he delivered Feiyan to her clan in unspoiled condition. Unmarked by blade, sickness, or even a stolen kiss.

Already he'd failed. She was soaked to the skin. Filthy with mud. And he'd be surprised if she didn't fall ill from exposure to the elements.

He dared not make that mistake again. She was probably the most treasured jewel in the Rivenloch clan. He had to treat her with the utmost care. Making her sleep in wet wool in the middle of the woods in a hailstorm was not acceptable.

He needed to find better accommodations, even if they came at a cost. There were more gemstones left in his dagger. Enough to afford dry lodgings and hearty fare. It would be wealth well spent.

He was calculating how many days until they reached the castle when she began to stir.

Feiyan snuggled closer to the warm body, absorbing its delicious heat. The sun filtered through her eyelids, beckoning her to rise. But she was comfortable as she was, dozing in a dreamy fog, only half aware of the waking world.

It was the soft breath on her face that finally roused her. When she blinked her eyes open in alarm, she realized three things at once.

One, she'd let down her guard to the man she'd targeted for assassination.

Two, she'd fallen asleep on his shoulder, practically on top of him.

And three, she'd be content to stay there a while longer.

The last thought was the most distressing.

With as much dignity as she could muster, she mumbled, "Good morn," and extricated herself from his embrace.

Immediately, the world felt colder and more hostile. The damp wool of her clothing clung to her like moss to a tree. The ground beneath her was spongy with rain. And in the gap left between them, the sudden rush of chill air made her shiver.

"Did ye sleep well?" he asked.

Was that a hint of amusement she heard? It was probably uproarious to him that the woman meant to murder him had slept in his arms all night.

She glanced up at him just as a shaft of newborn sunlight hit his eyes. Had they been so blue before? This morn, they were as vivid as a robin's egg.

"Aye," she croaked.

"Good." He swept his fingers through his black locks, trying to give them a semblance of order. "If we get an early start, we can reach The Stag's Head Inn by nightfall. Get a proper meal, a hot bath, a decent bed."

It was on the tip of her tongue to protest. She was a warrior maid after all. Viking blood flowed in her veins. She was no delicate flower requiring soft puddings, feather pallets, and...

A hot bath?

That did sound lovely.

She grunted in approval.

The offer was in the Westlander's own best interests, of course. He was no fool. Now that he knew she was a warrior maid of Rivenloch, he would do all he could to stay in the clan's good graces, including treating her like royalty.

Now that he'd promised her a few luxuries—luxuries that were sounding better and better with each passing moment—she was in no hurry to confess that the Rivenloch clan was not actually headed for Castle Darragh. Perhaps she would tell him the truth *after* she got that bath.

She made hasty ablutions at a spring that fed into the river while he packed up their things. She had just one request before they embarked on their journey. Something that would make her feel less vulnerable in his presence. Something that would make her feel like the empowered, competent, capable warrior maid she was.

"I'd like my *shoudao* back."

"Your what?"

"My sword."

"This?" he said, placing his hand atop the hilt of her weapon, already fastened around his hips. "After ye tried to kill me last night?"

She lowered her gaze. "I won't try again."

"Ye're a warrior maid" he scoffed. "Killin' is in your blood."

It sounded brutal when he said it that way. She wasn't a killer. Not really. The Rivenloch warriors only killed when there was no other choice.

She sighed. "I swear I won't harm you."

"Ye can swear all ye want. But 'twill be easier to keep your oath without the temptation of a blade." He turned to head down the trail.

She bristled and scurried up behind him. "Are you questioning my honor?"

"'Tisn't a matter of honor. 'Tis a matter o' sense."

"Sense?" She shoved past him, planting herself in the middle of the trail to block his way.

"Aye," he said, stopping inches from her. "I've got the sense not to arm a lass keen to slay me."

"You *wanted* me to slay you."

"Not anymore."

She scowled. "Bloody hell. I could have killed you last night. But I didn't."

The cocky grin that bloomed on his face was infuriating. "Och aye. But then ye couldn't very well snuggle in the crook o' my arm all night if I were cold and dead, could ye?"

Her cheeks flamed, and she couldn't sputter out a reply.

"Now," he said, "shall we go? 'Tis a long journey to The Stag's Head."

She stamped her foot. "Damn you! Not until you give me my blade."

He lifted his brows in disbelief. "Did ye just stamp your foot at me?"

"So what if I did?" she said, crossing her arms. "Your attitude is bloody vexing."

He clucked his tongue. "*My* attitude? If I return your blade, how can I trust ye won't thrust me through the next time ye lose your temper, foot-stamper?"

She could think of no response that wouldn't prove he was right. Which was doubly aggravating. Because he was wrong. Feiyan wasn't short-tempered. At least not under normal circumstances.

Now, however, his high-handed dismissal of her request had sparked something in her. A fiery fury bubbling under the surface. One that could rival that of her cousin Jenefer.

But she wasn't hotheaded Jenefer. She wouldn't succumb to anger. With a mocking smile and an inviting flourish of her arm, she stepped aside to let him take the lead as they continued down the path.

She wasn't finished with the debate, however.

"How am I supposed to protect myself?" she muttered at him.

"I'll protect ye," he said over his shoulder.

"What makes you think you can protect me?" she scoffed. She'd almost killed him three times. He could barely protect *himself.*

"I can't afford not to," he said. "Ye said it yourself. I'd be a fool to let harm come to a hostage."

"A hostage? I thought we were allies."

"Maybe. But I've heard no assurances o' that from the army o' Rivenloch."

She supposed that was true. But a hostage? She didn't feel like a hostage. Not after she'd *snuggled in the crook of his arm all night.*

She let out a cross sigh. She supposed what he said was true enough. He had to do his best to keep her safe. To do otherwise risked the safety of his clan.

Still, she hated not having her weapons on her person. They gave her a sense of security. Of control. As her cousins often claimed, Feiyan didn't need a weapon, because she *was* a weapon. But without her sharpened steel, she felt only half dressed.

"Fine," she decided. "For now."

Still, it rankled at her to see her *shoudao* hung from his hips, bouncing contentedly against his thigh.

It took her half a mile to stop seething. But she realized she needed to speak civilly to him at some point.

The sooner they got on with solving who was responsible for the Kirkoswald massacre—the sooner the mac Girics were absolved of the crime and she could assure Dougal of Rivenloch's help—the sooner she could have her hot bath, decent meal, and soft bed. Then she'd reclaim her precious sword. She'd reclaim *all* her weapons.

With that goal in mind, when the path suddenly widened, she skipped up to walk beside him.

"So we were discussing the details about Kirkoswald," she reminded him.

His face darkened at the memory. "Aye."

"You said you arrived there after the fire," she said. "After the perpetrators had gone."

"Aye."

"From where did you arrive?" she asked.

"Castle Darragh. 'Tis only a few miles."

"On foot? On horseback?"

"On Urramach, my charger."

"The horse you left with the crofters."

"Aye."

It was a shame he'd given the horse away. It was a fine beast and a fast runner. He'd probably covered the distance to Kirkoswald in no more than a quarter of an hour.

"How did you first learn about the fire?" she asked. "From the smoke?"

"Nay. Two o' my brother's men brought the news."

"Your brother? Who is your brother?"

"Gaufrid, the Laird o' mac Darragh."

She lifted an impressed brow. "You're kin to the laird himself."

"Aye."

"Oh." That was surprising. She'd assumed he was a lawless mercenary. She'd never dreamed he was...the son of a laird?

Bloody hell. She'd tried to assassinate the *son* of a *laird?*

The truth hit her like a blow to the belly. For a moment, she feared she might lose her supper.

Halting on the trail, she bent forward, bracing her hands on her knees.

"What's wrong?" he asked. "Are ye ill?"

She waved one shaky hand in dismissal.

"Weary?" he asked. "Should we stop awhile?"

"I'm fine," she choked out.

But she was not fine. She was mortified.

What if she'd succeeded at her mission?

What if she'd killed Dougal mac Darragh, the son of Laird Darragh himself?

Could she have instigated a full-scale clan war? One that might last for decades? For generations?

"Maybe we need to rest," he said.

"Nay, nay," she said, straightening and waving away his concerns. "I'll be fine."

She supposed there was no point in dwelling on what hadn't come to pass. But she'd have to be more careful in future about who she tried to kill.

"Are ye sure?"

"Aye," she said, mustering up a reassuring nod. "It's just struck me we're practically peers. You see, my mother is sister to the laird of Rivenloch."

Now the blood drained from *his* face. He looked ill, as if he'd eaten bad meat.

"Ye're...niece...to the Laird o' Rivenloch himself?"

"*Herself.*" She smiled proudly. "Aye."

Dougal pressed at his temples, where his head had begun to ache, and let out a long sigh.

Of *course* the Rivenloch lass he'd managed to capture wasn't a lowly foot soldier.

Of *course* she couldn't be one of the laird's distant cousins thrice removed.

Of *course* she was in the direct line of the laird. The Laird of Rivenloch. The most esteemed warrior of a warrior clan.

And of *course* that laird was a woman.

He was beginning to think he might have been better off to let Feiyan kill him quickly. If her aunt the laird suspected he'd mistreated the lass in any way, he was certain his death would be slow and painful.

He promised himself, once they got to The Stag's Head Inn, he'd order her a bath reeking of lavender, a meal fit for a king, and a pallet made of the down of a thousand swans.

"Shall we continue then...m'lady?"

She nodded.

Meanwhile, he'd try to work out what had happened at Kirkoswald. For the first time, he hoped it *wasn't* the doing of the mac Girics, after all. Then there would be no reason for him to visit vengeance upon the mac Giric clan. And no reason for the Rivenloch warriors to bother about declaring war on mac Darragh.

After they started down the path, he reminded her, "What else do ye need to know about the fire?"

She narrowed her eyes. "Did anyone in Kirkoswald have an enemy?"

"What do ye mean?"

"Were there any disputes over land or property? Quarrels with neighboring villages? Insults? Feuds? Matters of honor?"

He shook his head. The villagers of Kirkoswald were too

busy keeping their children from starving to concern themselves with neighboring villages.

She clasped her fingers and pressed them against her lips, thinking.

"Kirkoswald is under the protection of your clan?"

"Aye," he croaked. At least Kirkoswald was *supposed* to be protected by his clan. And guilt over his failure wedged like a stone in his belly.

"So any assault on the village is an assault on your clan."

"In a way, aye."

"So 'tis possible Kirkoswald was attacked as a way to wound Darragh."

Destroying the village *would* have an effect on the clan. Gaufrid depended on goods and crops from Kirkoswald. Without them, the Darragh coffers would suffer.

"Does your clan have enemies?" she asked.

He arched a cynical brow. "What clan does not?"

"Any who would resort to this kind of treachery?"

"Butchery of innocents? Nay, none."

"You're sure of that?"

"Our enemies reive coos and brawl o'er lasses." He clenched his jaw. "They don't burn people alive in churches."

She nodded and gazed pensively at the path. "That kind of cruelty... It seems more targeted. More personal. What about your brother?"

"Gaufrid?"

"Aye. Does he have any foes?"

Dougal furrowed his brows. Who *wasn't* Gaufrid's foe?

But if anyone wanted to hurt Gaufrid, it wouldn't be by killing the villagers of Kirkoswald. Except for the loss of revenue, Gaufrid would suffer no grief over their murder. He probably couldn't name a single one of the victims.

Victims who had worked from dawn to dusk to fill his coffers.

Victims who had slaved to pay for the laird's protection.

Victims who had died, screaming for his help.

He choked back the painful knot in his throat. There was no point in telling her all that. It would only muddy the waters.

"Nay."

CHAPTER 16

Feiyan had more questions for him. At the moment, however, her attention was on the five prowlers stealing through the forest surrounding them.

The Westlander hadn't noticed them. He was too preoccupied with the unraveling of the incident at Kirkoswald.

But for the last hundred yards, someone had been stalking them.

They were likely outlaws. Thieves roamed the Scottish woods. This wouldn't be the first time she'd encountered miscreants in the forest. But it would be the first time she'd done so unarmed.

She'd spotted the intruders at once. There were three to their left and two to their right. She couldn't tell if they had weapons. But the forest was definitely familiar surroundings for them. They were garbed in leafy green and muddy brown and crept through the brush with the silent ease of wolves.

The fact that she was already aware of these details while her companion continued to blather along the trail in blissful ignorance was just one reason he should have returned her *shoudao.*

It was too late now. She'd have to confront the knaves with her bare hands.

They would likely attack at the neck in the path ahead, where boulders flanked the trail, making it only wide enough for a single person to pass.

She wasn't worried about Dougal. He could defend himself well enough with her sword, even if it wasn't his usual claymore. Once he was alerted to the men's presence, he could take the two on the right.

But for Feiyan, without her weapons, overwhelming the three on the left would be challenging.

Most important, she needed the advantage of surprise. She couldn't let the intruders know she was aware of them. So she continued her conversation, watching them from the corner of her eye.

"Every laird has enemies," she said. "Maybe someone from Gaufrid's past?"

They were ten yards from the passage. Their trackers had melted imperceptibly into the forest.

"None that I know of," he said.

With the focus of a deer, she listened for sounds that would give away the outlaws' precise whereabouts.

"He wasn't indiscreet with any of the village maids?" she murmured.

"I doubt it," he murmured back.

Five yards. Positive the thieves were lying in wait just beyond the boulders, she made loose fists of her hands and edged in front of Dougal as the trail narrowed.

The last thing she expected was for him to seize her by the scruff of her neck and pull her back, shoving her behind him. But she didn't dare yell in protest. They were almost upon the outlaws.

She tried to hiss out a warning to him.

But he was already aware of the thieves. Perhaps he'd been aware of them all along.

Soundlessly, he slipped the *shoudao* from its sheath, all

the while rattling on, "O' course ye can ne'er be certain with Gaufrid, not when it comes to—"

Without warning, he slashed toward the right. A yelp of surprise came from behind the rock.

Meanwhile, Feiyan left the trail to circle behind the boulder on the left. Three men huddled there with daggers.

Stealing up behind the first, she circled her right forearm around his red-bearded throat and gave it a sharp squeeze, simultaneously jabbing him hard in the side with her left knuckles. He collapsed, choking and coughing, incapacitated for the moment.

When the second man turned at the sound, she seized his shoulder and swept her foot low, giving him a swift kick that knocked his heels out from under him. He fell flat on his back, next to the first man.

Mac Darragh seemed to be handling the other two outlaws. A quick glance told her one of them lay unconscious in the leaves. The second, a bald man with a black beard, knelt at the point of Dougal's sword.

But now the last outlaw was ready for her. He had an eating dagger, short and one-sided, but sharp. He also had a determined scowl on his gray-grizzled face. He didn't care that she was a woman. And he didn't care that his companions had met with misfortune. She saw weathered desperation in his red-rimmed eyes.

She braced for combat, flexing her knees and raising her hands.

He jabbed forward wildly with the dagger.

She dodged it with inches to spare.

He made another reckless slash.

She retreated again. But now the men close behind her were rousing. Judging the location of the first by his scuffling in the leaves, she spun, making a wide arc with her foot. It collided with the side of his head, knocking him back to the ground.

When she circled back, she wasn't quite quick enough to dodge the next slash of the dagger. The point grazed her cheek, just below her eye, leaving a stinging trail that made her recoil with a hiss.

Meanwhile, the red-bearded man she'd choked had recovered enough to grab her from behind. As his arms went around her waist, she smashed her elbow into his nose. He stumbled back with a wail of pain.

Emboldened at the sight of her blood, the man with the dagger slashed forward again.

She raised her left arm, intending to strike his wrist and dislodge his grip on the blade. But he changed his angle at the last instant, and the edge sliced through her sleeve and grazed her forearm.

More incensed by her damaged garment than her cut flesh, she staggered back out of range, unfortunately into the arms of the waiting thief, revived from her kick.

"Hold her!" the man with the dagger said.

Arms went around her, while from the ground, through his crunched nose, the red-bearded man snarled, "Don't kill her! She's mine!"

She attempted to escape her captor's grip, bringing her heel down hard on the top of his boot. She missed.

"You'll have to take the fight out of her first," her captor chimed in.

"Oh, I plan to," the red-bearded man promised as he struggled to his feet.

The man with the dagger paused to sneer in her face. "And after, we can throw her in the river."

Suddenly, from across the path, Dougal called out, "I've got your man! Let her go!"

There was a hesitation as the three outlaws turned to see their bald-headed, black-bearded cohort squirming at the point of Dougal's sword.

After a tense moment, the man with the dagger snorted. "Go on. Kill him."

"What?" The bald-headed man's face fell. "Nay, nay, nay, Robbie!" he squeaked out. "Russell? John?"

It seemed none of his fellows much cared if he lived or died.

"Don't kill me, sir," the man begged Dougal.

This time when Feiyan tried to crush her captor's foot, she felt the crunch of bone under her heel.

With a howl of pain, he hopped back, releasing her. But not before the man with the dagger could lunge forward to press the edge of his blade against Feiyan's throat.

She glanced at Dougal. His jaw tensed. The blood left his face. She sensed he was going to surrender. Lower his sword and let his captive go.

But she wasn't ready to yield. What Dougal didn't realize was Feiyan could do dagger defense drills in her sleep.

"Nay!" she shouted.

"Move," the man sneered at Dougal, "and I'll do it. I'll slit her bloody throat."

"Oh nay you won't," she bit out.

In the blink of an eye, before mac Darragh could lose his nerve and drop his weapon, she ducked back from the blade. Grabbed the man's wrist with her left hand. Punched him in the chin with her right. Kneed him in the groin. Then, when he bent forward in pain, she pinioned his dagger arm. A quick twist made him yap and drop the weapon.

But that was only one man. There were still two behind her. One of them intent on having his way with her before they tossed her in the river. Both of them too close for comfort.

"Feiyan!" Dougal barked.

He clouted his captive hard in the chin with the pommel of the *shoudao,* rendering him senseless, and then tossed the sword to her.

In one smooth move, she caught the blade by its grip and swung it around just as the red-bearded outlaw was advancing.

At that instant, all motion seemed to halt while calculations coursed through her head at lightning speed.

She could kill the red-beard. There was enough force and momentum behind the arc of the blade to do it. The *shoudao* was capable of slicing through a gambeson like a knife through cheese. If it didn't cut him in half, it was certain to deal out lethal damage.

And there was no question. The red-beard deserved death. He'd threatened to rape her. Rape her and drown her.

But there was something else. Dougal had said it. *Killing is in your blood.*

That wasn't true. And the fact that he thought it *was* bothered her. She might be a warrior maid. But she didn't enjoy slaughter. Not when it was unnecessary.

Perhaps it should have troubled her that she cared what mac Darragh—a Westlander she'd likely never see again— thought of her. But there wasn't enough time to consider the implications of that.

Instead, in that brief moment, gauging the speed of his advance and the range of her swing, she pulled back her reach by several inches. The tip of the *shoudao* slashed through just the front of the red-beard's gambeson, deep enough to penetrate the skin and scrape along his ribs. No deeper.

A line of crimson bloomed on the muddy linen. He shrieked, stumbling backwards in shock.

On the back stroke, as the second oncoming thief lunged forward, she shifted her angle to clap him on the side of his head with the flat of the blade, near the grip, where it was strongest. She struck him with enough force to knock him to the ground, leaving him groveling in the leaves for a stunned moment.

The third man, the one she'd disarmed, had scooped up his eating dagger again. After the good twist she'd given his shoulder, his right arm was worthless, so he raised the weapon in his left hand.

But while he sneered at her in challenge, the men she'd struck with the *shoudao* decided they'd had enough. They limped off into the forest to lick their wounds.

The man with the dagger ground his teeth. "Come back here, cowards!" he yelled.

While the man continued berating his fleeing companions, Dougal came up behind him and easily wrenched the dagger out of his hand. Defenseless, caught between the Westlander's weapon and her lethal *shoudao*, he opted to follow his fellow thieves. They didn't bother pursuing him. He'd likely never tangle with the likes of them again.

That left just two outlaws. The one willingly sacrificed by his friends and the one who was still unconscious.

"What about me?" the dazed fellow asked. "You won't kill me, will you?"

"Ye're free to go," Dougal said, "though if I were ye, I'd find new bedfellows."

"Thank you, sir. Thank you."

Dougal gave Feiyan a wink that made her glow as he added, "Be sure to warn everyone about the dangerous swordswoman who roams the wood."

"Oh...aye," the man stammered as he stumbled to his feet. "I'm much obliged. I won't forget your mercy."

Dougal smirked. "And I won't forget your face."

Once the man scuttled off through the woods in the opposite direction of his associates, Dougal turned back to her. He frowned at the injury to her forearm.

"That needs bindin'."

"'Tisn't as bad as it looks," she said.

"'Tis bad enough."

He picked up the deserted dagger and hunkered down by the last outlaw, who was still dozing. He cut the last foot of linen from the bottom of the man's shirt and tore it into two pieces. The larger one he used to bind her wound, pushing her sleeve back gently to wind the linen around her forearm. With the smaller piece, he dabbed lightly at the cut beneath her eye.

Despite the fact they were out of danger, her heart raced, and she wasn't sure it had anything to do with the violent encounter.

As Dougal tenderly touched her face, she held her breath. At this proximity, she could see flecks of indigo in his woad blue eyes. The small curve at the corner of his mouth that marked a history of smiles. The tips of his white teeth between his parted lips. The furrow between his brows. Every strand of his ebony hair.

"Ye were right," he murmured.

"Right about what?" Her voice was rough.

"Ye should carry your sword."

She smiled.

He shook his head in wonder. "I've ne'er seen a fighter—lad or lass—who had such skill with a blade."

Men she'd fought had praised Feiyan's swordsmanship most of her life. She'd trained hard for years. And as a warrior daughter of Rivenloch, she was expected to be a fine fighter.

But somehow Dougal's admiration meant more than a lifetime's worth of commendation from her clan. And now she was doubly glad she'd spared the outlaws. She glowed with pride as he continued.

"God's eyes! The way ye were able to disarm the fellow with the dagger, 'twas truly amazin'. I almost felt sorry for him."

Her grin widened. She winced as it tugged at the slash on her cheek.

He gave her a one-sided smile. "No wonder our borders are safe, with lasses like ye guardin' them."

Whether it was his words of acclaim, the heat of battle, his gentle touch, or his closeness to her, Feiyan's veins suddenly surged with a molten current of pleasure.

He caught her gaze then, and his fingers paused against her cheek. She saw her own evolving emotions reflected in his eyes. Warmth. Fellowship. Respect. Affection. Desire.

Then she lowered her gaze to his mouth—his wry, exquisite, enticing mouth, where the traces of a smile lingered—and she couldn't resist the call of adventure.

Feiyan had split, bruised, smashed, and swollen men's lips. She'd never once kissed them. She'd never before had the desire.

But now she was hot from battle. Flush with victory. Every nerve was alive and singing. A kiss seemed the perfect celebration of their triumph.

On instinct, she snagged the front of his gambeson and pulled him toward her. Then she closed her eyes and pressed her lips to his.

His mouth was softer than she imagined. Warm and yielding. Full and supple.

He put up no resistance as she discovered each new sensation with tentative care, like a child trying blancmange for the first time.

As she tasted more and more of him, a glaze of pleasure drizzled over her like honey. Her breath quickened. Her flesh tingled. Her head vibrated.

She began feasting on him, like a starving waif at a banquet. With a fierce need. Unable to cease. Unable to slow herself. Unable to get enough.

And then he responded.

CHAPTER 17

From the time he could grow fuzz above his lip, Dougal had been kissing lasses. Tall. Short. Plump. Thin. Ugly. Beautiful. As long as they'd been willing, he'd indulged in the pleasant habit. As often as possible.

But never had a woman so stunned him into submission. Whirled him into dizziness. Knocked him on his heels.

Maybe it was owing to the dregs of excitement from his recent battle.

Or the memory of her body pressed close to his all night.

Or the intriguing seduction of watching her wield a sword.

Whatever afflicted him, it caused him to cast aside all caution and return her kiss with equal fervor. Even knowing it was a hunger impossible to satisfy. A passion both desirable and dangerous.

Her lips—innocent in their exploration, tenuous in their pressure—drove him to seduction so swiftly, it took his breath away.

When he was finally able to respond, it was with none of his usual tenderness. Like a famished wolf, he fed on her with greedy abandon. Slanting his mouth over hers. Trapping her swollen lips between his own. Trespassing into her sweet, warm recesses with his thirsting tongue.

Yet despite his aggression, she welcomed him, kissing him as fearlessly as she fought. She coiled her fist in his gambeson. Ground her mouth against his. Delved deeper into the kiss.

Lust rose faster than a flooding river. Blocking out all sense. All space. All time. The world vanished around him. There were only the two of them and this thing between them. A sort of music or magic or magnetism that bound them together where their lips touched.

Where this raging river was headed, he was well aware. But it didn't stop him from mindlessly steering the vessel of his desire along the current. And she seemed content to embark on the same journey.

What would have ultimately happened, he never discovered. At that moment, the last remaining outlaw roused, scuffling at the leaves. The startling sound split them as neatly as an ax splitting firewood.

"What happened?" the thief asked, rubbing the bump on his head and frowning down at his torn linen shirt.

Dougal, perhaps angrier than he should have been at the interruption, snapped, "Go on! Leave! And don't come this way again!"

The man, seeing his fellows gone, scrambled to his feet and took off into the trees.

But for Dougal and Feiyan, it was too late. The mood had been broken. Whatever had possessed them was gone now. Each unable to look at the other, they squirmed in the awkward silence.

Finally, pretending to examine her blade, Feiyan mumbled, "I'm...sorry."

"Sorry?"

"For...for stealing a kiss."

He cleared his throat and hunkered down by the sack the outlaws had left behind, pretending to be fascinated by its contents. "Ye can't steal what's freely offered."

They exchanged glances then, and Dougal could see residual desire still glimmering in her eyes. Proof of the powerful attraction between them. Like banked coals, strong emotions burned under the surface. But in his heart, he knew stirring them again could lead to disaster.

They were playing with fire. And it was up to him to dowse the flames before they flared out of control.

It was up to Feiyan to stop this runaway cart of passion. She'd set it in motion, and she had to stop it from heading off a cliff.

What had possessed her to kiss him? She didn't know. Madness? Relief? Curiosity?

Whatever it was, she needed to put it behind her. Only a day ago she'd planned to murder the man. Now she was slathering her affections on him as thick as butter on bread.

Killing him? Kissing him? She needed to forget about both altogether.

She should focus on solving the tragedy at Kirkoswald so she could return to her comfortable life at Rivenloch, where raven-haired men with sparkling azure eyes didn't give her a second glance.

Despite her best intentions, her heart skipped a beat when Dougal pulled out several waxed linen parcels from the sack and smiled at her in triumph.

"Good news, m'lady," he announced. "Food."

Eager for the distraction—any distraction—she asked, "What kind?"

He unwrapped the parcels one by one. "Hard cheese. Bacon. Bannocks. Dried apples."

As he laid out the traveler's feast on his plaid, Feiyan's gaze kept drifting back to his mouth, remembering his warm lips, soft breath, intoxicating tongue. She thought she could will away desire. But it wasn't so simple.

Moments later, as she sat across from him, chewing on a slice of dried apple, she decided that rather than feigning the kiss had never happened, rather than pretending she didn't want it to happen again, she needed to confront the matter openly and settle it, as she would a dispute between foes. Put things to rest once and for all.

"We can't let it happen again," she blurted.

He glanced up from his bannock. "What? The outlaws? I don't think—"

"Nay, the...the...what happened between us."

"The kiss."

She blushed. "Right." It sounded so much more potent, more real when he said it aloud. "I just want you to know...I...didn't mean anything by it."

"Och aye. O' course not."

"'Twas likely only the excitement of the battle."

"Sure," he agreed with a nod. "Your heart was beatin' fast. Your blood was runnin' hot. 'Twas only natural ye'd...well..." He let his words trail off.

For some reason, what he'd said only made things worse. She choked down a half-chewed bite of apple. "I just don't want you to think..."

"Aye?"

"I don't want you to get the wrong impression."

"The wrong impression?"

"That I have...feelings...for you."

"Ah." Dagger in hand, he frowned down at the hard cheese. "Because ye most assuredly do *not*."

"Right. Aye." She hesitated. "I mean nay." Was he hurt by that? Did *he* have feelings for *her*? "That is to say, I don't *hate* you."

"Well, that's a relief," he said, carving off a slice of cheese for her. "'Twould be disappointin' to think ye go around kissin' men ye hate, ye know, just for spite."

She scowled. Was he toying with her? "I don't *go around* kissing anyone."

She swore there was a glint of amusement in his eyes as he replied, "Is that right? Because ye seem fairly skilled at it."

She wasn't sure whether to be pleased or insulted. "What's that supposed to mean?"

"I mean, if that's the way ye kiss a man ye *don't hate*," he said, handing her the cheese with a wink, "it makes me wonder how ye kiss a man ye have feelin's for."

She didn't know how to answer that, so she bit into the cheese, chewing away her dissatisfaction with the way the conversation was going.

As he cut off a chunk of bacon, he mused, "On the other hand, ye can certainly knock a man on his arse ere he knows what's hit him...'Tis amazin'."

She lowered her eyes to her lap. So he'd felt that as well? It wasn't only *her* world that had been turned upside down by the kiss?

"That kind of passion and focus," he gushed, "they're a gift."

Now he was making her blush. But his praise pleased Feiyan, who had more experience crushing men's mouths with her knuckles than her lips.

"When ye drew back just so," he marveled, "hesitatin' a moment before ye went all in, 'twas like a dance."

"Oh." Her cheeks flamed. Her heart raced. It *had* been like a dance. Pushing and pulling. Advance and retreat. Giving and taking. All to the musical strains of desire. But this discussion was hardly exorcising her lust. In fact, it was making things worse.

Completely abashed, she mumbled, "Aye, but... Well, enough about kissing."

"Kissin'?" he said in surprise, offering her a small chunk of bacon. "Och nay, I was talkin' about your fightin' skills."

Mischief glimmered in his gaze. The wicked knave had sown confusion on purpose.

She snatched the bacon out of his fingers, muttering, "For shite's sake."

But as vexed as she was, his low chuckle of response still curled around her ears like the intriguing purr of a wildcat.

Dougal couldn't deny it was entertaining to make the ferocious wee lass blush. But mostly it served his purposes to vex her. She wouldn't make the mistake of kissing him again. Given who she was, that would be better for both of them.

They ate in silence after that. He refilled his costrel with water from a spring that fed the river, and they continued their journey. No more thieves materialized to delay their progress.

Eventually, the excitement of battling outlaws and sparring with the lass faded. More pressing matters needed to be addressed. Kirkoswald. The mac Girics. And the Rivenloch army, marching inexorably toward his clan castle.

The sooner he unearthed the truth, the sooner Feiyan could call off the hounds of war. And that critical mission made it easier to speak about the unspeakable—the horrific carnage he'd witnessed.

"About Kirkoswald," he said as the trail widened through a glade of young elms, "I've racked my brain. But I can't fathom how killin' an entire village could have benefited anyone."

"What about someone from Kirkoswald?" she asked. "Could one of them have done it? Is it possible there was some indiscretion among the villagers? An unfaithful wife? An angry cuckold? An inconvenient conception?"

That was impossible to know. "Who can say what happens 'tween the linens in the dark?" Then he frowned. "But to slaughter the whole village…"

"'Twould require a great deal of rage," she agreed.

They both sighed. It seemed they were circling around and around and getting nowhere. And as they emerged onto a small glen in the middle of the woods, Dougal saw the sun was already heading toward the west. By his reckoning, they should be more than half the distance to The Stag's Head. He didn't want to miss the inn.

"We should find the main road," he said.

Traveling in plain sight was risky. If a Rivenloch warrior happened to spot the laird's niece ambling alongside the savage who'd ravaged the tournament at Creagor, he'd likely swing his sword first and ask Dougal his name as he lay dying.

CHAPTER 18

The mac Darragh horse, it turned out, didn't like bearing its two young riders any more than the two riders liked riding him—as Adam called it—in bare-backed, ballock-crushing discomfort.

But at least the beast cooperated as the cousins put him through his paces along the main westward road. He was a beautiful creature. It was hard to imagine he belonged to such an ugly master.

"We should keep him," Gellir decided.

"Aye," Adam said over his shoulder. Then he reconsidered. "Unless you think we *can* trade him for my sister."

"'Twill not come to that," Gellir assured Adam. "You'll see. She may be home already. 'Twould be just like Feiyan to turn up the moment the Rivenloch warriors are riding out the gates to search for her."

"Aye," Adam said uncertainly. "Maybe."

"Meanwhile, we'll have a fine adventure, you and me. Go to Darragh. Take a peek at the sea in the west. Then ride home with this prize of a horse."

"Sure."

Gellir didn't want to add that he didn't know what he'd find once they arrived. Feiyan hanging from a gibbet? A clan mourning the assassination of their most vicious Darragh warrior? Maybe both.

Whatever awaited them, they had to get there with all haste. Not only was time of the essence, but dark would be falling soon. Gellir didn't want to be caught without food and lodging in strange country.

"The road's straight here," he said. "Let's see how fast this beast can go, aye?"

Gellir gave the horse a nudge of his heels and nearly took a tumble when the animal shot into a full gallop, scattering pebbles and earth in his wake.

The dust was still settling behind him as he reined the horse to a walk at the curve of the road, a hundred yards later. If he'd hesitated a moment longer, he might have seen a pair of woodland travelers emerging upon the main road where he'd first spurred the horse to full speed.

But he was looking forward—toward the setting sun, to a room and supper, to finding Feiyan and putting his cousin's fears to rest.

"Someone's in a hurry," Dougal remarked as they emerged upon the main road.

He couldn't see the rider who'd just galloped around the bend in a cloud of dust. But he could hear the thundering hoofbeats of a horse being ridden fast and hard.

He didn't say what was on his mind—that he'd ride that fast and hard if he were a Rivenloch warrior seeking a valuable lass like Feiyan. He only hoped her clansmen didn't intend to take up lodgings at The Stag's Head. He had no desire to be murdered at a roadside inn.

If Feiyan thought the rider might be her clansman, she gave no indication. She wasn't much interested in the traffic along the road. She was still trying diligently to uncover who was responsible for the atrocity.

"You said there were no survivors from Kirkoswald," she said.

"Aye."

"But that's not quite true," she said.

He frowned.

"There were the two men who came to the castle," she explained, "who told you about the fire."

"Well, aye."

"What were they doing in the village?"

He blinked. That was curious. What *were* Fergus and Morris doing at Kirkoswald? Normally, unless there was a fair or a hunt, the Fortanach brothers kept to the castle, drinking, whoring, and playing at dice with his brother.

"I'm...not sure."

"But they escaped the fire."

"Aye. Barely." Their hair had been gray with ash. Their clothing had been charred and bloody.

"How did they get away?" she wondered. "If everyone else in the village died inside the church, how is it they alone were spared?"

He stiffened. He hadn't considered that. His only concern had been getting to Kirkoswald as fast as possible. Saving as many villagers as he could. Punishing whoever had set the fire.

In the end, he'd failed. At all of it.

"Maybe," she suggested, "they were just very lucky."

He grunted. Had they been lucky? Or had they fled like frightened mice from the ones who'd set the fire? Was it possible they'd watched the massacre happen and done nothing to stop it? Nothing to help the victims?

The idea was distressing. Especially because it was believable. The self-serving Fortanach brothers were not known for their heroism.

"They likely hid somewhere," he decided.

"Right. They probably realized they were helpless against a band of marauders armed with torches."

Maybe. But no matter how helpless the situation, *Dougal*

would never have hidden. "They saved themselves."

"Aye, but if they hid, they also may have seen who did it." Her eyes gleamed at the possibility.

He shook his head. "Most reivers wear masks and hoods. Besides, they found the clan badge. They know who did it."

"You can't be sure," she insisted.

He stopped and turned to her, taking her by the shoulders. "Look, m'lady. I know ye want the mac Girics to be blameless," he said. "So do I. Do ye think I want to face the wrath o' Rivenloch? But I've got all the proof I need. The mac Girics left clear evidence 'twas them."

She wrenched out of his grip. "I tell you 'twas not. And I'll prove it."

"And how will ye do that?"

"I don't know...yet. But once we reach your castle, I'll find a way."

"Once we reach my castle," he said, "it may be too late."

Feiyan knew he was wrong about that. His castle wasn't in danger. At least not from Rivenloch. Her clan wasn't coming to her rescue. They probably hadn't noticed she'd gone missing.

But she wouldn't argue with him. As long as he believed the Rivenloch army was already thundering toward Castle Darragh, she had leverage.

She suspected there was more behind the story of marauders. It seemed very convenient that two lucky villagers had somehow managed to escape and just happened to find the mac Giric clan badge. Still, she dared not voice her doubts yet. Not until she could puzzle things out for herself.

For that, forewarned was forearmed. She needed to skillfully pry from Dougal every bit of intelligence she could about clan Darragh. Their history. Their loyalties. Their castle defenses.

She waited until they had passed through a flower-studded glen, by a pair of squirrels making chase in a tree, past a spring trickling down a mud bank on its way to the river.

Then she engaged him in seemingly innocent conversation.

"So tell me about your clan. Do you have other brothers and sisters?" she asked casually. "I have one sister and four brothers. I'm the oldest."

"Nay, there's just Gaufrid and me."

"And are you close to him?"

"Gaufrid?" He smirked. "We're close in age, I suppose."

"So you don't get along?" she guessed. "My brothers are always fighting."

"I suspect 'tis the nature o' brothers."

"Nothing serious, though. Mostly words? A scrape? A black eye or two?"

His face darkened for an instant. "Nothin' serious. Not so far."

"With my brothers, 'tis always a fight o'er something ridiculous. Whose turn 'tis to right the quintain. Who gets the biggest slice of the roast. Which of them our mother likes best." She smiled. "Is it like that for you?"

"My ma and da are dead," he said stiffly.

"Oh."

"And my da made his choice. Gaufrid's laird o' mac Darragh now."

His words hung as heavy as fog. Was that bitterness in his voice?

"Is he a good laird?" She didn't expect the truth. A clan always defended its laird, no matter how cruel they were.

"As good as he's *capable* o' bein'," he replied.

What he left out spoke as loudly as what he said. And it put a new twist in the story.

Dougal didn't think his brother adequate for the role of laird. Perhaps he thought *he* deserved that role. It wouldn't be the first time sibling rivalry tore apart a clan. She wondered...

"You said you rode to Kirkoswald," she said. "Did your brother ride out as well?"

"Nay."

"Why not?"

A muscle twitched in Dougal's jaw as he gave her a curt reply. "'Twas *my* responsibility."

"Yours?"

"Aye," he snapped. "A laird can't be everywhere at once, can he?"

As soon as the words left his mouth, Dougal regretted his tone. It sounded exactly like something his brother would say. "Sorry."

It seemed the wee lass's wits were as pointed and accurate as her blade. In a matter of instants, she'd disarmed him and thrust a dagger into his heart.

She was right. It should have been the laird riding to Kirkoswald. Dougal wanted to believe his brother had saddled up a mount and followed soon after. But a part of him was aware of the truth. Gaufrid never did anything that inconvenienced him. And a fire was a definite inconvenience.

"So you and your brother's men rode to the village," she said.

"Only me."

"Alone?"

"I was already saddled and ready."

"But the others followed soon after?"

That he couldn't answer. He hoped so. But the more he considered how his brother had refused his request for knights to take to Creagor, the more he was convinced Gaufrid had never intended to lend him aid. Of any kind.

She continued. "Don't you want to know the truth? Don't you want to figure out who set the fire?"

He stopped to scowl at her. "I know who set the fire."

"Do you?" She poked him smugly in the chest. "Or do you only know what you've been led to believe?"

He swatted her jabbing finger aside.

But she was like a persistent fly.

"Did you see the badge?"

"O' course I saw the badge. They had it when they arrived at the castle."

As they resumed walking, he could hear a pair of slow riders approaching behind them, gradually closing the distance. He stiffened, closing his fist around the grip of his dagger.

They might be Rivenloch men. If so, they would surely recognize the warrior lass. He only hoped they would call out to her first rather than run him down straightaway with their war axes.

Feiyan paid them no heed, continuing her questioning as they ambled closer and closer. "Can you describe the insignia?"

He tightened his jaw. The riders were only yards behind them. "I didn't look at it that closely."

"Aha!" she crowed, startling one of the beasts into a bray that nearly stopped his heart.

She turned at the sound.

While Dougal hastily concealed his face in the shadow of his hood, she gave a friendly nod. "Good day."

As they passed, Dougal saw it was only a holy father on a mule, carting his belongings on a donkey.

Dougal released his breath and his grip on the dagger.

Feiyan resumed her interrogation. "So you didn't actually see the insignia."

He glowered at her. "Look, I didn't have time to study the thing. I was a wee bit preoccupied with a village bein' on fire. But that doesn't mean 'twasn't mac Giric that did the deed."

Feiyan suddenly grabbed his forearm to stop him and planted herself in his way. "Listen, mac Darragh," she warned, furrowing her brows. "You and I, we're on the same side at the moment. I may be able to help you. But you've got to be honest with me. About every detail."

He didn't particularly like the bossy minx getting in his face and dictating terms to him. Even if they did make sense. Even if she was offering to help.

"Perhaps we should be goin'," he muttered, setting her aside and continuing on. "Get to Castle Darragh before your clan blasts my home to kingdom come."

He'd heard the stories—that the Rivenloch army could explode trebuchets and loose fiery dragons that raced across the sky. He used to imagine they were exaggerations. But he wasn't willing to wager his clan castle on that.

"Is that it?" she said.

"Aye," he said. "I'd like to keep my castle in one piece."

"Nay, I mean, is that it?" She pointed to a thatch-roofed building in the distance with smoke wisping into the sky. "The Stag's Head?"

"'Tis."

In the excitement of reaching the inn, the lass forgot all about her ridiculously desperate line of questioning, which was fine with him.

The inn was large, clean, and cheery, just as he'd recalled. There was a wee garden and an orchard on one side, providing fresh fare for supper, and a small stable for horses in back.

When they arrived, however, the innkeeper had bad tidings for Dougal.

"Ye're out o' luck, I'm afraid, sir. I've just given away the best bedchamber." He leaned forward to confide in a pleased whisper, "A Very Important Guest has taken lodgin's at The Stag's Head."

Dougal frowned. It was on the tip of his tongue to inform the innkeeper that he had a very important guest with him—a Warrior Maid of Rivenloch. But disclosing that would have been foolish.

"Ye've got naught?"

The innkeeper shook his head. "Nothin' private."

"Shite."

Dougal glanced at the road-weary niece of the Laird of Rivenloch sitting by the fire. She was unwrapping the bandage around her arm to take a peek. He'd promised her a hot bath and a soft bed. It was what she deserved. He couldn't break this news to her.

Then another idea occurred to him. He drew his dagger and set it flat on the counter so the innkeeper could see the jeweled hilt.

"Do ye think your *Very Important Guest* could be persuaded to surrender his chamber for the right price?"

Normally, innkeepers were more than willing to bargain. For an extra coin, they would rent out a stall in their stables or a pallet by the hearth. But to Dougal's surprise, the man looked mortified.

"Och nay, sir," he said, his eyes round with shock. "That I cannot do."

Dougal glared at him in disbelief and nodded to the dagger. "Those are emeralds and rubies."

The innkeeper nervously licked his lips. "I'm sure they are," he murmured, "and I'd love to oblige, but this is a *Very* Important Guest." Then he looked around the room to make sure no one was listening and whispered, "Just between us..." He lifted proud brows. "'Tis the king himself."

Dougal only stared at him. That was unlikely. What would King Malcolm be doing in this remote part of Scotland? Without his retinue? Staying at The Stag's Head Inn?

"Alone?" he asked.

"Nay, he came with a servant."

If the innkeeper hadn't refused Dougal's offer of jewels, Dougal would have thought the man was mad. King Malcolm was still a lad. Unless he'd escaped his minders at Edinburgh, it was preposterous that the king would be traveling through the countryside unguarded.

But he had to believe the innkeeper was telling the truth. And he supposed it was possible Malcolm was secretly visiting the corners of his kingdom. He wouldn't be the first king to do so. More could be learned about the honest condition of things when a visit was unannounced.

But that led him to wonder, "Where is he headed?"

The innkeeper shrugged.

Dougal ran a hand over his stubbled chin. If the king was headed west, toward Darragh, his problems had just multiplied. The last thing he needed was to get caught in a conflict between Rivenloch, mac Giric, his own clan, and the king.

Meanwhile, the innkeeper was eyeing the jeweled dagger, chewing at the corner of his lip. "I could rent ye *my* quarters. I'd just have to let the wife know."

"Done," Dougal agreed quickly, before the innkeeper could have second thoughts. "And supper?"

"The wife's got it simmerin' o'er the fire."

"A hot bath?"

The innkeeper winced and sucked a breath between his teeth. "The wife would have to fill it."

Dougal nodded toward the dagger. "And what would the wife prefer for her trouble? An emerald or a ruby?"

A half-hour later, after washing down a sumptuous lamb pottage with too many foamy cups of strong ale, Dougal and Feiyan were ushered to their chamber by the sweaty-faced innkeeper's wife.

"I've changed the linens," she assured them. "There's a fire goin' and a wee bath with buckets o' hot water beside." Then, as she opened the door, she whispered to Dougal, "We've got a Very Important Guest on the other side o' the wall, so if ye and your wife could…" She pressed a finger to her lips.

Dougal didn't bother correcting her about "your wife." Nor did he argue that they'd be doing nothing to make noise. He simply gave her a nod, wondering how perilous it was to be sleeping one thin wall away from the King of Scotland, and then closed the door.

Already Feiyan was cooing excitedly over the steaming water and weaving as she walked toward the bed, stripping off her clothes.

Before he could hang up his cloak, she'd tossed hers onto the pallet.

As he placed his sheathed dagger on a table by the hearth, she kicked off her boots and peeled off her hose.

By the time he eased the satchel from his shoulder, she was down to her shift.

And when she pulled that last thin linen garment off over her head, the satchel fell from his fingers with a loud thump.

CHAPTER 19

Feiyan couldn't wait to get into the warm water. She was accustomed to bathing in the cool loch at home, and after the last few days of trudging through the mud, climbing through branches, and shivering in a hailstorm, a hot bath sounded heavenly.

As for disrobing in front of mac Darragh, perhaps owing to the strong ale she'd imbibed at supper, she didn't even think twice about it. She'd never been ashamed of what she possessed. Besides, to most people, she was generally invisible.

So when she glanced up as she was pouring hot water into the cold and saw the stunned Westlander staring at her with his mouth agape, she didn't understand at first.

"What's wrong?" she asked.

"Naught's wrong," he croaked.

But she'd glimpsed a different answer in his smoldering eyes, his flaring nostrils, his tense jaw. She might be invisible to others. But Dougal saw her. Saw her and desired her. No one looked at her like he did.

That was more intoxicating than the ale. She felt his gaze like a caress over her body, gliding over her shoulders, grazing her breasts, sliding down her legs, drifting back up to linger in the curls at the crux of her thighs, and then locking once again on her eyes.

He broke away then with a sharp cough, going to the hearth, stabbing at the fire as if it were a snake that needed killing.

But the effects of his brief perusal lingered, making every inch of her skin tingle. When she finally eased into the water, the prickling melted into a lovely warm glow, as comforting as the flame of a candle.

"This is heavenly," she sighed.

He frowned. "Take care with that gash."

"What gash? This?" She held up her arm for him to see. "'Tis a scratch."

He grunted in disapproval.

"You remind me of my cousin Gellir," she mused, drizzling water over her knees with the linen rag. "So serious."

"I'm on serious business."

"Oh aye," she said with a wink. "I keep forgetting I'm a hostage." She sighed, resting her shoulders back against the linen-padded edge of the tub and closing her eyes. "Though I doubt 'twill come to that."

"What do ye mean?"

She opened her eyes. She hadn't meant to let that slip. She had to be more careful. Her security depended upon him believing that Rivenloch was bearing down on Castle Darragh.

"I mean...after that scuffle in the woods with outlaws, we're allies now, aye? As Sung Li says, the enemy of my enemy is my friend."

"Sung Li?"

"My teacher. The one who taught me how to use those weapons." She nodded to the satchel.

"Ye must have had an interestin' childhood," he said, settling onto a chair by the fire and trying to keep his eyes averted.

"Oh aye. Sung Li was my mother's teacher as well, a

great master of fighting. 'Twas Sung Li who said I was destined to be as swift and elusive as a bird. I was named after an empress of China, Zhou Feiyan, the 'flying swallow.'"

When Feiyan had had too much to drink, she could be overly talkative. She would have to make sure not to divulge too much that could be used against her. Meanwhile, she needed to collect useful information about him.

"You were trained for battle as well," she said, dragging the wet rag up her arm, over her shoulder, under her breasts.

He began to focus intently on a spot between his feet. "I was."

"Alongside your brother?"

"Aye."

"But you're the better fighter, aye?"

He hesitated. "Aye."

She laughed softly. His candor was refreshing. She despised false modesty.

As she drenched the cloth and wrung it out, she suddenly wondered, "Were either of you fostered to the Giric clan?"

"Nay. We were brought up by our father."

"You really have no history at all with the Girics?"

He shook his head.

"Might your brother have quarreled recently?"

"With the Girics? Nay."

She frowned as she scrubbed at a spot on her knee. "Perhaps there was a mac Giric lass who scorned him?"

He shook his head.

"And you're sure he didn't want their land?"

"Land a hundred miles away?"

She furrowed her brows. Maybe he was right. Maybe his brother knew nothing about the Girics. Which only proved her point. The mac Girics couldn't have committed the crime.

She'd have to dig deeper once they arrived at Darragh. And if she was to infiltrate the castle singlehandedly, it was best to be prepared.

"Tell me about your home," she said, wringing the water out of the rag and dragging it along her collar bone. "Is there a loch nearby? Mountains? A forest? Does the castle have a moat? Or a palisade?"

"Ye want to know about my keep's defenses?"

She shrugged. "Aye."

He smirked. "Would ye like me to hang a banner to welcome Rivenloch as well?"

"You don't trust me," she said.

"Not completely," he said.

She gasped and replied by peppering him with a splash from the tub.

"Ungrateful knave," she scolded. "I defended you against outlaws."

"Hey," he protested, "don't be wastin' the water. I'd like a bath as well." The corners of his lip curled up in a grin as he added, "Besides, 'twas *me* who defended *ye* against outlaws."

She shook her head. He was a scoundrel. But she was enjoying the bath too much to argue with him. Even if he was completely wrong.

Sighing, she slowly sank beneath the surface, feeling the warm waves creep up over her chin, her cheeks, her brow, her head.

It was peaceful under the water. Calm. Soothing. Quiet. Nothing like the chaos above the surface. In the warm waves, she could indulge in what Sung Li called *mozhao*, silent meditation.

Indeed, she was so relaxed, she had almost floated away to serenity when she was abruptly yanked back to the surface by a pair of rough hands on her bare shoulders.

"What the devil are ye doin', lass?" Dougal demanded, staring down at her, aghast.

Her irritation at the interruption quickly gave way to amusement. "Nothing. What did you think I was doing?"

He didn't answer. He didn't have to. She could see the answer in his eyes. He thought she was drowning.

The look of concern on his face melted her heart. The strong ale loosened her tongue. "Ahh, you were rescuing me," she realized, gazing up at him with a grateful, drowsy smile. "Thank you," she purred.

He grunted in reply. "Och. Well. Ye're no good to me dead."

But she wasn't fooled by his harsh words. His expression as he hunkered down beside her told a different tale. He let go of her shoulders. But his gaze lingered there before slipping down to her breasts and farther, to her nether curls wafting in the warm current.

She flushed with a curious brew of strong emotion. Excitement. Danger. Pleasure. All blended into one.

"I like the way you look at me," she blurted.

Her words startled him, but that didn't silence her. When she'd been drinking, very little could stop her, once she began to gush.

"No one looks at me like that," she confessed. "No one notices me at Rivenloch. Sung Li says 'tis a gift. I can disappear in a crowd. Slip past enemy lines. Steal through the forest. I'm practically...invisible." The last word caught in her throat. Her gift sometimes felt more like a curse than a blessing. "But you... You see me, don't you?"

Dougal saw her. All too well. And if she didn't stop gazing up at him with those sultry silver eyes...cooing to him in those seductive, dulcet tones...tempting him with her strong, soft, lovely body...he'd never be able to achieve the detachment necessary to use her for leverage.

He shouldn't have had that last cup of ale. He was

having trouble averting his eyes from the beautiful lass before him. Hell, he'd had trouble releasing her shoulders. Her bare, warm, wet, slippery shoulders. And now, when he should be stepping away, returning to the fire, he couldn't seem to get his feet to budge.

Still, he managed to snarl out a gruff lie. "Aye, I see ye. I see ye as a valuable hostage."

But even as he said the hurtful words, he realized he didn't see her that way at all. In fact, he doubted he had the heart to harm a single hair on the lass's head.

She should have taken his words as he intended—as a dampening insult.

But somehow she twisted them into flattery. "You think I'm valuable?"

That he couldn't lie about. "O' course ye're valuable. Ye're a loyal clanswoman, a talented warrior, a beautiful lass..."

"Beautiful?"

She acted as if she'd never heard the word. Was that even possible?

He feasted his eyes on the breathtaking lass with eyes that gleamed like raindrops, a mouth to rival a rose, and a body that begged for a man's touch. Whether it was her beauty or the ale that left him besotted, he blurted out the truth. "Ye're the most beautiful lass I've e'er seen."

For a moment, she seemed stunned. Then she murmured, "No one's e'er called me that before. You really think I'm beautiful?"

He nodded. The beast inside his braies agreed. It roused at the sight of the lovely lass.

She lowered shy eyes and murmured, "'Tis what I thought of you as well."

"That I was a beautiful lass?" he asked with a one-sided grin.

She grinned back and flicked water at him. "You were not at all what I expected."

"What did ye expect?"

"A monster. A savage. But you weren't. You aren't." Her eyelids lowered with badly disguised longing. "Your eyes are so kind. Your mouth is so sweet. You're the most handsome man I've e'er seen."

He frowned. That could hardly be true. The ale was making her wax poetic.

"The first time I saw you," she continued, "sleeping there so peacefully, with the moon shining on your hair, your chest rising and falling with each breath, I knew."

"Knew what?"

"I couldn't kill you."

He sighed. He felt the same way about her. For the last few days, he'd tried to convince himself that when it came to protecting his clan, he'd let nothing stand in the way. Not daunting odds. Not a warrior clan on his heels. And definitely not a wee Border lass. He wanted to believe he was capable of cold, calculating negotiations and merciless justice.

But gazing at the lovely, innocent, vulnerable maiden, bathing like an enticing Siren in the dangerous waters before him, he recognized it was all just an empty threat.

That was going to be a problem when Rivenloch stormed the gates of Darragh. He didn't know if he could put up a convincing bluff, holding Feiyan hostage. Would her clan believe him capable of killing her? Even worse, was it possible she *was* invisible to Rivenloch? A pawn they considered worth the sacrifice?

He didn't want to think about holding a blade to Feiyan's throat. Indeed, at the moment, he'd prefer to leave a trail of kisses there.

As if she'd read his mind, she tipped her head back, baring her throat. Then she swabbed her neck with the dripping rag.

"I'm glad we're going to be working together," she said.

"What do ye mean, workin' together?"

"We make a great team."

They *did* make a great team. The way they'd out-maneuvered the thieves in the woods—two against five—had been masterful.

But he couldn't ally with a lass whose clan harbored outlaws. And until he verified what had happened at Kirkoswald, the mac Girics remained the most likely suspects.

At that moment, the lass lifted her leg out of the water and began rubbing at her shin. It took all his willpower not to seize the rag from her and do the task himself. He would have used more leisurely, languid, seductive strokes. He would have made her shiver with anticipation as he caressed the length of her leg, growing closer and closer to...

"Stealth is naturally the best option," she murmured.

For one startling instant, he feared he'd spoken his thoughts aloud.

Then she continued. "When we arrive at Darragh, we don't announce our presence. Not at first. That way we can gather information from the servants, crofters, merchants."

He was only half listening. Clearing his throat and adjusting his braies, he rose from his crouch and limped back to the chair by the fire. Perhaps the gentler flames would somehow cool his fiery lust.

As she chattered on, he removed his boots, studying them with an intensity normally reserved for chess.

"Servants always have the best information," she said. "They're invisible, like me."

He suddenly wished she *were* invisible. Even though he was examining the cracked heel of his boot, she was there in his peripheral vision, lifting her other leg with casual abandon, as if she didn't possess the limbs of a goddess.

Meanwhile she continued to think aloud. "Someone has

to know something about who did this. Maybe a squire. Or a stable lad."

She'd finished washing her legs now. She was sitting forward with her arms around her knees, tapping thoughtfully at her lip. At least, that was what he *imagined* she was doing, since all of his attention was on the spot of dirt on the toe of his boot.

"And as far as your brother…" she prompted.

"Gaufrid." The name came out of him like the croak of a frog.

"Aye, Gaufrid. As laird, he no doubt has a manservant. A steward. A mistress. Someone who may have overheard an important conversation."

Without warning, she rose from the bath, like Aphrodite from the sea. It took all his willpower to continue scouring his boot.

"I've dawdled long enough," she declared. "'Tis your turn."

He dared not watch as she emerged from the bath in all her naked glory. Soon afterward, to his relief, she shimmied into her shift. By then, he may have scrubbed his boot leather as thin as parchment.

"Here," he said gruffly, rising with a gesture. "Come take my place. Ye can dry your hair by the fire."

He needed her as far away from the bath as possible. At the moment, he had no control over what was happening betwixt his legs. He couldn't expose her to that.

Once she took his place at the hearth, he turned his back, undressing with as little fanfare as possible and immediately stepping into the tub.

He never heard her stealing up behind him. So when she suddenly said, "Here, I'll pour in more hot water," he started and stumbled, half-falling into the water with a great splash that sloshed out over the edge.

She squealed as the water drenched the bottom part of her shift.

All at once, he remembered the guest next door. The last thing they needed was a royal reprimand for the noise they were making.

"Sorry," he whispered, shielding his lap from view with his hands. "I didn't..."

"Hear me?" she said with a smug smile. "I know. I'm as stealthy as a cat. Say when."

It took him a moment to digest her words. He was utterly distracted by the fact that her shift was of such fine linen, she might as well be wearing nothing at all. As she poured water into the tub, he could see the curve of her waist where it flared gently into her hips. The silhouette of her modest breasts, their tips puckered with the cold. The damp, dark shadow where her thighs were joined.

Then he made the mistake of looking at her face. Her eyes had gone smoky, and she was biting her lip.

By the time he realized what she'd said, the water was growing too hot.

"Stop!"

She flinched, startled. "Sorry."

She put down the bucket. But he didn't breathe again until she resumed her seat at the fire and started combing her wet hair with her fingers.

He snapped up the rag. Maybe a brisk scouring could distract him from the lingering effects of her gaze. For now. But it was going to be a long night of torment, sleeping just a few yards away from a woman who put Aphrodite to shame.

CHAPTER 20

The key to being a supreme warrior, Sung Li always said, was discipline. That was why Feiyan still practiced *taijiquan* most morns. She repeated the same exercises over and over every day. Through discipline, persistence, and self-control, defenses had become second nature to her.

At the moment, however, whether it was due to her overindulgence in ale or the unsettling presence of her former foe in a most disturbing state of undress, Feiyan found her mind wandering in a most undisciplined manner.

She was supposed to be strategizing how to infiltrate Kirkoswald.

Instead, all she could think about was how the Westlander's bare skin would feel against hers. How his lips would taste. What it would be like to sink into the water and impale herself on that impressive dagger. That's what it had looked like to her when she'd stolen a glimpse. A powerful dagger, unsheathed and ready for battle.

It gave her a secret thrill to know she might be the cause of its state. That Dougal not only saw her as a warrior, but as a woman.

One of the pitfalls Sung Li had warned her about was pride, about falling prey to flattery and adulation. They were a dangerous distraction. A disciplined mind was weakened by too much praise. And a humble warrior was one who could more easily steal up on her enemy.

She was currently stealing glances at Dougal. As he sluiced water up over his shoulders, her mind felt weak indeed. She imagined sliding her hands over the broad muscle there. Pressing her lips against his warm, wet flesh. Surrendering to his desire and her craving.

A loud pop from the fire startled her—as effectively as the clouts Sung Li gave her when she lost focus. Flushing with shame and regret, she tried to force her thoughts back to the challenge ahead.

But it was so difficult when a naked warrior—a commanding yet vulnerable, eye-catching, heart-melting, breathtaking Highlander—bathed only a few yards away.

Somehow, against her best intentions, her gaze slipped again and again to his formidable form while she dreamed of possibilities. His midnight black locks, twining around her pale fingers. His chiseled jaw, manly and coarse, grating deliciously against her smooth cheek. His sculpted shoulders, flexing under her fingers. His indigo eyes, staring deeply into...

They *were* staring deeply into hers. Or they *had* been. Just for a moment. Yet in that brief splinter of time, she'd glimpsed a deep well of longing.

Her breath caught. Her heart fluttered. The silence crackled with unseen current.

For one precious instant, he'd seen her. Looked at her in a way no other man ever had. Peered into her innermost desires. Seen her naked emotions.

Though it felt like an eternity, the moment was fleeting. And when he began scanning the area around the tub, she feared his fleeting lusty glance might have been her imagination.

She followed his gaze and realized he was looking for his linen drying cloth. He'd left it on the bed.

Her initial wicked temptation was to force him to parade, naked and dripping, across the room to get it.

Courtesy won out, however, and she rose on quavering limbs to fetch the cloth for him. Which wasn't necessarily a better option.

As she held the cloth up before her, he faced away from her to stand, waiting for her to drape it over his shoulders. But she hesitated, biting her lip and letting her eyes follow a drop of water as it trickled down his well-muscled back. Past his tapering waist. Disappearing into the cleft between his firm buttocks.

When he cleared his throat expectantly, she thrust the cloth forward, lingering a moment as it clung to his damp shoulders.

She should have backed away then. Returned to her safe seat at the hearth. Averted her eyes and diverted her thoughts.

But she couldn't make her feet move.

Even when he slung the linen around his hips, tying it with a decisive knot, and turned to face her, she stood rooted to the spot.

And when his gaze strayed swiftly down the length of her, the heat of it impacted her so powerfully, she let out an audible sigh.

Then his jaw tightened, and he glared at the floor.

"Leave me in peace, m'lady," he growled. "Ye're playin' with fire."

He was right, of course. Damn him.

Surrendering to their passions would be a mistake of the worst kind. Not only a moral mistake. But a strategic one as well. How could he possibly use her for leverage if he swived her? And how could she maintain a warrior's emotional distance if she swived him?

Still, it stung to be so rebuked.

"I don't know what you're talking about," she said

stiffly, turning on her heel and marching back to the chair beside the hearth.

Grabbing the poker, she literally began to play with fire, cracking the coals one by one, pretending they were the black hearts of her enemies. She managed to distract herself enough long enough for him to finish drying off.

But he was still clad in only the linen wrap when he snatched the poker away from her.

"Easy, m'lady," he said. "Ye'll kill them all, and we'll have no fire for the night."

Her first impious thought was of other ways they could keep warm. But she dared not share that with him.

Even with the fire out, the shutters flung wide, and the covers off, Dougal wouldn't be cold. Not while the lovely lass was in the room.

But one of them had to throw a bucket of icy water on whatever was happening here. Not only was it improper. It was dangerous.

Until they learned the truth about Kirkoswald, they had to maintain an air of cautious alliance. The fate of three clans was at stake. He couldn't afford to jeopardize that arrangement with an ill-timed tryst.

Maybe later, he told himself. Maybe—if mac Giric was absolved and Rivenloch belayed their attack, once the real defiler was discovered and justice rendered—Dougal would celebrate with the wee warrior maid. Maybe then the two of them would consummate their mutual interest with a secret and rewarding tryst betwixt the sheets.

But they were still two days' journey from Castle Darragh. Two days from interrogating the Fortanach brothers. Two days from discovering what additional clues might be found at Kirkoswald. Until then, as difficult as it was, he had to maintain a safe distance from the lass who might or might not prove to be harboring outlaws.

That was the sobering truth of it, what convinced him to ignore his carnal cravings and focus on solving the crime. Though it was nigh impossible to imagine sweet-faced Feiyan being part of such a brutal act, he would be a fool to trust a wily warrior lass known for deception.

She came from a clan with no mercy, after all. A clan where women fought alongside men. Where slaying a man in his sleep was apparently acceptable.

He couldn't deny he looked forward to exonerating her, to proving her innocence...and, in a wishful corner of his mind, sampling her virtue. But he dared not let his desire for her cloud his judgment.

Meanwhile, the sooner they puzzled out what had happened, the sooner he could think about engaging in that much more entertaining pastime.

He propped the poker against the hearthstones.

"I'd like to ask ye somethin'," he said.

He'd noticed a useful thing about Feiyan. She was quite forthcoming when she'd been drinking. Which was convenient for him. Less convenient for a lass sworn to secrecy.

She gave him a cautious nod.

"How well do ye know the mac Girics?"

She straightened with pride. "Well enough. I know they didn't burn Kirkoswald."

"But how do ye *know* that?"

"The laird is a decent man. Well, mostly decent." Her brow crumpled. "He *did* hold my cousin Jenefer for ransom. And his right hand man Colban seduced my cousin Hallie. And they're Highlanders, of course." She lifted her eyebrows as if he would understand what that meant, as if he were not a Highlander himself. "But on the whole, they're good men."

Dougal arched a dubious brow. The world of the

borders must be very different from his, if she considered hostage-takers and seducers "good men."

"So tell me about the Colban fellow." Unless there was open clan warfare, it was unlikely the laird himself would perpetrate such a blatant act of terrorism. But he might leave it to his second in command.

"Colban an Curaidh," she said on a sigh of admiration. "That means the Champion, you know."

He stifled a smile. He *did* know. Gaelic was his mother tongue, after all.

She continued. "He's the one who brought Hallie back to life after you killed her."

He felt a twinge of guilt. But surely the woman's death had been an exaggeration if she'd been so readily brought back to life.

Feiyan lowered her voice to a whisper. "He wasn't born a mac Giric. He's a bastard and an orphan. The laird took him in as a lad, against the wishes of some in the clan. Hallie said his back still bears the scars of the whipping he got as a child. Can you imagine? Whipping a child? Yet he persisted and earned his honor."

This Colban fellow sounded like a candidate for sainthood, not an outlaw who would burn down a church.

Then she inclined forward, beckoning him close with a wave of her fingers. When he leaned down, he could see the gentle slope between her breasts, creamy and inviting, where her leine gapped open.

"And just between you and me," she murmured, "that nonsense about seducing my cousin Hallie? Hallie was always like a block of ice. Colban only warmed her up a bit."

He would have grinned at her revelation, but his own body was warming up a bit. Instead, he straightened to a safe position and continued his interrogation.

"What about the Laird o' mac Giric?" he asked. "What's he like?"

"Morgan? Oh, he's a man of honor, to be sure."

"I thought ye said he held ye for ransom."

"Well...aye...but 'twas for good reason." She explained. "You see, he figured Creagor was his by rights. But my cousin Jenefer thought it should belong to her. And when she feigned to be a spirit to frighten him off, he wasn't frightened at all. Instead, he took her captive. He took *all* of us captive. You know, in order to ransom us for Creagor. Only he couldn't do that until the Laird of Rivenloch returned from court. Meanwhile, I slipped past the guard and set off for home. But on the way, I spied English troops. So I mustered our knights," she said, finishing with a triumphant smile, "and we returned to do battle and save the keep."

Dougal's head was spinning. He understood almost none of what she was saying. Her enthusiasm, however, was adorable.

"So..." he guessed. "Morgan is a good man?"

"That's what I'm saying," she gushed. "He fought side by side with the army of Rivenloch."

"Shh." Considering who resided in the adjoining chamber, he thought it best not to mention Rivenloch by name. But he should have realized it was a mistake to muzzle a warrior lass.

"What do you mean, shh?"

"Naught. Go on."

It might have been his imagination, but it seemed her voice grew louder as she spoke.

"He was even decent when he took us captive," she said. "He kept us in Creagor's finest bedchamber. He confiscated all my weapons, of course, just as you have." Then she frowned. "You're going to give them back to me, aye? After you're done using me as a hostage?"

He flinched. He hoped no one next door heard that.

Mistaking the reason for his flinch, she demanded, "You

are giving them back, aye?" She rose to her feet, giving him a menacing glare that would frighten a wolf. "Those weapons are precious. They came from the Orient and cost me a fortune. If you don't return them—"

"Aye! Aye," he interjected before she could raise her voice any more. "I'll be givin' them back to ye."

"Includin' my *yan zi fei dao?*"

"Your what?"

"My swallow tail darts. The ones you left in the forest."

There was no hope of finding those. Not in the hundred miles of forest between Creagor and Darragh. Just as there was no hope of recovering the armor he'd ditched in the bushes.

"Sure," he lied.

"Because they're quite rare."

He believed her. He also believed she was going to get them both into trouble if they didn't stop talking about hostages and weaponry and Rivenloch.

"We were discussin' Laird Morgan," he said.

"Right. Aye."

"Ye think he's trustworthy?"

"Of course!" she scoffed. "Do you think the *king* would have betrothed him to my cousin otherwise?"

Dougal's eyes went wide. "Bloody hell," he muttered. That *king* was only a wall away.

"I'm telling you he *did,*" she insisted, thinking he didn't credit her. "Malcolm himself signed—"

"Nay!"

"What the devil?" she snarled. "You don't believe me? I swear it! The King of Scot-"

"Hush!"

She gasped. "Did you just hush me?" she asked in disbelief. Then she did the one thing he didn't want her to do. She raised her voice and named him. Loud and clear. "Dougal mac Darragh, how dare you—"

He didn't know what else to do. He had to stop her. Hushing her didn't work. In fact, it was having the opposite effect. So he cut off her speech in the only other way he knew.

Seizing her by the shoulders, he swooped down and planted a hard kiss on her disparaging mouth.

It worked. Her outburst was muffled by his onslaught. Her words subsided altogether after a moment. But he was well aware that if hushing vexed the lass, she'd be even more furious with this form of silencing.

Kissing her was only a temporary solution. A drastic measure taken in the heat of the moment when he'd had no other choice.

What he'd do next, he didn't know.

CHAPTER 21

Feiyan was seething. The infuriating Westland lout had just shut her up in the most belittling manner a man could choose. She was furious.

Nay, she wasn't. Fury didn't describe what she was feeling.

Disgust. Aye, that was it. She was disgusted that a man who purported to be honorable would force himself upon her. She was absolutely revolted.

Nay, it was more shock than revulsion. She was shocked by his behavior.

At least at first.

Not anymore.

Now she was puzzled. Why had he kissed her?

And what was he going to do next?

As the kiss continued, her emotions fluttered past like a swarm of motley butterflies. This one was rage. That one was shock. Then came panic. Then intrigue. Then curiosity.

Finally, after only a few moments, she settled on wonder.

In the satiated haze of a filling supper, a hot bath, copious ale, and good company, she was struck with a sense of wonder at the new feelings his kiss was engendering in her. Then she wondered what it would be like to pursue those feelings.

Casting caution aside, she hooked a possessive arm

around Dougal's neck, dug demanding fingers into the flesh of his back, and returned his kiss.

She was unprepared for the lusty surge that would sweep her up in its currents, conveying her toward a wild sea of desire. With breathless haste, she moved from sweet kisses to feeding ravenously upon his lips. His warm, supple, demanding lips.

The blood in her veins began to thrum. Her ears buzzed with a primitive vibration. Her head sang inside a sensual fog that softened the melody while sharpening her longing.

And then he responded.

Tilting his head, he slanted his lips across hers to deepen the kiss. He tangled his fingers in her wet hair and pulled her closer.

Through her leine, she could feel the heat of his skin against her breasts, soothing her, tempting her, compelling her to come closer.

When he teased her mouth open with his tongue, she sighed into him, relishing the wet, exotic, ale-spiced taste of him.

Her hands took their own journey, exploring the slick locks of his hair. The intricate curve of his ear. The rough edge of his jaw. The strong pulse in his throat.

She traced his collar bone. The sleek muscle of his chest. The flat nipple that responded to the brush of her palm. The lean ridges of his ribs.

He fed on her with wild recklessness. And she answered him kiss for kiss, as if they engaged in some mortal combat of passion.

Then he drew her even closer, and she felt the hard proof of his lust, pressing against her abdomen with wanton desire.

She felt lust as well. A current as powerful as lightning streaking through her. Tightening her nipples. Tingling with fire betwixt her thighs.

While their tongues fought an erotic battle, she gasped and arched and moved against him, pressing her burning flesh against the firm rock of his thigh, instinctively seeking comfort. Or satisfaction. Or release.

But it was to no avail.

She needed something more.

Something forbidden.

Something sinful.

Driven half mad with ardor and aroused to a fever pitch, Dougal scarcely knew what was he was doing. Where his hands were. Or how he was still able to stand.

Lost in a thick fog of desire that blinded him to reason, he kissed and caressed and feasted on the irresistible lass with mindless abandon.

He shouldn't have been surprised by her boldness. Feiyan was forward in every other way. Attacking him on the trail. Charging at outlaws. Demanding her weapons. Why would he expect her to turn timid when it came to trysting?

Still, when she suddenly and brazenly seized his member, he surged to new heights of irrepressible need.

He groaned as her fingers closed around him through the damp linen. She obviously knew what she wanted. There was no question about it. And no going back.

With a possessive growl, he swept her off her feet and conveyed her to the bed.

She tore off her leine.

He ripped away his linen wrap.

A primal moan of passion escaped her. And for Dougal, there was no sound more arousing. He clambered atop her, ready to plunge his aching dagger into her willing sheath.

But just as in battle, the minx wished to dominate him. With forceful determination, she shoved him over, rolling him onto his back beneath her. Holding him there with her deceptively strong arms and her hunger-glazed eyes, she sank onto him with a ragged gasp.

Overwhelmed by the delicious warmth bathing him, Dougal didn't notice at first that she'd gone abruptly still.

When he cracked open his eyes, he saw her hesitation. The tiny crease between her brows. The way her lip was caught between her teeth. And he knew.

She'd been a virgin.

Despite her lusty overtures, her impulsive drive, her aggressive mettle, her bold attack, she'd never waged this kind of battle before. And now the blow could not be unstruck.

"Och, lass," he whispered as despair and regret threatened to wither him. "I didn't know."

True to her nature, she didn't back down. Not for an instant. She only gave him a sly, smoky smile and said, "I did."

Then, before he could respond, she began to move against him. Tentatively at first. But she needed no training for this skirmish. Soon, despite her inexperience, her body learned how to strive against his. Soon she was lost in the battle.

And he was lost in passion again.

Unreserved and unabashed, she rode him slowly and without restraint, as if mating was as natural and innocent as breathing to her.

He responded, striving upward to meet her, blow for blow. With half-lidded eyes, he gazed up at her beautiful, bewitching face. With gentle fingertips, he sampled her alluring body—her slim throat, her silky hair, her puckered nipples, her firm buttocks.

He captured her head in his hands and kissed her again. As they moved together, he caught her sighs in his mouth and answered them with grunts of his own.

But soon he could no longer endure the leisurely pace she set.

With a groan of impatience, he heaved her onto her back.

She didn't fight him. Instead, she pulled him closer, wrapping her arms around his neck, her thighs around his hips. She strained against him, urging him on, panting as he plunged into her again and again.

When he increased the pace, she proved as hungry as he was, answering every thrust with an eagerness that rivaled his own.

Her gasps—erotic and compelling—swiftly launched him to new heights.

Just as he thought he could endure no more, she stiffened beneath him, and her mouth opened in wonder. He roared as the seed pumped from him with the force of a raging river, even as she cried out in rapture.

They shuddered back to earth together. Clinging to each other with the last of their strength. Collapsing in a tangle of boneless limbs and satiated flesh.

Once they rolled apart, they lay side by side, speechless, for a long while. The chamber was silent except for the rasp of their mingled breathing.

The soft crackle of the fire.

And the indistinct murmuring of someone in the room next door.

Dougal's breath caught as he remembered the Very Important Guest.

He and Feiyan had been anything but discreet in their lovemaking. They'd tested the squeaking ropes of the pallet to their limit. Bellowed out in sensual triumph like two warriors celebrating victory in combat.

What if the king complained to the innkeeper? What if he demanded to know who was making such a disturbance?

He let out a resigned breath. Yet as perilous as it sounded to annoy the king, it was nothing compared to the trouble he was in with Rivenloch.

Dougal was a dead man.

He knew that now.

There was only one rule in hostage negotiations, and that was that no harm should come to the hostage.

He'd just broken that rule. He'd trysted with his captive.

Worse, that captive had turned out to be a virgin. And she happened to be a member of the most fierce warrior clan in Scotland.

They would likely geld him before they hung him from the gallows.

And they might be right to do so.

This was his fault.

Aye, the lass had tempted him, kissed him, seized him bodily and practically demanded he couple with her.

But he could have said nay.

He could have resisted her charms. He could have set her aside. It wouldn't be the first time he'd gone to bed with aching ballocks.

What madness had possessed him? Was it the ale? Her beauty? The thrill of danger?

He didn't know. But he'd done the unforgivable. And now he'd pay the price.

He sighed, vanquished. He supposed there was no use in agonizing over what was already done. The most he could do was look to her comfort.

"Are ye all right?" he whispered, brushing a lock of hair back from her eyes.

Her eyes were closed, but her lips blossomed into a pleased grin. "Oh aye."

"I didn't mean to hurt ye."

"I've had worse."

"I didn't know ye were..."

"I know."

"'Twon't always be painful like that."

"Nay?" She opened her eyes then, and they gleamed with sultry challenge. "And do you intend to prove that?"

Did he? What was done was done. What difference would it make if he swived her once, twice, or a dozen times?

"Maybe," he said, returning her smile. "Later."

"That was lovely," she sighed.

"Aye."

But the lass had no idea how much better he could make it for her. And if he was going to cast caution to the wind and risk execution, he might as well spend his last night showing her how much more lovely it could be.

"I have a confession," she murmured, twining a lock of his hair around her finger. "About killing you? I could never have gone through with it."

"Is that so?" She'd certainly tried enough times.

"Aye. Once I laid eyes on you," she purred, "I think I knew I could ne'er hurt you."

He gazed at her kiss-swollen lips, her rosy cheeks, her eyes resembling silvery pools, reflecting back his own tender affection. And he made a foolish confession.

"I could ne'er hurt ye either. Not intentionally."

"You couldn't?"

He shook his head. Some hostage-taker he'd proved to be. And yet how could he do her harm now?

How could he bruise the lass who had gifted him with her maidenhood?

How could he batter the woman whose body had collided with his in the throes of passion?

How could he hold a dagger to the throat where her pulse had beat in lusty tandem with his?

"Ne'er," he confirmed.

Somewhere in the back of his mind, he realized that meant she was useless as a hostage. He had to let her go.

But in the next moment, as she bit her lip and ran a fingertip down the center of his chest, his good intentions scattered like chaff in the wind.

When she brushed her knuckles across his stomach, his mind turned to one thing, and one thing only.

By the time her fingers reached the lance between his legs, it was already primed and ready to charge.

CHAPTER 22

Dougal was right.

As incredible as it seemed to Feiyan, their second coupling was even better than the first.

He proceeded slowly this time, stirring her with tender kisses and titillating caresses.

He tormented her flesh with his tongue, nibbling his way up her neck. Circling the crevices of her ears. Suckling sensuously at her fingers. Bathing the sensitive backs of her knees.

She ached between her legs. But it wasn't an ache of pain. It was an ache of need. A sharp craving for the relief he could give her.

Once she tried to reach for him, eager to seize his dagger and plunge it into her body.

But he refused her with a throaty chuckle, drawing out her torture just a little more.

When he finally claimed her lips again, she returned his kiss with such frenzied fervor that he had to press her back down onto the pallet.

"Easy, lass," he murmured. "Soon enough."

Then he made a trail of kisses along her jaw, down her throat, across her bosom.

She arched in anticipation as he neared the delicate crest of her breast.

When he closed his mouth over her nipple, she moaned at the lovely sensation and felt a warm wave of longing gush through her, intensifying the throbbing betwixt her thighs.

But when he moved to her other breast, he simultaneously swept his hand down, separating her curls with his fingers, to touch the swollen nubbin at the apex of her desire.

She sobbed out, grinding against his hand, demanding relief.

Then, and only then, when her body was begging for satisfaction, did he finally give it to her.

With a groan that was half command and half surrender, he parted her nether lips, sliding his shaft into her hollow. Delving into her waiting wetness. And drawing a throaty gasp from her. Not of pain this time. But of pleasure.

Together they tussled, sweating with effort, shivering with need, gliding with heavenly friction toward the ecstasy awaiting them.

This time, when her body braced for release and she felt the fuse of their union sizzle and flare with white light, she opened her eyes to gaze up at him.

His expression—of agony and rapture, triumph and despair, power and vulnerability—touched her so deeply that she soared to a place beyond anything she'd ever imagined. A place where not only their bodies—but their souls—reveled in exquisite harmony. Where, like the ores of two metals, they were forged inextricably together.

Afterward, in the soft glow of blithe discovery, Feiyan clung to him. She had no regrets. This felt right. And she sensed it was meant to be.

Aye, they'd had questionable beginnings. He'd meant to massacre her clansmen. She'd meant to assassinate him.

But she could see now that had only been fate's way of throwing them together.

Like her cousins before her, Feiyan had found The One.

This was the man with whom she would tie her fortunes. Build a life. Make the next generation of Rivenloch warriors.

It all made sense now.

That was why she'd been curiously unwilling to kill him. Why she'd persisted in following him. Why she was driven to help him resolve the tragedy that had caused him so much pain.

She was in love with him.

They belonged together.

It was such a relief just to be able to admit that. To surrender to the truth of what her heart had been saying all along.

All she needed to do now was prove it to him.

Joining him in this glorious paradise of fulfillment was a good beginning.

Spent and sated, she drifted off to sleep in that beautiful place. Locked in his embrace. Dreaming of a destiny that included Dougal mac Darragh.

As Dougal gazed down at the wee, fey-faced goddess still slumbering in the first faint light of dawn, he felt a twinge in his chest, as if someone had taken a keen blade and scrawled "Feiyan" across his heart.

Her name would be engraved there forever, he knew. She was the most unique and fascinating lass he'd ever met. In another time, in another place, he would have clung to her forever. Held fast to the magic between them. Never let her go.

How she could ever imagine she was invisible was a mystery. She was beautiful. Bright. Soft. Strong. And aye, as she boasted, stealthy.

He would have to be even stealthier when he left.

He *had* to leave her. He knew that now. Now that he was sober, standing in the clear light of day. He had to go before he did any more damage.

He should not have succumbed to lust. He should have protected her against her own unwise desires. And by all that was holy, he should never have stolen her maidenhood.

Feiyan would deem him a coward for leaving. And perhaps she would be right. A better man would stay to face the consequences. Acknowledge his failing and suffer the punishment for ravishing a daughter of Rivenloch.

But more than just his life was at stake. He wasn't just Dougal. He was mac Darragh. He might not possess the title of laird, but he was responsible for his clan.

With the king so close, with blame directed at mac Giric, with Rivenloch bearing down on his home, he couldn't afford the luxury of surrendering himself when he was the only one who could save Darragh from harm.

It was best for Feiyan as well.

If he remained, if he admitted his crime, her honor would suffer.

She didn't deserve that.

By his leaving, none would ever learn of their indiscretion. She could keep it a secret. Eventually she would marry—a noble and courteous knight who'd never question her virtue. A decent man who'd give her a happy life and lots of children. And she'd forget all about the Westland knave who had stolen her innocence on a warm spring night.

He let out a shuddering breath. In his bones, he knew leaving her was the right thing. But in his soul...

He would never forget her.

He would never forget the wee outlaw dangling from his snare.

The sultry Siren removing his boots.

The sly assassin wielding her knife.

The storm-tossed waif shivering against him.

The fierce warrior battling thieves.

The breathtaking angel spiriting him to heaven and shuddering back to earth in his arms.

His throat ached as he took one last look at her.

Then quietly, before she could stir, he dressed and gathered his things. He left her weapons, as he'd promised. And he placed his dagger among them. She could use the jewels to pay for lodging when she returned to Rivenloch.

He owed her much more for what he'd taken from her. But that was a debt he couldn't repay. A wound he couldn't repair. An injury that, once inflicted, left a permanent scar.

Fighting indecision and choking back regret, he slipped out the door.

He needed to flee the inn before the king awoke. And he needed to get to Castle Darragh before Feiyan's clan came looking for their lost warrior.

Gradually the morning light, seeping through the crack of the shutters, beckoned Feiyan to leave her Eden of luscious bedlinens and toasty warmth. But she didn't want to rouse yet.

Sometime in the night, Dougal had awakened and tucked her under the covers. And that was where she wanted to stay.

She smiled. Once they were wed, she'd linger in bed *every* morn. She snuggled closer to where the Westlander had stretched out beside her last night.

But he wasn't there.

She was alone.

Panicked, she opened her eyes and flung off the covers.

The fire was cold. The bath was cold. And her weapons had been assembled neatly in the corner, looking as cold as the rest.

Every shred of Dougal's presence was gone. His clothing. His boots. His satchel. Erased, as if he'd never existed.

His abandonment hit her with crushing force, caving her chest, sagging her shoulders. Desolation squeezed her heart until it burst into a thousand pieces, like a fine glass chalice shattered in a mail-clad fist.

How could he have left her?

After what they'd shared together—the intimacy, the connection, the journey to a celestial realm—how could he turn his back on that and walk away?

A sob clogged her throat. Tears blurred her vision.

Had it meant nothing to him? Had *she* meant nothing?

Cursing under her breath, she swiped at her wet eyes.

She shouldn't be surprised. She *was* nothing. She was the kind of lass most people overlooked or ignored.

It seemed Dougal was no different. He may have made her feel special last night. But today, she'd become inconspicuous again. Easy to leave. Easy to forget.

Biting back foolish grief, she donned her clothes and hastily braided her hair. There was no point in lingering.

He obviously didn't want her help. Or her company.

Heartbroken, she consoled herself with the fact that at least she'd gotten her weapons back. As she slipped them into the pockets of her garb, she noticed the jeweled dagger he'd left behind.

She supposed it was payment for what he'd taken.

The more she glared at the shiny blade with its gems winking up at her, the more her hurt hardened into anger.

How dared he try to buy her forgiveness?

How dared he put a price on her virginity?

Like healing fire, rage suddenly swept in to sear and seal her wounds.

She wouldn't let him get away with that.

This matter of Kirkoswald was as much her concern as

his, curse him. The Rivenloch clan had married into the mac Girics, after all.

She'd be damned if she'd be shoved away and left behind.

If Dougal mac Darragh thought paying her off would somehow alleviate his guilt, drive her back home, and purge her from his mind, he was dead wrong.

She rushed down the stairs. Before flying out the door, she grabbed three oatcakes from the platter the inn-keeper's wife offered.

The woman clucked her tongue and gave her a conspiratorial wink. "Ye just missed him."

"I'll catch up to him," Feiyan bit out, "and when I do, I'll pummel him so fiercely, his ears will ring for a sennight."

The woman gasped. "The king?"

"What?"

"I mean..." The woman seemed flustered. "Nothin'. Ye didn't hear it from me. Just...take care with the pummelin'."

Feiyan's puzzled glance sent the woman scurrying back to her cauldron of frumenty.

Armed with all her weapons again, when she strode down the path, Feiyan began to feel like her old self. Strong. Confident. Capable.

She picked up Dougal's crack-heeled trail easily. But either the innkeeper's wife was mistaken about his recent departure, or he was tearing along the path, because she followed his tracks for half the day before she spotted him.

He'd stopped to sit on a moss-covered rock. Chewing on a hunk of cheat bread, he didn't hear her as she stole slowly through the elm branches above him.

She'd planned this encounter for hours now. Practiced what she would say. Imagined what she would do.

First, she meant to disparage him with vile curses. Call him ignoble. Dishonorable. Disgusting. The spawn of Satan. Lucifer's bastard. A minion of the Devil.

If he flinched from her onslaught, she'd spit on him and name him a coward.

If he fought back, she'd teach him a lesson. Clout him. Plow her fist into his noble nose. Split his lip. Blacken his eye. Leave him moaning in the dust.

That was what she'd planned. It seemed just, considering he'd betrayed and deserted her.

But now that she saw him, she knew she couldn't carry it out.

He looked so despondent. So dispirited.

She glanced at the hands holding the chunk of bread and remembered how his fingertips felt on her skin.

When a lock of ebony hair fell over his brow, she recalled how thick and silky it felt to her touch.

When he opened his mouth for a bite, she was reminded of the way his lips tasted. Warm. Sweet. Demanding.

And the sight of his legs—stretched out, knees wide— did strange things to her insides as she remembered how his thighs had hugged her hips, holding her in delicious confinement as he spilled his seed into her.

Her heart softened. Her resolve faltered.

Still, she wasn't about to forgive and forget. He owed her an explanation.

She palmed his jeweled dagger and, with a flick of her wrist, sent it flying. It thumped into the ground beside him, two inches from his boot.

He tumbled off the rock with a startled yelp.

Then she leaped down from the branch, landing before him. She glared down at him with her arms crossed and her expression crosser.

"You forgot something."

They both knew she wasn't talking about the dagger.

She expected a lie. A cruel challenge. Vicious words of rejection.

Instead, his face fell, and his expression was tormented

by remorse. Caught in the act and at her mercy, he sagged on his elbows, looked up at her, and told her the truth.

"I could ne'er forget ye. Ye're the most magnificent, beautiful, brilliant woman I've e'er known."

A lump lodged in her throat. Did he mean that?

She was suddenly grateful for her mask and hood so he couldn't see how her eyes shimmered with foolish hope.

"I had to leave, m'lady," he continued. "Don't ye see?"

She didn't see at all. But she supposed he deserved a chance to explain. "I'm listening," she choked out.

He sat up, placing his arms atop his knees. "I couldn't let ye suffer the consequences o' my recklessness. 'Twas my fault, I know. I should have reined in my urges. I shouldn't have led ye into temptation. But I failed. And after what I did," he said, shaking his head, "how could I allow *ye* to pay the price for—"

"Wait," she said, her hurt vanishing like mist. "After what *you* did?" A humorless bark escaped her. "Spare me."

She hunkered down before him, wrenching his dagger from the dirt.

"You're a cocky Westlander," she spat, flipping the weapon in her hand, "always trying to take credit for my deeds." She tapped the point of the dagger against her chest. "Last night was *my* idea. Whatever conceited notions you have that you somehow forced me—*me*, a warrior maid of Rivenloch—to do your bidding, I assure you you're wrong. No one tells me what to do."

Mac Darragh looked so stunned, Feiyan thought she could probably knock him over with a puff of air.

CHAPTER 23

Dougal hadn't realized until this moment just how much he adored the swaggering warrior lass.

Of *course* she would insist the idea was all hers.

Of *course* she would claim, not that he had seduced her, but that she'd manipulated him into doing her will.

Was it true? Did it matter? What was done was done. The only thing that mattered now was the consequences of their actions.

"What will ye do now?" he asked.

"We'll finish what we started. Find out what happened at Kirkoswald. Chase down and punish the devils who did this."

We. She'd said *we.* When he left the inn, Dougal thought he'd never see her again. He'd never realized how alone he'd feel without her by his side.

Miserable, racked with guilt, riddled with shame, forlorn, and unforgiven, he'd swallowed up the ground, hoping the distance would lessen his pain.

But from the moment he'd left, he'd missed her company. Not just the warm comfort of her body, but her bright eyes and mind. Not only her tempting lips, but her prickly, wicked tongue. He missed her refreshing candor. Her clever deception. Her quicksilver emotions. The way she made the journey swifter with her prying questions.

And how a coy wink from her could make his heart sing with joy.

He thought he might be in love with her.

He wouldn't tell her that, of course. She might laugh in his face.

His world had shifted last night, made him hunger for more lasting companionship. But for her, it may have only been a pleasant evening's diversion.

Before he could ask her what her intentions were, she straightened and offered him her hand, saying, "I want your word on one thing."

"Aye?"

"The Rivenloch forces live by a creed. Leave no clan warrior behind," she said. "Swear you won't leave me behind again."

He gazed into her dove gray eyes and somberly took her hand. "I swear." But even as made that vow, he knew he'd break it.

"Good," she said, hauling him to his feet. "Now enough chatter," she decided. "We have a crime to solve. And I have a new suspicion."

She returned his dagger, and soon they were striding down the path again, as if nothing had changed. But in Dougal's heart, everything was different.

He no longer thought of Feiyan as the enemy, a hostage, a wayward outlaw, an assassin. Now she was his to protect. All he cared about was keeping her safe.

Not that she needed his help. Though her weapons were hidden from view, he was certain she was armed now with her full deadly arsenal. He, on the other hand, had one jeweled dagger with which to defend her.

"There's an inn not far from the castle," he said. "We can stay there tonight."

He was already formulating a plan to keep Feiyan out of harm's way.

He didn't want her anywhere near the castle.

Though Dougal no longer intended to use her as a hostage, he couldn't say the same for his brother. If Gaufrid discovered the niece of the Laird of Rivenloch was within his reach, he might decide that ransoming her was a good way to refill the mac Darragh coffers.

So he absolutely intended to leave her behind. At the Ayr Arms. Where he knew she'd be safe. But until then, he'd go along with her plans.

"So what's this new suspicion o' yours?" he asked.

"First, I need to hear again about the two men who reported the fire."

"What more do ye need to know?"

"Say it all over. From the beginning. No detail left out."

"They staggered into the courtyard, covered in blood and ashes, sayin' there was an attack at Kirkoswald."

"They claimed they had just come from the village?"

He blinked. "How else would they know about the fire?"

"Right. And they're your brother's men?"

"Aye."

She rubbed a pensive finger across her lips. "Loyal to the laird?"

"O' course."

"What are their names?"

"Their names? I don't see how—"

"Indulge me."

"Fergus and Morris Fortanach."

Her brows lifted in surprise. "Are they brothers?"

"Aye."

"Hmm."

"'Hmm' what?"

"They didn't say anything about the attackers?" she asked. "How many there were? Two? Six? A dozen? Whether they were mounted or not?"

"There wasn't time."

"And these are the same men who brought you the mac Giric clan badge?"

"Aye," he said guardedly.

"Hmm," she said again.

"What do ye mean, 'Hmm'?"

She shrugged. "'Tis curious, don't you think?"

Dougal didn't think it was curious at all. "Who else could have found the badge but someone who was there?"

She waited a long while to answer. When she finally did, she spoke as if she were placing her words carefully amid broken glass. "Have you ever heard of...a false banner?"

He slammed his brows together. "Impossible," he muttered.

"What? That one clan would commit a crime and blame another?"

"Not my clan."

Bloody hell. Was the lass so desperate to vindicate the mac Giric clan, she'd cast aspersions on his own?

"Hmm," she said for a third irritating time.

Still, doubt began to seep in through the cracks of logic. Was it possible he'd been so concerned about the fire, so worried about the villagers, so devastated by the destruction, he'd never thought to question the brothers' story?

"False banners are common along the border," she said. "One clan is always stealing another's cattle and blaming the English."

The seeds of suspicion she planted began to take root in Dougal's brain. Just because no one in the clan had instigated a false banner attack before didn't mean it was impossible.

Had the Fortanachs been entirely forthcoming? Could they have invented a tale to cover their own malfeasance?

"It might have been an accident," she suggested. "My brother Gavand once overturned a lantern and set a storeroom on fire. He panicked and blamed my brother Tian."

"This was no accident," he said gravely.

Whoever had set the fire had waited until everyone was inside the church for the christening. Then they'd blocked the door and lit a torch.

He felt sick.

If Feiyan's suspicions were true, if it was an act committed under a false banner... Were Fergus and Morris more than just bearers of bad news? Were they more than witnesses? Could they be the demons who'd perpetrated the massacre?

The Fortanach brothers were the kind of men to lie, cheat, and steal to their advantage. But could they have darker, more ambitious plans? Plans they would kill for?

"I've got to get home," he bit out.

For all he knew, even now they could be poisoning Gaufrid and raiding the villages surrounding Castle Darragh, leaving smoldering embers in their wake.

"Wait!" she said, seizing his arm. "There's something more."

"I don't need to hear more. I need to get to Darragh. Confront them face to face."

"Right," she scoffed. "And what do you think they'll say?"

He scowled. "They'll have to tell me the truth."

"Will they? Or will they say anything to cast the blame elsewhere?"

She had a point. If there was one word to describe the Fortanach brothers, it was self-serving.

But this wasn't her fight. He'd be damned if he'd let her risk her life for something that was his responsibility.

"'Tisn't your affair," he growled.

"Listen, you pompous arse!" she snarled. "You can't go charging in, brandishing a blade and making wild accusations. Not until we have all the facts."

"The hell I can't," he snarled, wrenching his arm away.

Before he could take two steps, she somehow snagged his heel with her foot and kicked his leg out from under him.

He would have hit the ground hard, pounding his head against the hard-packed earth. But she grabbed his gambeson as he fell, instead easing him gently to the forest floor.

Leaning over him, she said, "We're doing this *my* way, with patience and planning. Attacking without provocation or proof will do more harm than good. 'Tis a situation for stealth, not strength. Forewarned is—"

"Forearmed?" he replied, vexed at being chided by a wisp of a lass. "Aye. I know."

Perhaps being swept off his feet had knocked a bit of sense into him. He supposed it *was* unwise to hurtle into the fray with an empty scabbard.

But there was equal benefit to acting swiftly, attacking unexpectedly before the enemy could prepare.

Still, it was hard to argue with the bossy wee lass when she was looming over him like a bloody Amazon warrior.

Feiyan extended a hand to help him up, half-expecting Dougal would growl and bat it aside.

She never dreamed he'd grab her sleeve and pulled her down on top of him. And once she collapsed there, it was easy for him to roll her onto her back, pinning her to the ground with his body.

Sparks flew as his indigo eyes drilled into hers. "But if ye think I'm goin' to dawdle back to Darragh while a pair o' murderin' monsters are on the loose, threatenin' my clan, ye're mistaken."

She narrowed her eyes and pressed the point of the *bishou* she'd slipped out of her belt against his ribs.

His eyes widened as she bit out, "Who said I meant to dawdle? But if *you* think I'm going to let the man I love rush into danger without a sword or a shield or any notion whatsoever of—"

"What? What did ye say?"

She blinked. "I said I don't intend to dawdle."

"Nay, after that."

She frowned. "You don't have a sword or shield. Or a plan."

"Ye said 'the man I love'."

She blushed. She *had* said that. But now she wished with all her heart she hadn't.

"Is that true?" he breathed.

It was true. And she hadn't realized that until she'd said it aloud.

But he obviously didn't share her feelings. She could see the amusement in his gaze. He probably thought it was naïve of her to fall in love with the first man who'd swived her.

Instead of answering him, she muttered, "Get off me."

He let her up, but his eyes were still dancing with smug humor as she sheathed her *bishou*.

Damn the swaggering knave. That was the last thing she needed. He had an advantage now. A weapon he could use against her.

"Shall we go on?" she said stiffly. "I thought you were in a rush. Or would you rather waste *more* time grappling?"

The gleam that flashed through his eyes said he was imagining a different sort of grappling. Which made her color even more.

Hiding a grin, he offered her his hand, and she let him haul her to her feet. Avoiding his gaze, she brusquely brushed the leaves from her gambeson.

She was a fool to confess her feelings for him. But it was too late to deny what she'd said. The best she could do was hope he'd dismiss her blurted words as impulsive and empty.

Dougal couldn't stop thinking about what she'd said.

The man I love.

Was it possible she actually cared for him?

The idea was intoxicating. Though they continued along the path in silence, his mind buzzed with visions of a future that included Feiyan.

Waking up to her beautiful face each morn.

Kissing her soft lips every night.

Caressing her gentle curves whenever he wished.

Making love and bairns and a life with her.

And then the image of an angry mob of Rivenloch warriors arose to dash those dreams. Telling him he was a monster. A berserker. A Westland knave who wasn't fit to polish Feiyan's sword.

He sighed. They might be right.

Who was he, after all?

His clan was in chaos.

His brother had depleted the treasury.

Gaufrid's army was being offered a reward to defeat Dougal.

The neighboring village had been burned to the ground on his watch.

And now it appeared there may be a plot afoot to destroy the clan from within.

Not only that, but the only time he'd met any of Feiyan's kin was when he'd stormed into the middle of their playful melee, brandishing a deadly claymore and leaving the daughter of the laird for dead.

Nay, now was not the time to pursue the lovely warrior maid.

Later perhaps, if by some miracle he managed to

untangle the threads of intrigue...remove the blame from mac Giric...make amends for the havoc he'd wrought at Creagor... If he proved himself a capable, principled, worthy husband...

It seemed an impossible task.

Despite her best intentions, Feiyan couldn't stop thinking about her reckless feelings for Dougal.

Of *course* it was naïve of her to imagine he'd feel the same way just because he'd swived her. With his handsome face, tempting form, and winning charm, he'd probably trysted with a hundred lasses. None of them had been so foolish as to believe they were in love with him.

She sighed. As Sung Li said when Feiyan went through difficult times, this was just another trial, one that would harden her for battles to come.

Meanwhile, she'd try to steer their conversation to more pressing subjects. There were still questions about Kirkoswald that needed to be answered.

She'd told Dougal there was more, and there was. The incident did indeed feel like the perpetration of a false banner. But one detail of the story was beginning to trouble her. Whoever had cast the blame on the mac Giric clan had specifically targeted Morgan Mor at Creagor when there was a much more likely candidate for the crime. There had to be a reason for that.

She feared an uncomfortable truth awaited Dougal at Castle Darragh.

A truth that might be hard to bear.

A truth that would put them in even more peril.

"Let me ask you something," she said when they'd gone several miles in silence. "Doesn't what happened feel just a bit too convenient?"

"What happened?" he echoed. His quick perusal of her

from head to toe told her all she needed to know about the bent of his thoughts. "Ye mean..."

She flushed, averting her eyes, and muttered, "Nay. What happened at Kirkoswald."

"Ah."

She cleared her throat and straightened her back. "Think about it. Your brother's men just happened to escape a fire that destroyed a whole village. They conveniently didn't see the ones who started it. But one of the attackers just happened to drop his clan badge. And they just happened to find it. That's too much happenstance."

He nodded. "Ye said there was more."

She took a deep breath. He was getting close to the crux of the matter. She would need to tread carefully. "I could be wrong, but..."

"What?"

"I've been assuming the reason for burning the village was personal. To destroy evidence. Cover up a crime. Eliminate a witness."

"Aye?"

"For that, any false banner would do. They could have blamed vagabonds. Miscreants. Outlaws. Heretics. Anyone available and believable." She shook her head. "But to accuse mac Giric... Why blame an old and honorable clan? And why Creagor? 'Tis a world away."

"So what are ye sayin'?"

"What if there was another reason? What if burning Kirkoswald was an attack on mac Darragh? You said 'twill harm the clan, aye?"

"Aye. 'Twill drain the clan's wealth. Deplete our resources."

"And weaken your defenses?"

He nodded.

"What if 'twas done to incite a clan battle?"

"With the mac Girics?"

"'Tis what you'd expect, aye?"

"Aye."

"But that's the strange thing. You said your clan has no history with the mac Girics."

"Right."

"No trade? No conflict? No contact whatsoever?"

He shook his head.

"Then who recognized the mac Giric clan badge?"

CHAPTER 24

Dougal stopped in his tracks, stunned.

An uneasy shiver slithered up his spine.

Who *had* identified it?

"Gaufrid," he remembered. "They showed the badge to Gaufrid. 'Twas my brother who knew it."

"Your brother?" Her eyes dimmed to a deep charcoal. "And is he the one who directed you to Creagor?"

He could only nod.

"But there's the other puzzing thing," she said. "Why Creagor?"

"'Tis the mac Giric stronghold, aye?"

"Nay."

He blinked. "'Tisn't?"

"The clan seat is in the Highlands. Creagor was awarded to the laird's *son,* Morgan Mor mac Giric. And he just married into the Rivenloch clan. That's who you were sent to face."

Dougal rubbed the back of his neck. What had his brother done? And why?

Gaufrid had instantly recognized the clan crest. He'd known exactly where Creagor was. He'd known how long it took to get there. Three days' ride, he'd said. He'd claimed he couldn't spare his men to ride along with Dougal. And Fergus and Morris had been quick to back up that claim.

Gaufrid must have known Dougal would be facing Rivenloch.

And he'd sent him there alone.

Alone.

His suspicions were slowly curdling into an insidious scheme that was bitter to the taste and hard to swallow.

The three of them—Gaufrid, Fergus, and Morris—had set him up.

He should have seen it. He should have known not to trust anything they said. If he'd stopped for one moment to think, he would have noticed small details that didn't make sense, asked questions that would have revealed the lie.

But his focus had been on Kirkoswald. On stopping the blaze. Rescuing the villagers.

As Dougal sorted through his recollections and tried to digest the incriminating facts, emotions struck him like blows of a war club. Disappointment. Dejection. Despair.

Just as he was defending himself against crushing self-blame, Feiyan gently confided, "I have to question your brother's motives."

So did he. And the sooner he found out, the better.

"I've got to get to Castle Darragh," he announced. "Now."

She seized his arm as he turned to go. "Nay."

"What do ye mean, nay?"

"Don't you see? 'Tis even more dangerous than we thought." She lowered her voice to a murmur and lightened her grip on his arm, as if to soften the blow. "I fear he may have meant to get rid of you."

Dougal gave her a bitter snort. "He's always meant to get rid o' me."

The words were harsh and shocking when he spoke them aloud. But he supposed he'd suspected the truth for a long time now.

Why else would Gaufrid offer a prize to the man who could best Dougal in combat?

Dougal had convinced himself the daily battles were only a matter of soothing his brother's wounded pride. But, goaded by his Fortanach companions, Gaufrid had increased the prize to a ridiculous amount, attracting more skilled and vicious warriors every day.

To what lengths would Gaufrid and his scheming minions go to be rid of him?

Was his brother aware he'd driven Dougal straight into danger? Into the swords of the most fierce border clan in all Scotland?

He shuddered.

That kind of betrayal—by his laird, by his brother—was too painful to accept.

Instead, he grasped at slender threads of hope.

Perhaps Gaufrid, conspiring with the Fortanachs, had simply failed to consider the consequences of his actions. It wouldn't be the first time he'd acted without fore-thought.

Perhaps he hadn't realized Dougal could be killed if he faced off against the combined forces of mac Giric and Rivenloch.

Perhaps in his drunken fog, he'd figured once Dougal was out of sight, he could banish him from his thoughts as well.

Perhaps it had all been a careless miscalculation on Gaufrid's part.

But with one gently whispered truth, Feiyan snipped all those threads.

"He sent you to an almost certain death."

The breath deserted his lungs.

She was *half* right.

"He didn't send me," he said, shaking his head in sad revelation. "He didn't have to."

Everyone in the clan knew Dougal couldn't resist coming to the rescue, whether it was defending the clan castle, saving a crofter from the tax collector, or coaxing down a wildcat stuck in a tree.

She nodded, understanding at once. "He must have known you'd have no choice but to avenge the villagers."

Even in the midst of devastating betrayal, he was struck by Feiyan's words.

"How can ye know that?" he said. "Ye barely know me."

"You're a man of honor and chivalry," she said, tugging him along to continue walking. "Fighting for what's good and just. A champion of the common folk."

He gave her a rueful smirk. "Two days ago, ye said I was a monster who needed killin'."

"I was wrong," she decided. "You're a hero."

"A hero?" he scoffed. "What sort o' hero lets a village burn? Brutalizes a tournament? Knocks a woman to the ground? What hero is haunted by hellish nightmares from what he's done?"

"Only a hero would ride alone halfway across the country to avenge the death of innocents," she said, ticking off his qualities on her fingers. "Only a hero would make a gift of his horse to a family of poor crofters." She held up another finger. "Only a hero would offer to pay half a year's lodging to try to reform an outlaw lass."

He frowned. This kind of praise made him flush.

"There's just one problem with being a hero," she said, bringing her gushing speech to an abrupt end. "You're predictable."

Her insult felt like a bracing slap in the face and humbled him at once.

"So if we're going to succeed," she continued, "you need to forget acting like a hero. You can't just march up to your brother with your head held high and your sword unsheathed and boldly demand the truth."

He bit the inside of his cheek. Damn the lass. That was

exactly what he'd planned to do. Which only proved her point. He *was* predictable.

He arched a brow at her. "I suppose ye have a less heroic plan?"

"I do."

Of course Feiyan had a plan. As Sung Li had taught her, ability was useless without wisdom, strength useless without strategy.

"Who do you trust at Darragh?" she asked.

He shrugged. "They're my clan."

"But I'm guessing the clan warriors owe their fealty to Gaufrid, aye?"

"Aye, though..."

"What?"

"Most o' my father's warriors are gone now. Replaced by mercenaries."

That was troubling. She'd hoped to assemble a small fighting force when it came time to confront Dougal's brother. "Are there any you can trust among them?"

"To take my side against the laird?" He shook his head. "They owe fealty to Gaufrid."

"As much as a mercenary's fealty means," she muttered. Then she asked, "What about servants? Do you have any loyal only to *you*?"

"To me?" He thought for a moment. "My stable lad, Campbell, I suppose. He looks after..." He broke off with a wince. "*Looked* after Urramach."

"Campbell," she repeated. "The stable lad. Got it. What about others? Servants in the keep itself. Kitchen lads who can keep secrets. Maidservants who would lie for you."

"There's Merraid, the new servin' lass." He smiled fondly. "She practically worships the ground I walk on."

"Merraid," she repeated. "Any others?"

"Most o' the servants were my father's. They serve Gaufrid, but not happily."

"But they love *you?*" She answered her own question. "Of course they do. Who would not? You're their hero, aye? So 'tis a good start."

He squinted. "A start for what?"

"As I said before, this is a matter for stealth."

"Stealth."

"Aye. 'Tis the best way. Sneak into the household. Interrogate the servants. Find out what's happened in your absence. Discover why they singled out Morgan and Creagor. Get to the bottom of what happened at Kirkoswald."

"I can't sneak into the household. I'm the laird's brother."

"Right, but I can."

"Nay!" he exploded.

"I'm practically invisible."

"Invisible, my arse," he bit out. "Why do ye keep sayin' that? By the Saints, lass, ye're anythin' but invisible. Ye're as eye-poppin' as a midsummer morn. As heart-stoppin' as a bloody rose. A man would have to be blind not to see ye."

His words of praise were at odds with his gruff growl. And she was well aware that none of what he said was true. But his flattery—so spontaneous, so genuine—made her heart go soft. No one had ever said such kind things to her.

"Nay," he decided. "Ye're not goin' near the castle. Not now. Now that I know what we're up against. Nay. Not on your own."

"How else do you think you're going to find out what happened?"

"There's got to be another way."

He never found one. At least not one that was better than what she had in mind.

As they ate up the miles, following the sun, he suggested a plethora of tactics. Telling Gaufrid he'd successfully slain Morgan Mor mac Giric. Challenging the Fortanach brothers to a duel. Threatening his brother with an attack by the Rivenloch warriors.

All his ideas were confrontational, doomed to fail. And none would effect the lasting change that needed to happen if what she suspected was true—that his clan was being destroyed from the inside. The malignant cancer eating away at the legacy of Darragh must also be removed from the inside.

She just had to convince him of that. She'd be perfectly safe. She'd performed dozens of spying operations just like this one. She'd be in and out of the castle before he knew it.

There was no point arguing with him now. By his long stride and determined scowl, he was in full battle mode. Each mile they came closer to Castle Darragh, the more fierce he looked. Keen to fight. Eager to punish.

Later, she decided, after their bellies were full of warm pottage and crisp ale, when a cozy fire crackled on the hearth, when he collapsed onto a plush feather bed in naked, sweating, breathless satisfaction beneath her— satiated with pleasure, softened with love—then she'd be able to persuade him that her way was best.

That was her plan.

But the Ayr Arms was packed to the rafters with guests.

There would be no romantic candlelight tryst this evening.

Noisy patrons crowded the common room, jostling for space and sloshing ale on the weathered timbers. A rosy-cheeked serving maid with an empty tray elbowed her way through the milling bodies. A pair of well-dressed merchants chortled together, absently brushing Feiyan with their velvet sleeves, while Dougal negotiated for lodgings.

"Well, let's see," the innkeeper yelled over the din. "I've got a chamber with two pallets ye'd be sharin' with eleven others. Or..."

Near the door, a trio of monks chortled into their ales. An ugly old man clutching a cat squeezed by her.

"There's a wee bit o' room by the hearth there," the innkeeper said with a nod. "'Twill be a late night ere the crowd thins, but ye'll keep warm enough. Or..."

"What about *your* chamber?" Dougal asked.

"'Tis already taken, I'm afraid," the innkeeper replied. "The wife and I will be sleepin' with the hens."

Out of the cacophony arose a familiar sound. A deep, unmistakable chuckle that pierced through the babble, making the fine hair rise at the back of Feiyan's neck.

She searched the crowd for the source of the sound.

There. The tall lad with the dark, tousled hair.

Her eyes widened. Her breath caught. It couldn't be.

But when he turned his head slightly, there was no mistake.

It was Gellir. Her cousin.

What was he doing here?

Quickly, before he could spot her, she turned away.

The innkeeper drawled, "There's room in the barn."

"We'll take it," she blurted out.

She plucked Dougal's dagger from its sheath, popped loose a ruby with her *bishou,* and dropped it into the innkeeper's palm.

"Let's go."

Dougal didn't question her urgency. He immediately ushered her through the crowd and out the door. Only when they were outside did he wonder what had startled her.

It would do no good to tell him the truth. To let him see her worry.

So when she turned to him, she had her panic in check and her wiles engaged.

She lowered shy eyes and bit her lip, tracing the middle of his chest with the tip of her finger. "I was afraid if we didn't take it, we'd ne'er be alone tonight."

An eager, pleased smile blossomed on his face. He took her hand to lead her to the stables.

Feiyan hated lying to him. She wished she could say he was the reason her pulse was pounding. But the truth was her heart raced, not in lust, but in alarm.

If Gellir was here, Rivenloch must have sent a force to Darragh after all. How many others were nearby? Did they intend to launch a surprise assault on the keep? Or did they mean to lay siege? Would they try to negotiate for peace? Or was this a mission of pure revenge?

Her first instinct was to announce her presence and call them off. But she couldn't do that without full knowledge of what had happened at Kirkoswald.

It was too difficult to explain to her kin why she hadn't killed Dougal mac Darragh on sight. How they were working together. And what sort of treachery was afoot in his clan.

At the moment, she needed to build allies on the inside. It was impossible to determine who would side with Dougal and who would remain loyal to Gaufrid when the mac Darragh clan was forced to choose.

She had to intercede ahead of time, before Rivenloch did something drastic. Figure out what had happened and who was at fault. Who deserved a second chance. And who deserved to die.

And she had to go alone.

Dougal would disapprove.

Which was why she wasn't going to tell him.

She'd steal away in the night. Right after she gave him a swiving that would leave no question as to where her heart lie.

As it turned out, trysting in a barn wasn't so bad. It was dim and quiet and not as foul as she'd expected.

One kiss from him, and she forgot all about the pair of oxen lowing in their stalls.

One caress of his hand, and the clucking hens faded into the background.

By the time they reached the pile of clean straw, the piglets snorting in the corner didn't matter. She tore off his gambeson, and the sight of his chest straining against his leine made her forget about their humble surroundings.

Their desire burned hot and fast, like a field fire in summer. The flames of passion leaped high and raced swiftly. Setting their hearts ablaze. Forging their two hearts into one. Purifying their spirits.

When they collapsed together onto the bed of straw, sighing in satisfaction, reveling in their reward, she didn't even mind that a goat wandered up to sniff at her hair.

But as the dust settled around them, he murmured three words that left her heart both thrilling with joy and aching with shame. "I love ye."

Her throat caught. Her eyes filled. She longed to whisper a sweet reply in his ear. Return his affections. And reassure him of her love. But she was too moved by gratitude to answer. Too choked by guilt to speak.

By the time the knot of tears in her throat loosened, he was already deep asleep.

Wearing remorse like a yoke about her shoulders, she slipped out of his embrace, dressed and armed herself, and set off without him.

Dougal had claimed to love her. But would he ever forgive her?

The next morn, when Dougal woke, he had a smile on his face before he even opened his eyes. He'd never been happier, sprawling in naked splendor in the bucolic comfort of a barn, with Feiyan nuzzling his hand in affection.

After their scorching tryst, he'd slept like a rock. No nightmares had invaded his sleep. He hadn't even roused enough to bother putting his leine back on.

But now he heard voices approaching from outside. They needed to get dressed.

"Quick, lass," he said, blinking his eyes open. "Someone's comin'."

When he rolled over, expecting to see the drowsy maid, a wee goat bleated at him instead.

"What the devil?" he growled, clambering back and wiping his wet hand on the straw.

The lass was gone. Her clothing was missing. Her weapons were nowhere to be seen.

And the voices were growing closer.

He cursed under his breath as he wrested into his leine.

Damn the conniving imp. He'd pledged his heart to her. Worse, she'd made him swear to never leave her behind, and she'd broken her own vow.

As the voices floated past outside, he recognized that of the innkeeper. "This way to the stables, Your Majesty."

Dougal frowned. Your Majesty? The king? Again?

Once they'd passed, he went to the barn door and opened it a crack.

The tall, dark-haired lad might be Malcolm. He seemed about the right age. He wasn't dressed in royal robes or wearing a crown. Instead, he'd chosen a fine woolen gambeson, one that would disguise him as a lesser-ranking noble.

The smaller lad might be his servant. He appeared younger than the king, though he too was clad in quality wool.

Still, it was curious there were only two of them. Had Malcolm indeed embarked on a clandestine tour of his lands? Or had he only fled his royal duties and run away from home?

Whichever it was, he was traveling west, straight for Castle Darragh. And somewhere between here and there, a willful lass with a bold tongue and a deadly arsenal was headed in the same direction.

Warring forces were about to collide.

Dougal slipped into his gambeson and braies, keeping an eye on the king.

At the stable door, the innkeeper bowed and left the lads to their business.

Dougal wasted precious moments rummaging through the straw, looking for his plaid, before deciding Feiyan must have taken it.

He tied on his once-jeweled dagger. At least the lass had left him *one* weapon with which to defend himself.

He peered out the barn door again. The young men were emerging from the stables, leading…

His jaw dropped.

Urramach.

He snapped his jaws shut again, grinding his teeth in outrage.

They had his horse.

That wasn't the king.

Too blind with outrage to consider the consequences, he burst out of the barn and confronted the startled lads.

"What the bloody hell are ye doin' with my horse?"

"*Your* horse?" the tall lad replied, tightening his grip on Urramach's lead. Then he muttered to his companion. "'Tis him. Mac Darragh."

The younger lad faced Dougal fearlessly, straightening his spine and drawing his sword. "What the bloody hell have you done with my sister?"

CHAPTER 25

Feiyan pulled Dougal's gray plaid closer around her face.

Past the mist, beyond the cliff, sounded the crash and hiss of the unseen sea. But before her, overlooking the firth, towered an imposing square stone keep. Surrounded by a curtain wall that was manned by at least six watchmen, Castle Darragh was well defended and nearly impenetrable.

Nearly.

But the magical morning mist kept her secrets. It softened the landscape, muting colors and obscuring her approach to all but the two guards at the gate.

The combat-toughened pair was not the sort to be swayed by a coy wink and a smile. They were rough-hewn, war-scarred, bitter-mouthed men. They wore bloodstained mail and wielded battle-nicked blades. She was certain they were from the mercenary stock who would side with Gaufrid in the fight to come.

Too little learning or too much fighting had left them thick in the head. They might be bulky with brawn, but they were barren of brain. And she could work with that.

"Hey!" she called out as she neared. "Let me back in, eh?"

The short, bald-pated brute glowered at her and grunted, "I don't know ye."

"I don't know ye either," she sneered. Then she shook her head as if in impatience and turned to the second man, a red-bearded giant. "But *ye...ye* remember me, aye?"

He looked uncertain.

"Ye sent me out last even," she reminded him. "To fetch the priest." She rolled her eyes. "'Twas a wasted trip. He's gone to the next village. Ye'll have to wait till the morrow."

"What?" He blinked.

"I said ye'll have to wait. Now are ye goin' to let me in? I got no sleep last night, thanks to ye."

"Hold on," the bearded man said. "'Twasn't me ye spoke with. I've ne'er seen ye before."

"Ye don't remember?" She clucked her tongue. "Well, to be fair, ye were in your cups and barely seein' straight."

The bald man cuffed him. "I told ye not to drink on the watch."

The red-beard squinched his piggish eyes. "I wasn't drunk."

"Why else would ye summon a priest?" the bald man scoffed.

"I didn't."

"Och aye, ye did," she told him. "Ye said ye needed to confess."

The bald man barked out a laugh.

Two red brows drew together. "Confess what?"

She shrugged. "Ye were cryin' in your ale o'er swivin' some other fellow's lass."

"What?" His face colored to match his beard. "I did no such—"

"Plowin' another man's field, eh?" The bald man chortled in amusement.

"Nay," the red-beard insisted. "I don't know what she's talkin' about. I ne'er—"

"Wait." The bald man's scowl darkened as he addressed

her. "Whose lass did he say he was swivin'? 'Twasn't Ivo, was it? Ivo's lass?"

"Aye, that's it," she said, brightening. "Swivin' Ivo's lass."

"What?" The red-beard's eyes grew round with panic. "Ballocks! She's lyin'. I swear—"

That was all the further he got.

Ivo—at least she *assumed* that was who he was—clouted the red-bearded philanderer in the nose before he could finish his sentence.

The blow rocked red-beard's head back and drew blood. But his injury didn't keep him from returning the favor. He gave Ivo a shove that sent him skidding across the ground on his arse and followed up with a dive that flattened his companion, Ivo, squirming beneath him, snatched at his beard, yanking until the man howled.

Stealing into the castle around the two brawling guards was child's play.

Once inside, she walked with purpose, as if she knew exactly where she was going. The true secret to blending in was appearing to be bored. So she sighed, pretending she'd rather be anywhere than traipsing through the courtyard at this early hour.

The bakers had been up for hours, of course. The smell of fresh-baked clapbread wafted through the air. Breezing past the ovens while the bakers were engaged, she casually tucked two of the cooling loaves under her plaid and continued walking.

When she found the stables, the stable lads were already up and about, feeding and watering the horses and mucking out the stalls.

From the wattle fence surrounding the practice field, she called out to the nearest lad. "Hist!" She beckoned him with a lift of her head.

The scrawny blond youth approached.

She showed him one of the loaves. "Here's breakfast for ye if ye can tell me which one's Campbell."

He didn't hesitate. Wiping his muddy hands on his trews, he took the bread and dove in.

"He's there with the dappled gray," he said around a mouthful, nodding toward the other side of the field, where a lad was tightening the girth on a horse.

Clutching the remaining loaf under her arm, she made her way along the fence to where Campbell was working.

He was plain, brown, and honest of face. Unlike the first lad, he was skeptical of a free meal.

She perused the practice field, which was beginning to fill with horses and stable lads. "Do you have somewhere... private...we can go?"

He looked mildly bothered. "With all due respect, m'lady, I've got horses to exercise. I've no time for..." He let the sentence dangle and turned back to brushing the horse's coat. "Maybe one o' the other lads will take ye up on your offer."

She colored. He'd clearly misunderstood her. "I just need to talk to ye," she hissed, wondering how often the lad was called upon for services other than grooming and saddling. "'Tis about Dougal."

That got his attention.

"Dougal? Where is he?" he murmured in concern. "Urramach's been missin' for days. No one knows where Dougal's gone. He rode to Kirkoswald, but—"

"He's fine," she said. "But he needs your help." She scanned the field. "Do you have somewhere we can—"

"Come," he said. He led her to a small open shed with an anvil for forging horseshoes. He sat on the anvil and offered her a three-legged stool.

"Dougal told me you could be trusted," she said.

Campbell nodded, obviously flattered. But he was also wise. "How am I to know *ye* can be trusted?"

"Fair point," she said. "All I can do is tell you what I know and swear to you that..." She grimaced. It was hard to express how she felt in words. "That I care for him as much as you do."

"Ye care for Dougal?"

"I do."

He still looked unsure. "Is that his plaid?"

"Oh. Aye. He...lent it to me."

By his mistrustful glance, he still wasn't entirely sure she hadn't killed him for the plaid.

Nonetheless she continued. "What I'm about to tell you is of vital importance and utmost secrecy. You must swear, upon pain of death, that you won't betray him."

"Betray Dougal? I would ne'er," he insisted.

"Even if it came to war betwixt Dougal..." she asked carefully, "and Gaufrid?"

He cleared his throat and lowered his voice. "Truth be told, 'tis Dougal who should be laird, not his brother. And I'm not the only one who thinks so."

"Right." That was exactly what she needed to hear. "You mean that?"

He nodded.

After a wee bit of persuading and half a loaf of clapbread after all, Campbell agreed to help her. He would speak to other trustworthy folk who were of like mind—men-at-arms, archers, craftsmen, servants—and let them know to be on alert for an uprising in the next few days.

She assured him, with growing confidence now, that the forces of the warriors of Rivenloch would take their side.

Then she asked him to identify someone who could readily enter and exit the castle. Someone whose comings and goings wouldn't be questioned. Someone known and liked in the villages surrounding Darragh.

Campbell humbly admitted that would be him. He often exercised the horses for the knights, riding them out to the villages. He confessed he sometimes pilfered food from Gaufrid's kitchens to give to the hungry crofters.

Only then did Feiyan realize just how dire the situation at Darragh had become and the extent of Gaufrid's cruelty.

A laird had one chief responsibility—looking after the clan. And the clan included anyone who resided on clan land. Villagers. Tradesmen. Crofters. Even beggars.

To rescind that responsibility, to withhold protection, or even worse, to starve and impoverish those reliant on the laird, was a crime of the worst sort.

Gaufrid mac Darragh had taken his villainy one step further. He'd murdered his own clan folk and driven off the one man capable of saving them. He'd tried to destroy their hero.

There was just one problem. Their hero had returned.

Feiyan's smile as she strode toward the great hall was grim and full of dark promise.

Dougal noted the resemblance at once. The dark-haired lad confronting him with smoldering gray eyes, a bold tongue, and a naked blade looked just like his sister.

"Ye're a Rivenloch," Dougal realized. "And *ye*," he said, eyeing the tall, somber lad holding Urramach's reins. "Ye're not the king. Ye're a horse thief."

The lad straightened proudly. "I paid good coin for the horse. 'Tis mine by rights."

He might not be the king. But the handsome lad had the royal bearing to carry off the disguise. It was no wonder he'd fooled the innkeepers.

"Where is she?" the young one asked again. "Where's Feiyan?" His voice broke over her name, and it was hard to tell whether it was from his awkward age or because he was worried about his sister.

It was futile to pretend Dougal didn't know what they

were talking about. They'd obviously been shadowing Feiyan for days, just as he'd suspected. Despite her insistence that no one would miss her, the people of Rivenloch had noted her absence at once and come looking for her.

And of course, they'd managed to show up at the worst possible time. When she was nowhere to be found.

"Answer him," the older lad growled.

Dougal didn't dare tell them what he assumed. That Feiyan had foolishly gone to confront Gaufrid on her own. The last thing he wanted was for the full forces of a warrior clan to descend upon Darragh without warning.

There would be a bloodbath.

Gaufrid knew nothing about hostage negotiations. Once whispers of "Rivenloch" circled the castle, the Fortanachs would likely desert him to save their own arses. And his brother, flustered by the responsibility of leadership, incapable of making rational decisions, would commit some heinous act that would cost lives and start a war.

"Answer me," the young lad demanded impatiently, brandishing his sword, "or I swear—"

"Adam!" the older lad barked, staying the younger's arm. "He's no use to us dead. Besides, he's unarmed."

Dougal held up his hands to show them he meant no harm.

"So were our clansmen," Adam snarled, "when he slashed through their ranks with his bloody claymore."

The lad was right. Dougal deserved every bit of the wrathful glare Adam was giving him.

"You owe us the truth," the older lad said.

"Just tell me, did you kill her?" Adam asked. This time the crack in his voice was from dread. "So help me God, if you hurt Feiyan, I'll—"

"Nay! I didn't touch... I didn't hurt your sister." He couldn't say he'd never touched her. Hell, he'd had his hands all over Feiyan. "As far as I know, she's unharmed."

He hoped that was true. But he could tell by the lads' dubious scowls that his claim wasn't very convincing.

"What do you mean, 'as far as ye know'?" the tall lad ground out. "Where is she?"

Dougal blew out a defeated breath and told them the only truth that would save his clan. "I don't know."

Despite Adam's brave countenance, a soft sound of despair came from his throat.

"Why should we believe you?" the older lad snarled. "You nearly killed my sister in the tournament."

Dougal's shoulders sank. "And I'll ne'er forgive myself for that."

"Nor will Rivenloch," Adam sneered. "When our clan army arrives—"

"Adam," the tall lad cautioned.

But it was too late. The lad had already leaked the truth.

"They're not here yet," Dougal realized. The lads had come alone.

The older lad compressed his lips.

Adam, mortified by his slip, blurted out, "But they'll be here soon. Give us Feiyan now." He grabbed Urramach's reins out of his cousin's hand. "And we'll give you back your horse."

The tall lad clapped a restraining hand on Adam's shoulder. He was old enough to understand, even if his cousin wasn't, that against an army, a horse was worth far less than a hostage.

The desperate young lad wrenched free. "Let me go, Gellir. She's not your sister."

Dougal realized then that everything Feiyan believed—about her worth, her invisibility, her significance to the clan—was completely wrong. These two lads—a cousin with courage beyond his years and a brother not yet able to grow a beard—loved her so much they'd purchased his horse and traveled halfway across Scotland to rescue her.

"Adam." He met the brave lad's worried gray eyes, so like his sister's. "Gellir." He faced the lad who bore the proud name of his legendary Rivenloch grandfather. "My name is Dougal. I know ye don't trust me. I don't blame ye. I can explain. And I intend to. Everythin'. But at this moment, Feiyan may be in danger. There's no time to waste. I need your help."

CHAPTER 26

K*now your enemy.*

Sung Li's wisdom echoed in Feiyan's ears as she entered the great hall of Castle Darragh.

It was risky to confront a target face to face. But in order to launch a successful assault against a laird who commanded an army of mercenaries, she needed to get the full measure of the man. Learn what drove him. Find out how competent he was. And where his weaknesses lie.

Besides, she was confident she'd be forgotten an instant after she was seen.

The castle perched dramatically on a cliff overlooking the sea.

The great hall, which took advantage of that view, was surprisingly beautiful. It was not quite as magnificent as Rivenloch's, of course, which was lined with the colorful banners of defeated armies and lit by dozens of sweet beeswax candles.

But it had arched windows on the west side to welcome in the sunlight reflected off the firth and a grand hearth on the east side to chase away the chill. The chalk-bright walls were painted with figures of sea creatures—fish, whales, shells, selkies—in shades of blue and coral, intertwined with strands of golden kelp and deep red dulce.

She found an unassuming place by the hearth to study the denizens of the keep.

Servants bustled about the hall. Lighting tallow candles. Stirring the fire to life. Strewing fresh rushes atop the old. Coming and going from the kitchens with clapbread and ale. They served the steady stream of castle folk arriving for a quick bite of breakfast before beginning their morning chores.

Several mercenaries arrived and left. Like rats infesting the sparkling hall, they slunk through the rushes with dull eyes and primitive instincts, heading toward the food. The sharp tang of tarnished metal, unwashed bodies, and rotting teeth wafted past her.

A motley army of mercenaries such as this presented a unique challenge.

She'd seen men like them before. Bitter. Empty. Lacking souls. They had no home. No clan. Nothing to live for. So they had no fear of death. Caring for no one, they served only to kill. And that made them extremely dangerous.

She hoped the clan folk of Darragh were up to the task of facing them down. When the time came for confrontation, would they have the strength to defy the mindless murderers? Or would they shudder and crumble at the last moment, like a wall beneath a trebuchet?

A trebuchet. Feiyan wished she had one of the rock-throwing war machines.

Her wee cousin Ian, a brilliant inventor, had made a miniature trebuchet. A full-scale version of that would have been useful in the coming battle. It was a pity there had been no time to assemble one.

On the other hand, Castle Darragh was an impressive keep. It would be a shame to slight it. Besides, if things went according to plan, Dougal would triumph and take over as laird.

She even dared to imagine she might one day rule beside him...if he ever forgave her for betraying him.

With that in mind, she continued with her scheme to gather information about the castle and its laird.

Weaving her inconspicuous way through the crowd, she crossed the hall and slipped into the kitchens. A maidservant emerged with a tray full of clapbread and butter.

"Here, I'll take it," Feiyan said smoothly, holding her hands out for the tray. "Ye're wanted in the chapel."

"The chapel?" The young woman blinked in surprise, but surrendered the tray and hied away.

At the bottom of the steps, Feiyan found two wee lasses playing with cloth dolls.

"Good morn," she whispered, bending to speak to them. "'Tis my first day bein' a maidservant. I'm supposed to take the laird his breakfast. Ye seem like clever lasses. Can ye show me the way?"

They jumped up eagerly to help, leading her up the winding stairs and pointing at the chamber door before giggling and running back to the great hall.

When they'd gone, she knocked softly on the door and called out, "Breakfast for the laird."

"Come in," someone said.

Despite her determination to remain nonchalant, when she entered the room, Feiyan caught her breath. In the shadowy chamber, the man lounging in his leine in the enormous bed looked so much like Dougal, it made her heart ache. He had the same black hair, the same wide shoulders, the same strong jaw and fierce gaze.

And yet she could see immediately he was nothing like his brother.

Dougal's mouth tended to drift into an easy smile. Gaufrid's seemed fixed in a permanent sneer.

Dougal's eyes shone with intelligence. Gaufrid's glittered with menace.

Dougal moved with commanding grace. Gaufrid puffed out his chest like a pigeon.

She closed the door with her hip and glided into the chamber. With sidelong glances in the dim light, she catalogued everything in the room. A massive oak chest hugging one wall. Red velvet draping the bed. Glowing coals on the hearth. Rose-painted shutters over the window. A lidded chamberpot under the bedside table as well as a curtained garderobe. An iron sconce with an unlit candle. A bare claymore propped beside the door.

Flanking the laird's bed were the two sharp-eyed sycophants. They must be Fergus and Morris, the Fortanach brothers, though they hardly looked like brothers. One was built like a wild boar, the other like a lean wolf. Their pale faces were freshly shaved. They wore ocher-colored coifs over neatly trimmed brown hair. Their expensive clothing was muted in color, as if to denote humility. But their good grooming couldn't disguise their oily manner. They alternated between hanging on Gaufrid's every gesture and glaring in jealous threat at her.

"Open the shutters, ninny," the boar snapped at her. "Would ye have the laird break his fast in the dark?"

Her jaw clenched. But she bowed her head, set the tray on the chest, and resisted the urge to stab the man with her *bishou* as she passed him on her way to the window.

"What will it be today, m'laird?" the wolf asked. "A game o' dice? A visit to the stews?"

Gaufrid let out a noisy yawn. "I need to wet my whistle first."

"Wench," the boar demanded, "bring us ale."

Shite. She didn't have ale.

Hoping to distract them, she threw open the shutter.

The bright light of the rising sun pierced the white mist and stabbed into the chamber like double-edged *jian*, slaying the shadows.

Blinded by the light, they bellowed in complaint.

Temporarily blinded herself, Feiyan never saw the blow coming as she whirled away from the window.

"Stupid wench!"

The back of the wolf's fist caught the side of her head. The world splintered, and she staggered to the ground.

"Wait," Gaufrid said. "Ye're not the usual maid. Who are ye?"

The boar bent down to look at her.

"Where's the wee red-haired lass?" the wolf snarled.

Stunned, Feiyan fought to regain her wits. Using the chest, she clawed her way back onto her feet. Unfortunately, her hand caught the edge of the tray, upsetting it and spilling clapbread onto the floor.

"Answer me," the wolf grunted.

She was fuzzy-headed, but this time she was prepared when he wolf lifted his arm to backhand her again.

She shoved his elbow away with one palm and punched him under the ribs with her other knuckles. He collapsed forward with an "oof" just as the door opened, admitting a timid young lass with a heart-shaped freckled face and orange hair.

"M'laird," she murmured.

Oblivious to the commotion, she bobbed to the laird with downcast eyes and hurried forward to offer her tray of clapbread and ale.

"There she is," the boar announced. "There's the redheaded wench."

"Then who is *she?*" Gaufrid jerked his head toward Feiyan.

Feiyan never got the chance to lie. The maid's pale blue eyes went round when she saw Feiyan. She gasped and dropped her tray. Her jug shattered on the floor, splattering ale over the tumbling loaves of clapbread.

"That plaid!" the lass cried in alarm. "I know that plaid. 'Tis Dougal's."

"Why should we trust you?" Gellir asked Dougal, narrowing flinty eyes.

"Aye," Adam chimed in. "Why should we believe anything you say?"

Dougal sighed. They were right to doubt him. He'd viciously attacked their clan. And they had good cause to believe he'd done some harm to Feiyan.

But that was the furthest thing from the truth. In fact, if he survived the coming battle, if he eluded death and delivered justice, if he proved himself worthy, he had quite different plans for the wee lass with the beautiful gray eyes and the invincible spirit.

He didn't realize it until this instant. But now his destiny couldn't be clearer.

"Because I mean to marry her."

For a moment, they only stared at him, speechless.

"What?" Adam blinked.

"You're not serious?" Gellir asked in disbelief.

Dougal straightened. "I am."

"Really?" Gellir snorted. "Does *she* know?"

"She won't have you," Adam stated.

"'Twas actually her idea." Dougal was fairly certain that was true.

"*Feiyan's* idea?" Gellir asked. He gave Dougal a cursory glance from head to toe, probably the same inspection he'd given Urramach before purchasing the horse.

Adam made an almost comical grimace of disgust. "'Tis absurd," he spat. "My sister would ne'er marry the likes of you."

Gellir made no comment. He apparently hadn't found Dougal as lacking in marriageable qualities as Adam did.

Dougal addressed the younger lad. "'Tis what I thought as well. Why would a lass as bright and beautiful as your sister wish to wed me? Aye, I'm the son of a laird. I'm the best warrior in my clan. And I did save her from outlaws in the forest, but—"

"*You* saved *her*?" Adam scoffed.

Dougal admitted, "To be fair, 'twas a mutual effort. Her fightin' skills are...impressive."

Adam raised his chin with pride, reminding Dougal of Feiyan. The lad still didn't like the idea of Dougal courting his sister. "Maybe she was only luring you in so she could finish you off."

It was Gellir who came to his defense. "Nay."

"What do you mean, nay? My sister would ne'er wed a bloody berserker. She'd sooner murder him."

"If Feiyan had wanted him dead," Gellir reasoned, "he'd be dead."

While that was unsettling, it was likely true. After long consideration, Adam accepted that rationale with a grudging sigh.

Gellir straightened. "So what do we do now?"

"I need ye to trust me," Dougal said. "There's no time to lose. Let me take the horse."

"Take the horse?" Gellir mocked. "Why? So you can ride off and we'll ne'er see you again? Nay." He echoed his cousin's earlier words. "All this talk about love and son of a laird and wedding my cousin. Maybe *you're* only luring *us* in so you can finish her off."

Adam gasped at that dire possibility.

Dougal scowled. How could he convince them he loved Feiyan and meant her no harm?

Suddenly inspired, he drew his jeweled dagger.

Adam replied by brandishing his sword.

Even stoic Gellir placed a tense hand on his hilt, ready to draw his blade.

"Nay, nay," Dougal clarified, "the jewels." He showed them the dagger, hilt-first. "These are rubies and emeralds. I'll pry them out and buy back my horse. Maybe then ye won't doubt my honor. How much did ye pay for him?"

"Thir-, forty pounds," Adam amended.

Dougal almost choked on the figure. "He's worth sixty," he muttered. He should never have given Urramach to crofters, who didn't know a destrier from a plowhorse. "These gems will earn ye more than that."

"Feiyan's life is not for sale," Gellir affirmed.

"O' course not."

Gellir scrutinized him with suspicion. "Yet you mean to buy back your horse. Is that so you can kill her with a clear conscience?"

"What? Nay. I only meant..."

Dougal sighed. He needed to find Feiyan before she found trouble.

"Here," he decided, tossing his dagger onto the ground before them. "Now I have no weapon at all."

It was a drastic measure. Dougal had a price on his head. And he'd be riding into Castle Darragh unarmed. But if it got him to the keep that much faster, it was worth the sacrifice.

"So?" Adam wasn't satisfied. "You could still—"

"Fine," Gellir said, scooping up the dagger. "Agreed."

"What?" Adam protested. "But what if—"

"He doesn't stand a chance against Feiyan," Gellir assured his cousin. "You know that."

"Then I want to go with him," Adam said.

"'Tisn't safe," Dougal said. "I need ye to stay here. 'Tis my fault she's gone. 'Tis up to me to get her back. I've done enough harm to your clan already. She'd ne'er forgive me if I dragged her kin into peril."

"So you *do* know where she is." The comment from Gellir was more of an accusation than a question.

"I suspect she's on her way to steal into Castle Darragh."

Gellir nodded. "Then you should make haste."

Still disgruntled, Adam shoved his sword back into its sheath.

Then Gellir handed Dougal the reins.

Urramach tossed his head and whinnied, glad to see his master and eager to run.

"I'll hurry back as soon as I can, I promise," he told the lads who would one day soon—God willing—become his kin.

Then he swung up onto Urramach, which was no easy feat, considering the lads hadn't purchased a saddle, and rode like the wind toward Darragh.

CHAPTER 27

It had never occurred to Feiyan, sneaking through the gates at Castle Darragh, that she might be found out.

For years, she'd mastered the arts of manipulation and clandestineness. Slipping in and out of chambers unnoticed. Following targets without their knowledge. Spying on suspects right beneath their noses.

She rarely failed to infiltrate and extricate herself without being seen.

But when the orange-haired maidservant recognized Dougal's plaid, Feiyan felt like her cloak of covertness was snatched away, leaving her as bare and helpless as a newborn babe.

She tried a feeble falsehood. "This old thing?" she said, lifting a corner of the plaid. "'Twas my ma's and her ma's before her. I don't know what ye're—"

The maid gasped in surprise. "'Tisn't true." She held out a trembling finger. "See at the bottom? There's a singed bit and a wee blood stain from his helpin' birth a lamb a fortnight ago."

Feiyan blinked. The maidservant certainly had keen powers of observation.

"Ye're sure?" Gaufrid sneered.

The maid nodded fretfully. "He was wearin' it when he rode to Kirkoswald."

"How did *ye* get it, wench?" demanded the Fortanach brother who wasn't clutching his bruised ribs.

She'd have to try another lie. "I-I found it. I didn't know whose it—"

"Where is he?" the maid asked frantically. "What have ye done with Dougal?"

"I don't know what ye're talkin' about," Feiyan insisted.

The boar shoved the maidservant out of the way and seized Feiyan by the neck. "Who are ye?"

By the gleam in his piggish eyes and the increasing pressure of his meaty fingers, he was looking for an excuse—any excuse—to squeeze the life out of her.

Instincts took over.

Locking her fingers into a rigid weapon, she punched forward and caught him hard in the throat. He gagged and released his hold instantly. As he staggered back, struggling to breathe through his bruised windpipe, she stomped sideways on his knee. He howled as his knee crunched and collapsed, sending him to the ground.

The wolf, still suffering from her first attack, nonetheless came to his brother's aid. No longer content to show his dominance with his fists, he drew a dagger. She backed out of range. He swiped back and forth with the blade, slicing the air with menace.

Observing his rhythm, she waited until he retracted his arm to strike and swept her dropped tray from the ground, raising it like a shield. Then, as he slashed forward, she swung the tray around, deflecting the dagger and smashing his knuckles.

With a curse of pain, he dropped the weapon. In one smooth movement, she swept it up and out the window. Then she returned with a second clout from the tray. This one flattened his ear with a resounding clang.

He shook off the blow and charged forward again.

Gripping her makeshift weapon in both hands, she

stepped sideways and used all her strength to bash the tray flat against his face. Blood streamed from his nose, and he lurched about in a daze for a few moments.

But in that small space of time, Gaufrid had stolen to the corner of the room and armed himself with the claymore.

"Surrender!" he ordered.

She ignored his command and weighed her options.

The claymore gave him the advantages of reach and power. But he was still vulnerable, clad in nothing but a leine, encumbered by a heavy weapon.

Did Gaufrid have his brother's strength? His agility?

Dougal had claimed he was the best fighter at Darragh. She hoped Gaufrid wouldn't prove otherwise.

"Drop it," he growled, "or I'll run ye through with my blade. I swear I will."

She dropped the tray then. Not because he'd told her to, but because it was useless against a claymore. Her chances were improved with both her hands free.

She didn't believe for one moment he'd have mercy on her. He was aware she was connected to Dougal now. The brother he'd sent to his death.

It was tempting to draw her *sais* and snap off his blade. Stab him through the heart with her *bishou*. Then whip out her *shoudao* and slice his head from his shoulders.

But Gaufrid was the laird of the clan. If it was discovered a heavily armed assassin had somehow sneaked into Darragh to kill the laird, she'd be hanged in the blink of an eye. Her mission would be compromised.

She had to rely on her wits and her bare hands. This was going to be a game of defense, not attack. She needed to disarm him and get out.

When he advanced, sweeping the point of his blade up toward her chin, she backed in retreat, angling toward the hearth. He followed her with the weapon, sneering in triumph as she was forced backward.

Eventually, her heel hit the plaster wall. She could go no farther.

Still he advanced. She shrank away, slowly sinking down the wall, cornered.

Gloating over his conquest, Gaufrid planted the point of the claymore between his spread legs and stared smugly down his nose at her.

She crouched before him, trembling and averting her gaze.

"Now," he said, "we're goin' to have a wee chat, ye and me."

Confident there was no escape for her, he lowered his guard, dropping to his haunches before her and resting the claymore across his knees. He never noticed she'd dipped her hand into the bucket of ashes beside the hearth.

"Who are ye, lass, and what have done wi-"

She threw the ashes into his face. He shrieked and tumbled backward, dropping the claymore and scrubbing at his eyes.

The moment she reached for the fallen sword, his groping hand closed around its grip again, reclaiming the weapon.

Blinded, he nonetheless swung the sword wildly about, nearly chopping the heads off the Fortanach brothers before they wisely scattered.

Dodging the slashing blade, Feiyan resorted to a risky tactic. Rather than retreating, she lunged toward him. Sliding to the ground, she skidded between his widespread legs to come to her feet behind him. Then, planting a foot on his buttock, she gave him a great shove toward the window.

He lurched forward and banged his head on the edge of the shutter, then caught himself on the stone sill.

Rushing up, Feiyan pounded her closed fist down hard on his sword hand. His wrist bent backwards, loosening his grip on the claymore. Simple momentum carried the weapon over the sill, and it plunged from the window.

No one screamed. It must have landed uneventfully.

When she turned back, she was facing three attackers. Their rage must have numbed them to the considerable pain she'd inflicted upon them. Blood dripped from the wolf's nose onto his snarling yellow teeth. The boar hobbled forward on his twisted leg. Ashy tears streamed down Gaufrid's cheeks. Yet revenge boiled in their eyes.

Gaufrid snatched at her with his undamaged hand. When she ducked away, it was into the path of the charging boar. He collided with her, stepping on the plaid. When she wrenched away, the plaid pulled free, revealing the hilt of her *shoudao*.

In her hurry to conceal the weapon, she retreated, unfortunately into the waiting arms of the bleeding wolf. But he'd already spied her sword. He reached across her waist and drew it himself.

The *shoudao's* sleek, honed edge glistened in the sunlight like a deadly silver snake. Her only saving grace was that they were all so astounded by the weapon, she was granted an extra instant to act.

There was no point in hiding her weapons now. And no time to hesitate.

The wolf tightened his grip on her blade. Feiyan pulled out her pair of *sais*. Her weapon might be valuable. But her life was more precious.

She caught the *shoudao* between the tines of the *sais* and wrenched upwards.

To no avail.

The *sais* could easily snap a Scottish sword. But the strong folded steel of the *shoudao* held. The most she could do was scrape the weapon aside.

Meanwhile, the boar spotted the ringed handle of her *duandao*, protruding from its leather sheath. With a crow of victory, he seized it, despite the quick elbow jab she gave him between the ribs.

Now she was in trouble. Outnumbered. Overpowered. Relieved of her two most formidable weapons. With only her *sais* and *bishou* for defense, she couldn't dodge their attacks forever.

It was then she remembered she had a hostage. The maid.

She hated to resort to such villainous tactics. But she had no choice.

Whirling her *sais* in a distracting display to hold off the men, she edged closer to the wide-eyed lass. Then she let the forked weapons fly.

They twirled through the air to opposite sides of the chamber, giving her time to whip her awl-like *bishou* from her boot.

Grabbing the lass roughly about the waist, Feiyan pressed the point against her throat.

The maidservant squeaked.

"Put down your swords," Feiyan commanded, "or I'll skewer her."

The lass made a small whimper of fear, shivering like a mouse under a cat's paw.

Gaufrid hesitated.

"Do it," Feiyan bit out.

He licked his lip in indecision.

"Do you want the blood of an innocent on your hands?" she challenged.

The lass's voice came out on a thin thread of sound. "Please, m'laird."

The boar, seeing Gaufrid waver, chuckled. "Go on," he invited. "Kill her. She's naught to us. Right?"

"Aye, that's right," the wolf said, giving her a bloody leer. "She's only a servin' lass, m'laird. Ye can get another."

Feiyan's heart dropped to the pit of her stomach. She'd never imagined they would throw down that gauntlet.

"But *you* don't want that, do you?" she asked to Gaufrid. "A real laird wouldn't let harm come to his clan."

If even a morsel of honor remained in Dougal's brother, shame would spur him to do the right thing.

But she'd given him more credit than he was due.

"Sorry, lass," Gaufrid decided, nodding to the maidservant. "Your sacrifice will be noted."

The lass stifled a sob.

Incredulous fury sizzled through Feiyan like a molten sword plunged into icy water. She'd thought Dougal a monster. But here was the real monster of Darragh. A laird who would casually and callously let the meekest member of his clan die for him.

She had no qualms now about ending his life. No remorse. No hesitation. She should have killed them all when she had the chance. Slain the three swine when she first walked into the chamber.

Now she had no choice but to surrender her hostage. After all, she wasn't about to murder an innocent lass.

She needed a more formidable hostage.

She released the maid and gave her a quick push out of the way. Then she faced the three brutes with her small and elegant *bishou,* which seemed pathetically powerless against the pair of folded steel swords they now wielded. Especially when the boar decided to disparage her weapon.

"What's that? Your embroidery needle?" He guffawed.

The wolf looked along the sharp edge of the *duandao.* *"This* is a keen weapon, though," he remarked. "Probably slice a man into neat ribbons."

"Or a woman," the boar said.

"We'll see."

"Wait," Gaufrid said. "She knows where Dougal is."

"So?" the boar asked. "I'm thinkin' she killed him."

The maidservant, cowering beside the bed, gasped.

"Maybe." The wolf nodded. "Maybe that's how she got his plaid."

Gaufrid shook his head. "He's not dead."

"Ye don't know that, m'laird," the boar argued.

The wolf sneered. "She could have murdered him and left him by the side o' the road."

The maid let out a soft sob.

"He's not dead, I tell ye," Gaufrid said. "Do ye think this scrap of a—"

If stealth was Feiyan's best asset, surprise was a close second. Before he could even finish his sentence, she sprang forward with the *bishou.*

She meant to press the point against Gaufrid's throat, to hold off the others by threatening the life of their laird. They might be willing to throw away a maidservant's life. But surely they wouldn't sacrifice the Laird of Darragh.

Unfortunately, Gaufrid's instinct for self-preservation was keen. With a squeak, he dodged aside. The point of the *bishou* grazed the side of his neck.

Knowing she had just one more chance before the Fortanachs came at her with her own *dao,* she drew back the *bishou* and prepared to try again.

Out of nowhere, something struck the back of Feiyan's head with a thud. Shards of bright lightning shot out and rapidly faded. Time crept to a halt as the day slowly dimmed around her and a dull throbbing began in her skull. The *bishou* dropped from her nerveless fingers. Stunned, she reeled sideways. The room spun as she began to collapse.

The last thing Feiyan glimpsed was the blanched face of the maidservant, still holding aloft the heavy steel chamberpot.

Then she slipped into darkness.

CHAPTER 28

The moment Dougal mac Darragh rode out of sight, leaving the Ayr Arms to look for Feiyan, Adam turned to Gellir.

"I don't trust him."

"I know."

"We aren't going to just let him go and wait for his return, are we?"

"Nay."

"So what are we *really* going to do?"

"Follow him, of course," Gellir said.

Adam shook his head. "He must think we're complete fools, letting him ride off like that."

"I suspect he's not thinking clearly at all. He's blinded by love."

Adam shuddered in disgust.

"Come now," Gellir chided, looping his arm around Adam's shoulders as they set off down the road. "All in all, he doesn't seem to be a bad sort."

Adam smirked. "We'll see what Feiyan has to say about that."

"She didn't kill him," Gellir said. "That has to account for something."

"Hist!" came an urgent whisper.

Feiyan wanted to rouse. But her head was heavy. Her tongue was thick. And her eyes wouldn't open.

"Wake up!"

She groaned and tried to lift her head. Pain pumped through her skull with every beat of her heart.

"Come on. I've brought ye ale."

Prying open her eyes, she managed to ease up to her elbows from the bed of packed sand. She blinked. Where was she?

The last thing she recalled was getting walloped with a chamberpot and sinking onto the floor of the laird's bedchamber.

Here the light was dim. The air was dank and musty. The odors of mold and rock and seaweed filled her nostrils.

"Where am I?" she croaked.

"Here." A cup of ale was pressed against her mouth.

Looking over its edge, she saw her visitor by the light of a candle.

"You," Feiyan accused. "You clouted me with a chamberpot."

"Drink," the maid urged.

Feiyan eyed the cup. "'Tisn't poison, is it?" she rasped out.

Though she was vexed at the conniving maidservant, Feiyan had only herself to blame for what had happened. She should never have dismissed the lass as helpless.

"Nay."

Feiyan reluctantly took a sip from the cup. Three swallows later, when she could speak properly, she sat up.

"What is this place?"

From what she could see by the candlelight, the walls were ragged, carved out of rock. The floor was made of sandy soil. And in the distance, she could hear the crash and sizzle of breakers upon the beach.

Instead of answering her, the lass posed a question of her own. "What have ye done with him? What have ye done with Dougal?"

"I don't know who you're talking about. Who is—"

"Don't lie to me!" The maidservant's cry was more of a sob than a command. "I know ye know somethin'. He wouldn't have willingly parted with his plaid. Ye must have done somethin' to him."

Feiyan frowned. It was one thing for Dougal's brother to interrogate her. But this was a lowly maidservant. What right did she have to question Feiyan? What concern was it of hers if Dougal went missing? Why would the thought of his absence drive the maid to tears?

Suddenly she recalled Dougal's claim about his most trusted servant. "You're not...Merraid...are you?"

"Aye," the lass replied. "How did ye know my..."

A breath of relief rushed out of Feiyan. Perhaps her mission wasn't compromised after all. Perhaps there was still a chance to unseat Gaufrid and his minions.

"Dougal told me about you," she said.

"He did? Dougal told ye about...me?" Merraid's expression wavered between disbelief and astonished pleasure. "What did he say?"

Feiyan wasn't about to waste time on flattering the lass with a gush of invented praise. "He said you could be trusted."

Merraid blushed and bit her lip. She was clearly besotted with the laird's brother. Feiyan couldn't blame her for seeing Dougal as a hero. Especially when the poor lass served a laird who was willing to let her be murdered.

"Then he's all right?" she asked.

"Aye."

"Where is he?"

Feiyan wasn't foolish enough to reveal that, even to Dougal's most trusted servant. The smitten lass might take it upon herself to seek him out and interfere with Feiyan's plans.

"He's safe," she said. "But he needs your help."

"*My* help?" Merraid's eyes took on a dreamy cast, as if Dougal had invited her to rule a kingdom by his side.

Feiyan nodded. Merraid's lovesick smile was mildly irritating. But if the lass could rally the clan folk loyal to Dougal, if she could assemble a small army for a rebellion, Feiyan would overlook the maid's hero worship.

"What does he want me to do?" Merraid asked.

It was tempting to make the silly lass spin round three times, eat a bug, and hack off her thick marigold tresses, since she seemed prepared to do anything for her beloved Dougal.

Instead, she told the lass the truth. "He plans to rise up against his brother."

Merraid gasped. "He's goin' to be laird?"

"With your help."

"O' course. What can I do?"

Feiyan finished off her ale as she detailed her scheme.

Merraid listened intently, nodding when Feiyan explained the need for utmost secrecy and careful preparation. When the day of the uprising came, she said, an army would arrive to join forces with those loyal to Dougal.

"An army?" Merraid asked, abruptly suspicious. "What army?"

Feiyan hesitated. The less anyone knew, the better. On the other hand, knowing they had a powerful ally might inspire the clan folk, giving them confidence to act.

She lowered her voice to a murmur. "The Warriors of Rivenloch."

"Rivenloch?" the maid asked in surprise. Even Merraid had heard of them. She regarded Feiyan with new respect. "Ye're one o' them, aren't ye? A Warrior Maid o' Rivenloch?"

Feiyan nodded. "I'm Feiyan la Nuit of Rivenloch, niece of the laird."

"No wonder ye fought with such skill," Merraid marveled, perusing her from head to toe. "Are all o' ye so fierce?"

Feiyan smiled with humbled pride. "Not as fierce as the maid who cracked my pate with a chamberpot."

Merraid blushed.

"So will you do it?" Feiyan asked. "Will you help?"

Merraid reclaimed Feiyan's drained cup and creased her brows as she gazed pensively into its empty depths. "E'en the forces o' Rivenloch may not be able to defeat Gaufrid's army."

"You haven't seen the forces of Rivenloch."

"If anythin' bad happens to Dougal, if he's hurt or k-ki-"

"Nothing will happen," Feiyan said, placing a hand of reassurance on the maid's forearm. "I swear it."

Merraid stared at her with earnest longing. "I'd do anythin' to save Dougal mac Darragh." Then, holding the cup and candle, she rose and turned away.

Feiyan stood to follow her. But a wave of residual pressure in her head dizzied her, making her sway on her feet. "Wait a moment." She pressed her fingers to her temple. "That clout you gave me has made a muddle of—"

Her words were cut off by a harsh scrape and a metallic clang. When she looked up, Merraid was on the other side of a gate of iron bars. The maid's face was solemn as she turned a key in the lock.

Feiyan's heart dropped. "What are you doing?"

For an instant, she gave Merraid the benefit of the doubt. Maybe there was a good reason to lock Feiyan in this cave of a castle gaol. Maybe his prisoner's sudden disappearance would rouse Gaufrid's suspicions.

But when she glimpsed the nervous spark in Merraid's heretofore innocent eyes, she sensed something else was afoot.

"Don't leave me here," Feiyan insisted, keeping her voice level. "I need to get word to Dougal."

"How do I know ye don't mean to keep him, ye and your Rivenloch army?"

"I give you my word."

"Why should I believe ye?"

"You *have* to believe me," Feiyan said, fighting back panic, trying to sound reasonable. "You have to let me go. Dougal is waiting for me."

"If ye're truly a Warrior Maid o' Rivenloch—"

"I am. I swear."

"Then ye'll make a valuable hostage."

The maid intended to trade her for Dougal. Merraid didn't realize that to Gaufrid, Dougal had no value.

Merraid tried to explain. "I can't lose him. He means too much to me. To the clan. Laird or not. I'm sorry."

It was Feiyan who was sorry. Sorry she'd trusted the maid. With a roar of frustration, she rushed at the lass, banging into the iron bars with such force that the gate clattered in its stony frame.

Merraid staggered back with a gasp, perhaps fearing Feiyan's rage would unhinge the cell gate.

"'Twon't work," Feiyan argued. "Don't you see? Gaufrid won't pay the ransom."

"Dougal is his brother. He'll pay."

"But he's the one who sent Dougal to his death. He's the one who set the fire at Kirkoswald. He knew Dougal would have no choice but to seek vengeance. Gaufrid sent him straight into the swords of Scotland's most formidable border clan. Alone."

"I don't believe ye."

Feiyan seized the iron bars, squeezing them in desperate fists. How could she convince the maid of the truth?

"Fine," she said, "Don't believe me. Believe your own

eyes. You saw what Gaufrid did when I threatened your life. You sampled his mercy. He would have let me slit your throat."

Merraid's resolve faltered, but only briefly. "I'm only a maidservant," she reasoned. "Dougal is his blood kin."

Feiyan felt a twinge of pity at Merraid's claim. How brutal was Gaufrid's rule that a maidservant would believe her life was expendable?

"I'm telling you, he won't make the exchange."

"I'm sorry," Merraid said, turning away.

"Nay!" Feiyan cried, then lowered her voice in a quiet plea. "Don't go. Gaufrid will kill me. And then he'll let my clan kill Dougal."

"Sorry."

"Nay!" Feiyan screamed after the maid as she scurried off, taking the light and hope with her.

Fergus was pleasantly surprised with the information the maidservant extracted from the prisoner. She'd been rather useful. On her own, without direction from him, the clever lass had managed to gain valuable knowledge, saving him the trouble of having to torture the captive for it.

Indeed, so useful was this information, he and Morris might reward the wee maid later with a lusty romp between the linens.

Of course, she had a very different idea about what he meant to *do* with this information. He had no intention of ransoming Dougal mac Darragh, no matter what the cow-eyed lass believed.

After all, he was now in possession of Feiyan la Nuit, a warrior maid of the illustrious Rivenloch clan, an ally of the mac Girics and the niece of the laird.

Once Dougal had arrived at Creagor, no doubt loudly

accusing the mac Girics of the massacre perpetrated at Kirkoswald, he'd probably been disabused of his belief at the point of a sword. Maybe the lass herself had slain him and kept his plaid as a souvenir.

That was for the best. Laird Gaufrid might pretend he was only getting Dougal out of his sight for a while. But Fergus and Morris knew better. And in his gut, so did Gaufrid. He had to know he was sending his brother on a suicide mission.

Now Fergus had earned a bonus for his trouble. A valuable hostage who would command a hefty price.

His only regret was that he wouldn't be able to pay the wicked wench back for the damage she'd inflicted. The cracked ribs. The bruised throat. The smashed knee. The crushed ballocks. Battered and humiliated by the wee slip of a warrior lass, he'd salivated over the idea of having her tied up and at his mercy. Imagined all sorts of painfully devious and deviant torments to subject her to while he feigned to care about and demanded to know Dougal's whereabouts.

Now he and Morris would have to forego their aberrant pleasure. Which was a pity. Unrequited revenge made one's injuries throb all the more.

But that couldn't be avoided. Perhaps they'd take their frustrations out on the wee maidservant later. As for the warrior maid, she would command a higher price if she was untouched.

Feiyan felt her way along the cave wall, running her fingers over the stony, damp surface, heading toward the sound of the sea.

Maybe there was a way out.

Several yards along, after unrelenting darkness, the passage curved to the right. There, light filtered in to speed her progress, allowing her to discern the knobby rock walls.

When she entered the last chamber of the cave and saw the bright beach and the misty water beyond through a narrow opening, however, the beautiful view was cleaved into squares by another iron grate that sealed the entrance. This one had no hinges.

The fresh, salty air kept the cell from feeling like a grave. But she wondered who had been imprisoned here before. Had they been starved? Forgotten to death? Antagonized by those strolling in delicious freedom along the beach? Were their unlucky skeletons cowering in the darkest corners of the cave?

She shivered. Eventually the cold and hunger would kill her, if Gaufrid and the Fortanachs didn't first.

She cursed herself for trusting Dougal's trusty maid. She might be faithful and devoted. She probably felt she was doing the right thing, saving her beloved Dougal. But she didn't have an ounce of good judgment if she believed Gaufrid would go along with her scheme.

She did an obligatory test of the iron bars. Forged into the rock, they didn't budge. She dug down through the sand. The grate extended farther than her arms could reach. It might as well have been anchored to the underworld.

Finally, she sighed and looked out through the rusty grate. White-capped waves of gray lashed the sand, leaving a frothy trail like a glimmering snail's path. Seagulls skipped along its edge, searching for breakfast.

Was Dougal searching for her? Had he discovered she was missing yet?

He'd realize at once where she'd gone. He would likely follow her. He might be on his way to Darragh even now.

If only she could give him a warning. Let him know that Gaufrid had discovered her identity. Make him aware that he had to feign disinterest in her. Otherwise, she would become leverage for whatever demands they wished to make of him. And those demands could be enormous.

Her eyes misted as she realized Dougal was the kind of man who would protect her with his dying breath.

She wouldn't let him do that. Not the man she loved.

Somehow she would find a way out of this cave.

Somehow she would find a way back to him.

Sensing they were heading home, Urramach raced along the road toward Darragh. Still, the sun was high in the sky by the time Dougal reached the castle. He'd hoped to intercept Feiyan before she reached the keep. Now he wondered if the sly lass had left him immediately after their moonlit tryst.

From the high towers, the guards shouted out a greeting at once. It was hard to miss Dougal's magnificent black charger churning up the ground toward the gates.

Once he was admitted, Dougal wasted no time. Word of his arrival would reach his brother's ears soon enough. He galloped to the stable yard, sliding from the horse's back to hand the reins to Campbell.

Campbell murmured, "We've missed ye...m'laird."

Startled by Campbell's address, Dougal frowned. "What's happened?"

"Your...friend...arrived," Campbell whispered.

"Feiyan."

"Aye."

"Is she all right? Where is she? She hasn't—"

He halted suddenly when one of the mercenaries lumbered past on his way to the stables.

When he'd passed, Campbell confided, "I've done as she asked. Ridden out to the villages and alerted the crofters to your plan."

"What plan?" Dread tingled at the back of his neck.

Campbell blinked, suddenly uncertain. "'Twas your plan, aye? She said ye were goin' to lay claim to the clan."

"Ah. Aye. I suppose." To be honest, Dougal hadn't thought that far ahead. That *would* be the ultimate outcome if he discovered his brother and his ilk had indeed committed the atrocity at Kirkoswald. But inciting a rebellion against a sitting laird was not a thing to undertake lightly.

Campbell's eyes grew moist as he added, "Those of us who remember your da and the days we were proud to be mac Darraghs, we intend to stand with ye."

Dougal couldn't help but be touched and inspired by his words. He supposed it was too late now to rein in the galloping horde. But he wondered what havoc the lass had wrought in her brash, singlehanded attempt to overthrow Gaufrid.

He gave Campbell a smile. "I'm glad I can count on ye."

Campbell grew nearly an inch, straightening with pride. Then he sidled close to whisper, "Is it true? Is the lass really a Warrior Maid o' Rivenloch?"

"Aye."

"And ye're goin' to wed her?"

"What? Did she say that?"

Campbell winced. "Nay. But she said she cared for ye. I assumed..."

"Well, that's still to be determined," Dougal decided. He didn't particularly care for the way she'd abandoned him, taken things into her own hands, and marched straight into danger. "What else did she tell ye?"

"Naught, but..." When Campbell furrowed his brows, Dougal braced himself for bad news. "I suspect she's in trouble."

Why did that not surprise him?

"What kind o' trouble?"

"There was a wee scrap with the laird and the Fortanachs."

Dougal bit the inside of his cheek. What had happened to Feiyan's insistence on stealth? "What kind o' wee scrap?"

Admiration shone in Campbell's eyes. "Accordin' to the maids, she left them with broken ribs, bashed faces, and bruised ballocks."

That sounded like his warrior maid. "And Feiyan?"

Campbell's face fell. "I fear Merraid laid her low."

"Merraid?" he asked in disbelief. What the devil did Merraid have to do with any of this? Why would she attack Feiyan? And how could a scrawny maidservant best a warrior maid? "Wee Merraid?"

"Drubbed her with a chamberpot," Campbell said.

"What?"

"'Tis true. Merraid said so herself."

"Where is she now?"

"Merraid?"

"Nay, Feiyan."

"I'm afraid they tossed her in the *dùn mara*."

Dougal's heart dropped. The *dùn mara* was what they called the chamber carved into a natural cave at the bottom of the cliff, underneath the castle. His father had used it for storage. His brother had turned it into a prison cell. It was dark. And dank. And there was no way out.

"Merraid said the laird was plannin' to use her to ransom ye from Rivenloch," Campbell added.

But Dougal knew better. "Rivenloch never held me. And Merraid's wrong about Gaufrid." If his brother recognized who Feiyan was, he would surely use her as leverage against a Rivenloch attack on Darragh. If Rivenloch didn't go along with his scheme, Gaufrid would kill Feiyan without batting an eye. And Rivenloch would retaliate, probably slaughtering the whole clan.

Dougal knew what he had to do.

Feiyan had tried stealth. It hadn't worked.

Now he would try *his* way. Confront Gaufrid face to face. Man to man. Demand answers. Threaten his conniving pair of minions. And inform his brother he meant to take control of the clan, once and for all.

With a nod of farewell, he wheeled and strode across the stable yard.

"Where are ye goin', m'laird?" Campbell called out.

"I'm goin' to take back what's mine," he growled.

CHAPTER 29

Dougal was no fool. He was well aware he couldn't simply march into Gaufrid's chambers and seize the lairdship from him.

But that was not his intention.

He meant to rescue Feiyan first.

News traveled quickly through a castle. By now, his brother would know he'd returned. Cowardly Gaufrid would likely linger in his bedchamber to avoid confrontation.

Dougal had to draw him out.

Seething with furious purpose, he stormed across the courtyard, through the crowd of shocked and whispering clan folk. With a great heave, he burst through the doors of the great hall.

"Gaufrid!" he bellowed across the cavernous chamber.

The dozens of servants and mercenaries bustling about the hall froze in alarm.

"Fetch Gaufrid!" he barked at a kitchen lad standing with his mouth agape.

The lad scurried up the stairs to do his bidding.

Dougal leaned back against the doors to close them, shutting out the daylight with a resolute thud. Then he slowly ambled to the middle of the great hall, keeping the mercenaries at bay with a menacing gaze. They didn't dare approach the brother of the laird, not without the laird's permission.

When the lad clambered back down the stairs, it was not his brother who followed him, but Fergus and Morris.

"What's this about?" Fergus demanded with feign authority.

"I asked for Gaufrid," Dougal bit out. "Gaufrid!" he yelled.

"He's unwell," Morris scolded.

"Why? Did ye poison him?"

The servants gasped.

"How dare ye," Fergus said.

Dougal crossed his arms. "Are ye tryin' to get rid o' him the same way ye tried to get rid o' me?"

The servants gasped again.

"What are ye blatherin' about?" Morris asked. "We've been naught but kind and carin' to the laird, lookin' after him in his grief."

"'Tis your fault he's unwell," Fergus said. "He's been worried sick about ye."

Dougal didn't believe that for an instant. "Then he should be glad to see me returned." He cupped his hands to his mouth and shouted, "Gaufrid!"

At last his brother stumbled down the stairs. He was a mess. He must have been drinking all morn. His eyes were bleary. His hair was uncombed. The two edges of his gambeson were mismatched, laced in a crooked tangle.

"What are ye doin' here?" he said, slurring the words.

"Look, Gaufrid," Fergus prompted him. "Your prayers have been answered. Your brother's returned."

Dougal's mouth twisted with bitterness. "Surprised to see me? After all, ye planned to have me killed, aye?"

"Ye? Killed?" The hall filled with anxious murmurs as Gaufrid mumbled out a denial. "Why would I do that?"

Fergus wiped his sweaty upper lip. "Quiet, Dougal. Can't ye see ye're upsettin' him?"

Morris, sensing the tension in the room, lowered his voice. "Why don't we go upstairs, the four of us, and have a wee chat?"

"Why?" Dougal asked, gesturing to the clan folk surrounding them. "Do they not deserve to know the truth?"

"What truth?" Gaufrid sneered.

Fergus clamped his jaw and grabbed Dougal's forearm to warn him to silence.

Dougal snatched it back. "The truth that ye set the fire at Kirkoswald."

Astounded whispers circled the great hall. But his stark accusation also drew the attention of the mercenaries, alert to any sign of threat to the man who paid their wages. Meanwhile, more servants crept into the great hall from the buttery and the chambers above, drawn by the commotion.

"Ye don't know what ye're talkin' about," Morris muttered, licking his lips nervously.

"Don't I?"

Fergus closed his eyes to cunning slits and gave him what sounded like a well-practiced, all-too-convenient explanation. "Impossible. Laird Gaufrid was at the castle all morn. Ye know that. He was watchin' ye spar."

"Oh aye, ye're right. My mistake. Gaufrid couldn't have done it," Dougal agreed. "But ye two... Why exactly were *ye* at Kirkoswald?"

Morris wasn't as good at lying as Fergus, so he chose to bluster. "'Tisn't your place to question us or the laird."

Fergus chimed in, "We were attendin' the christenin' on the laird's behalf."

That lie sickened Dougal. "The christenin'? Ye mean the christenin' where ye bolted the doors and set the church on fire?"

The servants' whispers rose to a horrified murmur.

"Enough!" Gaufrid decided, considering the temperament of the clan folk. "'Tis all lies. Guards! Seize him."

Two mercenaries immediately took Dougal's arms. He shook them off.

"What's the matter?" Dougal said. "Are ye afraid for the clan to hear what really happened?"

Two more mercenaries joined the first. One pair seized his arms, the other his shoulders. He tried to wrench free, this time to no avail.

"Are ye afraid they'll learn the depths o' your cruelty?"

"Stop it!" Gaufrid shouted.

"How ye had these fellows o' yours," he sneered, jerking his head toward the Fortanachs, "stage an attack under a false banner?"

"Ye're full o' shite!" Gaufrid screamed.

Another guard seized Dougal by the hair, dragging his head backwards.

"Damn ye!" Dougal cried. "There was a two-day-old babe in that church." His voice broke over the words.

"Shut him up!" Gaufrid ordered.

A meaty fist suddenly cracked the point of Dougal's chin, throwing his head back and scattering stars across the ceiling of the great hall. And then the world went black.

Transfixed by the silvery swell of the sea, Feiyan gripped the rusty bars of her prison. She scanned the beach for something more useful than the swooping seagulls and the wee crabs that scuttled across the sand.

If she could find someone—anyone—willing to take a message to Rivenloch at Ayr for a sizable reward, perhaps she could prevent all-out war.

But the narrow stretch of beach visible from this end of the cave was empty. And her calls for help were swallowed by the fog.

Suddenly, between the hissing surges of waves, she heard a noise from the back of the cave. She half-turned to hear better.

Someone was coming.

Was it Merraid again? Had she reconsidered her decision to abandon Feiyan? Or had the Fortanachs come to drag her out for some dark purpose?

Whoever made their way through the passage, it was with a great deal of grumbling and stumbling. If she could feel her way in the dark to the entrance, perhaps in the confusion she could slip out the gate.

The twitching light of a torch signaled someone's arrival. She melted back against the rock wall, out of sight. But she was too far from the entrance when the key rattled in the lock and the gate scraped and creaked open.

Before she could rush forward, she heard a muffled bark, a scrabbling that sounded like a struggle, then the dull thud of something heavy hitting the sand. By the time she eased forward out of the shadows, the echoing bang of iron on iron told her the gate had been slammed shut again.

The torchlight flickered and waned as the gaolers left, leaving her in utter darkness again. But this time she was not alone. She heard ragged breathing.

"Who's there?" she ventured.

There was no response. But Feiyan wasn't afraid. Whoever was in the cave with her was imprisoned just as she was. And a possible ally in an escape attempt.

"Are you hurt?" she asked.

No answer.

"Merraid?" she tried, creeping cautiously forward, inch by inch. "Campbell?" She hunkered down beside the silent form. "Are you all right? Are you injured?"

When there was no answer, she reached out to jostle the body. Gently at first, then with more force.

A loud rasp of breath alerted Feiyan that her fellow prisoner had roused. "Feiyan."

Her heart skipped at the familiar voice. "Dougal? What are you doing here?"

"I've come to save ye."

The great wave of pleasure and relief that had washed over her at the sound of his voice crashed and fizzled when she realized he was in no position to save her. The fact that he'd been thrown into this prison with her was proof he'd failed to defeat his brother.

Dougal was exactly where he meant to be.

He'd known—after his outburst in the great hall, standing up to his brother and the Fortanachs, announcing their crimes before half the clan, giving the laird's minions a verbal smack in the face—Gaufrid would have no choice but to imprison him.

"Are ye hurt?" he asked, pushing himself up from the floor. "If anyone's raised a hand to—"

"Me?" She sounded incredulous. "I'm fine. But what about you?"

"I'll live."

"What's happened? Why did you come to Darragh?" Her disbelief was beginning to wear off. Now she sounded peeved. "God's eyes, you could have been killed."

"But I wasn't."

"But you *could* have been. Bloody fool. I suppose you marched in, all full of outrage and honor."

"I did."

"And you threatened your brother, face to face, with his crimes?"

"Aye."

"And you expected he'd confess and concede to your greater wisdom?"

"Gaufrid? Nay. He'd ne'er do that."

"Then how did you...?" she sputtered. "Why did you...?"

"I had to see for myself that ye were safe." He found her hand, enclosing her fingers in a clasp of reassurance. "After all, I can't let harm come to my bride."

"Your bride?"

"Aye," he murmured, his heart in her hands, "if ye'll have me."

She was silent for so long after that, he feared he'd made a mistake. Misjudged her affections. Lost respect in her eyes. He wished he could see her face. See whether she was stewing in indecision. Laughing in mockery. Or weeping in happy relief.

"Well, I don't know," she hedged. "I'm not sure 'tis wise to tie my fortunes to a stubborn man who refuses to take my obviously superior advice."

His mouth eased into a grin. "I'll remind ye, your obviously superior advice landed ye in this gaol."

She sighed.

"Besides, I *did* take your advice," he protested. "'Twas trickery I employed to get my brother to toss me in here with ye."

"Trickery?" She sounded doubtful.

"Aye. Once I bellowed out his crimes for all the clan to hear, he had no choice but to put me here to shut me up."

"Clever," she admitted. "But now how do you propose we get out of here?"

"Ye're the stealthy one. I was hopin' ye'd tell me."

She sighed. "Come," she said, giving his hand a squeeze. "I've been tryin' to wave down someone along the shore."

He followed her, holding her hand.

As they fumbled their way through the cave, he said, "Ye should know your clan is on their way."

She stopped. "How do you know that?"

"I intercepted a pair o' them at the Ayr Arms. Your brother and cousin."

"You knew who they were?"

"They were ridin' my horse."

"Gellir and Adam stole your horse?"

"Well, to be fair, they bought him. Wait. How did ye know 'twas Gellir and Adam?" He frowned, answering his own question. "Ye saw them as well."

"That's why I had to leave. I needed to make certain we had mac Darragh allies on the inside before Rivenloch arrived."

He nodded. That made sense.

They continued along the passage.

"I only hope I did enough," she said. "I told Campbell to gather an army."

"He's already spread the word to the surroundin' villages."

"He has?"

"Aye," he said. "And he said ye met Merraid."

She let out a long breath. "Aye. You were right. She'll do anything for you."

He grimaced. "But cloutin' ye with a chamberpot? Why?"

"I suspect she was trying to keep Gaufrid and the Fortanachs from killing me outright before she could find out where you were."

"I'm grateful to her for that."

"Don't be too grateful. I made the mistake of trusting her. Once she found out who I was, she turned on me. She figured Rivenloch was holding you for ransom. So she convinced your brother to use me as a hostage to secure your return."

"She did? But Gaufrid would ne'er have made the exchange."

"That's what I told her."

"And?"

"She didn't believe me."

Dougal rubbed the back of his neck. "Gaufrid must mean to charge your clan a hefty price for your return."

"No doubt."

"Then we'll have to make his hostage vanish."

"How do we do that?"

"Haven't ye been sayin' all along ye know how to be invisible?"

Feiyan had never felt less invisible. Not because she'd been found out by Gaufrid. Not because she was about to be at the center of the battle to come. But because Dougal desired her.

He'd torn away her mask. Seen her at her most vengeful. Tasted the bitterness of her betrayal. And yet he'd returned.

He'd seen her flaws and foibles. Her drives and her stubbornness. She'd countered him at every turn. Usurped his authority. Lied to him. Abandoned him. Hell, she'd tried to assassinate him.

Still he saw her as a worthy woman. A lass who brought honor to Rivenloch. Victory to the King. And protection to Scotland.

But it was more than that. Dougal looked beyond her mask, revealing a lass she'd almost forgotten. A woman of passion and empathy. Of humor and heart.

The cave had grown light now as they neared the grate that faced the sea. He stopped and turned her towards him, giving her face a closer examination.

"Ye're certain they didn't hurt ye?"

She nodded and quirked up her lips in a crooked smile. "I didn't give them the chance."

He returned her smile. "Should I feel sorry for the Fortanachs?"

She arched a brow. "Possibly. The one who looks like a boar may never walk right. And the wolfish one's nose has been rearranged a bit."

The way he was staring at her mouth now made her heart flutter. There was a gentle hunger in his eyes. A sweet longing. His lips parted and his nostrils flared. When he drew in a deep breath of sea air, she sensed he was inhaling her scent as well.

A timid maid like Merraid would have lowered her gaze and blushed at the attention.

But Feiyan was hardly timid.

She thrust her free hand through his thick locks, catching the back of his neck and tilting his head down toward hers. When he sucked in a surprised breath, she covered his open mouth with a kiss.

CHAPTER 30

At the moment their lips touched, Feiyan felt the world disappear. The breeze caught strands of her hair and wrapped them around his face like a caress. The sounds of the sluicing tide and the screeing gulls receded, replaced by deep sighs of pleasure and soft moans of desire.

Had it only been hours since they'd joyfully quenched their lust in the barn and he'd fallen asleep in her arms? She was so ravenous for his touch, so eager for his body, it seemed like they'd been apart an eternity.

Her training as a warrior had made her a woman of strict discipline and control. Her every move was executed with purpose and intent. She's spent her life planning and practicing each step, each motion—meticulously, repeatedly—perfecting her attacks and defenses until they were as natural to her as breathing.

But this...this was unnatural. Making love with Dougal, she lost all sense of authority over her own body.

That should have frightened her.

Instead, it made her feel gloriously free.

Falling into his arms with unfettered abandon felt like diving into the sea itself.

She was rocked by waves of passion.

Tossed playfully about by the sensuous current.

Pulled under into the depths of desire.

In his embrace, she floated and swam and happily drowned.

She moved against him, delighting in his textures. The coarse stubble of his angled jaw against her cheek. The curl of his velvety locks around her fingers. The sleek muscle of his shoulder beneath her hand. The firm swelling against her belly.

He groaned as she pressed closer, and the sound awoke something primitive in her.

A sharp craving.

An intense need.

An undeniable imperative.

She deepened the kiss, opening his mouth with hers, letting her tongue swirl into his delicious recesses. His breath flowed into hers, warm and luscious and eager.

When his tongue whirled over hers in return, retreating and delving between her lips, his pulses were so evocative that she felt a white-hot current sear through her veins, jolting her to life with secret fire.

Gasping against his throat, she turned one hand to let it slide down his chest and over his abdomen. Seeking and finding the splendid bulge below his belt, she pressed her palm against him.

His response was half a grunt of victory and half a sigh of defeat.

But her gentle laugh of triumph quickly evolved into a helpless sob when he slid his fingers over her throbbing neck, descended to stroke the delicate flesh of her bosom, and slipped beneath her leine. His fingertips teased the top of her breast until she thought she would go mad with longing, and she arched toward his hand, aching with need.

With a low chuckle that made her ears hum, he brushed her nipple with his thumb, stealing her breath and sending sizzling sparks through her body.

Breaking the seal of their kiss, he moved his lips across her cheek and along her jaw, breathing flame upon her throat where her pulse raced.

She closed her eyes, collapsing against him as ecstasy washed over her like a powerful ocean wave.

Then she stiffened in alarm.

She wasn't sure what alerted her.

A sixth sense?

Her warrior training?

A survival instinct?

Somehow, in the midst of a sea of sense-stealing rapture, Feiyan suddenly felt, by the prickling at the back of her neck, they were not alone.

Someone was watching them.

Even as she reveled in the heaven of Dougal's hand fondling her breast and his lips burning a trail along her throat, she found the presence of mind to slip open the corner of one eye.

She only peeked for an instant. But that was all it took.

On the sand just beyond the iron grate, framed like a bright orange flower in the opening between the cave and the sea, stood Merraid. Wide-eyed and gape-jawed with shock and hurt and betrayal.

By the time Feiyan broke off the kiss to push away from Dougal and slipped the leine back up over her shoulder, it was too late.

Merraid had seen enough. She was already stumbling in abashed retreat. Blinking at Dougal in mortification. Turning as scarlet as a boiled crab.

Dougal was too busy frowning at Feiyan's abrupt rejection to notice Merraid.

Thinking fast, Feiyan whispered to him, "Push me away."

"What?"

"Do it," she begged. "Hurry."

When he stubbornly clamped his jaw shut, refusing to honor such a strange request, she was forced to take matters into her own hands.

Rearing back her arm, she cracked him across the face with a ringing slap that echoed in the cave.

"Don't you dare mention that maidservant's name again," she snarled. "She betrayed me. She betrayed *you*."

"God's eyes," he cried in surprise, cradling his offended cheek. "What are ye talkin' about? What maidservant?"

Feiyan scowled. "Who do you think?" She jabbed him in the gut, not too hard, just enough to get a decent cough out of him. "Merraid doesn't love you, you know," she sneered. "In fact, she hates you."

Dougal looked sick and confused as he clutched his belly. "What the devil has gotten—"

"She intends to turn you o'er to your murderous brother."

"Merraid?" he squeaked.

"She means to see you hang."

"What?"

Finally prompted to action by Feiyan's accusations, Merraid rushed forward and wrapped desperate fingers around the bars of the grate.

"'Tisn't true, Dougal. Don't listen to her," she pleaded.

Dougal's brows rose. "Merraid?" He blinked in astonishment, probably wondering how the maidservant had materialized so quickly.

"She's lyin'," Merraid told him, "I swear."

"Merraid!" he beamed, suddenly realizing Merraid could help them. "Och, lass, ye're just in time."

Merraid shot Feiyan a smoldering glare. "Just in time to save ye from this wench's connivin', 'twould seem."

Feiyan sniffed, crossed her arms, and leaned back against the wall.

Dougal glanced at Feiyan. It took him a moment to catch

on, but he finally gave her a subtle wink to let her know he understood her game.

He stepped forward to meet Merraid. He gripped the iron bars of the grate, letting the tip of his finger touch Merraid's.

The gesture wasn't lost on Merraid, whose eyes slipped briefly to the point where their fingers met. The soft sigh she released would have driven anyone but Feiyan into a jealous rage.

But Feiyan wasn't the jealous sort. Especially of a lovestruck young lass whose burgeoning affections were as changeable as the wind.

"'Tisn't true, is it?" Dougal murmured to the lass, furrowing his brows in concern. "Ye don't want to see me hang?"

Feiyan twitched back a smile at his tactics. She and Dougal *were* good partners. And Merraid was about to be wrapped around that finger of his.

"Och, m'laird," Merraid gushed, giving him the title he'd not yet earned, "not in a hundred years. 'Twould break my heart."

"Then will ye help me?"

"'Tis what I came to do, before..." She gave Feiyan another withering look.

"She means naught to me," Dougal muttered dismissively. "I was only plyin' her for information."

Feiyan stiffened. She might not be the jealous sort. But he didn't have to lay his lies on with such conviction.

Merraid's face brightened. "Och. Aye. O' course."

"So ye've come to help?" he reminded her.

She nodded. "I heard what ye said in the great hall. Is it true? Did Laird Gaufrid burn the church?"

"He had the Fortanach brothers do it."

"The Fortanachs." Her brow creased. "So they're not to be trusted?"

"Right."

She worried her lip between her teeth. "Because I told them..." She cast Feiyan a sideways glance and lowered her voice to a whisper. "I told them who she was...so they could ransom ye."

"Aye. So I heard."

"But now that ye're back..." She slipped her gaze to Feiyan again. "What will they do with her? Sweet Mary. They won't kill her, will they? I don't want to be the cause of anyone's death."

Dougal shook his head. "They no doubt mean to ransom her for coin."

"Will Rivenloch pay?" she wondered.

"I don't know."

Merraid's brow clouded. "I wish I'd ne'er told them." Her glance at Feiyan was softer this time. "I'm sorry, m'lady."

"Ye can make amends for that," Dougal told her. "Ye can help us."

"How?"

"Open the gate," Feiyan replied. "Let us out."

"Nay," Dougal said. "They'll see we're gone. And they'll know who let us go."

Feiyan nodded. "What then?"

Dougal paced, rubbing his cheek, which still stung from Feiyan's all too enthusiastic slap. After a moment, he decided, "I need ye to gather flowers."

"What?" Feiyan and Merraid said in unison.

"There are flowers in the field near the castle gates, aye?"

"Aye, but—"

"I need ye to gather flowers there," he said.

Their replies were simultaneous again.

Merraid said, "What kind o' flowers?"

Feiyan said, "What the hell...?"

"It doesn't matter what kind. I need ye to keep an eye on the road."

"All right," Merraid said.

"For what?" Feiyan asked.

"Two young men who followed me from the Ayr Arms."

He hoped he was right about that. Hoped he could count on the stubborn, rebellious nature of the Rivenloch lads.

Despite Adam vehemently disapproving of leaving his sister's rescue in Dougal's hands, Gellir had been suspiciously eager to capitulate to Dougal's wishes. If they were as deceitful as Feiyan, they hadn't capitulated at all. They were on their way here.

"I need ye to give them a message," he said. "Can ye do that?"

Merraid nodded. "What message?"

"What young men?" Feiyan asked.

"Gellir and Adam."

"What?" Feiyan blurted. "They're coming here?"

"I'm fairly certain they are."

"Alone?" Fear flickered briefly in her eyes, like lightning in a summer storm. "You told them to come alone?"

"I told them *not* to come," he said. "But I've learned that followin' orders is discretionary in the Rivenloch clan."

Feiyan sighed, but couldn't argue the point. "They'll likely come in disguise."

"Will they?" he asked. Then he frowned. "Hopefully not as the king again."

"What?"

"Naught," he said, shaking his head. God willing, there would be time to swap stories later. "Perhaps ye can describe the lads for Merraid?"

While Feiyan gave Merraid a detailed description, including several of Adam's favorite disguises, Dougal formulated a plan of attack.

It wouldn't be easy. He had to take into account the

ruthlessness of Gaufrid's mercenaries. The magnitude of Rivenloch's forces. And the vulnerability of the mac Darragh clan folk who would take Dougal's side in the battle to come.

But he had an idea. There were things about the castle Gaufrid didn't know. Secrets his brother had never shown an interest in. While Gaufrid wasted his childhood, Dougal had spent a lifetime shadowing their father, learning the names and faces of the clan and memorizing every nook and cranny of the keep.

Gaufrid might have known about the stairs leading from the ale cellar to the storage chamber, which he'd turned into a gaol.

But he was probably unaware of the *second* secret passageway—the one that led from the back of the buttery to the brink of the firth. And that could be the chink in his armor.

CHAPTER 31

Gellir wasn't pleased with his disguise. Not as pleased as he'd been as the King of Scotland. But Adam had done the best he could with what was available.

As he hobbled along in the tabard and cloak Adam had ripped to shreds and coated in filth, leaning heavily on his makeshift crutch, he wondered how angry his mother would be when she saw what had been done to his finery.

"Are you sure this is going to work?" he mumbled to Adam as they approached the well-guarded keep.

"All we need to do is get inside and stay unseen," Adam said, pulling his own hood farther over his grime-encrusted face. "Keep your face covered, and don't bark out any commands, and you'll be fine."

"I don't bark out commands."

Adam arched a brow at him that said otherwise.

"We're rat-catchers," Adam explained. "One step above a gong farmer. So stoop a bit, keep your head down, look no one in the eye, and, if we're lucky, we'll be given a bit of cheese for our trouble."

"Good," Gellir said as his belly growled. "I'm hungrier than a nun in Lent."

It was his own fault. They'd walked most of the day to get here. But when Adam had suggested they might trade the jewels in Dougal's dagger for food, Gellir had told him it wouldn't be right to trade away the possessions of a man who meant to wed his sister.

Of course, that had started a fight. Adam didn't want to think about his sister marrying...anyone, he supposed. That was understandable. Brothers didn't like to think of their sisters as objects of desire. Gellir hadn't been exactly thrilled when their Highland hostage began courting his sister Hallie.

Now, of course, Hallie's husband and he were best of friends, as well as brothers-in-law. Colban an Curaidh had turned out to be worthy of the title of champion.

Whether Dougal mac Darragh was deserving of Gellir's respect remained to be seen. He supposed he'd find out once they made it into the keep.

The sun was lowering, casting a golden glow over the green field in front of the castle. A few stragglers were making their way inside the gates before sunset. An old woman with a flock of geese. A lad lugging a cart of sod. A pair of maids bearing full milk pails. Gellir and Adam walked in their midst, trying to blend in.

As they approached, Gellir squinted up at the guards posted at the gates. They looked rough. He was glad Adam and he hadn't arrived after dark. It wasn't that Gellir couldn't have singlehandedly fought his way through them. But that would have given away their rat-catcher ploy.

"Adam?" some lass hissed. "Are ye Adam?"

Gellir kept walking. Nobody knew them here. She must be addressing another Adam. There was no reason to...

"Aye," Adam said, stopping. "I'm Adam."

Gellir frowned, pulling his hood farther over his face. "Come on," he growled. "We're going to be late."

"And ye must be Gellir?" she asked.

Gellir froze. Shite. They'd almost made it to the front gates.

"Aye, that's Gellir," Adam said.

Gellir fired a frosty glare, first at his cousin, then at the meddling lass—a freckle-faced, orange-haired runt of a thing with a basket of flowers and eyes as round and blue as a robin's egg.

She studied Adam's clothing. "So what are ye supposed to be? Turnbrochies?"

"Rat-catchers," Adam said.

She nodded. "I have an urgent message for ye," she whispered to Adam. "'Tis from Dougal mac..."

She stopped abruptly when she looked up at Gellir.

He wasn't surprised by her silence. His grim scowl often had a chilling effect. He found it quite useful. Sometimes he could stare down an opponent without even drawing his sword.

In this case, however, the maid wasn't cowering in fear. She seemed stunned with wonder, as if he were a curious creature she'd never seen before.

And then, as he continued to glower from the shadow of his hood, her face transformed. Her lips parted. Her cheeks flushed. Her eyelids dipped, and her eyes took on a dreamy cast, as if she'd grown suddenly sleepy.

His frown deepened. He sighed.

He wasn't stupid. He knew that look. He'd seen it on the faces of his little sister's friends. It was the look he'd been getting recently from every muddleheaded female at Rivenloch who wore her heart on her sleeve.

His father said it was because of his handsome Cameliard looks.

His mother said it was because he had the heart of a champion.

All Gellir knew was it made him uneasy.

He supposed it wasn't the maid's fault. Her condition seemed to afflict every lass he'd met of late.

"An urgent message?" Adam prompted, irritated by the delay.

"Wait," Gellir realized. "How did Dougal know we were coming?"

The lass gave him a shy smile. "He said he told ye not to...and that ye weren't much for followin' orders." Somehow she made it sound like a compliment.

"So what's the message?" Adam repeated, snapping his fingers in front of the dazed maid's face to get her attention.

She blinked, turning her focus to Adam. "Oh. He wants ye to know your sister is safe."

"My sister. Where is she?"

"She's in the *dùn mara.*"

"What's that?"

"'Tis a...gaol o' sorts."

"What?" Adam exploded, drawing attention from the passersby.

Gellir gave him a chiding cuff on the arm.

"What?" Adam repeated under his breath. "She's in a gaol? How can she be safe if she's in a gaol?"

But Gellir's mind was racing ahead. "Then where's Dougal?"

"He's in the *dùn mara* as well."

Gellir shook his head. "Well, that's lovely. 'Tis a good thing we came, Adam."

"Is that it? Is that the message? My sister is safe? In a gaol?"

"Dougal said he needs your help," the lass said.

"Does he?" Adam's sarcasm was as thick as butter.

"What does he want us to do?" Gellir asked.

"Follow me," she said. "I'll get ye inside the keep."

"And then what?" Adam asked. "Will they throw us in the gaol as well?"

Gellir could see Adam's harsh words were bruising the maid's feelings. He swatted Adam's arm to hush him. "What's Dougal's plan?"

"He said your army is on its way."

"Aye."

"He fears his brother will do somethin' reckless if Rivenloch attacks."

"His brother?" Adam asked.

"The Laird o' mac Darragh," she said.

"Something reckless?" Gellir said. "Like what?"

Adam's face darkened. "Like hurtin' Feiyan."

The maid nodded.

"So what do we do?" Gellir asked.

"He said ye must steal in," she said.

"We *are* stealing in," Adam said. "Or at least we *were* until you hailed us."

"Your whole army must steal in," she said.

"Our whole army?" Adam said. "'Tisn't possible."

"'Tis," she said. "If ye follow me. I'll show ye how."

With the lass to guide them, they passed through the gates without incident, mingling with the clan folk, and crossed the courtyard. But when they entered the great hall, they caught the eye of a pair of nobles drinking by the hearth.

Gellir watched the men from the shadows of his hood. They finished off their cups and made their way toward the lass. The skinny one had a swollen nose. The one with piggish eyes was limping.

"Who's this?" the pig-man snorted, giving Adam and Gellir a derisory glance.

"Rat-catchers," the lass said. "I'm takin' them to the buttery."

The skinny one grimaced and spit on the floor. "Rats."

"When ye're finished," the pig said to the lass, licking his greasy lips, "come up to the laird's chamber. We mean to thank ye properly for your good deed today."

The maid gulped, but managed a feeble smile. "There's no need to thank me."

"Nonsense," the skinny one said with a smirk. "We insist."

Gellir's stomach churned. What this pair of brutes meant to thank the maid for, he didn't know. But there was little doubt what they intended. And little doubt that the lass didn't want any part of it.

What he knew about swiving would fit in a thimble. But he'd been taught early on about consent. And he had no intention of leaving the lass to these wolves.

"We'll be waitin'," the pig said.

When they'd gone, Adam whispered, "What was that about?"

The maid was quick to dismiss him. "Naught. Come. This way."

The buttery was cool, dark, and deserted. The lass took a torch from the wall and led them to the back of the deep chamber. What appeared to be a wall cleverly concealed a set of stone steps.

"'Tis a secret passageway," she explained. "It leads from the castle down through the cliff wall to the seashore below."

"Brilliant," Adam breathed.

"And from the seashore up to the castle," Gellir realized.

"Right," she said.

Gellir's mind raced ahead. If there was a secret way into the castle, the army of Rivenloch could attack from inside the keep. The only problem was, judging by the size of the steps, they'd have to enter in a single line. It would be hard to launch an offensive when they could be picked off by enemy soldiers as they entered.

"Does Gaufrid know about this?" Gellir asked.

"Nay. Dougal said he's ne'er used it."

Lighting the way with her torch, the maidservant led them down stairs carved into solid rock. A few hundred steps later, they landed on sandy ground.

A diagonal crack in the rock let in a lance of sunlight that bisected a small cave. Shielding his eyes with his arm, Gellir blinked against the brightness of the setting sun as he moved toward the opening.

"'Tis a tight passage," Adam said.

"'Twill be tricky," Gellir agreed. A broad-shouldered warrior would have to turn sideways and lie back against one surface to pass through rock that was two yards thick. "But it can be done." Still they'd be reduced to squeezing through one at a time, hardly the ideal model for a surprise attack.

"How will they get to the beach unseen?" Adam asked.

"There's a landin' to the north, around the point," the lass said. "The ground there slopes to the shore. When the tide is low, ye can pass around the end o' the point to the beach below the castle."

Gellir grumbled. This plan was beginning to sound complicated.

Unlike Adam and his sister, Gellir wasn't fond of clandestine schemes and clever disguises. True, it had been useful to don the crown of royalty for the convenience of free lodging. And feigning to be rat-catchers had earned them passage into Castle Darragh. But sneaking an entire army into an enemy castle seemed impossible.

"What if they're spotted on the shore?" he wondered. "What if they're trapped at high tide? Where will they assemble? And how will they attack?"

"Dougal has a plan," the lass said, holding the torch aloft and picking up her skirts to climb the steps again. "Come. We must hurry."

"Now where are we going?" Adam asked.

"Ye want to see your sister, aye?"

Adam came to her heel faster than a well-trained hound.

They were out of breath by the time they emerged

again in the buttery, and the sight of the cheeses on the buttery shelves made Gellir's stomach growl.

The lass stifled a grin and handed him a small round of ruayn.

He thanked her and split the cheese with Adam.

While they ate, she grabbed a wooden tray and began loading it up with cheese and smoked fish.

"Come," she said. "The passage to the *dùn mara* is across the great hall."

She started forward, and Gellir caught her arm. "Wait. Let me."

He had no intention of letting that pair of brutish knaves get their hands—or even set their eyes—on the maid. He peered out of the doorway. Seeing no sign of the beasts, he motioned her forward.

She crossed the hall and led them to another hidden passageway. This one was carved into the back of the ale cellar. She handed a jug of ale to Adam to carry, took a large iron key from a hook on the wall, and beckoned them to follow her.

Gellir handled the torch this time as they descended dozens upon dozens of damp steps.

When they reached the iron gate at the entrance of the *dùn mara,* Gellir shivered. The dank, weepy walls, so deep beneath the keep, were shrouded in shadow, making the empty cell look as foreboding as a grave. He was suddenly glad Feiyan wasn't alone here.

"Dougal," the maid called out. "Are ye there?" She turned the key in the lock of the gate. "I've brought supper."

As soon as it was unlocked, Adam threw open the gate and called out, "Feiyan!"

"Adam?" came a faint reply. "Is that you?"

Moments later, brother and sister came together in an enthusiastic embrace.

Meanwhile, Gellir acknowledged Dougal with a cool nod.

"I thought ye'd come," Dougal told him.

Gellir smirked. "Rivenlochs ne'er leave clan warriors behind."

"So I've heard."

"Come with us now, Feiyan," Adam pleaded.

"I can't," Feiyan said.

"What do you mean? We have the key. We can slip out the gates, join the warriors, and return to Rivenloch. All you have to do is—"

"Nay," Feiyan said, casting an appreciative glance at Dougal. "I mean to win the castle back for its rightful laird."

Dougal shot her a look of earnest gratitude. Then he told them, "But we could use your help." He quickly scanned Gellir from head to toe. "Aye, I think ye'll do."

It was a mad scheme, this plan of Dougal mac Darragh's. Gellir didn't like it. Not at all. He was a skilled warrior, accustomed to being in the thick of battle. It seemed a waste of his talents to be relegated to the position of a useful but powerless pawn.

But since the ploy might save Feiyan, and since that orange-headed, dewy-eyed maid was fawning over him for his bravery, how could he refuse?

Still, he experienced an unsettling shiver of apprehension when Dougal pulled the hood of Gellir's cloak over his mud-smudged face to head up the steps after Adam, leaving Gellir to take his place in the gaol. He wasn't meant to be caged like an animal. Trapped here, he would be helpless to defend anyone.

As the maidservant turned the key in the lock, Gellir caught her sleeve.

Her quick intake of breath made him instantly release her again, though something in her face said she wished he hadn't.

"Those two men upstairs who spoke to you," he murmured. "Who are they?"

"N-nobody." She lowered her eyes.

"Don't go to them," he entreated.

"I'm a servant," she mumbled. "I don't have a choice."

He clenched his jaw. "You *always* have a choice." He could see his emphatic tone frightened her, so he softened his voice. "What's your name?"

"Merraid."

"Merraid," he repeated. "How old are ye, Merraid?"

"Ten and five."

He bit out an oath that made her flinch. What kind of monsters bedded a wide-eyed lass half their age? The thought sickened him, making him want to drive a dagger through their hearts.

"They're swine," he said. "They mean you nothing but harm. You stay clear of them. Promise me. *Promise* me."

She looked at him now with a dazzled sort of adoration, as if he'd asked her to promise him her heart. "I promise."

"Good." He nodded, satisfied. "Because I can't carry off this deceit if I'm fretting over what might be happening to you."

She gave him a wobbly smile, a smile that would sustain him over the long and frustrating night ahead.

CHAPTER 32

"**W**ait!" Fergus called out from the hearth as the pair of filthy rat-catchers slunk toward the doors of the great hall. "Where are ye goin'?"

They froze.

The short one bobbed his head and replied, "We're all finished, sir."

"Ye're sure ye got them all?" Morris asked.

"Och aye," the lad replied, hefting up a hemp bag as proof. "Quicker than cats we are."

"Because if I spot a single rat..." Morris threatened.

"Och nay, sir."

"Where's the redheaded lass gone?" Fergus asked.

The lad shrugged. "She bade us get rid of these straightaway."

Fergus squinted at the tall rat-catcher, the one who wasn't speaking. "What's wrong with him?"

Fergus saw the man's shoulders tense.

"He's a mute," the short one said.

Fergus frowned. Perhaps that explained the disquiet he felt, looking at the shrouded rat-catcher. He seemed different somehow, more threatening. But then Fergus had never gotten a good look at the man to begin with, since his face was hidden by that tattered hood.

After a long scowl, he waved them away.

He had more pressing matters to attend to, beginning with finding the wayward maidservant who'd given them the slip.

Laird Gaufrid was still at the high table, slumped over his pottage. He'd drunk himself into a stupor. Which was fine with Fergus. Gaufrid was much easier to manage when he was soused.

When it came to negotiating with Rivenloch over the hostage, Fergus didn't intend to let Gaufrid's cowardice, petulance, and childish pride get in the way of what had to be said.

That was why Fergus had had to take that business at Kirkoswald into his own hands. Left to his own devices, Gaufrid would have made a mess of things. Lacking ambition, the laird didn't have the nerve or the guts to do what needed to be done.

But Fergus and Morris were made of sterner stuff. They'd survived exile, after all. Forged a new life for themselves. Gathered a ferocious army around them.

And when the time came to demand ransom, Fergus intended to make the border clan pay, one way or another. Rivenloch would either reward Darragh with a chest full of silver, or he'd force them to watch while he took pleasure in killing their high-and-mighty warrior maid.

If they chose to wage war, Fergus was confident his ruthless mercenaries would make minced meat out of the self-righteous Rivenloch clan.

Afterwards, he'd murder Gaufrid's meddlesome brother himself and declare Dougal an unfortunate casualty of battle.

Feiyan and Gellir huddled together for warmth as they peered out the grate of the *dùn mara* toward the beach.

The sky was black. The air was clammy with sea spray. It was too cold to sleep.

Not that she could have slept. She was too busy watching for signs of the advancing Rivenloch army to doze.

"You're sure about this Highlander, cousin?" Gellir murmured.

"You don't trust him."

"He did try to kill half our clan."

"'Twas a mistake. A false banner."

"But he took you captive."

"Only when I tried to assassinate him."

"And now he's managed to lock up *two* hostages."

"We're not hostages," she protested.

"Aren't we?" he said, shaking the imprisoning iron bars. "What if he doesn't come back? What if his plan doesn't work? What if he fails?"

She frowned. "He's not going to fail."

"You only say that because you're in love with him."

She gave him a chiding punch in the arm. But his words shook her faith like a battering ram rattling a door.

Was it true? Had she wanted to believe in Dougal so much that she'd acted foolishly, entrusting him to carry out a dangerous plan while she and her cousin languished helplessly in a prison?

She gazed in silence toward the endless, empty black, searching for a rushlight, straining to hear the telltale rustle of chain mail. But all she saw was the rare shimmer of a wave when the moon's round face peeked out from the clouds. All she heard was the sound of waves slapping and pounding and hissing upon the shore as they scoured the sand.

Time dragged on and on with no sign of Rivenloch. Soon they were both shuddering with cold.

"We should go back where 'tis warm," she finally decided.

"What if they don't come?"

She answered him with an optimism she didn't feel. "They may already be here. You know Laird Deirdre. When the army arrives, no one will see them coming. Not even us."

Yet even after they retreated farther into the comforting warmth of the cave, Feiyan's thoughts were slowly poisoned by doubt. What if she *had* been wrong to trust Dougal with such a clandestine operation? Sneaking the forces of Rivenloch into the keep required deception and stealth. Neither were Dougal's strong points. And he'd never explained how he meant to hide an entire army under Gaufrid's nose.

What if his plan didn't work? What if he was unable to contact Rivenloch? What if he couldn't convince Laird Deirdre of the truth? What would happen if Gaufrid discovered he could demand ransom for not *one* Rivenloch hostage, but *two?*

Dougal might fail. And if he did—if Laird Deirdre was put in the unthinkable position of having to ransom both Feiyan and Gellir...

Feiyan didn't think she could live with the shame.

It was bad enough that she'd never measured up to her illustrious cousins. That she'd failed in her impulsive assassination attempt. That she'd caused her clan to march over a hundred miles to come to her rescue.

But to think that the laird might be forced to drain the Rivenloch coffers for her return...

These troubling thoughts kept her awake, staring sightlessly at the bleak cave walls long after Gellir dozed off.

Far past midnight, she finally fell into a fitful sleep. Her slumber was riddled with nightmares of disappointment, dishonor, and disgrace.

When the guards came for her, it was impossible to tell what time of day it was and how long she'd slept. But she awoke with a gasp as ragged as the harsh grating of the prison door. She sat up, blinking raw and gritty eyes against the torch light. She instinctively patted her hip, searching for her missing *duandao*.

"On your feet, wench," someone growled.

"Where are you taking her?" Gellir demanded from the shadows.

They didn't answer.

She straightened, quickly assessing the situation. There were three guards. The one holding the torch had a scar down his cheek. The two behind him wore hoods. One was burly. One was tall. If they were unarmed...

"Where are you taking her?" Gellir asked more loudly.

"Just the wench," the one with the torch snarled, seizing her arm.

She reacted out of habit, levering her arm free. Then she made a grab for the torch.

But the guard was ready for her. He swept the torch out of reach. "Take her."

She could have overcome one guard, even unarmed.

Against two, she might have triumphed, given enough space to move.

Even three mercenaries weren't impossible to vanquish.

She got in a few good blows—slamming her elbow into ribs, driving her knuckles into a windpipe, and kicking at a shin. But eventually two of them trapped her arms. And when the third held a knife to her neck and his torch close to her face, she decided the best option was cooperation.

"Feiyan!" Gellir cried out.

"Stay back!" a guard barked.

"I'm fine," she said between her teeth as they muscled her forward.

"We'll come for *ye* later," one of the guards grumbled at Gellir, punctuating his dire promise by slamming the gate closed again.

They dragged her up the steps to the great hall, where mercenaries were buckling on armor and strapping on weapons, preparing for war.

She gulped. Had Rivenloch arrived? Was Laird Deirdre here? Where were they? Where was Dougal?

Dozens of servants scurried about, responding to the commands of the soldiers, offering bread and ale to break their fast.

For one brief moment, she spotted a head of marigold hair—Merraid rushing toward the ale cellar—but was unable to catch her eye before the guards hauled Feiyan across the hall and up more steps to the wall walk.

The sun was just peering above the horizon, casting cold morning light through the haze enveloping the keep. At the parapet's edge stood Laird Gaufrid, disheveled and drowsy-eyed. Flanking him were the Fortanach brothers, the plump boar and the lanky wolf. The boar's eyes glittered as he glared at her. The wolf sneered, his gaze flat and dull.

Gaufrid beckoned her near. The guards wrested her forward until she was pressed against the stone of the parapet.

Feiyan glanced down, and her heart sank.

Rivenloch hadn't made it into the keep after all. And now she saw why. Laird Deirdre had brought only a handful of mounted clan warriors with her. They were no match for the mercenary army of mac Darragh.

"Before we discuss your so-called mission of vengeance, Rivenloch," Gaufrid called down, clasping the back of Feiyan's neck in one viselike hand, "I may have somethin' of interest to ye."

Feiyan bit back a sob of humiliation and rage.

This was all her fault.

She had meant to distinguish herself in the eyes of the clan. But not like this. Not as a helpless hostage that the laird had to travel a hundred miles to ransom.

She'd intended to bring glory to her clan. To right the wrong done to them. To prove to them she was worthy of their respect and honor.

She'd planned to avenge the poor folk of Kirkoswald. To punish the villains who had sullied the name of Darragh. To help Dougal reclaim his legacy.

Instead, she'd disgraced her clan. Disappointed Dougal. And cost her laird time and coin.

It would have been better to remain invisible.

"Return her to us," Laird Deirdre intoned, "and swear never to return to Creagor, and we'll consider the matter settled."

Gaufrid laughed at that. "Return her? Just like that?"

"Give her back, and we'll withdraw our forces."

"Forces?" he scoffed. "What? All twelve o' ye?"

Feiyan fought to keep her chin up. It was obvious from the dearth of Rivenloch warriors that the laird didn't consider her worth fighting for.

"Nay," Gaufrid said smugly. "If ye want your warrior lass back in one piece, ye'll have to ransom her."

Gaufrid gestured to the hooded guard holding her. The brute wrapped a powerful arm around her waist and raised a dagger to her throat.

"And if I refuse to pay?" Laird Deirdre asked.

Feiyan bit her lip. Of course the laird would refuse to pay. One person was a reasonable sacrifice to make. The Warriors of Rivenloch hadn't earned their fearsome reputation by yielding to the demands of rogue clans.

Gaufrid, however, strangled on outrage at having his plans thwarted.

The pig of a Fortanach leaned close to Gaufrid to murmur, "Tell her ye'll slay the lass. We'll take their horses. They're probably worth more than the wench anyway."

Gaufrid thrust out his jaw. "I'll kill her," he promised. "I'll do it."

Feiyan choked on panic. Not for herself. Sacrificing herself for the clan was one thing. She'd caused this trouble. She'd pay the price. But once Gaufrid killed her, he wouldn't stop there. He'd go after her clansmen as well. And then Dougal.

"Run!" she blurted out. "He has dozens of mercenaries, m'laird! Save yourse-"

The guard restraining her gave her a sudden squeeze, cutting off her words.

"That's right," Gaufrid repeated. "If ye won't pay the price, ye'd better run. I'll kill her, and then my men will chase ye down and kill every last one o' ye."

To her relief, Laird Deirdre stood her ground. "I will not be threatened," she declared. "The Warriors of Rivenloch do not negotiate with outlaws."

"Fine then," Gaufrid said, giving the guard a nod.

Feiyan gasped.

The guard's restraining arm tensed around her waist. Then he bent close to her ear and muttered under his breath, "Be a good lass and die when I slash your throat."

Then he swept his arm swiftly and violently across her neck, and she felt cold steel slide across her flesh.

CHAPTER 33

Killing Feiyan was the hardest thing Dougal had ever done.

He hadn't really killed her, of course. He'd used the flat of the blade, ensuring that not a drop of her blood was spilled. There was no pain. No injury. Just a harmless caress of blunt steel.

But even that innocent gesture felt like drawing a dagger across his own heart.

Fortunately, the lass collapsed against him. Whether it was from his instructions or simply shock, her performance was convincing enough to inspire a chorus of astonished gasps from her clan folk. Indeed, so convincing was she, for a moment Dougal was unable to breathe.

Quickly, before Gaufrid had a chance to discover his hostage was alive and unharmed, Dougal gave a subtle nod to the Laird of Rivenloch.

On his cue, Laird Deirdre let out a cry of rage. "Forward!" she commanded. "Storm the gates!"

"They can't be serious," Gaufrid chortled as the Rivenlochs spurred their horses forward.

"Idiots," Morris sneered.

"Where do they think they're goin'?" Gaufrid said.

A moment later, as Rivenloch approached the gates,

Fergus assured Gaufrid, "No worries, m'laird. They won't get past the guard."

"Right," Morris agreed. "And if they do, they'll be met by a courtyard full o'—"

"Shite," Fergus muttered. "Shite!"

Dougal concealed a satisfied smile. Their scheme was working.

"How the devil did they get through the gates?" Morris wondered.

"Someone opened them," Fergus ground out.

"Who?" Gaufrid growled. "I'll murder the traitor."

Feiyan stiffened in Dougal's arms. He gave her a warning squeeze. It had to be torture for the lass, pretending to be dead, unable to see what was happening. But if Gaufrid saw that she was alive, she'd become a hostage in earnest, and the next guard tasked with slitting her throat would actually do it.

Despite the Laird of Rivenloch's virtuous speech about not negotiating with outlaws, Dougal knew from speaking with her last night—when he'd finally convinced her of his innocence and they'd come up with this daring plan—that Laird Deirdre would sacrifice all she owned before she'd let harm come to one of her clan. The Warriors of Rivenloch would fight to the death for Feiyan.

"Don't worry, m'laird," Morris said with confidence as he sauntered to the inner wall overlooking the courtyard. "An army's standin' ready for them in the yard."

Gaufrid joined him at the wall.

"See, m'laird?" Morris said. "The mercenaries are goin' to—"

Gaufrid, joining Morris at the wall, spat out a foul curse.

Morris echoed the curse.

Fergus shoved his way between them to see what was happening. A primal growl of frustration rolled up from his throat before he bit out, "Go."

With a spate of vile oaths, Gaufrid and his minions fled along the wall walk to the far end of the keep.

After they'd gone, Dougal whispered, "Ye can join the livin' now. 'Tis safe."

Feiyan opened her eyes in alarm and sprang back to life. "What's happening? My clan…"

"They're fine," he assured her. "Everythin's goin' accordin' to plan. Here." He reached inside his gambeson and handed her the dagger she'd lost.

She frowned down at it. "How did you…?"

"Adam retrieved it, searchin' for rats in Gaufrid's bed-chamber." She furrowed puzzled brows at that. But there was no time to explain. "Come on."

She flipped the dagger once in her hand, clearly eager to use it. "What do we do now?"

"The battle has begun," he said, nodding toward the yard below.

Her face fell as she peered down at the chaos in the courtyard. "Twelve of my clan against an army of mercenaries?"

"Not exactly." He threw back his hood and gave her a wink. "Follow me."

Fergus couldn't understand what had gone wrong.

How his perfect plans had gone to shite.

He'd wasted two years of his life kissing Gaufrid's arse while carefully keeping him under his thumb.

He'd proved his loyalty, incinerating an entire town under a false banner just to rid Gaufrid of his meddlesome brother.

He'd sent Dougal to certain death at the hands of the savage Rivenloch clan. And though the devil had inexplicably dodged that fate, Fergus had at least managed to lock him behind bars.

Fergus had assembled a host of mercenaries unlike any in the Highlands. An army to strike fear into the hearts of anyone who even thought of infiltrating Darragh. Bloodthirsty thugs, miscreants, and outlaws who wouldn't squirm when it came to ruthless slaughter.

He'd unmasked the pesky wench who'd followed Dougal home and managed to leverage her as a hostage against one of the richest border clans in all of Scotland. And even though Gaufrid had had to spill her blood when Rivenloch refused to ransom her, Fergus would still profit handsomely off their horses and armor, once they were defeated.

They *would* be defeated. They *had* to be.

Fergus was admittedly shaken by the fact that someone on the inside had let Rivenloch through the gates. Still, there were only a dozen enemy warriors. Darragh's forces numbered over a hundred. Defeating the piddling company should be child's play for his mercenaries.

Why then was he staring down at a bloody tangle of perplexing mayhem in the courtyard?

As he hurried along the perimeter of the wall walk with Gaufrid and Morris, insulated by burly guards at their fore and aft, he squinched his eyes at the pandemonium below.

And suddenly he saw it.

Servants who should have been cowering in corners, hiding inside the hall, hunkering down in the safe havens of the stables and storerooms, were instead pouring out of the keep to join the fray.

At first, he assumed it was some sort of spontaneous uprising. Weary of subservience, the peasants were apparently taking advantage of the attack on the keep to stage an overthrow.

Their efforts were doomed to fail, of course. They would die, as any untrained commoner would, on the blades of hardened soldiers, crushed by the boots of men who lived and breathed warfare.

But looking closer, he saw that was not the situation. And when he perceived the truth, it felt as if claws of ice clenched his heart.

The servants throwing back their hoods to join the fray looked like no peasants he'd seen before. If he'd given them a second glance, entering the great hall this morn, he might have noticed they were not the usual servants.

These men and women wore chain mail beneath their cloaks. They were broad-shouldered and tall in stature. They brandished, not the mallets of blacksmiths or the fire irons of kitchen lads, but the fine steel swords of seasoned warriors.

A half dozen, then a dozen, then more of the armored fighters unsheathed and engaged his mercenaries. Some wore grizzled beards. Some were beardless youths. Some were maids, as fierce and vicious as the men. They roared and charged, lunged and slashed, felling his knights as if they were pawns in a game of draughts.

"What's happened?" Gaufrid squeaked as they scurried toward the stairs at the remote end of the wall walk.

Fergus, too upset to explain, merely growled at the whimpering laird. "Just go!"

"Where are we goin'?" Morris asked.

"Down the stairs," Fergus snapped.

Where they would go after that, he didn't know. It was clear something had gone very wrong. Who the imposters were, he could guess. It had to be Rivenloch's forces that had infiltrated the ranks of the mac Darragh clan.

But how? And how many were there? Enough to overwhelm Gaufrid's army? Enough to seize the castle? If Rivenloch had managed to steal inside the keep, was the castle surrounded? Were there more of them lurking in the wood?

As they scrambled down the steps, he could hear

Gaufrid's petulant whining in the stairwell. "I'm not goin' a step farther until ye tell me what's happenin'."

Fergus suddenly felt in full force the months of sycophantic fawning he'd spent on the laird. All the compromising and placating. Enduring Gaufrid's tantrums. Easing his fears. Massaging his ego. Licking his damned boots.

It had all been for nothing.

And Fergus would suffer the fool no longer.

Elbowing his way down the steps to seize Gaufrid by the scruff of his neck, he slammed him back against the stone wall.

"Hear me well, ye pulin' churl!" he snarled, spittle gathering at the corners of his mouth. "'Tis o'er. Ye've lost your keep. Ye've lost your clan. If ye don't want to lose your life, I suggest ye keep your tongue in your head and obey my orders."

His threat worked. Gaufrid stared at him, wide-eyed, his mouth gaping like a landed trout's.

Sneering in disgust and releasing the laird like the rotten fish he was, he slipped down the last few steps and peered out carefully.

At the moment, the mercenaries were holding their own. They might have been caught with their braies down. But once they engaged in combat, they were like wild boars. Murderous and merciless.

Still, there was no way to tell how long they'd survive. Rivenloch was rumored to be the most ruthless and rabid border clan in Scotland. If anyone could cut down the mac Darragh army, it was these warmongering Lowlanders.

Even before he finished that thought, a mercenary came staggering across the sward to fall at Fergus's feet. The man clutched at his bleeding throat, then opened his maw in a silent scream as his eyes went glassy with death.

Fergus glanced past the fallen warrior. A lass with a long blond braid and a bloody sword nodded in icy satisfaction before wheeling to face her next foe.

Fergus shuddered, realizing Rivenloch's reputation was earned. There was no way mac Darragh would escape unscathed. He needed to concentrate on self-preservation.

"Come on!" he barked over his shoulder.

As Gaufrid sidled past the fallen mercenary, his mouth twisted in a grimace of disgust. Fergus felt a similar disgust for Gaufrid. The laird might have a taste for power, but he didn't have the stomach to do what it took to gain it.

Fergus and Morris did. They had always done what was necessary to better their lot. From whipping that upstart mac Giric bastard so many years ago to kissing the arse of this worthless laird to burning the church at Kirkoswald, they had done what needed to be done.

And so they would now. Even if it meant stealing what resources they could, cutting their losses, and surviving to fight another day.

He wouldn't give up on Castle Darragh. As long as he kept the laird alive, the keep belonged to Gaufrid. With Gaufrid in tow, Fergus and Morris could lie low for a while, bide their time, wait until Rivenloch left or grew careless, and return in triumph to take back what was rightfully theirs.

There was only one complication. They'd neglected to kill the rival laird. If Gaufrid left now, clan loyalty might swivel to Dougal. And that would be calamitous.

"Morris," Fergus muttered as they edged along the inside of the courtyard wall, well away from the chaos of clashing swords and bloody savagery. "Go now. Kill the prisoner."

Morris glanced at Gaufrid in concern. After all, the laird might have something to say about Morris murdering his brother in cold blood.

But the laird was too dumbfounded at the sight of a claymore-wielding Rivenloch warrior hacking the sword hand off one of his mercenaries to notice.

"Dougal?" Morris mouthed.

Fergus nodded.

Morris left to do his bidding, dodging his way across the courtyard to slip unseen through the doors of the keep.

Fergus tugged on Gaufrid's sleeve. They too had to get to safety. The pair of guards accompanying them had keen eyes and naked blades. They would defend the laird with their lives. But that didn't mean they were infallible.

Moving Gaufrid, however, wasn't easy. He seemed stupefied by the battle raging before him. He stood frozen in place—his eyes wide, his jaw slack—as his men fell, one by one, under the swords of the invading army.

"Come on, m'laird," Fergus snarled, wrenching at Gaufrid's elbow. "There's no time to waste."

Privately, Fergus entertained the idea of throwing Gaufrid into the fray to see how long he'd last, defenseless against the towering warriors and vicious vixens who would love to see the Laird of mac Darragh chopped to bits.

They were halfway around the courtyard, heading toward the keep when Morris burst out of the doors. He was red-faced, sweating, and out of breath.

"He's gone," he wheezed.

"What do ye mean?"

"He's not there."

"Are ye sure?" Fergus bit out the words as calmly as he could when he felt like screaming. "'Tis a large cave. Did ye look in the shadows and—"

"He's not there." His next words made Fergus's irritation congeal into icy fear. "The door was open. He's gone."

CHAPTER 34

When the wee maidservant came rushing down the steps to unlock the gaol door, Gellir was so glad to see her, he actually grabbed her by her orange-topped head and planted a quick kiss on her surprised brow.

After that, he couldn't get much out of the tongue-tied lass about what had happened. But as they wound their way back up the stairs, he managed to learn that Feiyan was safe and that the army of Rivenloch was fighting the mercenaries in the courtyard.

As soon as he emerged in the ale cellar, of course, he was eager to join the battle.

"If I only had a weapon," he despaired.

"Och!" Merraid exclaimed. "I forgot. Dougal left this for ye." She reached behind a barrel and dragged out a sword, handing it to him hilt-first.

Gellir grinned. "He's thought of everything." He swished the blade through the air, testing its balance. "I suppose I won't mind him marrying into my clan after all."

Merraid blinked. "Dougal? Marryin'?"

"Shhh," he whispered with a wink. "You didn't hear it from me."

She looked mildly stunned, but he didn't pay much heed. After all, there was a battle to wage, and if hotheaded

Hew had come, his cousin would need all the help he could get.

Still, he took her hand before he rushed off.

"You stay out of danger, aye? A wee lass like you could get hurt."

She nodded, and he pressed a chivalrous kiss on the back of her hand—one that left her speechless. Then he bowed in salute and turned to exit the ale cellar. Loping across the great hall, he gave the sword one last trial swing, and then burst out of the doors into the thick of battle.

The skirmish raged below while his cousin Jenefer and her archers stood on the wall walk, firing arrows down at the enemy.

In the midst of the courtyard, his mother Deirdre fought back-to-back with his sister Hallie as they fended off two mac Darragh mongrels.

Past them, Morgan mac Giric and Colban an Curaidh wielded claymores against a trio of warriors armed with axes.

Near the gates, his uncle Colin spun and slashed with catlike grace at a huge but clumsy mercenary.

Across the field, his father Pagan lunged and skewered a bellowing attacker who'd come at him with a war club.

Then Gellir spied Hew feverishly fighting a man built like an ox. Unbeknownst to his cousin, another giant was lumbering toward him with a mace.

"Nay!" Gellir cried, leaping from the steps and charging across the field to intercept the giant.

He got in several good blows and, between Hew and him, brought the Goliath to ground. After that, the battle continued until Gellir's brow dripped with sweat and his clothing was spotted with blood. Most of it had come from the enemy, though Gellir's lack of proper armor meant he earned several cuts and bruises.

When he glimpsed a pair of brutes stealing toward the Rivenloch archers on the wall walk, he raced up the stairs and singlehandedly fought them off. Colin and Morgan eventually joined him, hacking at the attackers. Hallie, arriving with a chilling slashes of her lightning-fast blade, sent one man leaping over the outer wall and another scrambling down the steps.

As the mercenaries scattered, Gellir gazed breathlessly at the courtyard below. Slinking furtively along the far wall was a small party of mac Darraghs.

"Where's he's going?" he wondered.

"Who?" Colban asked.

"Gaufrid, the Laird of mac Darragh."

"Coward," Hallie sneered. "He's fleeing. Who's that with him?"

"The Fortanachs," Gellir told her.

"The ones who implicated mac Giric with the false banner?" There was frost in Hallie's voice. She'd become especially protective of the clan, now that she'd married into it.

"Hold on," Morgan breathed, staring intently at the group skulking toward the keep. "I know them."

"You *know* them?" Hallie asked.

"Colban." Morgan nudged his friend. "Isn't that...?"

Colban narrowed his eyes. "It can't be."

"Their name isn't Fortanach," Morgan said.

"Fergus? And Morris?" Colban whispered. As if on reflex, he reached over his shoulder, touching his back, and gave a brief shudder.

"How do you know them?" Gellir asked.

"They were in my clan," Morgan told him. "They were mac Girics."

"Were?" Gellir said.

Colban had gone pale. "They were exiled."

"'Tis them, isn't it?" Though Hallie pressed a tender

hand on Colban's shoulder, there was a deadly chill in her tone. "The ones who...the ones who whipped you?"

Gellir had heard a bit of the story, though Hallie didn't like to talk about it. Her husband Colban, a bastard and an orphan, had been tormented as a child by a pair of older lads who thought he needed to be beaten into submission. They had been banished for their brutality. But Colban still bore the scars of their cruelty.

"They must have changed their name," Morgan realized, "and found safe harbor with a kindred spirit."

Suddenly, Gellir heard men charging up the steps. He turned away from the courtyard to greet them, raising his blade. Colban and Morgan followed his lead. But as they prepared to engage this new foe, he heard Hallie make a bone-chilling vow.

"Before the day is out, I mean to slay both of those villains."

"Are we going to hide in the buttery for the whole battle?" Feiyan asked Dougal.

At least they'd have plenty to eat, she thought, scanning the array of cheeses stacked on the shelves. But surely she could be of more assistance. Dougal had a claymore with him. If he could get her some sort of weapon, they could both join the fighting.

Before he could answer her about the buttery, she added, "What the devil did you say to convince Laird Deirdre to trust you? And how did she sneak the entire bloody army of Rivenloch into the castle? What happened to the servants? Where are Gellir and Adam? And tell me again why you had to kill me?"

Dougal had smuggled her past the guards and into the buttery under his hooded cloak. Now that they were safely out of sight, Feiyan had questions.

He replied, not with words, but with a blinding smile that took her breath away. And suddenly she didn't care about answers.

Once she gazed into his sapphire-blue eyes—eyes filled with relief and adoration—she melted into his arms. Sighing against his chest, she tipped back her head until their mouths met. The world glowed as they lingered over a kiss full of solace. And gratitude. And longing.

When they at last reluctantly drew apart, Dougal said, "Not the whole battle."

"What?"

"Ye asked me if we were goin' to hide in here for the whole battle."

"Oh. Aye." It seemed a distant memory.

"And as far as earnin' Laird Deirdre's trust," he said, "I didn't have to say much."

She raised a skeptical brow at that. "You attacked our clan. You nearly killed her daughter."

"Your brother Adam explained. Once he told her my actions had been the result of a false banner played against mac Giric, she understood. And when he told her ye had plans to marry me—"

"What?" Feiyan's heart dropped to the pit of her stomach. "You told her?"

"Adam told her."

She caught her lip under her teeth. How could her brother have betrayed her like that? This was a disaster. "I don't know how you do things in your clan, but in Rivenloch, we seek permission to wed. From the laird. And from the king." She closed her eyes and shook her head. "No wonder she wouldn't pay the ransom."

"Och, ye o' little faith," he scoffed. "She knew 'twas a deception."

"Are you sure?"

"O' course I'm sure. Don't ye realize it yet? Ye're a

precious gem in the crown o' Rivenloch, Feiyan la Nuit, no matter how invisible or expendable ye think ye are."

His words pleased her, even if they weren't true. They warmed her heart and flushed her cheeks.

"Indeed, 'twas your laird who insisted I had to kill ye," he added. "She didn't want Gaufrid to have any leverage over her when she invaded."

Feiyan nodded. She supposed that made sense.

"How did they do it? How did they get in?"

"There's a secret tunnel at the back of the buttery, just there," he said, gesturing with his head toward the place. "Last night, they climbed up from the beach. One by one, they traded clothing and replaced the servants."

"And no one noticed?"

He shook his head. "Gaufrid wouldn't recognize half the clan. The Fortanachs pay no heed to servants. And the mercenaries were asleep, restin' up for the battle to come."

"What happened to the real servants?"

"Some took refuge in the villages. The bravest remained. Most of them are waitin' in the woods, armed with scythes and hayforks."

Feiyan was impressed. For a man who preferred to meet his foe head-on, he'd managed a complex and brilliant deception.

"What about Adam and Gellir?" she asked.

"Adam the rat-catcher?" Dougal smiled. "He left last night after he collected the pointy-toothed 'rat' in Gaufrid's chamber." He nodded, indicating Feiyan's *bishou*. "As for Gellir, he's likely free by now."

"How?"

"I let him out," came a voice from the buttery entrance.

When Feiyan whirled and recognized Merraid, she took a judicious step away from Dougal. Merraid might only have a fleeting infatuation with the man Feiyan meant to marry, but it probably felt real to the lass. And if Merraid had freed Gellir, she owed the maid a measure of courtesy.

But Merraid swept into the room with a bright and dreamy smile. "Congratulations," she gushed.

Feiyan frowned, not understanding.

Merraid raised her brows. "On your weddin'?"

Feiyan scowled at Dougal. "Does everyone know?"

Dougal shrugged. "Thank ye," he said to Merraid. "So Gellir's safe?"

Merraid's melting gaze at the mention of Gellir's name told Feiyan everything she needed to know. No longer infatuated with Dougal, she'd obviously fallen prey to Gellir's charms, like so many lasses of late. Feiyan didn't understand it. To her, Gellir was her serious, sullen cousin who lived for battle and hated losing to a lass.

Then Merraid's gaze faltered. "I hope he's safe. I gave him the sword like ye asked," she said to Dougal. "He ran to the courtyard to join the fightin'."

Feiyan took pity on the worried maid. "Gellir will be fine. After all, he survived a bout with Dougal and lived to tell the tale."

Both of them lifted their brows at that. Dougal apparently didn't remember, but he'd attacked Gellir at the Creagor tournament.

"There's no one like Gellir with a sword in his hand," Feiyan said.

"Unless 'tis ye, m'lady," Dougal said. Then he turned to Merraid. "Were ye able to—".

"Och, aye!" Merraid exclaimed.

She lowered the satchel she'd been carrying, carefully emptying its contents onto the floor and unbuckled the belt fastened diagonally over her shoulder.

She'd brought the rest of Feiyan's weapons. Her *shoudao.* Her *duandao.* And her *sais.* And buckled across her back was Dougal's claymore, which Laird Deirdre had returned in good faith.

"Find him," Fergus snarled as he burst through the keep doors into the great hall. Snagging Gaufrid's upper arm to keep him securely at his side, he stabbed his finger at two of the guards. "Ye. And ye. Check the keep. He can't have gone far."

He scoured the great hall, which was teeming with servants. He cursed his own carelessness, which prevented him from being able to discern the real mac Darragh servants from possible Rivenloch warriors.

Then his gaze fell on the orange-headed lass stealing from the stairwell toward the buttery. That one he recognized. She'd been at the keep for a month at least. She was the one who'd told them their captive was a warrior maid of Rivenloch. He'd been intrigued by her fresh face and the rumor that redheads were as hot as fire between the linens. But the wayward lass had shunned his invitation to come to his bedchamber last night. And now she was creeping about like an outlaw.

She also had a key to the gaol, since she'd been taking meals to the prisoners. The satchel she was lugging might contain food. But what was buckled across her back was hardly provisions. It was a sword.

He could have stopped the maid with a shout. She might be a sly vixen, but she was also timid. One sharp bark from him, and she would have dropped her burden and likely wet her skirts.

But she was definitely going somewhere with that sword. And he could guess who she was taking it to. The meddling Dougal mac Darragh, whom she'd been swooning over for weeks. The man she'd undoubtedly just freed from the gaol.

Fergus's lip curled into a smile. The stupid wench was leading him right to his quarry.

He let her proceed. Once she ducked behind the buttery screens, he waved Morris forward and tugged Gaufrid along with him, motioning the laird to silence.

He had her cornered now. He had *both* of them cornered. The maid and her hero. He'd catch them unawares, before she had a chance to hand over the weapon. Then he'd get rid of the lass and take Gaufrid's brother prisoner. That was better than killing him anyway, in the event Gaufrid didn't survive.

That was his plan.

Unfortunately, when Fergus burst into the buttery, he didn't foresee coming face to face with a dead woman. A woman whose throat he'd just seen slashed.

His heart caught. His eyes widened in disbelief. The breath that scraped across Gaufrid's drunken throat at the sight of her was loud enough to wake the dead. And perhaps that was what he'd done. For before them, as whole and hale as ever, stood the lass that the Laird of Rivenloch had refused to ransom.

Unlike Gaufrid, Fergus didn't waste time trying to figure out how she was still alive. Instead, he wanted to make sure she stayed dead this time. Shoving the laird out of the way, he bolted forward and seized the sword belt out of the maidservant's hand. Unsheathing the blade, which he recognized as the curious sword he'd confiscated from her, he turned his attention to Dougal.

"Ye're comin' with us," he said, pointing the sword point at Dougal's belly.

"Nay!" the Rivenloch lass cried.

She dove toward the floor, where the satchel lay, its contents strewn on the stones. When she came up, she had steel forks in each hand.

CHAPTER 35

For one instant, it occurred to Feiyan to try the ploy her cousin had once used on her husband to frighten him away—feigning to be a ghost. But despite Gaufrid's gasp of fear at seeing her come back to life, the Fortanach brothers seemed to be the kind of men who believed in only what they could reach out and throttle.

So she used one of her *sais* to shove Fergus's weapon away from Dougal. With the other, she defended herself against Morris's dagger.

Dougal raised his claymore. But in the tight quarters of the buttery, he could do little with it.

While her *sais* was still tangled with Morris's dagger, Fergus came back at her with the *shoudao*. Fortunately, he didn't realize the sword was single-edged. The blow that struck her shoulder hit with the dull side, leaving a bruise, but not a cut.

She managed to catch the *shoudao* again. But as she attempted to break Fergus's blade between the tines of her *sais,* Morris thrust forward with a second dagger. Dodging just in time, she collided with the shelves, knocking several blocks of cheese to the floor.

Meanwhile, Dougal walloped Morris's head with the hilt of his claymore, distracting him. Feiyan dropped her *sais* and drew the *bishou* hidden in her gambeson.

Fergus took a swipe at Dougal's neck with the *shoudao*, but Dougal was quick to block it with the flat of his claymore.

Thwarted, Fergus slashed again, this time aiming for Dougal's shoulder, missing by only an inch.

On Fergus's third attempt, Merraid, who had been cowering in fright against the buttery wall, scooped up two of the fallen cheeses and sent them bowling toward Fergus's feet. He stumbled over them, catching himself with one hand on the wall. But the *shoudao* swung wide, ruining his attack and giving Dougal a moment to recover.

Time seemed to stand still as Feiyan studied the situation around her.

While the Fortanachs were spitting and thrusting, banging into shelves, slashing wildly at everything in reach, Gaufrid had stood aside, looking on with a dazed and slow-witted stare, as if his clansmen were performing for his entertainment.

Now a cruel and amused sneer curdled the laird's face. An expression that was greedy. Entitled. Self-serving. Everything that Dougal was not.

She also saw that Gaufrid was unguarded. Unarmed. Vulnerable.

Dougal could have easily struck him down.

Yet he didn't.

And she realized in that frozen instant of time that Dougal was incapable of raising a blade against him. Gaufrid was his brother. And his laird. His own father's death was too fresh in his mind to dishonor that memory with familial bloodshed.

Feiyan, however, had no qualms about ending a monster's life. She was an assassin. She had a heart of steel. She could do what was necessary.

Dougal had never seen her as a coldblooded killer. Never imagined she was capable of deadly violence. Now he would witness it with his own eyes.

He would be horrified. And he'd probably never forgive her.

But it was the right thing to do. For Dougal. And for his clan.

Too much was at stake to think of her own interests and what future she might have had with the charming Westlander.

Mac Darragh needed a new laird. His clan *needed* Dougal. More than she did.

And it was that thought that gave her the resolve to thrust forward with the *bishou,* aiming with killing force at the spot just under Gaufrid's ribs in order to give the villain a quick and merciful death, a kinder death than he deserved.

But it was not to be. As Morris shook his head to clear residual daze, he staggered over the spilled cheeses. His flailing hand bumped Feiyan's arm and ruined her aim. Instead of piercing Gaufrid's heart, the needle of her *bishou* sank into the flesh of his side.

Gaufrid wailed like a stuck pig, stopping everyone in their tracks.

Feiyan would have withdrawn the *bishou* and given him a second thrust to end the ghastly noise. But he retreated out of reach, staring in horror at the weapon protruding from his side.

Fergus was the first to recover. Infuriated by the interfering maidservant who continued to bowl cheeses at them, he turned toward that easy target. Raising his meaty left fist, he punched her in the face.

Merraid crashed into a shelf, cracking her head on the crockery, and sank bonelessly to the floor. Blood poured from her broken nose, dripping onto her pale bosom.

With an oath, Dougal dropped his claymore and surged forward, falling to his knees beside the moaning maid.

"There 'tis," Fergus said with a nasty chortle. "Your weakness. Ye've got a soft heart for helpless creatures."

"Ye mons-," Dougal snarled.

That was all he got out. Using the pommel of the *shoudao,* Fergus struck Dougal's chin with full force. Dougal's head snapped back, his eyes rolled, and he fell into oblivion.

Feiyan felt his defeat like a blow to her chest. But there was no time for heartache. She had to quickly reassess the situation.

She was unarmed. Dougal and Merraid were incapacitated. Fergus had her *shoudao.* Morris had two daggers. And Gaufrid was still screaming.

Morris came at her slowly, leering as he brandished his pair of daggers, forcing her to retreat. When her back hit the wall, he bared his teeth in triumph.

Then a slight breeze from the passageway beyond swept up the stairs and ruffled his hair. His eyes slipped to the secret entrance.

"Hey!" he called over his shoulder to Fergus. "I think there's a tunnel back here."

"What?" Fergus barked over the sound of Gaufrid's wails.

Antagonized by the laird's caterwauling, Fergus wrenched the *bishou* roughly and suddenly out of his side. Gaufrid screamed and clutched his hands over the oozing wound. Fergus dropped the weapon, having successfully reduced Gaufrid to whimpers of disbelief.

"What kind o' tunnel?" Fergus asked.

Before Morris could answer, Feiyan took advantage of his inattention. With her left foot, she kicked his right arm aside. Then she seized his left hand between both of hers, digging her thumbs into his tender wrist.

He yelped and reflexively dropped the dagger.

But he still wielded the second blade. When he came round with it, she ducked back. The point swished past, a hair's breadth from her face. Before he could make another slash, she caught his wrist. Giving it a hard twist, she pinioned his arm behind his back.

"Let him go," Fergus warned.

Feiyan held fast. She had Morris subdued for the moment. She could use him for leverage and force Fergus to let them all go.

Then she glanced over at Fergus. He held the tip of her *shoudao* against Dougal's neck. One tiny slip, and his life would be over.

"Nay," she gasped.

"Let him go," Fergus threatened, "or I'll send this one to the devil."

They were at an impasse. She had Fergus's brother—his companion-in-arms, his partner in crime—at her mercy. But Fergus held hostage the man who meant everything— the sun, the moon, the stars, the world—to her.

"Well, well," he gloated at her hesitation. "It looks like I've found the chink in your armor as well, haven't I?"

She sighed. He had.

And now she had no choice.

She couldn't let Dougal die. She had to surrender.

Her shoulders slumped in frustration and defeat as she released Morris, who stumbled away from her, aggravated and humiliated.

Fergus pulled his blade back an inch, but he could still slay Dougal in a heartbeat. "Where does the passage lead?"

It was tempting to lie. But it would do no good. Closing her hands into fists of impotent rage, she muttered, "To the beach."

Fergus pinned her with wolfish eyes. "That's how Rivenloch got in," he realized. "And 'tis the way ye planned to escape."

She didn't answer. She didn't have to.

Fergus slapped Dougal, trying to wake him. At Dougal's groggy mumble, Fergus cracked him hard across the face. Dougal sat up at once, disoriented yet aware of the blade at his throat.

Meanwhile, Fergus called out to the laird, "Come along, Gaufrid. Stop groanin' o'er your wee cut. We've got to go." To Morris, he said, "Help me. He's goin' with us."

"Why?" Feiyan demanded, her heart in her throat. "He's of no use to you."

"Maybe not, but he's o' use to *ye,*" Fergus said, "so if ye want to keep him alive, ye'd better not follow us."

Feiyan didn't trust him. Once they were safe, Fergus would most likely kill Dougal. After all, he was Gaufrid's rival. But she was helpless to do anything except stand by and watch as they dragged Dougal down the steps.

When they faded from sight, descending into the darkness, she whipped around and rushed to the slumbering maidservant.

"Merraid," she whispered, patting lightly at the lass's cheeks. "Merraid. Wake up."

When the maidservant roused, it was with a soft moan of pain. The lass touched her damaged nose, which looked slightly askew, then withdrew shaking fingers stained with blood.

"What happened?" she asked.

"How can I get down to the beach?" Feiyan asked.

Merraid nodded to indicate the passageway. "There."

"Gaufrid and the Fortanachs just went that way with Dougal."

"Dougal?" Her brows creased with worry.

Feiyan nodded. "Is there another way down?"

"'Tis a cliff," Merraid said. "Ye can't get down."

Feiyan's thrumming heart didn't want to hear the word "can't." If she couldn't find a way down, she'd make one.

She retrieved her bloody *bishou* and wiped it on her skirts. There was no time to waste. She just needed to know one more thing.

"Where do you think they'll go once they reach the beach?"

Before she could answer, Gellir burst suddenly into the buttery. His sword was drawn. His face was smudged with grime and sweat. His chest was heaving.

"Where are they?" he demanded. "Where are the Fortanachs? I saw them come in here after Merraid."

"Gellir?" Merraid purred.

His gaze fell to the lass with the bright orange hair, sitting in a sad heap on the floor with a bloody nose. His jaw tensed and he fell to his knees before her.

"What happened?" he demanded, wavering awkwardly between compassion and outrage. "Did they do this? Are you all right?"

"You can chat later, Gellir," Feiyan said. "Right now I need to know where they're going."

Merraid screwed up her forehead, thinking. "If I were them," she finally replied, "I'd steal a boat."

Feiyan nodded. "Right." She considered several strategies. As always, stealth was her best option. "Give me your clothes," she said to Gellir.

"What?"

"Quickly."

"But..." The idea of undressing in front of Merraid clearly discomfited him.

"Please. Hurry."

She began stripping down, and he reluctantly removed his clothing as well. Merraid averted her eyes, for the most part.

Then Feiyan donned his oversized garb, tucking her *bishou* into her belt. She grabbed a kitchen lad's sooty cap from a hook on the wall. Tucking her braid inside, she shoved the cap down over her brow. Wiping more soot on her face, she looked askance at Gellir.

He nodded in approval. "Good. But what am I to wear?"

"You're not coming."

"The hell I'm not."

"I need you to stay here. Look after Merraid."

Gellir was a good lad. He wouldn't let his disappointment show. Not when a wide-eyed lass was depending on him.

"Fine then," he said. "Go to the south wall. Most of the fighting's at the north end."

She left, pulling her cap down to conceal the vengeance brewing in her eyes.

As it turned out, scaling down a cliff wall was not the same as clambering through the branches of a forest. Feiyan's heart pounded as she searched for footing on the slippery rocks, wet with sea spray. Once she skidded down the steep face several feet, muddying Gellir's clothes and scraping her palms. She lost her grip several times. Each time she was certain she would fall and dash her head on the stones a hundred feet below.

But her fear for Dougal outweighed her fear of falling. Eventually, despite the mist obscuring the sand below, the gulls' startling squeals as they swooped past, and the muscle-straining, nerve-rattling climb that seemed to have no end, she found her footing on the solid ground of the beach.

Praying she'd arrived before the Fortanachs, she shuffled through the sandy rubble, heading north along the cliff.

Half a dozen fishing boats slumbered together on the shore, waiting for high tide and their masters to pull them into the firth. Feiyan chose the nearest one, untied it from its moorings, and began to drag it across the sand. When she was halfway to the water's edge, she stopped and waited, tugging her cap down over eyes that restlessly scanned the beach for intruders.

She didn't have to wait long. The Fortanachs' quibbling voices announced their presence well before they materialized in the mist. Fergus was still prodding Dougal along at the point of a sword. Gaufrid hobbled along in pain. From snippets of their conversation, she learned that Morris was skipping ahead to look for suitable transportation.

Keeping her head low and schooling her voice to a low, gravely tone, she called out to Morris. "Mornin'!" she grunted as he approached.

"Is that your boat?" he asked.

"Aye."

"We're goin' to need it."

It was tempting to simply hand it over. After all, that was her plan. The boat was bait. If she gave them the easy means to escape, they might release their hostage.

But surrendering it so eagerly might seem suspicious.

So instead she grunted, "B'longs t' me."

"I don't care if it belongs to Lucifer himself," Morris ground out. "I'm takin' it."

"How much'll ye give me for it?" Feiyan grumbled.

"What?" Morris exploded. "I'm givin' ye naught, ye—"

"What's the trouble now?" Fergus asked. He sounded irritated, as if Dougal had fought him every step of the way, which pleased her immensely.

"Stupid piker wants to be paid," Morris said.

"Oh, he does, does he? We'll see about that." Fergus waved Gaufrid forward. To her satisfaction, the laird looked wan and agonized as he gripped the place where she'd wounded him. "Do ye know who this is?"

Feiyan glanced over, feigned a gasp of surprise, and gave Gaufrid a deep bow. "M'laird!" Pretending to be flustered, she handed the rope to the boat to Morris. Then she rushed forward with a bowed head as if to pay her respects.

But instead of kissing Gaufrid's hand, she whipped out her *bishou* and held it against his ribs. This time, if the worst happened, she didn't intend to miss.

Gaufrid raked in a ragged breath when he saw the familiar blade and paled when he saw her familiar face.

"Shite!" Morris exclaimed. "How did ye...how did she...?"

"Let Dougal go," she said calmly, "or I'll finish what I started."

"Feiyan, nay!" Dougal called out. "Put it down."

Feiyan thinned her lips. Of course he would say that. He didn't think she should risk her life for him. And he didn't believe her capable of following through on her threat.

He was wrong on both counts.

"Please, Feiyan," he begged. "Save yourself."

Fergus smirked. "Och aye, Feiyan, please save yourself," he mocked. "And whate'er ye do, don't let harm come to my dear brother Gaufrid."

Then, with a shocking play that took her completely by surprise, Fergus gave Gaufrid a hard shove forward, impaling him on her blade.

CHAPTER 36

Dougal was stunned.

What had just happened?

In the space of that horrible instant—where his brother and laird was alive one moment and dead the next—emotions raced through his head. Disbelief. Shock. Horror. Dread. Relief. Sorrow. Anger. Malice. And ultimately fear.

Feiyan.

He had to save Feiyan.

If Fergus could so easily kill his closest companion, the man he'd sworn to protect, what would he do to her?

"Nay!" he bellowed, wrenching away from Fergus's blade, anything to distract the brute from the precious lass within his reach.

But Fergus wasn't interested in Feiyan.

He wanted Dougal.

With a vindictive snarl, he lashed out with the *shoudao*.

The blade caressed Dougal's flank with sharp steel, slicing into his flesh as if it were butter. Dougal didn't even feel it at first.

Feiyan screamed. That didn't seem real either. He'd never heard Feiyan scream before. Even facing the outlaws in the forest, she'd never cried out.

As Fergus turned away, a searing pain swept down Dougal's side, and a wet warmth trickled down his abdomen.

The world slowed, and he suddenly felt like he was slogging through a bog.

He wanted to move. Wanted to go to Feiyan.

But his legs were weighted. His arms were as heavy as anvils.

Feiyan cast aside Gaufrid's limp body, revealing her beautiful face. Her silky hair was tucked into a cap, and her rosy cheeks were smudged with soot. But she was still his Feiyan. Still the woman he had dreamed of wedding.

That wouldn't happen now.

He was a dead man.

But he could still save her.

If he could live long enough.

She looked distressed. Her brows were furrowed. Her eyes were wide. Her mouth was open in a silent cry.

He tried to give her a reassuring smile. But he couldn't. And he couldn't get to her.

Then, from the corner of his eye, he saw Fergus and Morris frantically moving the boat toward the firth. Dragging it across the sand.

They were fleeing.

Of course they were.

They had only ever been interested in their own fortunes. They'd sunk their claws into mac Darragh—befriending Gaufrid, replacing the army, impoverishing the clan—solely for their own benefit.

Having failed, they were fleeing, Leaving a trial of blood and devastation in their wake.

Then he saw the others. Hordes of villagers armed with axes and scythes charged onto the beach, spilling out toward the firth. With fierce cries of "Mac Darragh!" they chased after the escaping villains.

They were mac Darragh folk. Crofters, merchants,

maids, youths. People he knew and loved. His heart swelled with pride. They had come to defend the clan.

Shadows began creeping in at the sides of his vision. He tried to blink them away. He refused to close his eyes until he was sure Feiyan was safe.

She came to him then, just as his legs collapsed beneath him and he sank onto his knees in the sand.

The Fortanachs were far away now. Out of the villagers' reach. But that was good. They were too busy escaping to hurt anyone. If they were wise, they would never return again.

Feiyan wrapped her arms around him. Her eyes filled with tears of despair.

But Dougal was beyond sorrow. The danger had passed. Feiyan was safe. She would live. Numb relief slowly filled his veins.

He tried to raise his hand. To brush the locks of hair back from her worried eyes. But he hadn't the strength to even lift a finger.

She slipped behind him, easing him onto his back, cradling his shoulders on her lap.

The sky was clearing now, turning a shade of blue-gray that matched her wet eyes. He felt a warm drop on his hand that couldn't be rain.

He licked his lips. They were dry. But he had to speak to Feiyan. She looked so aggrieved. He had to tell her it would be all right.

He wouldn't be there to share the future with her.

But he wanted to tell her that she had a long and happy life ahead of her.

He wanted to remind her that Rivenloch had shown up in force to defend her, proving she was anything but invisible.

He wanted to tell her that her efforts had surely saved his clan from destruction, and they would be forever grateful.

And he wanted to assure the bright and beautiful lass that she would one day find a husband who would love and honor her as much as...

Nay, he thought. No one would love Feiyan as much as he did.

He wanted to tell her all that.

All he could manage was three weakly whispered words.

"I loved ye."

Loved? *Loved?*

The possibility of losing Dougal had left Feiyan crippled by hopelessness. Mired in misery deeper than any loch, she had succumbed to despondency, sinking into an abyss of anguish.

But that word—*loved,* not love—was like a slap in the face, awakening her to reality. For Dougal, dying was not just a possibility. It was a certainty. And the thought that he would surrender so easily dissolved her grief like the sun burned away the mist, turning it from weak despair to fiery resolve.

The Fortanachs might be getting away with murdering Laird Gaufrid. She didn't give a fig about that. But she'd be damned if she'd let Dougal die.

"Don't you leave me," she said. "Don't even think about it."

His eyes were dimming even as she spoke the words. She shook him back to life.

Her throat clogged with tears as she lectured him with an unshakable confidence that was as full of pretense as her disguises.

"I didn't follow you all the way from the border—scrambling through the trees, sleeping on the cold ground, battling outlaws—just to lose you on a Westland beach."

She clenched her trembling jaw.

"I didn't risk my honor and my name and my neck just so you could slip away."

She sniffed back a sob.

"I didn't give up my mask and my virginity and my...my heart, just so you could break your vow."

He started to fade again, and she shook him once more.

"Listen, mac Darragh. You promised to marry me," she told him, "and you're bloody well going to keep that promise. Do you hear me? Do you *hear* me?"

She wasn't sure he did. His eyes glazed over, and he sank into darkness.

For Gellir, confined to the buttery, it was torture not knowing what was happening outside. Chivalry demanded he look after the wee lass with the broken nose. But he wasn't a physician. All he could do was comfort the maid with words of reassurance.

Even that was humiliating, considering he was clad in next to nothing. While his cousins battled the foes outside, he was stuck here, placating an innocent lass whose gaze kept straying to his linen braies.

He cleared his throat. "My brother Brand once broke his nose."

"He did?" Her eyes dipped to his bare chest.

"Aye," he said, casually crossing his arms to block her view. "And he's still the comeliest of all of the Cameliard brothers."

"How could anyone be as comely as ye?" she gushed.

He glanced at her in surprise.

She blushed and clapped a hand over her mouth. Clearly she hadn't meant to speak that thought aloud. "I mean..." she said through her fingers, but she couldn't figure out how to finish the sentence.

He frowned. He knew what she meant. She was blinded by affection. He'd stayed with her in her time of need. And now she saw him as her handsome hero.

She was wrong. He might do the noble thing when it was required. But he was no one's knight in shining armor. Bloody hell, he wasn't even wearing armor. Pesky Feiyan had left him with little more than his undergarments. Thank God no one in the clan could see him now.

An instant after he sent up that thanks, his cousin Hallie burst into the buttery like a snowstorm, trailed by her husband Colban and his friend Morgan. Their faces were covered with the sweat of battle. Their swords were flecked with blood.

Gellir immediately covered his manly bits with his hands, emitting a very unmanly gasp. "'Tisn't what you think," he tried to explain, suddenly aware of what it looked like.

But they didn't seem the least bit interested in what he was or wasn't doing with the redheaded lass with the bloody nose.

"Where are those fiends?" Hallie bit out. "That pair of gutless savages. I saw them come in here."

"Who?"

"Those two conniving Highland knaves," she muttered, making Gellir wonder if she'd temporarily forgotten she was married to a Highlander.

"Fergus and Morris," Colban said.

"The Fortanach brothers?" Merraid asked.

Hallie curled her lip. "Whatever they're calling themselves, they're bloody swine. Did they escape through the passage?" She was aware of the secret stairs since Rivenloch had made use of them last night.

Merraid nodded.

Gellir, leaping at the chance to lend aid, replied, "But they said they'd kill Dougal if anyone followed them."

"Shite!" Morgan spat. "We'll have to go the long way around the point again."

"And hope we're in time," Colban said.

It was on the tip of Gellir's tongue to ask if he could go as well. But just then Hallie hunkered down beside Merraid as if noticing her for the first time.

"Did they do this to you?" she asked.

Merraid nodded.

Hallie gave Gellir a grim smile. "Well, you've got the best champion a lass could ask for. Gellir will take good care of you."

Gellir clenched his teeth, forcing a smile. Inside he was seething. But after his cousin's compliment, he could hardly ask to be relieved of duty.

"You go to the beach," Hallie said to Colban and Morgan as she rose. "Now that the bulk of the fighting is over, I'm going to take up a position atop the cliff, see what I can manage from there."

They departed as quickly as they'd come. Gellir sighed. He'd missed the battle. And now he was left alone with a lovesick lass.

After a moment, she murmured, "Ye can go if ye like."

He looked up sharply. Was his frustration so transparent? "Nay," he replied, though he had to admit he'd been tempted for just an instant to take her suggestion. "I'm a warrior of Rivenloch," he said, straightening with pride. "We don't turn our backs on those in need."

Saying it aloud felt like reclaiming his honor. It made him realize battles like this were not a trial of his skill at arms, but a test of his mettle as a man.

The mighty army of Rivenloch would triumph, with or without him. But to a wee lass with a broken nose, he was everything.

Dougal had bid the world farewell.

Yet here it was again, staring down at him in expectation.

Peering up through a bleary veil, somewhere between life and death, he discerned the familiar faces of his clan folk, murmuring in soft concern. Here were the men who fished the firth. There were the crofters who plowed the fields. The maidservants who tended to the castle. The villagers who marketed their goods.

They were carrying hayforks and scythes, axes and spades. For what purpose, he didn't know. But they looked as if they'd deserted the fields mid-harvest to come stare at him on the beach.

Bending close over him, as blurry as a fish glimpsed in the shadowed depths of a loch, was the face he most longed to see.

Feiyan. Beautiful and fierce.

How could he leave her?

How could he face the thought of never seeing her again? Never gazing into her adoring eyes? Never kissing her welcoming lips? Never holding her tightly as they shared the joys of passion?

Someone jabbed his side, and a current of blinding pain brought him awake with a groan.

"He'll live," someone announced.

Cheers and prayers of gratitude went up all around.

Dougal was in too much pain to appreciate them.

But then he heard a voice that made him smile through the pain.

"Don't you dare try to leave me again," Feiyan threatened. "You're going to be a Rivenloch now. And Rivenlochs ne'er leave clan warriors behind."

Was it true? Was he going to live? Would he become the next laird? Would this incredible, brilliant, devoted, beautiful woman become his wife?

It took all of his strength, but he managed to croak out a reply. "Aye, m'lady."

Another round of cheers erupted from his clan.

Then he frowned. He was still on his back on the sand. How long had he been lying there? Where were the Fortanachs?

While someone tended to his wound, poking and prodding, he drifted in and out of consciousness. But once when he opened his eyes, he was greeted by an impossible vision. By the exclamations of wonder around him, he realized he wasn't the only one seeing the curious phenomenon.

Against the azure sky, he saw a strange flock of birds fly past. Golden phoenixes. Fiery-feathered beasts racing across the heavens and then diving down, as if to douse their flaming wings in the sea.

Turning his head, he watched the trajectory of one of the magnificent creatures. Its feathers smoked as it arced toward the water. But this one didn't disappear beneath the surface.

Instead, it crashed onto a small sailing vessel in the harbor, engulfing the craft in flames.

"Got it!" someone cried.

"Burn in hell!" yelled someone else.

"They'll burn or drown!"

"To Lucifer with ye!"

"Despicable demons!"

"That's for Kirkoswald!"

"Ye'll meet the devil for what ye did!"

The strange fire blazed on and on. Burning as if by magic atop the water. Sending black clouds roiling into the sky to foul the bright blue.

The last thing he saw before he succumbed again to the shadowy relief of slumber was his beloved Feiyan's face, wreathed now in a smile despite her tear-filled eyes. It was a face that would grace all his dreams. Dreams that could now come true.

"Welcome home, Laird Dougal."

EPILOGUE

The victory feast at Castle Darragh might have been delayed a week while Dougal recovered and supplies could be fetched. Once begun, however, it lasted long into the night. All the mac Darraghs, all the Rivenlochs and mac Girics, all the crofters and villagers from the surrounding lands, and even a handful of reformed mercenaries crowded into the great hall.

Feiyan couldn't have been happier.

The enemy was vanquished. The dead were buried. Dougal was well on his way to recovering from his wound. And her fears had been put to rest.

All her life, she'd believed she was of little import to her illustrious clan. Imagined she was hardly more than a wee cog upon which the machine of Rivenloch turned. True, without that cog, the machine might fall apart and cease to operate. But it was up to her to keep it running, smoothly and discreetly.

Dougal had shown her that wasn't true. Feiyan might be smaller, less bold, less brazen than her cousins. She might fight her battles behind the front lines, using stealth and wit rather than might and muscle. But her efforts didn't go unnoticed.

More than once, Laird Deirdre asked her to tell the tale of their encounter with the outlaws. Her cousins Jenefer and Hallie delighted in her account of Dougal catching a fish. And Gellir, Brand, and Adam couldn't get enough of her descriptions of the fights she'd had with her bridegroom-to-be in the woods.

Halfway through regaling her uncle Pagan with the amusing story of how Dougal had tried to sell her house-keeping services to the innkeeper, she was interrupted by a dagger that landed with a jarring thunk in the middle of the high table.

Everyone shot to their feet, their eating knives at the ready, seeking out the one who'd flung the dagger.

"'Tis yours, I believe," her brother Adam called out to Dougal.

"'Tis," Dougal replied.

"What's this about, Adam?" Laird Deirdre wanted to know, motioning everyone to return to their seats and put down their knives.

"I've returned what's his," Adam explained. "Now he must return what's mine."

"What's...*yours?*" Laird Deirdre asked.

"Aye. Feiyan," he replied. "My sister."

Feiyan's lips twitched. Adam's face was set in a somber expression, but she saw a telltale glimmer in his eyes.

Dougal, who wasn't yet aware of Adam's impressive talent for deception, frowned. "Ye would stand between your sister and the man she's chosen to wed?"

"Not me," Adam said. "But she has to seek permission from the king."

"Och." Dougal nodded. "Aye."

Dougal couldn't know it, but an ancient clan like Rivenloch, guardians of Scotland, loyal warriors of the king for centuries, were unlikely to be denied their will when it came to marriage, especially when the alliance between east and west would fortify the southern border against invasion. The king would be mad not to wholeheartedly endorse such a marriage.

"Oh!" Gellir yelped. He'd been staring at the redheaded maid as she bent near to refill his cup, and he suddenly whipped around as if Adam had kicked him. "Right. As King of Scotland, I grant permission for you to wed."

Relieved laughter erupted all around. Once Dougal understood the jest, he joined in. But it was Adam's grin that was the widest as he lifted a cup in Feiyan's honor.

Laird Deirdre's words, however, touched her most of all. "'Twill be an enormous loss to us," she said. "Feiyan is one of our most skilled warriors. A wee lass with a gigantic impact. A quiet fighter with a bold heart. But it gives me enormous satisfaction to spread the legacy of Rivenloch, and I know she will sow the seeds of greatness across Scotland." As the clan cheered, she gave Feiyan a wink and murmured to Dougal, "And for each seed you sow, I shall replace one of the gems lost in that dagger of yours."

To Feiyan's delight, Dougal blushed. But she grinned and winked back at her aunt.

Laird Deirdre's message stayed with her as she took Dougal's hand much later that night, grabbing an armful of furs and leading him down to the gaol at the foot of the castle. If they were going to sow seeds, they might as well start tonight.

This time when they locked the gate, they took the keys with them, navigating by torchlight to the far end of the cave.

Feiyan had never seen anything quite like the silvery ribbon of light that rippled across the limitless expanse of black as the moon began to sink toward the sea. Even framed by the crude iron grate, it was a breathtaking sight.

They spread out the furs on the soft sand while the

torch flickered nearby, illuminating the naked longing on Dougal's face, which she was certain mirrored her own.

She had to be careful. Dougal's injury was still bandaged, and he winced with a twinge of pain as he removed his leine.

When he was undressed, Feiyan pressed him back on the furs to remove her own garments, relishing the smoldering in his eyes and his body's eagerness to mate.

As the sea kissed the shore, so did she brush her lips against his flesh, grazing his brow, his neck, his shoulder, and moving lower.

He shivered as she gently lapped her way across his chest and down his abdomen. But he groaned as she neared that part of him that hardened with desire. And when she would go farther, he grunted with primal need, rolling her over onto her back, rising above her like the breaker of an incoming tide.

With her head on the fur-covered sand, she felt the strength of the sea thundering beneath her. And yet it was not as powerful as the love she felt for the Westlander. The savage she'd nearly killed. The man she intended to cherish for the rest of her days.

When they joined at last, it was with a sigh that echoed the lovely whisper of foam on the sand. They drew apart and together, their movement as natural as the moon tugging on the current.

When they crested together, it was with a crashing of waves that drowned their breathless cries. A splintering of stars that rivaled the bright scattering across the dark heavens.

Like the surging sea beyond, waves of pleasure lapped at her again and again, pounding her into welcome submission and leaving her sapped upon the shore like stranded seaweed.

Afterward, as they snuggled together in the furs, gazing

out at the moon, which danced now upon the edge of the endless firth, she thought she would never tire of making love in this lovely land beside the sea.

"'Tis beautiful," she whispered.

"Beautiful and dangerous."

"Aye."

Only a week had passed since the Fortanachs—or rather the mac Girics who had been exiled by Morgan's father—had met their end in this very harbor. No one would ever be sure whether they were swallowed by the firth or burned alive by the missiles of Greek fire Hallie had launched onto their boat, but she had claimed credit for their demise.

After witnessing the terrible substance that burned on water and could not be extinguished, Laird Deirdre had proclaimed that her inventive son Ian was no longer allowed to make the stuff. She'd decided it was too destructive and too inhumane to use in civil warfare.

"Where are your thoughts?" Dougal suddenly murmured, tipping his forehead to hers.

She didn't want to tell him she was thinking of murder and mayhem. Instead, she said, "I was wondering how long my cousin Gellir can keep that orange-haired maidservant at bay."

He chuckled. "He doesn't seem quite certain what to make o' her."

"The lovesick lass cleaves to the practice field fence all morn, watching him."

"Well, he won't be here fore'er. He's already makin' good progress, trainin' my army."

She nodded. "Maybe he'll stay till winter."

"By then he'll have fallen out o' favor, and she'll be showerin' her affections on someone else. She's young. Her heart is as variable as the currents." He nuzzled her neck. "Not like mine."

"Nay?"

"My love is steadfast," he confirmed. "There's only one lass for me."

"Is that so?"

"Aye," he said. "I'm steadfast and straightforward. When I want a kiss, I'll ask for it. When I need nestlin', I'll say so. And when I require swivin'..."

Before he could finish, she slipped clandestine fingers across his hip, letting them delve between his thighs, where he roused at her touch with a ragged gasp.

"You know," she whispered against his ear, "there's somethin' to be said for stealth."

One caress led to another, and their inevitable coupling was magical and meaningful.

Feiyan seduced him as slyly as the moon slipping into the sea.

Dougal surged against her as boldly as an ocean wave.

And by winter, their love would manifest in a child born to unite their clans and create the next generation of Rivenloch warriors.

The End

THANK YOU FOR READING MY BOOK!

Did you enjoy it? If so, I hope you'll post a review to let others know! There's no greater gift you can give an author than spreading your love of her books.

It's truly a pleasure and a privilege to be able to share my stories with you. Knowing that my words have made you laugh, sigh, or touched a secret place in your heart is what keeps the wind beneath my wings. I hope you enjoyed our brief journey together, and may ALL of your adventures have happy endings!

If you'd like to keep in touch, feel free to sign up for my monthly e-newsletter at www.glynnis.net, and you'll be the first to find out about my new releases, special discounts, prizes, promotions, and more!

If you want to keep up with my daily escapades:

Friend me at facebook.com/GlynnisCampbell
Like my Page at bit.ly/GlynnisCampbellFBPage
Follow me on Twitter @GlynnisCampbell
Follow me on Instagram @glynniscampbell
Follow me on Goodreads @glynnis_campbell
Follow me on Bookbub @glynnis-campbell
And if you're a super fan, join facebook.com/GCReadersClan

ABOUT THE AUTHOR

I'm a *USA Today* bestselling author of swashbuckling action-adventure historical romances, mostly set in Scotland, with more than 20 award-winning books published in six languages.

But before my role as a medieval matchmaker, I sang in *The Pinups,* an all-girl band on CBS Records, and provided voices for the MTV animated series *The Maxx,* Blizzard's *Diablo* and *Starcraft* video games, and *Star Wars* audiobooks.

I'm the wife of a rock star (if you want to know which one, contact me) and the mother of two young adults. I do my best writing on cruise ships, in Scottish castles, on my husband's tour bus, and at home in my sunny southern California garden.

I love transporting readers to a place where the bold heroes have endearing flaws, the women are stronger than they look, the land is lush and untamed, and chivalry is alive and well!

I'm always delighted to hear from my readers, so please feel free to email me at glynnis@glynnis.net. And if you're a super-fan who would like to join my inner circle, sign up at http://www.facebook.com/GCReadersClan, where you'll get glimpses behind the scenes, sneak peeks of works-in-progress, and extra special surprises.

www.ingramcontent.com/pod-product-compliance
Lightning Source LLC
Chambersburg PA
CBHW021345130726
47899CB00018B/2948